AND AFTER

UNTIL THE END OF THE WORLD
BOOK TWO

SARAH LYONS FLEMING

For Will, who knows that the way to my heart is through water filters and crossbows.

And who loves me in spite of (or maybe because of) it.

CHAPTER 1

It's still dark when I wake for my breakfast shift at the restaurant—that's what we call the dining area here at the farm. Most people dread breakfast, but I like it. This past year has brought me a new appreciation of the dawn. I like the way it rubs off on me, the way it makes me feel quiet and peaceful.

What I don't like, however, is the cold, and it's plenty cold in here. I push down the blankets and shiver when the air hits my skin. The farmhouse is always freezing by morning, no matter how much wood they load into the furnace. I drape a scarf over the light when I get back from the bathroom, so as not to wake Adrian, and inspect myself in the mirror. My hair is its usual puffy morning mess. I smooth it down and wind it into two buns. I might not have to keep it out of reach of zombies here at Kingdom Come, but I'm pretty sure no one wants a strand of long, brown hair in their oatmeal.

I walk to Adrian's nightstand to retrieve my hat. I don't kiss him goodbye; Adrian is not a morning person, despite his many tranquil qualities. He's sleeping bare-chested, with the blankets at his waist. I don't know how he can stand it. We wage a silent, half-asleep battle every night in which he kicks the blankets off and I pile them back on.

Adrian's fingers wrap around my wrist. I drop my hat and quash my scream. "Holy crap! You scared me."

"Sorry," he says, his voice sleepy. "How do you get prettier every day? What's your secret?"

I return his smile and ignore his question. "You're a cheery fellow this morning."

"Because I got to see you. You didn't answer my question."

Adrian's hair is rumpled and he has pillow creases on his cheek, but with his green eyes, olive skin and strong features, I think he's the one who's beautiful.

"Well," I say, "you'll be thirty soon, and your eyesight fails just a tiny bit more every day. It's an illusion."

He lets go of a dramatic sigh, the one he throws around when I won't act serious. "Can't you just take a compliment?" I pull away, but he tightens his hold. "Take the compliment."

"Thanks," I mutter.

His dimple is at maximum depth now, although his calloused fingers haven't loosened a bit. "And now answer the question."

"Don't push your luck."

He releases me with a chuckle. "That wasn't so hard, was it?"

"It was horrible." I brush back his dark hair and kiss his forehead. "I can't believe you made me do that. See you at breakfast?"

"Two eggs, over easy," he orders. "Bacon, toast and hash browns."

"You wish," I say with a laugh. We're low on eggs at this point in the winter; most of the eggs are in the incubators, making new chickens. "Oatmeal. Buckets of oatmeal. I'll make it just for you."

I tiptoe down the creaky stairs and into the night. My boots crunch on the leftover snow, of which we had a record amount this past winter. Not that anyone keeps records anymore. A lot has melted, but the enormous piles that have been shoveled to the side all winter might need a week or more.

The restaurant is off to the right—a barn-like building whose windows glow with the warmth of electric light. We have real bulbs in the farmhouse too, while people in the cabins and tents have to make do with oil lamps, candles or battery-powered lights. I pull off my boots once I'm through the back door and wave to Mikayla, who's started the fires in the wood cookstoves.

She sets a giant bag of oats on the floor and smiles. "Morning, Cassie."

"Morning."

The kitchen is a huge room with a pantry, three wood cookstoves and a long counter in the middle for food prep. I hold my hands over one of the stoves and soak in the warmth. Mikayla's ringlets have already escaped the confines of her ponytail and stick to her temples. Her skin has a golden glow and her cheeks are flushed from the heat. That's another reason I love breakfast shift— by the end of it we're in tank tops and bare feet like it's summer.

"Want to start the oatmeal?" she asks.

"Sure." I retrieve a giant pot and grab the milk out of one of the freezers that are modified to run as refrigerators on the solar.

"We've got a bunch of eggs," Mikayla says. "Enough to make frittatas. I'm so excited!"

She bounces around, collecting ingredients. Only Mikayla could be this excited about eggs. She was on the farm before Bornavirus destroyed the world; she'd planned to start her own farm one day.

"Where's Ben?" I ask.

Ben and Adrian were partners in what was a sustainable farm called Kingdom Come Farm. It's now Kingdom Come Safe Zone, although we're still a farm. You have to be a farm these days, if you want to eat. Fully-stocked grocery stores are a thing of the past. Mikayla and Ben began dating in the fall, and now they're inseparable.

"Guard duty. He'll swing by after. He made me promise I'd hide some frittata for him. Hey, are you going on the final run? They found a group of Lexers over to the west."

"Yeah, I think we're leaving after breakfast."

We've spent the winter killing all the infected we could locate. We'd waited, fingers crossed, until winter came, hoping the infected would freeze. And when they did, we made it our mission to seek them out and finish them off. We'd also hoped that the cold would destroy them once and for all, but it turns out there's a fifty-percent survival rate when thawed, based on our own experiments and reports from a few other Safe Zones. It's better than nothing.

I put on water to boil, set home-canned fruit on the serving tables in the dining area and then start on today's bread. I love making bread, although making it in such large quantities is more work than pleasure. We have it down to a science: it's measured, kneaded and tucked by the heat to rise by the time Toby and Jeff fall through the door. Jeff has a crooked ponytail and bags under his eyes, and Toby's blond dreadlocks are rattier than usual.

"Rough night?" I ask.

"I'm too old to be sleeping in that tent," Jeff says. He turns to Toby. "Unlike you, I am no longer twenty-six. You young whippersnappers may be able to stay up all night, but we old folks need sleep."

He's only in his forties, but I know what he means. The guys in that tent are all lovely human beings, but they're loud. "I don't blame you," I say. "I wouldn't want to be in there."

"There's an empty bed in the old timers' tent," Jeff says. "I'm switching today."

Toby points a finger. "You thought you could hang, old man, but you were mistaken."

Toby was an employee on the farm before Bornavirus. He's so laid-back he can appear lazy, but he knows the farm and all its animal and vegetable residents intimately, including the once-illegal herbs he grows just outside the fence. He might prefer hanging out to work, but he does more than his fair share, and he's good on patrol. Jeff mutters something and pushes Toby into the dining room to set up tables and chairs.

A moment later, Penny rushes in and hangs her coat on a hook. Her dark hair is in a haphazard bun, and her eyes are puffy with sleep. "Sorry I'm a little late. James practically had to push me out of bed."

Penny walks to where I'm stirring oatmeal and wipes her fogged-up glasses on her shirt. "I'm late," she says with a frown.

"Geez, Pen, you're allowed to be late once in your life."

She pushes the antique glasses up her nose and whispers, "No, I'm *late*."

"Shit." I drop the spoon into the pot. The oatmeal sucks it down like quicksand. I try to fish it out without taking my eyes off Penny. "Crap."

She nods at my eloquence and takes a deep breath. Her normally light brown skin is almost as pale as mine. I inspect her for any other signs of pregnancy, but her soft curves haven't changed in any significant way.

"How late? How do you feel? Are you freaking out?"

Penny points at where I'm slopping oatmeal all over and runs a shaky hand along her glasses' earpiece. "I'm over a week late. I'm tired and, like, not quite right. And of course I'm freaking out!"

"So how can we find out? Didn't they used to inject rabbits with urine? We can't do that. There are rabbits here, bu—"

"Well, we could murder a rabbit," she says with a look that tells me I'm insane, "or I could go to the infirmary and get one of the tests. James and I are going to get one after breakfast. Maureen's filling in for me at school."

"That probably makes more sense." I laugh and squeeze her arm. "I'm excited. Can I be excited?"

Penny's brown eyes shine. "Yeah. I'm kind of excited."

Sometimes I think about a sweet, tiny baby that Adrian and I have made. But then I think about how I would have to protect it.

How I would have yet another person to worry about. How babies cry and make noise and you can't tell them to keep quiet. And then I stop thinking about babies. Besides, I've got Bits.

This is the next best thing, though, so I focus on the positive: A tiny Penny-and-James baby. Quite possibly the smartest baby ever. I whisper this to Penny when she passes on her way to the pantry, which gets me an eye roll and a giggle.

By the time Ben and Dan arrive, the dining area is filled with people eating oatmeal and day-old toast. Only the early birds and those in the know got frittata this morning. And me—I think I ate four eggs' worth. Barnaby, a dog with some Golden Retriever but no brains to speak of, follows them in. He sniffs my leg, tail wagging madly, and then plops his butt on my foot where I wash dishes at the trough sink. There aren't many dogs around, since Lexers eat animals. Maybe a lot of dogs were eaten by their owners before they figured out they should have run.

"I heard I could score some real eggs," Dan says.

Mikayla bustles over to where she hid the last of the frittata. "You heard right."

"I tried to lose him, but he followed me like a lost puppy once he heard," Ben says. He takes off his winter hat to reveal a curly mop of brown hair. Mikayla tousles it and gives him a kiss.

Dan puckers his lips at Mikayla. She grins, hands him a plate and says, "Not gonna happen."

"Worth a shot," he says to Ben, who doesn't look all that amused. Ben's a very nice person, but he's unbelievably serious.

Dan inhales his frittata by the sink while Barnaby pants beneath his plate with hungry eyes. Dan's a carpenter and good-looking in a scruffy, dirty-blond, young-weathered-thirty-something kind of way. He's never hurting for company, and he's an incorrigible flirt; he puts Ana to shame.

"Here you go," he says to Barnaby and drops a bite of frittata on the wood floor. Barnaby scrambles to his feet and wolfs it down.

"Don't let Mikayla see you do that with real eggs," I say. "She'll kill you."

"I couldn't resist. Look at that face."

Barnaby's tongue lolls out of the side of his mouth while he shifts his gaze between me and Dan. This dog eats anything, barks at everything and manages to get himself filthier than I thought possible. He doesn't know a single trick.

"That is the dumbest dog ever," I say, and give him a scratch. I love Barn, but it's true. "It's a good thing he's cute."

"Well, he's not fixed. So, if we find a girl who's not, maybe we'll get puppies."

Barnaby horks up something he's scavenged, and what looks like crumpled paper hits the floor in a pool of dog drool and frittata. I look at Dan. "That's the future of domesticated dogs? We should just cut our losses and move on."

Dan laughs and wipes it up with his cloth napkin, which he then throws into the laundry bin. "You're going on the run with us later, right?"

"Yeah. You're going? You just got off guard. Don't you need any sleep?"

He drops his plate in the sink and pats his stomach. "I'm going to get a couple hours right now. I'll be good to go."

"Well, that's dedication." I'm decent at killing zombies, and one of the few who are willing to do it, but I don't like it.

He winks. "Nah, I heard you were going and didn't want to miss out."

"Must you bother *me*?" I ask. "Aren't there tons of other girls you could flirt with on this fine morning?"

"Yes," he says, "but they don't blush like you do. I can't help myself."

I threaten to squirt him with the water nozzle and say, "Go to sleep, you. I've got people to feed without you bugging me all morning."

He salutes me and marches out the door. I leave to retrieve the next round of never-ending dishes. These people can eat.

CHAPTER 2

There are clothes under my clothes, but it's still freezing on the back of the snowmobile. I grip Adrian's waist and bury my face in his back to keep out of the wind. We come to a stop fifteen miles from the farm, where a group of Lexers was spotted on one of Dwayne's flights in the plane.

Dan checks his map and points into the trees. "Right down there."

Ana shakes out her short, chestnut hair before pulling her cleaver off her shoulder. The cleaver-shaped blade on one end of the shaft is perfect for decapitation, and the dull spike on the other end slides into an eye socket or the soft spot right below the skull. It's still our favorite weapon, although my Ka-Bar knife is a close second. And my revolver. I love my Smith and Wesson.

"C'mon!" Ana says, bouncing on the balls of her feet.

She heads down the incline without waiting for a reply. Dan races her down the snow-covered slope with his snowmobile partner, Toby, following behind. I take off my mittens and pull on the leather elbow-length gloves that I use to deal with Lexers.

"Go ahead," I say to Adrian. "I have to get out the rubber gloves and stuff." He nods and joins the others.

"Why are we here again?" Peter asks from behind me.

He leans against his snowmobile, eyes as dark as his black hat. I finish pulling latex gloves over my leather ones and grab my cleaver.

"To preserve the human race," I say, only half joking.

"No, I meant *we* as in you and me. We hate this." He blows into his hands before pulling on his own gloves.

"Well, I certainly don't love it." I point to Ana. "Not like your other half. But I think she does it solely for the outfit."

Peter sniffs in amusement. Ana wears black leather gloves and a black leather jacket. They match the black leather pants she's tucked into tall, fur-lined boots. She's not tall, but she's strong and gorgeous with her small features and dark eyes. We watch as she brings her cleaver forward in a swift, effortless and deadly motion.

"We do it because it needs to be done," I continue. "I'm not going to sit at the farm, worrying about whether or not people come back, are you?"

There may be nothing worse than not knowing what's happened to someone you love. This new world is full of stories, of lives, with no ending. People have survived, died, turned—there's no way to know. My brother, Eric, was supposed to meet us at my parents' house last summer. He never showed. Everyone has a story like that these days, and I couldn't bear to have another.

"I know," Peter says. He frowns in Ana's direction. "They're going to thaw soon. You know she's going to want to be out here all the time."

Ana is brave to the point of stupidity. Last fall she took on six Lexers by herself. She's used herself as bait. And, in true Ana fashion, she always escapes unscathed, so she doesn't see what the problem is.

"We'll be there, too," I say. "I'll keep her under control."

"You may be the only person who can."

Ana and I make a good team because we can usually anticipate what the other's planning. Not only do we keep each other safe, but I can usually deter her from doing asinine things like fighting six Lexers who could be ignored. Unlike her, I don't have a death wish. She listens to me. Occasionally.

"I'll do my best. Now, come on, or we'll be accused of shirking our duties."

Peter drapes his arm across my shoulders while we walk. It's not awkward, even with our past. In the past year he's become one of my closest friends. I can tell him anything, the way I can with Penny and Nelly. Sometimes I tell him more; the Peter who never discussed anything profound is practically a philosopher now.

"Thanks, Cassandra."

"Welcome, Petey."

He squeezes my shoulder. Peter's the only person left in the world who calls me Cassandra, but I'm the only person who has ever called him Petey.

We come face to face with over a hundred frozen and thawing zombies at the base of the hill. Some of the half-thawed ones are dead—really, finally dead. A few are thawed enough to gurgle and twitch, but the below-freezing nights seem to have kept their cores frozen. Dead or undead, they all get a spike in the eye or a knife in the head. I move to where one slumps against a tree like he's taking a rest on a nature walk. Something black and fuzzy grows on the gray skin of his cheek. "Hey, look at this," I call out.

Everyone peers at the mossy growth. Adrian scrapes off a patch with his knife, revealing spongy flesh beneath. I hand him a latex glove. "Put some of it in this."

At the sound of my voice the Lexer's eyes shift in their sockets. It sees all the potential food and an urgent sound rises from its lipless mouth.

"Oh, shut up," Ana says. She uses her spike to make a hole in his skull and flashes me perfect white teeth, while Peter flashes me a look that reiterates his concern.

I follow Adrian to where a dozen of them stood before they succumbed to the cold and punch my spike into an eye socket. The crunching sound used to be disturbing. I'm used to it now, which is disturbing in a different way. Killing things has become just another day at the office. I try not to think about who they once were—like Eric.

"Here's more of that moss," Adrian says. He crouches for a closer look at a bloated, cracked body half-covered with a sweater of black fuzz. "Maybe this is some kind of decay, finally."

"Maybe something's finally going to eat *them*," I say. "Maybe something's evolving along with the infection."

"I hope so." Adrian looks up, knife in hand and eyes hopeful. "Nothing's ever grown on them before. It's got to mean something."

We spin at Toby's yell of surprise and race to where a group of fifteen Lexers lay in the snow. Toby had been stepping his way through the bodies, spike in hand, but now he's on the ground kicking at one that's managed to sink its mouth into the cloth above his boot. Adrian slams his knife into the base of its skull and pulls Toby to safety.

Toby clutches his calf, and when he finally releases his hands, we gasp at the rip in his cargo pants. He leans back on his elbows and screws his eyes shut. "Did it break the skin? Just shoot me in the head if it did, man. I don't want to know it's coming."

"There's no blood on your pants." I kneel down and pull my knife off my belt as the others gather round, their faces pale. "I can't see the skin. I have to cut it wider."

Toby nods, eyes still closed. He's a lot calmer than I would be, although he's trembling so badly that I have to steady his leg when I slice the cloth. The marks are deep and some are more red than pink, but there's no opening, no blood. I inspect carefully, and Ana crouches for a second opinion. Even one tiny break in the skin might mean certain death.

"You're okay," I say in a rush. I don't know what I would've said had he not been, and I'm relieved I still don't. "It didn't break the skin. But don't move. Let's wash off any virus in case it does open up."

Everyone sighs in relief. Toby drops his head to the snow and stares up at the trees. "Holy fucking shit. Holy shit. Douse me in bleach, man, I don't care."

I wipe it down with cleaner and ointment while the others finish off the remaining bodies. They're careful in case more Lexers are thawed through, but there's only the one which Toby had the misfortune of stepping past with his guard down.

"You are officially alive," I tell Toby when I'm done. "So live it up."

He gives me a quick patchouli-scented hug. "You bet your ass I will. Jeff's gonna be glad he left the tent tonight."

CHAPTER 3

I can still smell the bodies when we get back to the farm. It sticks on your clothes and in your sinuses. The frozen Lexers don't splatter the way thawed ones can, but they still stink. We park the snow machines quietly, well aware of how close a call that was. Toby dashes off to begin his celebration of life, quite possibly the least solemn of us all. Now that the Lexers are thawing, it's only a matter of time until the pods come. They'll find us eventually. They may not communicate, but they follow each other looking for food. Looking for us.

I haven't forgotten what the ever-present terror of millions of zombies feels like, but it's had a chance to fade since the autumn. The winter gave us time to heal from shell-shocked survivors back into the people we once were, barring the visible and invisible scars we all carry. We've grown used to not worrying. The rustle of the trees really has been the wind, every snap of a branch heavy snow or ice. We haven't become complacent, but it's time to get back into that old mentality—the world has never been more of an eat-or-be-eaten place than it is now.

Adrian kisses me and heads out to whatever's on his to-do list. Ana and I wash our blades in bleach water, dip our boots in the foot bath and mist each other with a virus-killing spray. I'm not the neatest person, much to Adrian's chagrin, but when it comes to the virus, I'm all for sterility.

"Let's go find my sister and see if she's knocked up," Ana says when the others are gone.

"That's my first stop," I say. "I can't believe she might be pregnant."

"I think she is. I would die if it were me. Imagine?"

Ana gives a dramatic shiver as we leave the shed. I bring her to a halt by her arm. "Ana, don't say that to Penny. Believe me, you won't be telling her anything she doesn't already know."

"Cass, I wouldn't say that!"

I stare at her until she drops the innocent, doe-eyed expression. "I'll only say how happy I am," Ana says. "Promise. I am happy, you know. I've always wanted a niece to spoil. It's a girl, I know it."

Cows low from the barns on our left, and the goats rest their front legs on the barnyard fence, looking for a handout. We turn right and weave through the large outfitter tents to the grouping of small cabins, where Ana and Peter share a cabin with Penny and James.

"I'm happy for her, too," I say. I don't tell Ana I agree with her on the other stuff. Like I said, we all know.

We burst into the cabin's tiny main room. The golden glow of the wood walls, the woodstove and the shelves stocked with books make the room cozy. Penny looks up from the loveseat that sits under my painting of our old neighborhood in Brooklyn. I try to imagine what it must look like now and wonder if Penny and Ana's mother, Maria, is still alive. She would love to be a grandma.

Ana raises her hands and shouts, "Well?"

Penny holds up the little plastic stick. "Two lines. Positive."

Ana and I shriek. After I've hugged Penny, I notice James staring into the distance, light brown hair tucked behind his ears and thin face paler than usual. James is nothing if not pragmatic, and I know his mind is traveling down some seriously dark baby-zombie roads right now.

"We're still trying to wrap our heads around it," James says when I congratulate him. "But it's good."

"It's great," I say with what I hope sounds like absolute confidence. "It's going to be fine."

He rubs at his forehead before he nods. We both know I could be wrong, but we have to take pleasure in these moments that could otherwise be ruined by what's outside the fences. If we don't, we might as well give up. Penny's face is soft and buoyant, and James reaches for her hand, mirroring her expression. My resolve not to have a baby weakens a tiny bit, but I shore it up with the image of the frozen Lexers today.

***

I make my way to the farmhouse to change before dinner, planting my feet carefully in the muck at the lowest part of the farm. Today might herald the start of mud season, that time of boot-sucking bogs and dirty floors. I extend my arms to keep from falling when my leg slides out from under me. I should've stuck to the graveled path.

"How is it that anyone wants you, of all people, on patrol?" asks a wry voice.

I turn to where Nelly leans against one of the cabins with his arms crossed and an eyebrow raised. "Why are you following me?"

"I saw the windmill arms and had to get a closer look."

He mimics my arms with a look of desperation. I laugh so hard that my foot slips again. Nelly grabs my elbow and sighs, but his blue eyes twinkle.

"Thanks," I say. "And I'm glad you find me so entertaining."

"Me too, darlin'."

Nelly's unruly blond hair sticks up all over the place, and his cheeks are pink from working outside with the livestock. His left arm never entirely recovered from that bad infection last year, so he doesn't do patrol unless we're short of people. He argues that it's fine and that he's right-handed. Truthfully, Nelly's always been broad and strong, so his weakened arm is probably still stronger than most, but I like it this way. It gives me one less person to worry about.

"Want to come to the house with me?" I ask. "I have to change."

"Sure. I'll flush the toilet for fun."

Those who don't live in the farmhouse make do with the composting outhouses. And unless they're in one of the tents lucky enough to have its own composting toilet, they have to brave the cold to use them. Nelly lives in one of the men's tents, along with John. The cabins were given to families and couples. Being the boss's girlfriend has its perks, besides the obvious one of being in love with him.

"So, did you see Penny?" Nelly asks.

I know he's under orders not to ruin the surprise. "How crazy is it that she's pregnant?"

I'm staggered that Penny, my best friend since the age of ten, is having a baby. We'd planned—when we were twelve and still sure we could order up the life we wanted—to have kids together, so they'd be best friends, too. That's not happening, but some of that hazy future has just arrived with a bang.

"Yup, it's crazy all right," Nelly says. "What did you think happens when you have unprotected sex?"

He's happy, though; I can see it by the way he tightens his lips so as not to smile. "Oh, stop! Can't you just be excited?"

"Oh, my God, I'm so psyched!"

"You're an ass. I know you're happy."

He pats my hand and grunts, which is as close as I'm getting to agreement.

The restaurant clangs with the sounds of dinner, and my stomach growls at the drifting aroma of marinara sauce. I haven't eaten since breakfast. Killing the infected kills my appetite as well, but now I'm ravenous. I'd sneak in and grab something, but people avoid you when you're wearing your Lexer gear. There's no way they'd let me in.

We take off our boots in the sunroom. The white farmhouse has a porch that spans the front and old windows that let in tons of cold air, although they're lovely to look at. I poke around in the kitchen pantry, but someone's eaten the cookies I stuck in there. The bread is gone, too. I'd hoard food in my room if it weren't for mice.

"Scavengers ate my cookies!"

"I'll bet anything that scavenger's name was Bits," Nelly says.

He throws himself onto the couch in the living room and puts his feet up on the coffee table. "I'll be watching the game," he says, picking up an imaginary remote control and aiming it at an imaginary television.

"I'll make you and the guys some sandwiches when I'm changed, honey."

I climb the stairs to the bathroom, where I wash up and bundle my jeans for the laundry. Adrian's already been back to our room: his gloves and leather jacket hang on their hooks, with his spotless boots underneath. The room was his, but I've added my own touches since last summer—namely in last night's pajamas thrown over the desk chair, the teetering stack of books, the papers where I've scribbled lists or notes or doodles and the art supplies that I find impossible to keep organized.

There's also the addition of a twin bed in the corner, where Bits sleeps when she's not with Peter. Peter and I joke that we have split custody, and she comes and goes as she pleases. Adrian hadn't expected to become a father-like figure to a now eight year-old girl, but he loves Bits dearly.

Bits was orphaned by Bornavirus LX, although her parents died at the hands of men who weren't infected. Her father died in an explosion at the school where they'd taken refuge from the Lexers. Her mother wasn't so lucky—a group of men fed her to the infected while Bits watched. I don't often think of Neil, the leader of those men, and how his head exploded out the back when I shot him, because it's never exactly pleasant. Except for the fact that he's dead. That is kind of pleasant.

I shake my head to banish the image and look out the windows. The ring of mountains that surrounds us is still white with snow, their peaks bristly with the branches of barren trees. The mountains of the Northeast aren't huge, but they're tall enough to offer some semblance of protection and a feeling of security. Sometimes I feel like nothing can touch us here, with our fences and weapons, but I know it's not true. It's dangerous to think that way. I sigh and pull on my shoes.

CHAPTER 4

I watch people eat their spaghetti and meatballs and entertain the idea of grabbing a plate out from under one of them. I've reached a new level of hunger since breakfast, but I'm very aware that I don't know what real hunger is. There must be people out there who are starving, who died of starvation over the winter, while I've had three, or at least two, squares a day.

A dinner roll floats over my shoulder and jiggles in the air. I turn to find Adrian attached to the other end and take a bite. "That is so good," I moan through a mouth full of the yeasty bread I kneaded this morning.

"You were practically drooling. I thought I should feed you before you did something you'd regret." Adrian always notices things like that, and not just with me. That's why everyone loves him.

"I was so hungry," I say, and rip off another bite. "Thanks."

"Are you ever not hungry?" Nelly asks. "Seriously, it's flabbergasting."

"I like food. Would you rather I have that Body Dysmorphic Disorder thingy? I have a healthy approach to food."

"Yeah," Adrian says, "any food you approach, you eat."

Nelly laughs. Sometimes when we're all together it's like having two big brothers.

"I can't help that I grew up eating good food and appreciate it."

"A lot," Nelly adds, and turns to Adrian. "So, did you hear the news?"

"Penny?" Adrian asks. His eyes widen when I nod. "Wow."

Bits races in the door, with Penny, James, Peter and Ana in tow. I offer her the last bite of roll and lift her petite body in the air. At times, because of her size and nightmares, I forget she's eight. She's grown up a lot this winter, but she still has a paralyzing fear of Lexers, and I'm worried about the summer that will assuredly bring more.

"How was school, Bitsy?" I ask.

"Penny's pregnant!" she says into my ear. It was supposed to be a whisper, but her enthusiasm makes it more of a yell.

I kiss her freckled cheek. "I know. But I think she wants to keep it a secret for now."

"It's a lost cause," Penny says with a shrug. "When I was leaving the infirmary, I dropped the test and at least four people saw it. Everyone has to suspect by now."

Sure enough, people glance at her quickly and look away smiling. It's impossible to keep a secret while living in such close quarters, and their suspicions are not laid to rest by Adrian's congratulatory hug.

She pats her stomach ostentatiously. "Might as well give them something to talk about."

John and Maureen enter the big door just after we've sat with our food. They're often together, and I think it's only a matter of time before something romantic develops. It might have already—John is the only person who could keep it from the other one hundred people here.

They sit in the seats we've saved for them, and John bows his head for a silent grace before digging in. His salt-and-pepper beard is whiter than last fall, and he's filled out more due to all the farm work. If Adrian's the manager of the farm, John's the foreman, and he runs a tight ship.

Maureen has a brown bob, laugh lines, and round cheeks that get plumper when she smiles at the other tables. She and John are surrogate grandparents to the fifteen kids who live here. Sixteen, if you include Penny, and I don't think she'll be the last. We have little to no contraception left; it's one of the first things we need to find when the snow melts. Maureen taught us how to chart our monthly cycles, but if Penny the straight-A student is any indication, it's not foolproof.

"Cassie, I know I said I was staying with you tonight, but can I stay at Peter's again?" Bits asks, spaghetti dangling from her lips.

"Suck up that worm, baby bird," I say. She slurps it up and licks the sauce off her lips. "Sure, as long as it's okay with them."

Peter nods. "Sure. Any reason why?"

"Well, when will I be able to feel the baby move?"

"It'll be months, Bits," Penny says with a laugh.

Bits frowns but then shrugs and swings her feet that don't hit the floor. "Aren't you supposed to read to babies? I could read to it if you want."

"I bet it'd love that."

"*Her*," Ana says. She twirls pasta on her fork. "Not *it*."

"You're going to be disappointed if it's a boy," Penny says.

"She's not, so I won't." Ana swings a leg up onto Peter's lap, completely confident in her prediction. This baby wouldn't dare be a boy now.

Dan stops at our table with a plate loaded with spaghetti and a mound of meatballs. "Hungry?" Adrian asks him.

"Just a little. You're going to Whitefield in the next couple of days, right? I was wondering if you could bring a letter there for me."

"Sure. Just drop it off at the house."

"Love letter?" Nelly asks. Dan smiles but says nothing.

"A girl in every port," I say. "How do you find the time?"

"Granted," Nelly says to me, "there are ninety-nine point nine percent less girls than there used to be, but still."

Dan eats a meatball and chews slowly while we tease him. He swallows and points his fork at us. "Chicken coop plans, people."

"Well, we were right about it being for chicks," Nelly says.

Dan laughs and moves to his table, where he commences eating with a gusto that may rival mine. The talk turns to Whitefield, the Safe Zone in New Hampshire. The 157th Refueling Wing of the Air National Guard evacuated to the tiny airport last year. We help them with their farm in trade for fuel, but it isn't all about barter. They're our closest neighbors, and we help each other out the way neighbors should, even if we are eighty miles apart.

"I want to get that moss there," Adrian says. He explains what we found today, and the faces at the table turn hopeful when they realize what it could mean.

"Are you going?" Nelly asks me.

"Yep. I'm sure you're going."

I wink at him, and he shrugs. "I have to. They need help with the cow inseminations."

Adam lives in Whitefield. Nelly's never been serious about anyone he's dated and, true to form, refuses to admit he likes Adam. He dodges my inquiries by saying that he doesn't have much choice, since Adam's the last gay man on Earth. But I know they would have hit it off even if the world hadn't ended, and I'm pretty sure Nelly's in love.

"Right," I say. "What do you know about cow inseminations that they can't read in a book? For instance, are cows more likely to get pregnant in the winter or summer?"

"Summer." It's obvious he's guessing. He grew up with cattle on his parents' farm, but unlike his brothers, he never had much interest in them.

"Ha!" I yell. "Winter!"

"I had a fifty-fifty chance." Nelly narrows his eyes at me. "What the hell do *you* know about cow inseminations?"

"That's the only thing. I heard someone say it one day. So, are you coming to Whitefield, or do you want me to bring a love letter for you?"

"I'm coming," he mumbles.

I pinch his rosy cheek, glad I'm not the only one around here who blushes.

***

I read on the bed while Adrian organizes himself for the morning. His jeans and shirt are draped over a hanger and he's set out his hunting knife and the random things—a lighter, little pliers and a spool of wire—that he always carries in his pockets. It's hard to not feel lazy when you live with someone so neat. I look at my various piles and try to feel inspired, but I'm dead inside when it comes to organization.

When Adrian's done, he sits on the edge of the bed and squeezes my ankle. "We always said we'd have a baby sometime around now."

I toss my book to the side. "The idea of a baby is nice. The reality is very different."

"I know. We'll have one someday. A little pink baby with freckles, like you."

"Only someone who hasn't spent their whole lives burning and peeling and getting sun poisoning would wish that on a child."

"I like your pinkness." His hand travels up my leg and under my shirt. When it gets higher, he asks, "What's going on here?"

I kneel and pull my shirt over my head. This lacy purple bra—which still had the tags on, because wearing a dead person's sexy underwear just feels weird—cost me four laundry shifts and assorted other favors, but Adrian's face makes it worth it.

His hands move under the straps. "I like it."

"You were supposed to. You should see the matching underwear."

"Yes, I should," he says. I strip off my pants, and he runs a finger down my stomach and hooks it in the top of the purple lace. "You're so hot."

I stick out my tongue and cross my eyes, and he tickles my side. "Especially when you do that. Any guy here would love to be with you. You know who has a crush—"

"Could we not discuss the legions of apparently invisible men who are dying to get in my pants? There's only one person I want in my pants."

Adrian isn't the jealous type. It was a little weird when Peter showed up at the gate last fall, but it was worse for us than for Adrian. He was over it in days, while Peter and I tiptoed around for weeks and tried not to look too friendly. The lack of jealousy would almost be offensive if it wasn't because he knows he has nothing to worry about.

"I'm just trying to get a rise out of you."

"Well, I was trying to get a rise out of *you*." I turn to crawl under the covers. "But, obviously, you'd rather discuss other things, so I guess I'll just go to b—"

He drags me into his lap and says, "It looks like we've both accomplished what we wanted."

I can feel what he means. He pushes me onto my back and props himself on his elbows so his face is only inches away. I use my toes to inch his pajama pants down. "Hi, gorgeous," he says.

"That's why I don't take your compliments, you know," I say. I press my chest against his warm one. Even with the furnace going, this purple outfit isn't cutting it. "You throw them around like confetti. *Blah blah blah gorgeous. Blah blah blah beautiful.* How am I supposed to believe anything you say?"

"So, what, I should tell you what's wrong with you?" Adrian runs a thumb along my cheek, lips curved, and his smile widens at my nod. "Fine. You're a slob."

"That's more like it." I run my hand down his side and around to his stomach. His dark lashes flutter and he lets out a hiss of air as it moves lower.

"Your hair is insane in the morning." He ruffles it with a hand and twines it through his fingers. "And your breath isn't much better."

"Hey! Try waking up next to yourself."

I laugh and attempt to roll out from under him, but his arms are immovable. He raises a bored eyebrow at my struggle, and I stick my feet on the backs of his bare legs in retaliation.

He clenches his teeth and growls. "And your feet are fucking freezing. Good enough?"

"There's got to be more than that."

His mouth moves along my neck, and I sigh when his teeth graze my earlobe. "There's plenty more. But I'm kind of busy right now."

I move against him, and not because I'm cold. The furnace could be broken right now, and I don't think I'd be chilly. "So, get in my pants already."

CHAPTER 5

The white plane waits on the runway just outside the east fence. It looks huge on the ground, but feels tiny when we're up in the air, like the flick of a finger could knock it out of the sky. We would drive the eighty miles to save on plane fuel, but the roads are still blocked with a winter's worth of snow.

We load the veggie starts from our greenhouse into the cargo area. It's too early for planting, so we'll transfer them to Whitefield's tiny greenhouse. Months of canned and dried fruits and vegetables have us all eager for something fresh, and these will produce a bit earlier than the ones they'll sow directly in the ground.

I choose a seat close to our pilot, Dwayne. He twirls the ends of his bushy mustache while he and Jeff, Dwayne's sort-of copilot, run through whatever pilots do. Dwayne's been teaching Jeff to fly and help to navigate. The plane may have state-of-the-art GPS, but since the satellites went out of whack in no time, it's completely useless.

Adrian sits across from me, legs bouncing. Nelly and John squeeze into seats next to us and buckle in as we roll. The trees that circle the fallow field flash by, and then the rumbling under the wheels ceases. I look down as we gain altitude. In a few months the fields outside the fence will be filled with oats, wheat and corn. The vegetable garden inside the fence will be lush and green. But for now, Kingdom Come is a mottled white and brown. Smoke rises from stovepipes and people stroll in groups of two and three. Everyone gets along for the most part—there are petty jealousies and problems, of course, but most of the time we remember how lucky we are.

Together, Kingdom Come and Whitefield have just over two hundred-fifty souls. Moose River Safe Zone, in Maine, has five hundred. They're pitiful numbers when you think of how many people the Northeast used to hold. I know we're not the only ones; there have to be people out there who've found places to hole up, who've survived the cold and the Lexers. Maybe they'll chance traveling when the snow melts and before the Lexers start their endless roaming.

Nelly sips from his murky looking bottle of mint tea—the closest he gets to his beloved Pepsi these days.

"We'll have to go back to Whitefield again soon," I say to him, raising my voice above the drone of the engine. "To bring the chickens once the snow's gone. You could stay for a while."

"Yeah," he says, pulling the brim of his baseball cap down so I can't see his face. "I was thinking about it."

I yank off his cap and arrange his hair in a good messy way, instead of the crazy messy way his hair prefers. "There, now you look handsome. Adam likes you without a hat."

"How do you know?" he mutters.

"Because he told me." Nelly's mouth opens. "Yep, I know all kinds of things. Adam *loves* me."

Nelly looks irritated with my teasing, so I poke him in the chest and continue. "And do you know why Adam loves me? Because I love you, and so does he. So we love each other. He does love you, you know. And he's awesome, so don't screw it up."

He fights to keep his frown in place. "How do you always redeem yourself just when I want to kill you?"

"Love you, too."

We chat until the plane banks left for a landing. Whitefield isn't completely surrounded by mountains like we are, and the towns surrounding it were larger, so they have more unwanted visitors than we do. But they also have real soldiers and a lot more ammo. The fact that I'm considered a soldier of sorts at Kingdom Come may surprise Nelly, but it astonishes me. You do what you have to nowadays, and although I'd rather paint or read, I can't do either of those if surrounded by Lexers.

Smoke pours from the stovepipes of the hangars and buildings, and the snow has finally melted on the runway and concrete surfaces of the airport. Everything outside the fence lies under an undisturbed blanket of snow. The plane hits the runway, and we slow to a stop in front of the main hangar. The large hangars that have been converted to living space sit behind four smaller hangars that house the communications, weapons, storage and mess hall.

We leave the soldiers to unload the plants and head inside the communications hangar. The wall to our left is all radio equipment. A couple of uniformed soldiers sit at stations wearing headphones.

Whitefield mans the radios at all hours. We do, too, but we have one or two people sitting at our small station in the building with the solar equipment. This place broadcasts daily.

Whitefield can afford to blow through gasoline for their generators, since they scored a tanker full of fuel last fall. That's what the soldiers do—head into previously populated places for all the things that make life easier. We're lucky they share so readily with us, although the oats and corn that we gave in trade came in handy over the winter.

People scribble furiously in the row of desks on the right side of the hangar. They keep track of communications from Safe Zones all over the country, as well as Whitefield's food and fuel supplies. Will Jackson gets up from his desk nearest the glassed-in room in the back, once the airport's office but now called Command. Will gives the impression of being four feet wide and seven feet tall, with the biggest laugh I've ever heard.

"Cassie, a pleasure, as always," he says, and envelops me in a hug that makes me feel like a tiny elf instead of five foot seven. "How's it going?"

I smile into his uniform shirt, somewhere down by his navel. "I'm good, Willie. How're you?"

Will's laugh rings out, and he releases me. He's nothing but kind to us, but being on his bad side doesn't look like much fun. I've seen him reduce men bigger and angrier than him to tears. He's tough but fair, and if you don't love him, you have to respect him. But I love him.

"Come on into Command," Will says.

The room, with its long table and chairs, reminds me of the conference room at the non-profit where I used to work. Instead of inspirational messages, though, giant maps of the United States, Canada and Mexico are tacked to the wall, peppered with pushpins. The red pushpins are Safe Zones that still stand. The green are the ones that have lost contact with Whitefield. The black are those that are known to be gone. There aren't many to begin with, but it looks as though there are more green pins than a few weeks ago.

Adrian goes still, eyes locked on the wall. The pin in Idaho, where his mom and sister are, is green. No contact. Three weeks ago it was red. I take his hand and in my most hopeful tone, say, "It's still green."

Will comes up behind us with a sigh. Adrian pulls his eyes away from that lonely green pin.

"I was hoping to have better news for you today," Will says. "We haven't heard anything in two weeks. But all that could mean is they lost power. Maybe a generator died, or they ran out of gas. They don't need fuel to live. I know they had supplies laid in for the winter. I'm not worried."

There's no doubt in his voice. Will has a wife and two kids in Boston. He fought his way home, but they weren't there. He still talks about them in the present tense. Adrian nods. There's nothing more to say, and everyone looks away to give him a private moment.

"I'm sorry," I whisper.

Adrian squeezes my hand twice, our code for *I love you*. I do the same. He blinks—a long, slow blink—and then takes a deep breath. "So, what else is going on, Will?"

There's nothing to do except move on. To file it under Fear or Grief or Overwhelming Sadness. To only let it out when you absolutely need to, and then, only in small doses. You laugh and joke about the terrible things, even when those jokes are in awful taste. At least that's what we try to do, but it's not always that easy.

I sit at the glossy brown table between Adrian and Nelly. I wish there was a big box of donuts, like my old boss Julio would bring in. Right now I'd take one with rainbow sprinkles and a Boston cream. My stomach growls at thought of all that processed sugar.

Nelly hears it and shakes his head. "Didn't you just eat?"

I rub my stomach. "Baby's hungry." His eyes widen until he catches Adrian's grin, and then he shoves me.

"This reminds me of work," I say.

"Mm, Julio's donuts," Nelly says. "I'd kill for a glazed."

"Rainbow sprinkles," Adrian says. This is why we're perfect for each other.

"So," Will says, and points at the maps, "we've lost contact with some other Safe Zones, too."

We were so busy looking at Idaho that I didn't think about the green pins in the bottom of the map.

"All south of us," he says. "Southern Louisiana and San Jose de Morilitos in Mexico. Morilitos had lost contact with two Zones south of them before they went dark."

"Could be they've run out of fuel to power the generators," John says. He steeples his fingers on the table and glances at Adrian. "If people have a choice between vehicles and radios, they'll choose vehicles every time."

"True," Will says. "I just want you all to know where we stand. Which is to say we don't know a goddamned thing, as usual. Sometimes trying to keep all of this together is like pissing in the wind."

Will rubs the back of his neck with a meaty hand and stares at the map. "Approximately twenty thousand people. That's all we know are left. Out of what, three hundred million? There could be thousands we don't know about, but we can't afford to lose a single one."

"If something's moving north, we'll know soon enough," John says. "One of the Zones is bound to contact us, if that's the case."

I've never seen Will so discouraged. None of us has, and we watch as he pulls himself together with a shake of his head. Adrian slides him a paper. "Here's a list of the starts we brought you today. I'm working on plans so you'll know where and when to plant."

Will glances at the paper and hands it to Ian, his right-hand man. "You're getting the short end of the stick here, A. Like I said, you don't need fuel to live, but we damn sure need food. Whatever you need, man, say the word."

CHAPTER 6

"Lunch won't be fancy, but it'll be food," Will says on the way to the mess hall. "People may bitch about oatmeal every morning, but they know they're lucky to have it."

"Same with us," Adrian says, "and we've got more variety. Oh, that reminds me—soon you'll have more chickens than you'll know what to do with."

Will thumps Adrian's shoulder. Adrian's tall and lean, but his shoulders are broad and arms muscular. Even so, Will knocks him forward an inch.

"I don't think we would've made it without you," Will says. "Not all of us. The food rationing would've been pretty tight."

Adrian shrugs. "You'd do it for us. And as long as there's fuel, we can farm as much land as we need to. We're going to try using livestock this year, too. The gas won't last forever."

"Sure as shit won't. But there's plenty of it for now, as long as we can get to it. Only good thing about how this went down is that it happened too fast to burn up all the fuel. We might as well use it up before it degrades any more."

This hadn't been an issue last summer, when the fuel was a few months old. Without stabilizers, however, gasoline goes bad. Sometimes it degrades in a few months; sometimes it's still usable a year or more later. The problem is, aside from a marked change in color and smell, there's no way for us to tell until we use it. We have additives that can help restore old fuel, but those are finite as well. By next summer, or the one after, we'll have to rely on steam and solar power, as well as draft animals.

Will watches the plume of snow the wind carries from the top of Mount Washington, the highest peak in the Northeast. He wears the look people get when they're thinking of the ones they've lost: the thousand-yard stare. "Wish I had better news about your family, A."

Adrian claps his back in turn. "I know."

"We've got a good thing going," Will says. He turns to John. "John, I wanted to show you something the guys have been working on. We'll see you all at lunch."

A flat carpet of snow covers the tall grass that was tilled last fall to prepare for this summer's crops. Whitefield will produce enough food to feed themselves this year. And it was all under Adrian's tutelage. The farmers in the area had turned or left by the time the 157th arrived.

"You're amazing," I say to Adrian. He brushes off my praise with a wave of his hand. "And *I* should learn how to take compliments? You heard what Will said—they wouldn't have made it without you. You deserve anything in the whole wide world. That's how amazing you are."

"Anything?" he asks.

I spread my arms expansively. "Anything!"

"Well, how about a girlfriend who picks her underwear up off the floor?"

Nelly snorts. He's lived in a room with me and knows the score. I get him with a swift kick to the ankle.

"They're *clean*," I say, because there's no way I can promise something so unlikely. I only make promises I can keep. "And they're usually on a chair." Adrian lets out a *humph*. "How about the purple ones?"

He gooses me. "The purple ones can stay out unless Bits is there."

"All right," Nelly says, "that's my cue to leave. This is not something I need to hear."

"Have fun with Adam. Oh, I mean the *cows*," I yell after him. He flips me the bird without looking back. I grin at Adrian and pull my coat tighter. The sun may be out, but the breeze is cool. I tilt my head toward the mess hall. "So, lunch?"

I take a couple of steps without waiting for an answer, but Adrian lays a hand on my arm and spins me around. He's so still and serious that I feel a pang of worry. He rubs a hand on the leg of his jeans and clears his throat. "How about a fiancé who picks her underwear up off the floor?"

I stare, unsure if I heard correctly. He fumbles to get his hand into his jeans pocket and watches me closely. His eyes are gray-green today, but they're as warm as ever.

"What?" I try to say more, but nothing comes out. It may be silly to feel nervous after all these years, but my smile trembles and I can barely hear over the wind rushing in my ears.

He reaches into his pocket and pulls out the engagement ring I returned three years ago. I've never asked what he did with it. It didn't matter; I've only ever wanted him.

"Will you marry me?" It comes out in one breath. He's as nervous as I am. My mouth opens, but he holds up a finger. "If I promise I'll never ask you to pick your underwear up off the floor or any other completely inappropriate surface."

I laugh so loud it echoes off the buildings and all my nervousness dissipates. Adrian rubs the dark stubble on his jaw and rocks on his feet. He's waiting for an answer, but I can't imagine he doesn't already know what it is.

"Yes," I say. "Of course." I laugh again, this time from the light feeling that's flooded my chest and the relieved look on his face.

"Good." He closes the space between us. "I love you until the end of the world."

"And after," I say.

He takes my left hand and twists off the ring I wear—the silver band with a tiny star that he gave me in college. It's one of the only things I have left from my old life, besides people. He moves it to my right hand and slides the little antique diamond on my bare finger. It still fits, just like us. When he's done, we stand inches apart, smiling like self-conscious teenagers. This may be the second time we've done this engagement thing, but we're not much more sophisticated at it this go-round.

"You sure?" he asks, still holding my left hand.

"Yes! What'd you think?"

He shrugs, his smile embarrassed and sweet, like a little boy. I pull him in for the kind of kiss I don't usually dole out in public. It's just getting good when three passing soldiers catcall, and we break apart.

I lean my head against his chest and sigh. "You know, this whole communal living thing can really cramp one's style."

"Yes, yes it can," Adrian says. He tickles the small of my back with the hand that managed to creep under my coat. "Later?"

"Maybe," I tease, and pull back to look at him. "Why were you walking around with a ring?"

"I've had it for a week. I've been waiting for the right moment."

I try not to show my amusement that the right moment was in the middle of the tarmac at Whitefield while talking about underwear, but it's impossible.

"I know," he says. "Underwear. Can I pick a moment or what?"

"It was perfect."

"Bits wouldn't have been able to hold it in much longer, anyway. I cleared it with her first."

Adrian would think of asking Bits, who's probably planned the wedding down to the hideous white dress by now. That he would do such a thing makes me love him more than ever.

"I can't believe she kept it," I say. "Bits is horrible with secrets."

Adrian mumbles something at the ground. I could swear it has the word *kitten* in it. I pull his arm. "What? Did you just say something about a kitten?"

Bits is desperate for a kitten. She plays with the cats in the barn all the time, but figuring out what to use for kitty litter—or, even worse, how to housebreak a cat—is not at the top of my to-do list.

"I promised her one." He runs a hand through his hair and looks at me sheepishly. "I said it could live in the house with us."

"No, you didn't! You're such a sucker!" I crack up. I knew one of us would break if she asked long enough. I'm just glad it wasn't me.

"But you love me anyway."

"Nope, that's why I love you. You're my sucker, lollipop." I plant another kiss on his lips and then wag my finger. "But you are totally in charge of potty training and litter recon."

Adrian pulls my arm through his. "I know, I know. Now, can I offer my fiancé some lunch?"

"Only if you don't call me your fiancé. It sounds so pretentious. How about *my intended*?"

"Right," he says, "because that's not pretentious at all."

CHAPTER 7

Lunch isn't fancy, but the bread is warm and the soup is hot. Adam sits across from me, thin, boyish face aglow. He's on the shy side, but he manages to hold his own with Nelly. "So when do you think you'll get married?"

"I don't know," I say. "Whenever we don't have to eat soup for the thousandth time?" I look to Adrian, who slurps up the last of his soup and gives an agreeable shrug.

"Your excitement is contagious," Nelly says. "Does one of you need a Green Card or something? Why bother?"

Adrian and I laugh. Years ago, we'd planned on a simple service at my parents' cabin. We'd already pledged ourselves to each other, but we wanted to do it before the people we loved. It would almost seem pointless—since so many of those people are gone, since we're already married in every way that counts and since the end of the world doesn't exactly lend itself to wedding ceremonies—but it doesn't feel pointless.

"Maybe it's important to keep doing the things that used to be important," Adrian says quietly. He's put into words what I couldn't, and I lean my head on his shoulder. Then he holds his thumb and index fingers a centimeter apart and shrugs. "Plus, I'm almost positive I love her."

"No one else would take her," Nelly says. "So there's that, too."

"Exactly. I didn't want her to feel bad."

I roll my eyes and turn to Adam. "Are you sure you want to become a part of this dynamic? You'll never be safe."

"Well," Adam says, and tugs on the front of his short, brown hair, "I asked around, and no one else will date Nel. I thought I was doing him a favor."

I lean across the table for Adam's hand. "I'm positive I love you. Let's you and I get married and leave these two to their own devices."

"I do," Adam says with a grin.

"Sorry, sweets, I'm already taken," I say to Adrian. I turn to John, whose blue eyes have been twinkling ever since he received our news. "John, will you perform the ceremony? It would mean a lot to us."

John lumbers up from his chair, and his bear hug feels the same as the ones my dad used to give. John's been like a dad to me ever since my parents died. Even more so, now that he's lost contact with his own kids.

"It would be an honor," John says. "Your mom and dad would be so happy for you. Both of you."

"Let's do it in July," Adrian says. "There's no soup in July."

"Okay. But, why?"

"He wants to snap you up before you get away," John says.

"Well, I should marry you while I'm still twenty-nine," I say. "I've got to snag you while I'm young and fresh."

My birthday is in August, but I'm not dreading thirty. I want to make it to eighty, at least, and the chances of that have gotten a lot slimmer in the past year. I'm just hoping it's an improvement on last year's birthday, which ended with us surrounded by a pod of Lexers and my parents' cabin burning down.

"Fine, but once I see a wrinkle, you're out," Adrian says. He runs a finger along his throat in warning.

I punch him and say, "Thank you, John."

John's not the most demonstrative person, but he sniffs and the skin around his eyes has gone pink. "Like I said, it's my pleasure."

I spot Zeke on the other side of the room and excuse myself to ask him a question. Zeke's beefy frame sits in front of a huge bowl of soup and half a loaf of bread. His gray-streaked hair is in a ponytail, but when he leans close to the bowl his beard comes away dripping.

I rest my hand on his shoulder. "Hey, Zeke."

"Cassie!" he says, and gives me a blindingly white grin. He may look like an outlaw with his long hair and tattoos, but we learned he's a dentist when we met him last summer on his way from Kentucky to Whitefield. He earned the name Z.K. on that trip, for Zombie Killer, and now everyone calls him Zeke instead of his given name, Martin. "What brings you to our fine establishment?"

"I missed your handsome face."

He leans back in his chair with a bellow. Nothing about his slightly squashed features is remarkable, but the kindheartedness that shines through makes him attractive. I'd love to find him a nice biker lady. "If only that were true. How's Bits?"

"She's great. I wanted to ask when you were coming over to Kingdom Come. She's due for a cleaning—" I lose my train of thought when I spot a familiar figure filling his bowl at the soup pot. He turns and sets his bowl down at an empty table, and I let out a gasp. I leave Zeke staring and run through the tables. "Hank?"

Hank's eyes are still huge behind his glasses, and he's as skinny as ever, but he's sprouted tiny dreadlocks and a couple of inches in the past year. He blinks like I might disappear. "Cassie!"

I know ten year-old boys don't like hugs, but I wrap my arms around him anyway. "How long have you been here? Where's—"

"Cassie?" Henry's voice comes from behind.

Henry always had the slightly weary look of a man used to hard work, but the past year has aged him even more. The lines around his eyes have deepened and the look in his eyes is more sad than tired. But his face is bright when I pull Hank his way for a group hug.

"When did you get here?" I ask. "I'm at Kingdom Come, but we were here three weeks ago."

"We snowshoed in a few days ago. Decided to do it before traveling would be riskier." Henry shakes his head slowly. "I didn't think I'd ever see you again."

"I thought about you guys all the time. Are Corrie and Dottie—" I stop at Henry and Hank's identical expressions of grief. "No. No, I'm so sorry."

"Come sit," Henry says.

I wipe my face with a cloth napkin as the tears roll. He leads me to the chair next to his soup bowl. I'm crying for Corrie and Dottie, for Eric, for Maria, for Adrian's mom and sister. Once you let the tears out, they have a way of taking over.

"It was late last summer," Henry says. "We got to the camp and found some other people there. Since we were waiting on family, we decided to stay. They were a nice group, but there wasn't enough food. By the time we decided to make our way to you, the pods were everywhere and there was no more gas. We started out on foot—we thought we'd walk until we found a car, but we ran into a group of them. Corrine and Dottie..."

Dottie was quiet and strong, and Corrine so sensitive in spite of all her tween bluster. Corrine had looked just like her mother, petite with dark skin and striking light eyes, and the vision of what they must look like now rises in my mind. I shove it back down and hope that Henry and Hank don't have that firsthand knowledge.

I can tell he doesn't want to continue, so I fill the empty space. "We had to leave the house in August. A pod came there, too."

Henry nods. "Hank and I found an old hunting cabin and enough food in the houses close by. Then, when it got cold enough to freeze them, we'd snowshoe until we found a new place to stay. We'd use up all the food and move on again. We thought Whitefield would be easier to get to, since we could follow the highway most of the way."

Henry smiles at Hank. I don't know where my brother is, but the rest of my family—my adopted family—has made it through unscathed. I know how lucky we are. I can't imagine losing Bits the way Henry lost Corrine. The thought is so bleak I can't dwell on it for more than a moment or I'll start to cry again.

"I'm so sorry. And I'm so glad you're here. I missed you. Especially you, Hank. I've got a little girl now. Her name's Beth, but we call her Bits. She's eight, but she's crazy smart and loves to read, just like you. I bet you guys would get along great."

"Does she like graphic novels or comics?" Hank asks. His eyes light up at my nod. "I've got some really cool ones. There's one with this guy, well, he's not really a guy, he's like a..."

He goes on and on, but Henry and I only half listen. Henry rests his work-roughened hand on mine. I squeeze it, overcome by a rush of happiness. We may have only spent a few days together last spring, but I feel like I've reclaimed another piece of my family.

CHAPTER 8

I tried to convince Henry and Hank to move to Kingdom Come, but Henry is an electrician, something that's sorely needed in Whitefield. Whenever they have a problem they call Adrian or James to talk them through. Henry doesn't want to leave them in the lurch, but I made him promise to consider the idea. Adrian was disappointed too, because once they started talking about electricity and solar power you'd have thought they'd known each other forever.

That was a week ago. And yesterday Mother Nature decided to dump two feet of snow on us in April. I'm in no hurry to start the summer, so I don't mind. Summer might mean fresh food and warmth, but it also means zombies.

Ana looks up when I stamp my feet off in the greenhouse at the north end of the farm. "Cass, you have to see my tomato sprouts. They're super cute!"

"Ana, you are an enigma wrapped in a mystery. How can someone who has no mouth filter and kills with more glee than I thought humanly possible also coo over seedlings?"

"Because they're my babies. And mamas love their babies." She wrinkles her nose. "What do you mean I have no mouth filter?"

"You say whatever comes into your head," I say, and admire her seedlings. They're impressive; even plants do her bidding.

She shrugs. "Yeah, so?"

"Normal people don't do that. Their brain relays the message to another part of their brain, which then decides if it's something that should be said out loud. Your brain opens the gate and lets the horses run."

Ana tucks her hair behind her ear and laughs. "Are you saying I'm a bitch, Cass?"

"You're a bitch with a heart of gold, Ana. I love you, horses and all. And, by the way, those seedlings are super cute." She's not really a bitch. Just blunt. Like a two by four.

"I love that!" she says. *"Bitch with a heart of gold.* It could be my slogan."

"We'll get some business cards printed up."

I water the hundreds of seedlings and check the fire in the stove. This is my favorite place to work. It's quiet and warm and smells like moist earth and tomato leaves. The peas are growing like crazy. They need to get out there soon.

"Why aren't you complaining about the snow?" Ana asks.

"Because it keeps things frozen. Things I'd rather not have thaw out."

"True. But I wouldn't mind a little patrolling."

I point a stake at her. "I am under orders to keep you reined in this summer. You are not allowed to do anything stupid."

"Peter." Ana sighs. "He wants me in the kitchen, barefoot and pregnant."

"Ana, no one, anywhere on Earth, wants *you* in a kitchen. He just wants you alive. Remember your quarry idea?"

The old quarry sits a half mile south of us, tucked in among the farmland that's quickly becoming forest. You can see it from the top of the mountain we use to watch for pods of Lexers moving north. The quarry's been dormant for decades, and the three immense holes have filled with water. It would be a great place to swim, if it didn't have Lexer corpses floating in it.

Ana had a plan to lead a pod of Lexers there with our ambulance, sirens blaring and lights flashing. She thought if she could get them to follow it along the narrow road that snakes between the pools, they'd fall in. But if they caught up with her, or more came from the other side, so would she.

"It was a great idea!"

"Well, it probably would have worked," I admit. "But that doesn't mean it was a great idea. How's Penny? She wasn't at breakfast this morning. I'm going over there when I'm done."

"She's either puking or about to puke. I am so not having a baby. Ever."

"You might want to talk to Peter about that. Since he wants you barefoot and pregnant and all."

She lifts a plant and kisses it. "Who needs a baby when I have my beautiful little plants?"

CHAPTER 9

I convinced Penny that coming to dinner would make her feel better, but now that she's here, head on the table, I'm thinking that maybe it wasn't the best idea.

"Oh my God." Penny lets out a moan. "Move the food away."

Ana pushes Penny's bowl of soup to the center of the table. "I didn't think people got sick this early."

"Doc says it's a good sign," James says. "The baby's strong."

Penny raises her head. She's pale, with dark circles under her eyes. "The baby is not strong. The baby is kicking my ass. This is awful. I don't know why people have babies, if this is how they feel." She looks at James. "We are never having sex again."

"Okay," James says. "Never again."

"Stop agreeing with everything I say." Penny's head clunks back down.

"Okay, I mean, no."

Penny's hand rises from the table, middle finger extended. Ana and I laugh. This new Penny may feel like crap, but she's entertaining. She's usually so well-mannered. It must be exhaustion; she can barely drag herself to the little school cabin every morning.

"How are my three favorite ladies?" Dan stops to ask. He looks at Penny, who groans. "That bad, huh? Be right back."

Five minutes later he returns with a glass packed with fresh snow and another glass with yellow liquid. He pours the yellow liquid over the snow. "Here, drink this."

Penny lifts her head and sips from the glass. "That's not bad. What is it?"

"Ginger lemonade. It's what my sisters drank when they were pregnant," Dan says. "I thought it might work, even though it's powdered. It won't make it go away, but they didn't throw it back up. Most of the time."

"How many kids did they have?" Penny asks.

"Jen had two and Christy had three."

"They must've been crazy to do this more than once."

"It'll get better. Promise." He motions to my ring. "So, I hear Adrian's making an honest woman out of you. Congratulations."

"Thanks. When are you going to settle down with some lucky lady?"

He points at the three of us. "My top choices are all taken."

"Well, you're my second choice," Ana says. "I'll let you know if the first spot opens."

"I'll be here."

Penny rolls her eyes at me. Those two can flirt for hours.

"Are you propositioning my girl?" Peter asks Dan. He sets his bowl down next to Ana and takes a seat.

"*I* was propositioning *him*," Ana says.

"Well, that's a relief." He smiles when Ana kisses his cheek.

I wave over Nelly and Adrian. "Why don't you sit here tonight?" I ask Dan. "We'll push tables together. You can sit at the old married people's table for once."

Dan agrees, and by the time everyone's arrived it's become an impromptu dinner party.

"This soup is really good," Jamie says. "Better than usual."

"Well, you didn't make it," Shawn, her husband, says. "It's got that going for it."

Jamie gives him a friendly smack with her spoon. She's mid-thirties, five foot nothing, with an ample chest, curly black hair and olive skin. Shawn has a scruffy beard, a tree trunk chest with arms to match and a sarcastic manner. It's obvious they love each other, but they also love to shoot each other down at every opportunity.

"That's because it's Peter's recipe," Ana says. "He can cook anything. Oh, Maureen, I wanted to ask you—I keep signing up for kitchen duty, but I always end up assigned somewhere else."

Peter chokes on his soup. Maureen says, "It's just that you're so good at other things, Ana. We try to assign everyone based on their strengths."

It's a diplomatic reply, but it doesn't escape Ana that Nelly and Adrian are overly focused on their bowls and everyone else has gone silent. She narrows her eyes. "I'm not allowed to work in the kitchen? There's actually a plot to keep me out?"

"No, Ana," Nelly says, "there's a plot to save us all from death. It just requires that we keep you out of the kitchen. Especially after the *arroz con pollo* incident."

That had been the worst meal ever. Ana had tried to cook Maria's famous dish, but it had fallen short. Way, way short.

"It wasn't that bad! Cassie ate it. Right, Cass?"

"Yes," I say. "Yes, I did. I did it to be nice. And I paid the price, believe me."

Ana crosses her arms and her lip juts out. "So it wasn't the best *arroz con pollo*—"

"More like *arroz con peo*," Penny says. She even smiles a little. Maybe that drink's helping.

Bits informs the table, "*Peo* means fart!" She's had Penny teach her every semi-inappropriate Spanish word there is. Everyone roars with laughter.

"Remember how bad it was, Adrian?" Bits asks. "Cassie ate so much of it, too."

I can see where this is going. Good Lord. I swear Adrian has a tear of laughter snaking down his cheek. "We almost had to kick her out of the room, right, Bits? It—"

"Enough!" I say, my face on fire. "This is where I draw the line! It's bad enough everyone knows everything about everyone else. Can we please keep the two secrets that are left?"

Even Ana is laughing now. I kick Adrian under the table and drop my head into my hands. "New topic, please!"

"Let's play *I Miss*," Bits says.

It's a game where everyone names something they want but can't have. We never mention people, which is what we all want most of all. It has to be a thing, sometimes frivolous, sometimes not, but it's never, ever a person.

"I miss orange juice," Bits says.

"I miss not being pregnant," Penny mutters.

"Pepsi!" Nelly calls out.

"A Caramel Macchiato," I say.

"The internet," James says. "But not Facebook."

"Red Sox games," Dan says.

"Music," Adrian says. "All the music on my phone."

"Why don't you charge your phone?" Dan asks. "You could, couldn't you?"

Adrian shakes his head. "It wouldn't be fair. And if we had everyone charging phones and iPods we wouldn't have juice for anything else. We can barely keep the lights going as it is."

He doesn't even charge it occasionally. I've told him he should. It's his farm and I think he and Ben have every right to a little extra power, but he refuses. He's given me an idea, though. I barely listen to the rest of the answers while I mull it over.

***

A few days later, I find James in the solar barn, where he would probably sleep if he didn't have Penny warming his bed at night. He hands me a small box wrapped in a cloth, and I hide it in my bag after I hug him in excitement.

"It works, I tested it myself," James says. "You know, he'll never agree to this."

"I think I have that part covered," I say. "Thank you so much, James. This is the best birthday present ever."

CHAPTER 10

The snow melted in days, and the past week has been unseasonably warm for April in the Northeast Kingdom. Now that the roads have cleared, we visit what we call the lookout twice or three times a day. We drive up a dirt road to an abandoned house and then hike the short trail to where we've cleared trees on the summit. The view is beautiful, but it's also strategic. If anything's moving in the fields or near the quarry, we can see it in what's close to a 180 degree view.

We can't see into the woods, though, and we have no way of surveying north of the farm without the plane, which would probably attract more Lexers. So, when the radio in the greenhouse crackles and Jamie announces that seven Lexers are approaching the north fence, I'm not surprised. Ana and I grab our gloves and walk the short distance. I wear my shoulder holster and my knife on my belt. We'd stopped carrying weapons in the winter, but everyone is armed now that it's warm.

Jamie is winding her hair up into a knot on top of her head when we arrive. She hands Ana her binoculars. "They just came out of the tree line. Taking their sweet time, but they're definitely heading this way."

She swings her spike and hops from foot to foot. Jamie's almost as crazy as Ana. Maybe you have to be somewhat crazy to have survived this long.

"Oh, yeah," Ana says. "There's another three behind them, too."

It's impossible not to make noise while living on a farm with so many people. Farm machinery, chopping wood, voices, kids playing, drifting stovepipe smoke—they all serve as zombie beacons. It's pretty much a guarantee that anything close is going to stop by eventually.

"I've got Ana and Cass," Jamie says into the radio. "Ten Lexers now. We're all good here." She turns to us, hands on hips. "You know a guy is going to come anyway, right? No way three girls can kill ten Lexers through a fence."

Footsteps sound behind us, and Shawn appears. Jamie raises the radio in the air. "Did you or did you not hear 'All good?' "

"Oh, I thought you said, 'Send a strong man,' " he replies, and flexes a furry arm.

"Then why'd *you* come?"

"I was in the north barn, light of my life. I thought maybe I could help. I know you can kick anyone's ass, including mine."

"That's right," Jamie says.

The Lexers are halfway to us, and there's nothing to do but wait as they plod across the muddy field, laboriously pulling their feet out of the muck. A tall, thin Lexer takes a fat one down with it when it falls, in a Laurel and Hardy-esque routine.

I giggle, which may be callous, but I can't stop. The others join in. It was nowhere near as funny as the level of hysteria we reach. Shawn hangs on to the fence to stay upright, and Jamie wipes away tears. These are officially the first Lexers of the season, and the tension it causes has to come out somehow. When the first two are twenty feet from the fence we quiet down to hiccups and gasps.

"I've got one," Jamie says.

Ana holds her cleaver like a javelin, spike side toward the fence. "Me, too."

The rasping moans start when they hear our voices. Coarse, wrinkled, gray skin is mottled by open wounds edged with black. The one that has lips bares his teeth. They hit the fence and the chain-link bends, but I'm not worried. Those posts are sunk deep; it would take many more to push it down.

The lipless one tightens its fingers around the links. The metal sinks into his skin where some black moss has taken hold, and a dark fluid trickles out. They usually don't drip unless you cut them with something sharp, and even then it's more of an ooze. The moss must be breaking down his tissue.

Ana glances at the liquid on her boot and says, "Gross." She lines her cleaver up with his eye and pushes.

Jamie drops her spike and releases her hunting knife from the sheath on her belt. The other one has his head pressed sideways, and her knife enters his ear and comes back out with a popping noise. Five more have reached the fence, including Laurel and Hardy. Laurel's mud-covered mouth is open wide. I hold the spike of my cleaver at the closest opening and give a quick jab to the spot where jaw meets neck. I yank it out and do the same to Hardy, who falls with a meaty thud. Maybe I shouldn't be so sweaty because I'm quite safe behind here, but seeing them on the move has reminded me that I'm not safe. None of us are.

When the last three are down, Jamie picks up her binoculars and scans the field. "That's it. Good job, people." She looks behind us and sighs. "I *said* we had it."

Thirty people stand there, probably all the adults who heard the radio and could leave their posts. But I know they're not there because they doubted us; they wanted to see it with their own eyes. I think we all harbored some shred of hope—one that we knew would never be realized—that the winter might end this. That the fifty percent who'd survived the cold wouldn't be able to walk far on damaged muscle, or that they would rot away. We hoped for something, anything, other than the alternative. Something other than this.

CHAPTER 11

We've heard from the Safe Zone in New York City. They'd stopped broadcasting in the winter, but they're up and running again. I'm not sure how they've made it this far—hundreds of people vs. eight million or so Lexers. Maybe only half that number of Lexers now, due to the winter, but they roam the city in endless circles since no one, including the survivors, can leave.

Maria's not with them, we checked again to be sure. The New Yorkers live in the sky, on the tops of buildings. They drink rainwater and grow what they can on rooftop gardens and in backyards, but they say there's still a lot of food to scavenge even though those promised FEMA food drops never arrived. From their vantage point, with high-powered telescopes, they've seen a few pods across the water in Jersey, pods that might end up here later this summer.

Over thirty have come out of the woods in the past week. It may not be a lot, but one group came to the fence while the kids were outside. We spotted them right after they left the trees, but so did the kids. Bits was so scared that her nightmares returned, and she's just had another one starring her mother.

"What if you die too, Cassie?" she asks me with trembling, tight lips. "I'm scared you're going to die."

I kneel at the edge of her bed and find her hand under the blankets. I wish I could promise her it won't happen, and I lower my head to hers. "I'm planning to be here a long time, honey. I can promise you that."

She attempts to hold in her tears, but one makes a glistening track on her cheek in the moonlight and then drops to her pillow. "But what if you do?"

"You'll always be taken care of. There are so many people who love you, you know. I wish I had as many people as you do. I have, like, five, and you have a million."

"There aren't even that many people here."

"That's what makes it so amazing," I say. Bits rolls her eyes and lets out a soft giggle. "Don't worry about me. And don't worry about you. Let me worry about that, okay?"

I press my lips to her forehead, and she closes her eyes. I sit on the edge of her bed to wait for the even rise of her chest. Her eyes flicker under their lids, and even in sleep her hand clutches the locket I gave her. It's big as lockets go, a little less than three inches long, the kind in which Victorians would put miniature paintings of their loved ones. I painted a tiny image of her mother this winter, from my memory of the photograph we left behind. Bits cried because she'd forgotten what her mother had looked like.

"You look just like her—beautiful blue eyes, heart-shaped face and cute nose," I'd said. "All you ever have to do is look in a mirror." But still, she carries it everywhere.

I kiss her forehead and creep back to bed. Adrian pulls me close with a sleepy arm, but I can't fall back asleep. Bits lies motionless in the moonlight. I've watched her sleep enough times to know that I can't always see her breathe, but suddenly I'm convinced that she isn't. The fear rises up so fast that I throw Adrian's arm to the side and rush to get my hand on her chest. Once I feel the up and down of gentle breathing, I let out my own breath and cross the floor again.

Adrian's eyes are open. "What's wrong?"

"I thought she wasn't breathing," I say softly. "I know, it's ridiculous."

"It's not ridiculous."

I get back under the covers and whisper, "So I'm not crazy?"

"You're a little crazy."

He chucks me under the chin, but I can't shake the panicky feeling in my belly. There's so much that can go wrong, and I feel like it's only a matter of time before our luck runs out. We escaped Brooklyn. We made it here. I'm in bed with Adrian, something that should have been impossible. A person can only be so lucky. I feel tears brewing and clench my teeth. I barely cried all winter, but this time I lose the battle.

Adrian pulls me to him. "Don't cry, sweetie. We'll be all right."

I nod into his chest. I want to cross my fingers, knock on wood, throw some salt in the hope of keeping bad luck away. I know it won't do any good, but there are two things I don't think I could stand to lose, and they're both in this room with me right now.

CHAPTER 12

Ana's been on duty at the gatehouse all night, and now she rushes into the kitchen. "There's a pod of Lexers at the tower."

Adrian's at the tower, the little cabin on stilts before the first gate. I drop the fork in the bacon pan and turn to Mikayla, who shoos me out with wide eyes. I wrestle my gloves over my sweaty hands and pick up my cleaver at the door. We rush out the back door and into the lot that holds the vehicles. Ana opens the ambulance door, and I take the passenger's side.

"Caleb's gone to the tents to wake everyone." She hands me her radio. "Here, call. They're fine. Nothing can get to them up there."

I press the button. "Adrian? We're coming!"

"Cass, we're fine," he says in a calm voice. "There's only fifty of them, and the ladder's up. Relax."

He's surrounded by Lexers, and he's telling *me* to relax. Nelly opens the rear doors and climbs in with Jamie, Shawn, Dan, Caleb and Marcus. Ana thrusts the key into the ignition and revs the motor. She'd barely driven before Bornavirus, and now she drives like she does everything else—maniacally. There are thumps and curses from the back when she does a donut and races down the driveway. She slams on the brakes beside Peter at the first gate, which results in several more thuds from the back.

"What's the plan?" he asks.

Killing them through the fence is easy, but taking on fifty in a clearing is a good way to get killed. I speak into the radio. "Adrian? What do you want us to do? Should we come down and lead them away?"

"They'll just come back. We're going to spike them and then shoot the ones we can't reach. We've got plenty of ammo. Might draw some others, so we don't want you guys out here. We're fine."

It's killing me how calm he is. Doesn't he know this is when a person is allowed to freak the fuck out? I stare at the radio and grit my teeth.

Nelly kneels in the opening that connects the back to the cab and rests a hand on my leg. "He's fine, darlin'."

I take a breath and speak into the radio. "Okay. We're up at the gate. Tell us when it's safe."

"We will."

We sit in silence. The entrance that allows vehicle access to the farm is corrugated metal, with a viewing platform on either side. I climb one and stand in the early morning light, wishing I could see what's happening a quarter of a mile down the road. But I can only stare at the trees while I imagine them dropping the long spikes into the top of the Lexers' skulls from the cabin's walkway. I jump at the first gunshot; now they must be going after the ones they can't reach.

Movies make you believe that head shots are easy. Point, pull the trigger and you're good. Center mass is easy, but it's a lot harder to get a head shot in a moving person than they would have you believe. Head shots can be tricky on paper targets, but add in the movement, fear and lack of time to properly sight, and they become extremely difficult. Adrian's good at this, though, and he has time on his side. I know he's safe, but it's out of my control, and I hate that feeling.

Nelly climbs up next to me. His hair is crazy and his clothes are askew, but his eyes are sharp.

"Who's with him?" I ask "I can't remember."

"John," Nelly says.

It doesn't make me any happier that two of my most favorite people in the world are down there, but my heart slows; John's the best marksman I've ever seen. Now that I know it's him, I can tell by the reports that carry our way. Slow and steady. Boom. Boom. Boom. Nelly puts his arm around my shoulder when I shiver.

"They're fine," he says. "Don't worry. Talk to me about something."

"Okay. How's Adam?"

He shakes his head and snorts.

"It was your idea, Nelly!" I say. "The least you can do is talk to me about it."

"Okay. He's fine. I like him."

I keep my eyes on the road. "*Like* like?"

There's no response. We have to be close to twenty shots now, but those head shots are hard. "Nelly!"

"Yes, Cass. *Like* like."

"So, what base—"

"Cass?" Adrian's voice comes through the radio.

"I'm here."

"They're all down. You guys can come help with clean up. But be careful, there might be others in the woods."

I close my eyes. "Okay, we'll be there in a minute."

***

Bodies cover the grass around the lookout. Adrian and John lean on the walkway railing, looking very pleased with themselves. I climb the ladder they lower, and when I get to the top Adrian pulls me to him. I grip the back of his coat and exhale.

"I was fine, sweetie," he says.

"I was still scared. What if it'd been me here?"

"I would've been terrified."

I let go of Adrian and hug John. "Good job, you guys."

"It was fun," John says, smiling under his beard. "I've missed the range."

"Awesome. Well, let's not make a habit of it." I look around the clearing. The others have begun to drag the bodies into a pile, and the trailer's on its way down to move the bodies to the field we use for that purpose. "I don't think we should have anyone down here anymore. It's not worth it. Any people who show up can come to the first gate."

"I think you're right," John says, and starts down the ladder. "I'll help with disposal."

"We should go clean up, too," I say to Adrian.

"Okay," he says. He pecks my lips, and a familiar smell carries over the aroma of rotten brain cavities that permeates the air.

I open my mouth in shock and put out my hand, palm up. "Give me one."

He puts on a puzzled expression. "Give you one of what?"

"I know you have Twizzlers! I can smell them." We have a bit of a candy habit, and there's not much of it left around here.

"I found them in the bottom of the food locker," he whispers. "Don't worry, I saved you one."

"One? One lousy Twizzler? That's worse than none! And after I raced down here to save your life."

Adrian winks. "So little faith in me. I saved most of them for you and Bits. I'll give them to you later."

The guys toss the bodies into the trailer while Ana, Jamie and I watch the woods. This is one time when I take full advantage of being female—if I don't have to lift a heavy, stinking body, I'm not going to complain. A branch snaps, and I spot movement in the trees. Ana's head whips my way when I make the short whistle we use to call each other. There's another flash of something pale, coming closer now that they've locked on us. There are five of them, so I hold up five fingers right before they step into the clearing. Some Lexers seem to move at the same speed as last summer, while others seem to be dragging their feet even more than they did. Thankfully, this group is the latter.

My stomach churns with the usual mixture of fear and disgust. I'm not like Ana—I always want to run away, but I've trained myself to stand and wait when it makes sense to do so. Still, it's difficult to fight against your body's survival instincts. I tell myself that there will be five fewer Lexers in a minute. That every one counts. The Lexer I kill might have been the one who would've bitten Bits, or Adrian, or anyone else on the farm. We're fairly safe there, but we have to leave—to get wood, to farm, to find supplies—and five fewer might be the difference between making it home or coming to the fence as one of them.

Ana and I situate ourselves next to each other, cleavers in hand, so they'll come at us together. We won't use guns unless it's unavoidable. More noise makes more Lexers, and it can become a never-ending cycle. When they're close enough, we split apart and move around to either side. It takes the Lexers a moment to work out what's happened, and by then we've finished off one each. Cleaver in, cleaver out.

Two move toward me, one to Ana. I put the cleaver edge under the next one's chin and shove. What would have taken all my strength last year is like a gentle push in comparison, due to all the practice I've had. It kills her and pushes her backward into her one remaining friend, who's knocked to the ground. I move forward, but

Adrian rams his machete through its head before I get there. He leaves it there, hilt up, and raises a hand in the air.

"You couldn't have moved back and let us all take them?" he asks through a clenched jaw.

"We were here." I knew we had them, no matter how shaky my hands were. "They were extra slow, did you notice?"

"No, I didn't notice, because I was watching you do something completely idiotic."

He stares past me into the trees, eyes flinty. I glance around to gauge everyone's reaction, but no one else looks particularly upset. They do look interested, though.

"Can we talk about this later?" I ask in a low voice.

"Fine," he says, but he still won't look at me.

Ana gives me a sympathetic look when Adrian stalks off. She gets this all the time, and not only from Peter, but I never do. I stare down at the bodies in confusion, and then I get angry.

***

After we've taken care of the Lexers and cleaned up, Adrian and I head to our room to change. He hasn't said a word to me since the clearing. I stop in the bathroom first, and by the time I've made it to our room I'm ready for a fight. I walk in and hang my jacket on a hook.

"Wow, you're actually hanging up your coat?" he asks from where he sits on the bed.

I spin around, fists clenched. "What the hell is your problem?"

"My problem is that you're so worried about everyone's safety, but when you have seven other people to help, you decide to take on Lexers by yourself."

"I wasn't by myself! Ana was there, and—"

"Yeah, yeah, I know all about you and Ana, the two-girl zombie team."

I take a breath at his comment, which is completely unfair. He knows how I feel about all of this, how I'm nothing like Ana. "That is not what I was going to say. I was going to say that Ana was there, and I knew you all had our backs. All I had to do was move back, run, anything like that. They were slow."

He glares at me from the edge of the bed. He's not giving an inch. I don't know what's gotten into him. It's not like I haven't done this before, and with his blessing, not that I need it. I want to scream, but I decide to go with common sense.

"Do I ever do anything dumb, really put myself in danger?" I ask. "Even when Ana does?"

He shakes his head grudgingly, but he still doesn't say anything.

"I have a freaking caution sign on my forehead!" I yell. "Why are you acting like this?"

"Because I fucking love you!" he yells back. "You're not the only person who worries, you know!"

His eyes redden before he looks at his feet. I think of his mom and sister. He insists he's fine whenever I've tried to bring them up, but there's no way that's true. All the fight leaves me. I sit beside him, lace my fingers through his and squeeze two times.

He squeezes back and rests his head on my shoulder. "I'm sorry. I knew I was safe up there, but you weren't safe. You didn't seem to care that they were coming right at you."

"You know I cared that zombies were coming to eat me. I would've run if I'd thought we couldn't kill them. I would've left Ana in the dust." He sniffs at my joke. "You were the same way on the radio. I wanted to kick you because it seemed like you weren't taking it seriously."

"I was, I swear," he says. "I just wasn't freaking out."

"Exactly. I don't do anything stupid because I always want to come back to you and Bits. I wouldn't do anything to jeopardize that."

"I know."

"Plus, you don't need to worry, not with my expertise in karate." I shoot out my hand in a faux karate chop, which accidentally knocks half of my stack of books on the nightstand to the floor.

"That's not helping your case," he says with a reluctant smile, and his shoulders come down a notch. "I really am sorry, sweetie. I shouldn't have taken it out on you. I just love you so much."

"I love you, too." I push him with my shoulder. "Even though you're a jerk."

He pulls a little paper bag out of his coat pocket and waves it in the air. "Would a jerk have saved you the last Twizzlers in the world?"

CHAPTER 13

"Trouble in Paradise?" Nelly asks, when I sit at the lunch table.

"Oh, shut up," I say. "He got worried and didn't handle it very well. So you can feed that to the rumor mill before it has us breaking up and moving to opposite sides of the farm."

Dan and Liz, another of our patrollers, laugh.

"I didn't think you guys ever fought," Dan says.

"Of course we do," I say. "How can you live with another human being and not get annoyed at them at least some of the time?"

Dan points a finger at me. "*That's* why I don't settle down. I always end up annoyed out of my mind."

"Want to hear my theory?" I ask.

Nelly groans. "Here we go—Cassie's Theory of Relationships."

"It's true!" I turn to Dan and Liz. "Everyone is going to annoy you somewhat. The trick is to find the person who only annoys you a little, and where what you love about them outweighs what you don't love. They'll never be perfect, but they'll be perfect for you. The problem is that people think it has to be perfect all the time, and that's not possible."

"That's actually a good theory," Liz says to Nelly, who shrugs.

"So, anyway, Nels," I say. "We never got to finish our conversation about Adam. I mean, you admitted you *like* like him, but you never told me—"

"Right now what I don't love about you is outweighing what I do love about you," Nelly says.

"You love me so much that the good could never be outweighed by the bad. You can tell me later. *In private*," I whisper loudly, from behind my cupped hand.

"I hate you," Nelly says. I blow him a kiss.

"So, are we really closing the cabin?" Liz asks.

"It doesn't make sense to have anyone down there if they're going to have to be rescued," Dan says. "Or waste ammo. It's better to wait for the Lexers to come to the fence."

Liz nods. She's in her early thirties, thin and tall, with short dark hair and muscled arms. I was a little afraid of her at first, but she laughs easily and is nice once you get past her tough demeanor.

Caleb and Marcus pull out chairs. They're brothers, but they could be twins with their platinum ponytails, snub noses and matching mannerisms. Caleb is nineteen and Marcus is twenty-two. They made it here last summer, after traveling home from college to find their parents dead. Well, they weren't actually dead. They had to finish them off.

"You can't see shit from the cabin, anyway," Marcus says. "Hey, we need to go on patrol soon. We're running out of stuff."

Patrol is when we leave the farm for supplies. It takes a lot of gas to run what little machinery we use, and all the little things—like toothbrushes, medicine and random equipment—are out there.

"We need feminine hygiene products," Liz says. "I don't know about you, Cassie, but this menstrual cup thing sucks."

"I don't mind it," I say. "My mom used one. It's better than the cloth pads."

Liz frowns at the mutters of the men. "What? It's perfectly natural. The female body is a beautiful thing." Caleb looks at her almost non-existent chest with a snort. "Yes, Caleb, I am a woman." She grabs his head in the crook of her arm. Caleb writhes and twists but can't escape.

"A woman who can kick your ass, Cabe!" Marcus calls.

"I've got to go. Art class." I look at Nelly. "So, we'll discuss later?"

"Nope," he says.

***

The cabin that was pressed into service as the school isn't cordoned off into rooms the way the others are. It's a modern pioneer schoolhouse, with desks, a wall painted chalkboard-black and projects hanging everywhere. Once winter set in, Penny insisted we start a school for the kids, and the weapons that once lived in here were moved to the solar barn.

"That's great, Jasmine," Penny says to a little girl with a long brown braid who holds out a piece of paper.

Jasmine is Bits's best friend. She towers over Bits, but she's shy and reserved where Bits is spunky. Her eyes light up at Penny's compliment. "Thank you, Miss Diaz."

"You really don't have to call me that, Jasmine."

"My mom says I should, at school."

Jasmine's mom, Josephine, is very strict. I don't blame her. She had three kids and a husband, and Jasmine's all that's left. She still jumps at the smallest noise and spends more time worrying than I do. Sometimes I catch her peering through the school windows until she catches sight of Jasmine and relaxes enough to head back to her shift.

"Hello, Miss Diaz," I say.

Penny waves half-heartedly. She still feels sick, but we've been filling in on her other shifts, so she's been getting more rest. I've upped my art classes from two to four days a week. I make them extra long and force her to lie down in the corner.

The fifteen kids, who range in age from five to sixteen, sit at tables working on projects or read in the pillow-strewn library area. I catch Bits's eye and wink. She returns it but stays put. Penny may be sweet, but she doesn't let them take advantage. She has the teacher stare down pat.

"Cassie's here!" Jacob, a ten year-old, says.

The kids mark their pages in books, return projects to their cubbies and come back to the tables with soft murmurs.

"They're like robots," I say to Penny. "How do you do that?"

"They listen to you, too."

"That's only because I do fun stuff. If I taught math they'd be throwing spitballs at me. Now go lie down."

Penny flops on the pillows in the library. I think she's asleep before she gets there.

"We're going to start working on self-portraits this week," I say. "Who knows what a portrait is?"

Ashley, who's sixteen and arrived here last summer with her surrogate mom Nancy, says, "A picture of a person. And a self-portrait is a picture of yourself."

"Right."

"Cassie painted me a portrait," Bits tells them. She pulls the locket out of her pocket. "It's of my mom."

I pull out the art supplies while they pass it around. Some of the kids look at it longingly, and I'm sure they wish they had something similar. Chris, Doc's twelve year-old son, had been on their annual father-son fishing trip to Vermont, and they never made it home to Mom. Even though Ashley has Nancy, she lost her parents. And the list goes on. I'd paint one for each of them, if only I knew their parents' faces. Maybe if I teach them well enough they'll be able to make their own before they really do forget.

On my way to the front, I notice a photo of me in the locket, opposite the portrait. Adrian must have cut up an old picture for her. I know Bits loves me, but she kind of has to, since she has no parents. That she would put me into her locket, next to her real mom, makes my chest tighten—in a good way. I take a breath and turn to the class.

"We're going to make portraits of ourselves, like these." I open the Frida Kahlo book to a self-portrait, one with Diego Rivera painted on her forehead. "We won't only draw what others can see, but what's inside, too. It can be anything—something that has meaning, something we love, even something we don't like."

"She has a man on her head!" Chris says.

"He's not *on* her head," Ashley says. She tosses her dark gold hair and raises her eyes to the ceiling. "She's thinking about him." Chris blushes, his unrequited love for Ashley apparent.

"Let's look at more of her paintings and talk about why you think she painted what she did."

They crowd around the book I set on the front table. Bits's freckled face is serious; she loves art of any kind. And she's good at it, like I always hoped my daughter would be. I smile and hope it conveys how much I adore her. And when she beams back, I think it must.

CHAPTER 14

I jolt awake when Bits leaps onto the bed.

"It's your birthday!" she screams into Adrian's sleeping face, and his eyes snap open.

"Yes," he says, slowly coming to. "Yes, it is. And I can't imagine a better way to be woken up than by such a pretty girl screaming in my ear."

Bits wiggles between us. She was ten times worse on her birthday. And this is before she has cake. "Party time! We took a vote, and we're going to watch *Ponyo*."

The party is just dinner with something special for dessert, like we do for everyone's birthday. But we always fire up the generator and let the kids watch a movie. They think it's because we love them, but it's to get them out of our hair while we drink a bit of alcohol.

"That sounds great," Adrian says. "But first, do you want your birthday present?"

"It's not *my* birthday," Bits says.

"Well, it's mine. And I can give out birthday presents to anyone I choose. So, do you want it?"

She stops bouncing and looks around the room. "Um, yeah! What is it? Can I have it?"

"It's not in here. It's in the barn."

Her eyes grow round. "My kitten? I'm getting my kitten? Holy crap!"

"Bits, language!" I yell, but she pays no attention, probably because I'm laughing.

Adrian gives me a lazy smile. The kind that makes me want to stay in bed and do things. Things you can't do around the eight year-old who just landed on me with a scream of joy.

I wink and mouth, *Later*, then tickle Bits under her armpits. "Okay, let's go get that kitten, potty mouth."

***

The gray-striped kitten's name is Sparkle, and she's unbearably cute, with her tiny white paws and pink nose. Actually, the kitten's name is Sparkle Moon Rainbow, which is what happens when you let a fairy-obsessed eight year-old name a cat.

I've just finished work at the laundry, which is the worst job here, barring anything related to zombies. It may not be as bad as Ma Ingalls had it, with the huge drums that we agitate using belts and a generator, but it still involves copious amounts of hot water and heavy lifting. We ran out of toilet paper months ago and switched to cloth. Thankfully, today was not a poop wash day because on those days I'm in the shower within eight seconds of the end of my shift.

Now, back in my room, I hold Sparkle in the air and talk to her while her tiny purr motor runs. "I'm sorry about your name, but I figure we can call you Sparky. That's not so bad, is it?"

Adrian enters and I deposit her in his outstretched hands. "Oh, I love you, Sparkle Moon Rainbow."

"I'm going with Sparky," I say. Adrian rubs Sparky against his cheek, and both of them close their eyes in pleasure. I have a sneaking suspicion he wanted this kitten as badly as Bits did. "So, is the cake almost decorated?"

"Nope, Bits just threw me out of the kitchen. She's waiting for it to cool." I lock the door. Adrian places Sparky on Bits's bed, and his eyes gleam. "Hi."

"Hello," I say. "She's going to be there for a while. She'll want to sleep here tonight with the kitten, and we'd be evil if we said no. You shot yourself in the foot with that one."

Adrian laughs. "I realized that, but it was too late. We'll work out custody arrangements with Peter tomorrow."

"So, do you want your present now or later?"

"I thought this was my present."

"Nope."

"It's all I want," he says. "What else could you have gotten me?"

I peel off the damp shirt I wore to the laundry and look in the dresser for something halfway decent to wear. Everything is so boring. I'm not a clothes horse, but something special would be nice every once in a while.

"You'll never guess," I say. "Now or later?"

He comes behind me and runs his hands down my sides. "Later. Definitely later."

***

I put on my only nice shirt, a black one that shows some cleavage, and sit on the edge of the bed. "Come here."

Adrian sits next to me, and I hand him the first box, which he rips open like a little kid on Christmas morning. He holds his iPhone in the air. "My phone?"

I nod and give him the bigger box. He pulls out the charger that James made. It has a USB port and a solar panel that flips open, but it folds down to be carried in a backpack.

"Sweetie, I can't. I love it, but I—"

I make a shushing noise and thrust his card into his hand. The glitter on the front drifts to his jeans as he reads the inside aloud, "We, the people of Kingdom Come Farm, insist you charge your phone and listen to music whenever you want. Love, everyone." He looks up with a furrowed brow. "Did you make everyone here sign this?"

"Every single person. Even Penny's baby signed it." I point to the tiny baby foot in the corner. "And I didn't have to make them. They wanted to, I swear. Turn it on."

When the home screen appears, I press the music app, and then all his music is there, in his hand.

"So, what are you going to play first?" I ask.

"I—" he says. My heart falls when he grips his phone silently and presses his lips together. It's not going to work, even with the card. I mentally line up all the arguments I prepared. But then he gives his biggest smile—the one with teeth and dimple and shining eyes. "Wow."

I bounce up and down on the bed. "You'll use it?"

"Yeah, I'll use it."

"And please don't feel guilty. Everyone really, truly wants you to have it and James said that panel wouldn't work in the system anyway and it was the thing you named in *I Miss*—"

He covers my mouth with his hand. "Okay, okay. Thank you, I love it. It's the best present I've ever gotten."

"Play something already!"

He scrolls through his millions of songs and chews his lip. Adrian lives for music the way I live for books, and he's looking for that first perfect song.

"Here," he says. He touches the screen, and "In the Aeroplane Over the Sea" begins.

"Good choice."

"It's for you. I don't know what I did to deserve you." I start to argue, but he silences me with a shake of his head. "You are the kindest, most beautiful person I've ever known, inside and out. Don't ever think I don't know how lucky I am."

For once, I decide to take the compliment. It's the best one I've ever gotten.

CHAPTER 15

Art class is over when Ana arrives at the school. The self-portraits are coming along nicely. The kids put away their sketches and line up at the door like good little robots, but you can still see their excitement. They love Ana, partly because she gets them out of the cabin and partly because she's so enthusiastic about being their PE teacher.

Today she's set up boards to jump over and scramble under while she has them run. She made up a game that the kids named Dodge Tag, but which we privately call Zombie Tag. In this game almost everybody's "it," and the few who aren't have to escape them. It may be called PE, but it's not just for fun; they're learning to evade, although they don't know it. They have no idea that Ana's obstacle courses give them stamina and the crazy ball games improve their reflexes.

We try to protect them from the worst of it, but they all know how to aim and fire a gun. They also know how to use a knife, and everyone knows where to stab it. But mostly, we make sure they know how to run. We want them fast and tireless. If they didn't have such short legs, they'd probably be faster than me.

"Okay," Ana says as they file out the door. "Get on your teams and get ready. You're not getting dinner unless you win."

She winks at me when they giggle. I follow them into the sunlight and talk to Ana while the first team finishes. Ashley stands next to us and crosses her arms.

"I don't see why I can't do patrol," she says. "I'm sixteen. I don't know why I have to sit in school with all the little kids."

"It's *because* you're sixteen," Ana says. "You should be learning, not spiking zombies."

"You could use me. I'm trapped in there all day, and I hate it."

"If you do patrol, you have to do poop day and all the other gross jobs, too," I say. "I'd rather be in school. And every teenager hates being trapped in school all day. It's part of being a teenager."

She isn't convinced, though, and she narrows her eyes. "That's when school was normal. There's not even anyone to hang out with." She makes that teenage noise in the back of her throat. "I hate my life!"

"How about I talk to Maureen and Nancy about letting you do guard every once in a while?" Ana asks.

"Really? Oh my God. Thank you, Ana!"

Ashley rushes off to join her team, and I turn to Ana. "They're never going to let her do it."

"I know. But it'll be their fault, and she'll love us and hate them."

"You're diabolical. I'm so glad you're on my side."

Ana grins and calls the kids over. "All right, now we're going to go for a run. Cass, want to come?"

I back away slowly. Ana made me run with her all winter and stab things in ice-cold barns. I gave in because I didn't want to get out of practice, but there's no way I'm running now that we have Lexers to kill. Not unless I'm being chased.

"Shucks," I say, and snap my fingers. "I've got dinner shift. See you later, everyone."

***

I stand behind where Adrian splits wood under the cover of the trees behind the barns. Summer may be coming, but we need wood for the kitchen year-round, and it takes a lot of wood to keep everyone warm in the winter. Cords of firewood are under the barns' eaves in tarp-covered stacks, with more waiting in piles to join them. I take a moment to admire the way Adrian's t-shirt sticks to his back. He wasn't a slouch in the muscle department to begin with, but now with the farm work we have to do by hand—it's one of the silver linings in a very dark, zombie-shaped cloud. Barnaby sits by his side and squeezes his eyes shut every time the axe falls, due to the fact that with every third strike a wood chip smacks him on his head.

Adrian looks down and nudges him with a boot. "C'mon, Barn. Move it."

Barnaby gives him a doggy grin and stands his ground. Adrian pats him on the head and then pushes him, but Barnaby leans into his hand and pants happily. He's not budging.

"Well," Adrian says, "if you're not going to move, then I can't be held responsible for what transpires."

Adrian positions both hands on the axe and swings. I wait for a lull and call out his name, but he doesn't turn; he must be wearing his ever-present earbuds. When he stops to swig water, I sneak up and pull the old fourth-grade trick of pushing the back of his knee with mine. He spins around in surprise and pulls out his headphones

"If I were a zombie, I would've bit you," I say.

Adrian laughs. "Art class over?"

"Yep. I'm on guard tonight, and I'm filling in for Penny at dinner, so I wanted to give you a goodnight kiss."

He grabs my hand and makes loud kissing noises up and down my arm. "But how will I sleep without you, sweet cheeks?"

"Snuggle with Barnaby."

Barnaby wags his tail and looks receptive to the idea. He arrived last fall with his name tag still on, otherwise we would have named him something halfway normal. It said he'd lived down south, near Manchester. How such a clueless animal found his way to us, I'll never know, but he immediately decided that Adrian was his Person.

"You will, won't you?" Adrian asks him, and kneels down for dog kisses.

"Maybe I don't want that goodnight kiss after all. God only knows what's been in there today."

"Old Barn and I have an understanding. He's even learned a trick."

He stands and points his finger at the ground. "Sit, Barnaby." Barnaby looks at Adrian's finger and remains on all fours.

"He did it earlier. Sit, Barn. Sit!" Barnaby continues to watch him blankly.

"Great trick," I say.

"Stand, Barn. Stand up." Barnaby wags his tail, and Adrian gives his head a pat. "Amazing, isn't it?"

"You're a dog whisperer. The likes of which have never been seen."

"I know."

The light filters through the branches and casts highlights on Adrian's cheekbones. His eyes are green against the brown tree trunks, and his smile is so broad that I want to freeze the image.

"Let me see your phone," I say. "I'm taking a picture, so be good."

He pulls it from his pocket. Usually, he balks at having his picture taken by himself, but he keeps smiling until I've finished.

"Perfect," I say. "We should take more pictures, now that we can."

I decide to behave when he turns it on me and then move around so we're both in a shot. He drags his tongue up my cheek as he presses the shutter.

"Yuck!" I yell, and scrub my cheek with my hand. "I don't want your germs on me!"

"That's not what you said the other night."

I push him. "One more. A nice one this time."

Dan comes around the barn and when he sees what we're doing he insists on taking the shot. He hands it back and picks up an axe.

"Hey, Dan," I say, and point it his way. "That's a keeper. I'm definitely putting you two in the Hunks of Kingdom Come Calendar."

They laugh, and I turn to Adrian for a kiss. "I've got to go. Goodnight, my little puppy dog."

I wave goodbye, and as I walk away I hear Dan ask, "Can I call you puppy dog?"

"Absolutely," Adrian answers. "If you want to be banished for life."

CHAPTER 16

I tip my head to watch the stars in the night sky down at the first gate. The thin, white streak of a meteor moves across the sky and fades away.

"I just saw a shooting star," I say. "Everyone make a wish."

"You know, it's not really a star," Nelly says.

"Yes, Mr. Spoilsport, I know it's not really a star. Forget it—I'm not sharing my wish with you."

Peter laughs from his chair. The three of us pulled night duty tonight, and I've been looking forward to it all day.

"So, Peter, Ana hasn't been asking to do patrol constantly," I say. "Did you talk some sense into her, or what?"

"I wish. It's the garden," Peter says. "She's too busy bossing Adrian and Ben around. She's driving them crazy."

May is days away, and although the last frost date this north isn't until the end of May, it's time for the cool season vegetables to go in. We still have potatoes left in the root cellar, but I want a big spinach salad and carrots in the worst way.

"Adrian can handle it," I say. "Remember, he knew her for years. He likes that she's into the garden now. And she grilled him on it all winter, so she does it his way, mostly. Ben, on the other hand, might be losing his mind."

I was out there today, and watched Ana stand Ben down about whether the carrots should be sown closer together. Finally, just to get rid of her, Ben let her plant some of them her way to see if it worked better.

Footsteps crunch on the road behind us. It could be our hot drink delivery; sometimes someone takes pity on us and sends us food and drink.

"It's Dan." He appears in the lamplight and sits in an empty camping chair. "What's up?"

"You on tonight?" Nelly asks.

"Nah, I was bored."

"You were *bored*?" I ask. "Bored enough to come to the gate and *work*? That's really, really bored. Stupefyingly bored."

Dan chuffs out a laugh and shrugs. "Well, I wanted to get out of there."

"Out of where?"

"The tents."

"Why?" I ask. Dan shakes his head and looks at the ground.

"Cass, can't you tell when a guy doesn't want to talk about something?" Nelly asks.

"Of course I can. I just don't care." Dan snorts, and I put my palms together and beg. "C'mon. Tell us!"

"It'll never leave this table?" Dan asks. We nod solemnly. I like to know what's going on here, but I don't spread it around. "Well, Meghan and I have been hanging out a lot."

"What does that mean?" I rest my chin in my hand and furrow my brow. "This 'hanging out' that you speak of? Are you guys playing Parcheesi or something?" Nelly snickers.

"Parcheesi," Dan says. "We're definitely playing Parcheesi."

"So, do you like her?" I ask.

"Yeah," he says, but he stretches it out, so it's more like *Yee-aaah*. "She's a really nice girl."

The three of us groan. Dan raises his shoulders. "What?"

"That's the Dan Death Knell of relationships," Nelly says. "That's what you say about everyone you date, right before you break up with them."

"It usually lasts three to five weeks," I say. "Then you're done."

"What number is Meghan?" Nelly asks me.

"I don't know. Four, maybe?"

"What the hell, do you guys keep track?" Dan asks. Nelly and I nod; we're not ashamed of what we do for entertainment around here. The lines around Dan's eyes deepen. "So I'm that predictable?"

"Yup," Nelly says. "You could set your watch by it."

We fall into a comfortable silence and watch the sky. That's pretty much all we do out here, interspersed by small moments of craziness when we have to kill things that were once people. We still haven't had any refugees.

"There's no one keeping track of the sky anymore," I say. "You know, like what star has burned out, or where the asteroids are or anything."

"Maybe we should do that," Nelly says, "instead of keeping track of Dan's love life."

Dan punches Nelly's shoulder and says, "My dad would be, if he were here. He knew all the constellations. He'd quiz all us kids whenever we went camping."

"I've always wanted to learn the constellations," Peter says.

"Me, too," I say. "Show us some."

Dan leans back and points out the Big Dipper, then shows us how to follow it to the Little Dipper and the North Star.

"I thought the North Star was brighter," Nelly says.

"It's brighter than most of the stars around it, but it's not very bright. See those stars that make a W? That's Cassiopeia. She was beautiful, but so vain that she was punished and sent to the sky where she'd hang upside down for half the year."

"Those Greeks really knew how to punish folks," I say. "They were so creative."

"I'd say a world full of zombies is a pretty creative punishment," Nelly says, and looks at his watch. "Time to walk the fence. I'll go east."

"You want west or to sit on your butt?" I ask Peter.

I'm uneasy when I walk the fence alone in the dark. Usually, I take Barnaby with me, but he's nowhere to be found. It's entirely possible he's snuggling with Adrian, Bits and Sparky tonight. Adrian will let him in, even though Barnaby is filthy and it goes against every tidy bone in his body—he's a sucker for those sad doggy eyes.

Barn's more afraid than I am, but at least he whines when he smells them, which is before I see them. Otherwise, I'm unprepared when I see that sudden glow of a white face, even when I think I've steeled myself beforehand. Their hisses and the rattle of metal gets me every time. I've never told a soul, but Peter knows me well enough that he's probably guessed. Or he knows I'm lazy, which is also true.

"I'll walk," Peter says. "You sit on your butt."

I gesture to myself. "Done and done."

He salutes me with the radio and disappears into the darkness. The guards assigned to other fence sections also walk the line in their area. That way the entire fence is inspected at least three times a day.

"More stars, please," I say to Dan. He points out more constellations, until we've seen all the ones that the clouds don't cover. "Thanks. You'll have to show me them again sometime. I'll never remember all that."

"Sure, anytime."

I shiver. The temperature feels like it's dropped five degrees in five minutes.

"Cold?" Dan asks.

"My middle name is Cold. I'm starting the fire." I move to the metal fire pit and begin to arrange the kindling.

"You want help with that?" Dan asks.

"No, thanks," I say, but he gets up anyway.

He breaks up a few sticks of kindling and his hand nears my carefully arranged pile. "You know, maybe if you put—"

"Don't do it," I warn, and tap on his outstretched hand with a stick.

"Do what?"

He really doesn't know. Why must every man within a two-mile radius of a campfire try to take over? "Don't be the guy who tries to show the little lady how to build a fire. I was building fires when you were knee-high to a grasshopper."

"I'm older than you," Dan says. He lets the kindling fall with a rueful smile. "But, point taken. You make a damn good fire."

"Damn straight."

The kindling takes off and shortly thereafter the fire is roaring. I hold my hands over the flames. "So, when are you going to brave the tents again?"

Dan pokes the logs with a stick. I ignore his surreptitious rearranging—it must be inbred. "When everyone is sound asleep. I don't know how I end up in these situations."

"What? Yes, you do! It's because you sleep with multiple people who are all trapped inside a circular fence. There's no way that can end well."

"I guess you're right," he admits. "I don't feel trapped, though."

"Me neither. I feel safe."

"Me, too."

The radio crackles and I pick it up. "Cass, I've got a few at the fence," Peter says.

"How many? Need help?"

"No, only three. I'll radio when I'm done."

"Copy that."

I imagine Peter using one of the metal spikes we keep at the fences for just this purpose. They slide through the links—and skull bone—easily. On the parts of the fence that are wood or concrete we have to entice them to an area that's chain link.

"Okay, all clear," Peter calls. "On my way back."

"See you in a few."

I set the radio down and rifle through my bag for lip balm. It's sunk to the bottom, so I pile all the other junk on the table until I can reach it. There are mittens, toothbrush and toothpaste, a pair of socks, water, a hat, a container of cookies, two books and a smaller bag that contains toiletries.

Dan looks it over and smirks. "You travel light. You know you're still on the farm, right? Toothbrush? Two books?"

"We may have a dentist, but he doesn't have much novocaine."

"Good point."

"And two books, in case I finish one. I get nervous if I don't have a book on me."

"I should go by the library. I need a new book."

We moved the tiny town library here, along with any other books we've found and had space for. Ana tries to collect clothes when we're on patrol. I try to collect books. I win every time.

"Hey, you know what you might like? *A Short History of Nearly Everything*. It's in there. It's about the universe and space."

"Cool. I'll check it out."

"No pun intended," I say, to which he groans.

Peter walks out of the woods and inspects himself in the lamplight for splatter. I double check, but he's clean. I write down the time and location of the Lexers in the log book and notice that it's been increasing steadily. Except for that big group that surrounded Adrian and John, they've still been no more than a dozen at a time, but they're getting more frequent.

James has calculated that they walk about one mile per hour, faster when they're after something. They don't always walk, though. Sometimes they seem to be in a trance-like state until they find something to follow. But since they can walk without stopping, even the ones in the Deep South, none of whom froze over the winter, could make it here before next winter. A pod will find its way here soon enough. If it weren't for the fact that we need the summer to grow food, I'd prefer to skip the season entirely. I try not to worry about it because there's nothing we can do.

Nelly comes out of the east and falls into his chair with a yawn. "And now we wait and do it again."

"I like working nights," Dan says. "Staying up until dawn."

Nelly stifles another yawn. "I love to wake up at noon. After a night of drinking."

"That world is over," I say. "At least until you'll be so old you won't want to do it anymore. Sorry, buddy." I pat Nelly's head and point a finger at Dan. "You know, you'd like sleeping at night if you had someone you liked to sleep with."

"There are lots of people I like to sleep with," he says. Peter and Nelly chortle.

"Ha ha. You know what I mean. Someone you *like* like. We have to find you someone."

"I'm good, believe me." I frown at Dan, and he turns to the guys. "Is she always like this?"

"She practically tied me and Ana together," Peter exaggerates.

"She," Nelly makes air quotes, " 'accidentally' locked me and Adam in the storeroom at Whitefield overnight."

"That *was* an accident!" I say. "I just didn't rush back when I realized. And it was three hours, you liar. I like people to be happy."

I point at the two of them. "You're both happy, right?" I get two nods, and say, "So, what's the problem? Oh, and that reminds me, Nelly, we never finished our convers—"

My bag's contents are still on the table. I duck for cover when Nelly lobs my mittens at my head, followed by my socks and hat.

CHAPTER 17

"I think we're going on patrol this weekend," Ana says from her chair where we watch the west fence. "Maybe around Montpelier."

I knew it was coming. All the early plants are in the ground, and Ana's been itching to do something.

"What's in Montpelier?" I ask.

"Walmart."

"Why do we have to go so soon?"

"Health and Beauty stuff. We're low on conditioner."

"You and your conditioner," I say. "You don't even have long hair anymore."

"That doesn't mean I don't want it soft and shiny." Ana swings her head like she's in a shampoo commercial. "Doc says we could always use more meds. We need contraception and soap, razors—all that stuff. Plus whatever food we can find. Please say you're coming."

I think of the promise I made to Adrian. Not only do I want to keep it, but I also don't want to risk my life for no good reason, even without having promised. If we were in dire need of food or medicine I would, but I know we're not. "I don't think so."

"Why?" Ana screeches. "I need you!"

"Banana, you don't need me. You want me there, but you don't *need* me."

She thrusts out her lower lip and drums her fingers on her jeans. We sit by the part of the fence that's chain link, but down and back from the barns it's made of logs, like a fort. I walk to the fence and lean my head against the metal to get a view. I can just make out something standing near the middle of the wood section.

"Lexer behind the logs, Banana."

Ana jumps up and strolls toward the section. "Here, kitty, kitty."

We stop where metal turns to wood. Ana wiggles two gloved fingers through the links and clicks her tongue. A head lunges at her hand, and its teeth bite the empty air where her fingers were a second before.

"Shit!" Ana says. She shakes her finger. "You're a sneaky fucker."

What was once a woman in a flowered wraparound dress throws herself against the fence. She bites the steel with such venom that I take a step back. I know they don't have any emotions, but sometimes the hunger looks so much like hate it's disconcerting.

Ana ignores the woman's growls and points at her clothes. "That was a nice dress once. I wish we had some nice clothes. We should go on a clothes patrol."

"I wouldn't mind new clothes, but that is the worst idea I've ever heard. Unlike you, I'd rather be alive than have clothes. Now, move out of the way so I can put this poor lady out of her misery, or are you going to do it?"

It not only frightens me, but it also makes me sad to see what people have been reduced to. I want her dead and gone.

"Oh. Yeah." Ana pierces the woman's eye with a handled spike and turns away from the body. "Well, we'll need new clothes eventually, so why not nice ones?"

I look from Ana's unruffled expression to the heap on the ground. I don't expect her to be remorseful, I know I'm not, but a split second of something—fear, sadness at the state of the world, even shortness of breath, for God's sake—would be a nice reminder that Ana's human. I know it's in there; I just wish she wasn't reluctant to show it. "Do you even care that you just did that?"

Ana doesn't answer as we walk back to our chairs. She drops the spike in the bucket of bleach water with a splash, and when she turns her eyes are dark. "No, I don't because she was already dead. They want to *eat* us, Cass. I'll save my feelings for all the people who are actually alive, you know? Lexers wanna start shit with me, I'm gonna fuck them up."

"You just sounded so Brooklyn." Penny, Ana and I grew up there, but only every so often does one of us say something that gives it away.

She laughs and sings, "*Boricua* in the house!"

Ana hides it well, but on her face I just saw the same desperation I feel. The need to protect everyone she loves, even at her own expense. And with her recklessness she's bound to do something stupid because of it. I should be there to stop her.

"Maybe I'll go on patrol," I say. "If Adrian goes, too. Don't get your hopes up, though."

Ana bounces in her boots and squeals.

CHAPTER 18

W e're woken up before dawn by an urgent knock at the door. Adrian grumbles and turns facedown into his pillow. I open it to find John fully dressed and pacing the creaky floorboards.

"Whitefield was attacked," he says.

"What?"

"Lexers. No one's sure exactly what happened, but a lot of them are dead. Will, maybe all of the 157th, and some more. They're not sure how many yet."

Adrian curses and pulls on pants. I stand with my mouth agape and wonder how that could have happened. They have more guns, ammo, and guards than us.

"We'll leave in half an hour?" Adrian asks.

"That'll work," John says. He turns to me. "Can you go wake the others? Maybe seven or eight of us should go."

I have a million questions, but I get dressed and head to the cabins. Peter and Ana are ready in minutes, and Ana races off to score coffee from the kitchen for our trip. She and Penny have a coffee addiction, and it kills Penny that she can't drink any now that she's knocked up. Coffee is heavily rationed and saved for patrol and guard, but we always sneak Penny some. She mutters under her breath about herbal tea and the apocalypse.

"You can have coffee, Pen," I say. "People drank coffee when they were pregnant for a million years. I'll get Ana to bring some back for you."

"No, no," she says. "I'm just being grouchy. Sorry."

The line between her eyebrows deepens, but she looks at Bits and doesn't say anything. I'm worried, too.

"Do they need help with the electrics?" James asks. "I'll go if they do."

"I don't know, but Adrian's coming anyway," I say. I think of Henry and pray that he and Hank are okay. "But we'll have to go back again once we know what they need. They might want you then."

James ignores Penny's pointed look and rubs his hands together; he's always up for an adventure, but he doesn't get out much. He's not the best shot with a gun, but his lack of fear and ability to think under pressure are great attributes. Plus, he can fix anything. He's already learned everything there is to know about electrical systems, and now he's moved onto cars with Shawn.

Bits clings to me like a baby monkey when I say goodbye. We've told her as little as possible, although enough to know that we have to help Whitefield.

"I love you, Bitsy-poo," I say, and wonder if any of the kids at Whitefield are dead. The thought makes me bury my face in her hair. "Until the end of the world."

"I love you, Cassie-poop," she says with a giggle. Nothing's funnier than poop to this kid. I should get her to help at the laundry one day; it might cure her of it forever.

"Be good for Penny, okay?"

I give her one last kiss and hand her to Peter, who lifts her up to the cabin's ceiling like she's a feather. One thing that zombie fighting and farm life don't do is make you weak. Slightly crazy and tired, respectively, but not weak.

"Okay, baby girl," Peter says, "we'll see you later, or in a day or two. Don't you dare get any more freckles while I'm gone, or else."

"I'll try not to," she says, and squeals when he pretends to drop her.

"I love you," Peter says. "Now, go back to bed or brush those teeth."

Penny hands Bits her toothbrush and looks at us with wide eyes. "Please be careful."

We promise we will. I walk out into the night with Peter and turn to look through the open doorway. Penny is exhausted, but there's no way she'll go back to sleep now. Bits talks nonstop around her toothbrush. She looks so small and vulnerable in her pajamas, and I want to hug her one more time. Peter watches her, too. We have this in common: a love for Bits so deep that sometimes I can't believe we didn't make her ourselves in some strange alternate universe. I almost blurt out how scared I am—for all of us, for Bits, for Whitefield—but I shut my mouth with a clacking of teeth.

"You okay?" Peter asks.

"Yeah. I just hate leaving."

"I know."

Bits spits out her toothpaste and wipes her mouth on Penny's proffered towel. That won't have been the last time I'll ever hug Bits, I tell myself, and walk away. Sometimes it takes a huge effort of will to drive through those gates, and I know if I go back in, I'll never leave.

CHAPTER 19

Whitefield is a wreck. Bodies are strewn everywhere, smoke rises from the charred heaps of buildings and the air smells of burning flesh and raw meat. They're too shell-shocked to have gotten a plan in place. A few people load bodies into the beds of pickups, but the rest stand and watch them in tight groups.

"Holy shit," Adrian says, after we get out of the van. "I didn't think it was this bad."

"Me neither," Peter agrees.

I hear a piercing wail and look for its source. It's Christine, whose husband, Brett, was in the 157th. I assume he's one of the bodies. The blond hair that she pulls into a silky ponytail sticks out like straw, and her plain but pleasant farm-girl face is screwed up in agony.

"Go," I say to Nelly, who scans the crowd, and point to where Adam loads bodies.

Nelly nods and strides off in his direction. I hear him shout over the roar of a generator, and Adam moves toward him eagerly. Nelly knew he was okay because John asked via radio.

Ana's eyes flicker from the bullet holes in the main hangar's window to the blackened remains of the barn, then to the blood that runs along the concrete. Her lips tighten and her neck moves when she swallows. Ana hardly ever cries; she gets pissed and flies off the handle instead. Zeke and Kyle step through the door of the main hangar.

"Thanks for coming, y'all," Zeke says. "Jesus Christ, can you believe this?" He surveys the airport and twists his beard.

"What the hell happened, Zeke?" Adrian asks.

"The fences are solid, man," Zeke drawls, his Southern accent deepening. "Only thing I can think is we had four new people come in yesterday evening. They seemed well enough, but we didn't check them—I asked one of the guards who was on and he said they didn't.

Maybe one of the arrivals was too scared to admit he'd gotten the virus."

I don't know how you could do that, knowing you'd kill other people. I'd blow my head off before I'd let that happen.

"Best I can tell is it started in the men's barrack while we were sleeping. Someone must've opened the door, and then they got out. No alarms, nothing. I was in my office last night and didn't hear a goddamned thing. Not until it was—" He sweeps a hand in the air at the devastation. "We got it under control pretty quickly, once we figured out what was happening, but they'd gotten into the main hangar and the soldiers' barrack. I think people opened doors to see what was going on. None of us thought of Lexers."

"You know I sleep in the family barrack," Kyle says. He has a four year-old daughter, Nicole. "That's the only reason I'm here."

Kyle, who shaves his head bald, rubs his hand along the gleaming brown skin as if for luck. He was from a different unit of the National Guard, although he came to Whitefield with the 157th.

"Almost everyone in the men's barrack was infected," Zeke says. "The families are okay. A lamp must have burst in the soldiers' barrack during the fighting. They became fucking human torches. The chicken coop and barn burned. Half the food was in the soldiers' barrack and over another quarter in the barn. It's all gone. We won't make it on what we have until the summer crops."

"Don't worry about that," Adrian says. "We'll bring you everything we can spare. There's always North Conway. Will was talking about making a trip there."

"Almost all the patrollers are gone," Zeke says. "We've got me and Kyle. We're all that's left."

"We'll come," Ana says.

Kyle crosses his arms and assesses the survivors. "We'll need you. We've got to train some people—if we can find them."

We have the same problem at Kingdom Come. People don't want to risk their lives. They're scared, and rightfully so. Last fall, a patrol went out and never returned. Thirty people left for Moose River, Maine, after that, along with the people at the farms we'd helped to fortify. They thought it'd be safer, since it's the largest and most remote Safe Zone in the northeast. It made the winter easier in terms of food and fuel, but there's strength in numbers, and ours have dwindled.

We don't have enough ammo to teach people how to use guns, although a blade of some type is sufficient. But a blade requires the nerve to jam it into a head, and I've been surprised to find that not everyone will do that unless they absolutely have to. Even on someone who's already dead. They had to do it on the way to the farm, maybe, but now they avoid it, even through the fence. There are just over a dozen of us who will go on patrol. The other adults will guard, but they won't step beyond the gates except to help with body disposal.

Zeke nods his thanks. "What we could use is some help with the bodies. Burying one or two on this side of the gate would be fine, but I don't like the idea of all that infection in here. I'm meeting some resistance on that. I don't blame them, but I don't know what else to do."

"Nothing *to* do," Kyle says. He turns to us with sympathy in his eyes, but his mouth is set in a line. "It's the families. They want somewhere to visit inside the gates."

I've never been fond of graves. My parents were cremated, and I liked knowing they were scattered on their land, free to be anywhere. But I could see where having one would be comforting, especially these days. It's important to know for certain where someone is.

"We've got two spaces where the ground could take them. One's by the water," Zeke says, talking about the irrigation pond that they use for crops, "the other's by the big field. I don't feel good about burying seventy infected people in the ground next to something we put in our mouths."

"They'll come around," Adrian assures him.

"I hope so. I never wanted to be head of this place, but Will asked if I would step up if he, Ian and a few others were gone. I agreed, but that's 'cause I never thought it would happen. Never in a million years."

I could imagine almost everyone in the world dying, but not Will. He seemed indestructible. Zeke shakes his head repeatedly and watches the ground. When he turns to us, however, his jaw is set. There's a reason he made it all the way from Kentucky to Whitefield, rescuing people along the way. That's why Will insisted he be in charge.

"He knew you'd do a good job," I say. "And you are. You're thinking of everything."

"I sure hope that's true, sugar," Zeke says. He lets go of a sigh and raises his bushy brows. "Adrian, you're gonna have to show me the ropes."

***

It takes three people to move Will's body. His skin is ashen and he has blood around his mouth and between his teeth. There's no way he would have let himself turn, so he must have died and turned quickly. I say a silent goodbye when the truck holding his body pulls away and the weight in my stomach worsens. This could have been us.

Whitefield has lost every soldier but Kyle and over thirty other residents. Henry, Hank and all the other kids are okay. That leaves eighty people; eighty people who can follow orders but don't know how to run this place day to day.

I stand next to Henry and Hank, who I've found outside the main hangar at an electrical box, surrounded by tools, circuit boards and wires. Henry looks as surprised as everyone else, but his hands are steady as he fixes the ruin caused by a rogue bullet.

"I can't believe this," I say. "Thank God someone locked the family barrack."

"It was my dad," Hank says proudly.

Henry grimaces and throws his screwdriver into his tool bag. "I knew something was wrong. I should've gone outside to help."

"No, you shouldn't have," I say. "Someone needed to protect the kids."

Henry isn't convinced, though, and he stares at the wet spots from the water they used to put out the fire and wash away the blood. The patches of dirt that are stained dark with blood won't be gone until the next soaking rain.

"You did the right thing, Henry," I say, and touch his shoulder. "Can you imagine if someone had opened the door to see what was going on?"

"Yeah, I guess you're right." Henry catches Hank's nod. "Hank's been telling me that all morning."

"Dad, I'm always right," Hank says. "You should know that by now."

Henry clamps his lips together, since Hank is completely serious and his adult expression is incongruous with his big glasses and skinny arms. "Guess I should, huh?"

"You should always listen to Hank. I know I do," I say with a wink. "I said I'd help in the men's barrack. But I'll see you guys later."

I catch Adrian just before he heads into the barrack, and it's hard not to feel better when I see the soft smile that's reserved for me.

"Hey, pretty girl," he says.

"Hey, handsome."

He hands me a pair of yellow rubber gloves like the ones he wears. My engagement ring catches, so I pull it off and hold it out. I wore black leggings with no pockets because I didn't want any of my three pairs of jeans bloody.

"Hold this for me?" I ask, but snatch it away before he can reach. "I want it back, though. No changing your mind or anything."

"We'll see." Adrian plucks it from my fingers and puts it deep into his jeans' watch pocket. "I might need some convincing later. You can show me just how badly you want it."

"Oh, I want it pretty badly."

"Maybe you can wear that holster later, too."

I found a thigh holster with its own elastic belt in the weapons room. Usually, I wear a shoulder holster and my knife on my waist, but this holds my knife without needing a belt. I have to admit, I felt a little like a badass when I put it on. It's probably how Ana feels twenty-four hours a day.

I let out an exaggerated sigh even as warmth floods my abdomen. "Is there anything you don't find sexy?"

"Not on you." He shakes his head like it's a lost cause.

"Seriously, y'all," Nelly says from behind me. "You are so annoying."

He and Adam stand hand in hand. Nelly makes a sound of disgust, but Adam cocks his head. "I think it's nice."

"Hang out with them long enough," Nelly says, "and you'll be singing a different tune."

But I see the way his thumb strokes Adam's. I bite my tongue and pull on my gloves. I may like to tease Nelly, but I don't want to scare him away from acting like a human with real emotions.

My first thought when we enter the men's barrack is that it might have been better if it'd burned, too. Even with the open windows, the smell of blood hangs in the air and many of the mattresses are stained beyond redemption. They're all garbage now, since it might be infected blood.

The body of someone I don't know, maybe the one who started all this, is just inside the door. I reach down for an ankle while Adrian grabs the other. We pull him outside and hoist him into the pickup's bed. The sun is warming up the day nicely, and the newly tilled fields are a rich brown. A perfect spring day, ruined by Lexers.

We grow quieter and quieter as we move the bodies. We know all these faces: they're people we've spoken to, laughed with. There's something deep between survivors, even if we don't know each other well. It must be similar to when veterans meet up—they may have had different units, different battles, but the war was the same.

We leave the blood and bedding for the cleanup crews. Most people are willing to do that, and I can't blame them for not wanting to touch their family members and friends. That's why we're here. Thankfully, although the ground is muddy, it's thawed enough to dig a hole in a nearby field. Digging separate graves would be too dangerous and time-consuming out in the open. The bodies are gently lowered into the ground while John says a few words.

I'm given the task of watching the surrounding fields while much of Whitefield stands over the mound of dirt. I don't want to see it anyway; listening to John's soft, deep voice and the sobbing is bad enough. Christine stands next to me. I wonder why she's not with the others, since Brett's in the ground, too.

"I killed him," she says suddenly.

I turn, startled, but her face is blank like she hasn't said anything. Just when I think I've imagined it, she speaks again. "He bit me through the blanket. Woke me up. At first I thought he was playing. Then I heard the screams. I ran for his knife."

She's reciting the chain of events like a grocery list. *I need milk, flour, sugar, and butter.* Her lack of emotion is more alarming than a complete breakdown because I know it's buried in there.

"His blood got everywhere. Then I hid under the bed. The only one I ever killed, you know. I made it all the way here with the 157th and never had to kill a single one."

"I'm sorry," I say. "I'm really sorry. Can I do anything for—"

She steps back, the blank look replaced by tears. "I don't know what I'm going to do."

I raise my hand to touch her or offer her a hug, but she runs to catch a truck that's heading back. I hope she has someone to talk to. Or, at the very least, something to live for.

***

"You sure you don't mind?" Nelly asks.

"They need you here," Adrian says. "We'll start on organizing supplies to bring back. Marcus doesn't want to miss Caleb's birthday."

Nelly, John, Liz, Peter and Ana are staying to help with cleanup. The bodies are buried, but things need to be rebuilt and disinfected. Food needs to be catalogued, along with ammo.

"But we're gonna hold off on the party until you guys are home," Marcus says. "I wouldn't deprive you of the bonfire and alcohol."

"You're a good man," Liz replies. "Tell your snot-nosed brother we say happy birthday."

"I will. He'll be happy to know you're thinking of him." Liz snorts in a most unladylike fashion.

"See you in a few days," I say to Nelly. "Adam, maybe you could come back for a visit."

"I don't want to leave the kids, especially now," Adam says. "But I will soon. Maybe during summer break."

"Do kids get summer break in the apocalypse?"

"It's like the old days," Adam says. "They get to break their backs doing farm work."

I laugh because it's true. Poor kids.

"So long, lollipops," I say to Peter and Ana. It's what we say with Bits, instead of *So long, suckers.*

Peter smiles, but it's a tired one. "Safe home."

Ana makes a murmur of agreement; even she looks worn out. This day has worked itself under everyone's skin.

I nod before I get in the van. "Of course."

CHAPTER 20

Wr've seen Lexers on the side of the road and a crowd in the biggest town we passed through, but otherwise the ride to Kingdom Come has been peaceful. Marcus is behind the wheel, singing under his breath, while Adrian and I sit in the seats behind him and figure out what we can spare for Whitefield. I know the kitchen pretty well, since I do inventory with Mikayla. And I know that even with all those people gone, they're going to be short on food. And now we are, too. I have a feeling many patrols are in our future, and I don't like the idea at all.

Adrian looks up from the list he scribbles in a notebook. "We'll search everyone who comes from now on. Maybe even quarantine them for twenty-four hours."

We haven't had any new people so far this spring, but I remember when we showed up at the farm last year. They'd asked about Nelly's wound, but they'd believed us when we told them what it was.

"People might not like that," Marcus says.

"Well, then they can leave," Adrian says. "Ask me if I give a shit."

Marcus howls. Adrian can give the mistaken impression of being docile. He might sing ridiculous songs to kittens and let mangy dogs in our bed, but he never shrinks from a fight.

Adrian holds up a finger. "One. That's all it took to do that to Whitefield. One fucking Lexer. We're not taking any chances."

"I'm in charge of the strip searches," Marcus calls out.

He turns onto a road that will bring us north and drop us on the main road to the farm. Another three miles and we'll be home in time for dinner. I'm wondering what's on the menu when Marcus shouts. Dozens of Lexers are gathered on the right side of the road ahead. There's room to pass, and when we do I see that they're bent over a meal. Bloody hands reach into a body cavity I can barely see and come away dripping. My fear fights with the revulsion in my stomach at their blank stares and mindless eating.

Marcus cranes his neck to look behind us. "Could you tell what that was? A deer? I hope it wasn't someone trying to get—"

Adrian and I call out when the van veers to the right. We hit the shoulder, and the passenger's side bumps down into the steep ditch. Marcus guns the engine in reverse, but the tires spin and the motor revs, to no avail.

"Stop, stop, you're digging us in," Adrian says. He climbs over and rolls down the passenger's side window. "Maybe we can push it out."

I spin around, hands clammy, but the road behind us is still empty. The Lexers are just around a bend. They may be busy enough not to have heard the noise of the engine over the sounds of their eating.

Marcus sucks in his cheeks. "Shit. Fuck! I'm sorry."

"Let's try the farm." Adrian calls on the handheld radio, which is all we have in this van, but it's dead air. "We're too far, with the trees in the way."

A flutter of dread beats in my stomach. It's bad enough we're in a ditch, with Lexers just behind us. But I thought—no, I *knew*—the radio would get someone here within ten minutes. We could last ten minutes. But no one's coming.

"They'll come looking for us," I say. I can hear the high, hopeful note in my voice that sounds close to panic.

Adrian glances down the empty road and back at me. "At some point. But if they trap us in here...We should at least try to push. If it doesn't work, we'll walk and call when we're closer."

The thought of walking three miles down a dirt road with Lexers nearby makes my throat close. I'm not walking anywhere. I'm running.

"Marcus and I will push," Adrian says. He lowers his forehead to mine. Either he's not panicked, or he's hiding it well. "You reverse, gently, when I tell you."

I nod and clench to stop my teeth from chattering. My eyes skitter around for threats while they line the mud under the tires with whatever they can find for traction. Once that's done, they place their hands on the hood and lower their heads with the effort of pushing, while I lower my foot to the accelerator and pray. The wheels spin in the muddy ditch until Adrian raises a hand for me to stop. His face pales and he elbows Marcus.

I spin in my seat to find that the first few have rounded the bend. We were quiet, but the sound of spinning wheels carries in the forest. Or maybe they were following the van to begin with. It doesn't matter; the only thing that matters is that they're making a beeline for us. Adrian and Marcus fall in the side door and close it with a soft click. The Lexers are moving quickly, more quickly than they do if they don't have a destination.

"Down," Adrian says, just before the first Lexer hits.

There's a thump and a hiss. I crawl to sit in the aisle next to Adrian, under the cover of the seats. I want to close my eyes, like a little kid who thinks no one can see him if he can't see them. The Lexers might lose interest if we're quiet and hidden from sight, and then we can wait it out until help arrives. Someone from the farm will be here before night; they know we're coming.

Adrian covers where my hand grips the denim of his jeans. He tries to keep his hands steady, but I can feel the tremble. You have to be scared, though. If you're not scared, then you're stupid. It's not a bad thing.

But this is a bad thing. Because they know we're in here. They must, by the way they hammer on the windows. A streak of black liquid runs down the glass and a forehead leaves a smear along a side window. There are more dragging footsteps, more groans, and then the sound of denting metal on the road side of the van grows more insistent. One of the windows cracks with a sound like a gunshot, but it holds for now.

Marcus clamps a hand over his mouth when we slide farther sideways into the ditch. The van will end up on its side if they push hard enough, and then they'll be in here. I imagine their arms reaching through broken windows and the way they'll slither through and land on us, and I bite my tongue so hard that the metallic taste of blood floods my mouth.

"Run?" Marcus asks in a low voice.

Out the door on the forest side may be our only chance. The slope is steep enough that they haven't come around yet. I nod when Adrian looks to me and then fumble for my cleaver and check my knife and gun.

Marcus raises himself eye level to the window and comes down with a face whiter than before. "They're in the woods."

Adrian points up the road. There aren't that many on the road ahead, and three miles to the farm. I've run farther with Ana, and although I've hated every minute of it, I could run a marathon if it meant getting home.

The van shifts again. Marcus grabs the door handle, takes a breath and throws it open. I glance at the woods and my breath disappears, not that there was much of it to begin with. Scattered Lexers stumble through the trees, coming for us. We're in the middle of the largest pod we've seen this year.

We stop at the hood of the van when Lexers flood out of the woods on the left side of the road. They've cut off our escape. Normally, I can find my calm inner space in the center of the storm, but right now there's nothing but the certainty that this is how I'm going to die. Marcus points to a path through the trees, where the Lexers are spaced out. We scramble down the incline just as the van lands on its side with a thud and a shattering of glass.

I swing my cleaver at everything that comes our way. I stop for an eye socket when its fingers fasten around Marcus's coat and a neck when one stands in front of us with its arms out. It's happening so fast. I can't look in every direction, so I run alongside Adrian and stare straight ahead. If we barrel through them fast enough, they won't have time to get a handhold.

Marcus's foot hits the heel of my boot, and I stumble into a Lexer. The moss that moves up its arm and under the tattered sleeve of its shirt hasn't affected its strength thus far. I scream when it sinks its teeth into the leather sleeve of my jacket. They couldn't have gone through, but I drop my cleaver from the pain. I can't reach my knife with my left hand, and the tips of my fingers have just grazed my pistol when my left arm is yanked from behind. Another Lexer pulls me in the opposite direction like I'm the rope in a game of tug of war.

Adrian tries to come to my aid, but he's stopped by three Lexers that surround him. He yells something over his shoulder, and the twisted faces of the Lexers snarl, but I can't hear anything but my grunts and the pounding of my heart. I push them away whenever they get close, my arms growing more exhausted with every shove.

This is how I'm going to die.

The calm hits just before I've reached full-scale panic mode. I need to be mad and scared, not frozen in terror. I need to take them one at a time. That's how John says to do it—one at a time. I let the first one's mouth come for me and headbutt him in his chest. There's a crack when my head sinks into his sternum, and a rush of fluid soaks my scalp. I'm probably more stunned than he is by the blow, but he stumbles back from the force and loses his grip. My right hand free, I pull my knife from my holster to bury it in the eye of the other.

Adrian's machete goes under the chin and out through the top of the first one's skull. I snatch my cleaver off the ground and we run. Marcus pulls ahead and disappears into where the ground forms a natural bowl, and seconds later a high-pitched wail echoes and cuts off. We skid to a stop at the edge of the bowl. Marcus lies on the ground, covered with Lexers like flies on a corpse, and the ones not eating begin their approach.

They're coming from the road, from ahead of us, from the left and right. Adrian glances at the hundreds of bodies circling in with an expression that's almost vacant. He takes my gloved hand, and I notice his hands are bare; he'd taken his gloves off to make that list and had never put them on again.

He squeezes my hand twice, and then he says, "Run."

I start in a sprint toward a grouping of trees that might offer some cover. His hand slips from mine, and I spin, terrified I'll find him on the ground like Marcus. But he's running in the other direction.

"Adrian!" I scream.

A Lexer with long hair grabs me from behind. I spin to stab my cleaver in her forehead, and by the time I turn to follow he's too far gone, moving east from the farm. The Lexers are giving him chase now. I press my back against a tree, the adrenaline that had been spurring me on replaced by an icy tingling that has me frozen to the spot.

"Cassie, run!" Adrian calls. "Run! I'll meet you there!"

He yells it again and again, making noise to attract them, to pull them away. And it's working; the Lexers are passing me by. But I don't want to run. I won't leave him here. Adrian fires his pistol and steps backward through the trees. His jacket has gone missing, and his white t-shirt is bright against the pale, colorless clothes of the Lexers. They're closing in on him, hundreds of Lexers I could never fight off myself.

I scream his name. He can fight his way back. We can run together. I want to tell him that, but all that comes out is another scream. Something in my throat gives, and the next is nothing but an exhalation of air. I scurry out of reach of a straggler I've alerted to my presence and duck behind another tree. A group of five Lexers lumbers toward me with interest. Adrian's pulled most of them his way, but there are still too many. They're bound to notice me, no matter how still I am. I have no choice if I want to live. I don't know that I'll ever forgive myself, but I run.

CHAPTER 21

I slap at branches and stumble through a thicket to avoid another small group. They're moving in the direction of the gunshots that reverberate through the trees. Those shots mean Adrian's still alive. He'll circle around and meet me at the farm, like he promised. I hold onto that hope while I try to figure out where the farm is. I don't know these woods, but I'm sure I started in the right direction.

I've run a mile, maybe more. I stop to get my bearings and listen for the sounds of someone moving fast, but all I hear is a slow shuffling to my left. A Lexer moves past, unaware of me, and just beyond her is the unbroken stream of sunlight that means road. I leave the safety of the bushes and hit the dirt road just below the turn to Kingdom Come. It's only another mile; I've gone farther than I thought. My feet pound the earth now that nothing stands in my way, but I stop when a truck comes into view. The blue pickup screeches to a halt beside me.

Dan throws the door wide and steadies my shoulders while he looks me over. "We heard the shots. What's happening? Are you okay?"

"Adrian," I rasp. It hurts to talk. I point down the road. "Marcus."

He bustles me into the back and takes off after I tell him where to go. Toby and Liz stare at me with wide eyes. "What happened?" Liz asks.

I want to tell Dan to go faster, but a look at the speedometer tells me he's going faster than I'd dare.

"The van's in a ditch," I whisper. "We had to leave it. Marcus—" I shake my head, very glad that Caleb isn't in here.

Toby raises a hand to his forehead. "Fuck!"

"Adrian's in the woods. He ran the other way."

The underside of the van comes into view. Lexers still stand beside it, but most have left for the woods. For Adrian. I haven't heard a gunshot in a while. I tell myself it doesn't mean anything; he'd had no reason to make noise once I was gone. He could focus on saving himself.

The Lexers wander over to the truck. Dan rolls thirty feet past and lowers the window. "Adrian!" he calls. "Adrian!"

The Lexers follow, and he reverses, paying no mind to the thumps when he collides with them. He calls again, but there's no answer.

"He ran southeast," I say. "Maybe he came out on the other road."

Dan puts the truck into drive. "Wait!" I say.

I search for a white shirt and exhale when I see only the browns of the forest and the Lexers' clothes. I catch Dan's eye in the rearview and nod for him to go.

***

The roads are empty. We might have missed him. He could be moving through the forest. Maybe he's at the farm already. I press my knees together to stop the tremors that run through me in waves. At the gate, I promise the universe that I'll do anything, anything at all, if only Adrian is on the other side. Caleb slides the gate open, looking so much like Marcus that for a moment I'm bewildered, then hopeful, then crushed again. Adrian isn't here. Caleb thrusts his head through the window and scans our faces. He stops at me and his mouth gapes.

"Where's my brother?" he finally asks.

I don't want to tell him from inside the truck, although his trembling chin tells me he already suspects. I open the door and face him on wobbly legs. "We went into a ditch and had to run. They caught—he couldn't get away."

He runs his knuckles up his cheek. "Is he dead? Tell me he's not one of them."

"I don't know," I whisper. "I'm sorry. I don't know."

"Fuck!" he screams. He kicks the side of the truck hard enough to leave a dent. Then he kicks it again. "Fuck!"

We watch while Caleb beats the shit out of the pickup, until the side is full of tiny dents from his steel-toe boot. Finally, he crosses his arms over his face and howls. We stand helplessly, unwilling spectators to his private moment of anguish, until they trail off into silence.

"Where's Adrian?" It's muffled, but I can make out his words.

"I don't know. He went the other way."

"Probably dead," Caleb says.

Those two words slam me back against the truck. He's right. Adrian's probably dead. I might never know for sure.

Caleb drops his arms and digs his fingers into my shoulder. "I meant Marcus! Cass, I meant my brother."

I hold my hand to my mouth and stare at him. He may have meant Marcus, but it doesn't matter. Adrian's dead, I can feel it. He might be walking through the woods right now, but he isn't alive.

CHAPTER 22

"Please," Penny says, "will you come and clean up?"

I stare at the gate. The day has become dusk, and I've been in this chair since we returned. I'm not leaving until I know for sure. He'll come here, or I'll go out looking for him. Either way, I'm going to find out. I won't have another loose end.

"You look—"

I know how I must look. My forehead and cheek crackle with dried blood whenever I speak, which hasn't been often, since my throat feels as though someone's taken a sander to it. I don't care that the blood in my hair is infected. If it finds a point of entry, so be it.

"Bits wants to see you." Penny twists her hands together. "She's scared. And she'll be even more afraid."

My hands tighten on the arms of the chair. She's afraid I'm going to lose it, but she's managed to say the one thing that could make me get up.

"I'll get you," Caleb says from the chair next to mine.

"Promise?" I don't trust anyone else will. They'll want to protect me, but Caleb understands.

"Promise."

Penny trails me to the second floor of the farmhouse, where I falter to a stop outside my bedroom door. I don't want to go in and see our stuff how we left it this morning, sure that we'd be back soon.

"I'll get clothes," Penny says softly. "Do you want anything else?"

I shake my head and shut myself in the bathroom. My buns are cemented with Lexer blood, so I step into the warm water and let it work its way through. It takes three lathers before what runs down the drain is clear. Penny's laid out my clothes, and I emerge from the bathroom to find her slumped over the banister. She brushes my shoulder as I pass her down the stairs. "He could be okay."

I want to scream at her to shut up, but then I *will* lose it. Right now I'm in a holding pattern. Something bad is coming, but I can't think of anything except what I'll have to do when I see him. I should do it; it's only right. We're supposed to take care of our own. I walk out the door and back to my chair.

***

The others arrive in the dark and make their way to me. At my request, Ben radioed them to stay at Whitefield until morning, when it would be safer to travel, but I wouldn't have listened either. I fall out of John's rough embrace and into my chair before I dissolve into tears. I won't cry until I know for sure.

Nelly crouches and takes my hand. "What happened?"

"The van went into a ditch. We had to run. He ran the other way and called them so I could escape."

The tone of my voice is eerily similar to Christine's. We should have run together. And if we were going to die, die together. He knew I never would've agreed to split up, which is why he didn't even say goodbye.

"Maybe—" Ana begins.

"No," I say. It's loud in the quiet.

Ana looks away. I'm relieved when her eyes stay dry. She drops her bag, pulls a chair over on my other side and sits. Nelly lowers himself to the dirt, clutching my hand in his.

"Bits is with Penny," I say to Peter. I've sent Penny and Bits to bed. All Bits knows is that Adrian's in the woods—which upset her enough.

He's been waiting behind the others, and now he bends over me. "I'm sure she's okay. I'll stay."

I look up when I hear the thickness in his voice. He presses his lips to my forehead before he moves to Ana's other side. He takes up her hand, and we wait.

***

Dan brought a tent for me and Caleb, but every noise snaps us out of sleep. Every radio call makes us jump. I know he'll come, and not because I think he'll come back to me or something similarly idiotic. We're plowing the fields and the noise draws them from the surrounding woods. That pod has been making its way here, and it's only a matter of time.

Nights are quieter, since the farm is quiet. On the second night I lie in the tent next to Caleb, who unzips his sleeping bag and wraps his fingers around my wrist. "Cassie?"

He sounds so young, and I remember that he's only nineteen. Or he's twenty now—we were coming back for his birthday. I squeeze his hand as he continues. "What will you do when..."

"I don't know." My voice is back to normal. "You?"

"I don't think I can."

"Someone will. Don't worry."

"Okay."

We lie in silence until his hand relaxes in my grip, but I don't let go until I drift into sleep at dawn.

CHAPTER 23

I'm walking back from the bathroom when I hear Caleb yell from the east fence. My hands grow cold, and I stumble over the gravel path. I thought I'd run when I heard, but it's a struggle to make myself move toward the noise. The rattle of the fence is punctuated by more shouts. Nelly emerges from the trees that stand between the restaurant's rear lot and the east fence. He directs people back into the building and speaks into Jeff's ear. Jeff nods and plants his feet apart, arms crossed like a sentry.

Nelly's blotchy face and rounded shoulders tell me all I need to know. He closes the distance between us, but I back away when he tries to touch me. "Don't," he says. "You don't want to see."

It takes every bit of determination I have to take the next step. I shake off Nelly's hand, ignore his pleading and put the other foot forward. I do it again and again, forcing myself not to think about where I'm heading. I have to know. I've always needed to see the wound, inspect the stitches, pick at the scab. Sometimes imagining is worse than reality. Most of the time, actually. So I keep walking.

***

It comes to me in flashes, each one forcing the air from my lungs until it feels as though they've collapsed. His shredded white t-shirt, now a dried-blood brown and covered with the mulch that lines the forest floor. His filthy, gray fingers threaded through the links of the fence. The flesh that's been torn out of his arms.

But it's his face that makes a groan rise from somewhere under my stomach. His olive skin is sallow and his eyes rimmed with brown. Something black drips from a hole in his temple. He looks at us sideways and pushes his mouth against the fence. It looks like it hurts. I want to tell him to stop.

I plod forward with Nelly at my elbow. The others stand in a group ten feet away from the fence line and part at my advance. Barnaby, silent for once, lifts a paw and drops it, as though trying to figure out why this Adrian is on the other side. Dan holds Caleb back from where Marcus stands with one cheek missing, head cocked and teeth bared.

"Caleb," John's voice carries forward. "Let one of us—"

Caleb screams something unintelligible and rips from Dan's grip. He races toward the fence, knife raised, and rams the blade through the links. He follows Marcus down, every jab linked to a shriek so shrill and piercing that my ears ring, and then he sinks against the fence. He reaches a finger through to touch where Marcus lies on the ground. There are other, freshly killed Lexers outside the fence. They didn't touch Marcus and Adrian, like we asked.

When I'm a few feet away, I stop. Adrian's eyes are a dead silvery green. His teeth grate on the metal when he tries to connect with the hand I hold up. I'd thought maybe I'd say something to him, but I'd rather talk to his lifeless body than this creature. This isn't him—it's a germ, a virus, a fucking parasite.

Without lowering my eyes, I fumble in the bucket for a spike and wrap my fist around the handle. Another step and I'm close enough to do it. I raise it to my ear, but I can't make that initial thrust, can't find the power that I'll need to crush it through bone, especially the tougher bone of someone so recently turned. I've held these spikes hundreds of times, pushed them through the fence into eye sockets, the backs of throats and the bases of skulls, but I can't do it to him. I could if he were coming at me, if there wasn't a fence between us, if there were no one here but me. I can't do it this way, though, not if I ever want to sleep again. I don't want to be a coward. I thought I was stronger than this.

"Cass." Nelly's hand closes over the spike. "Don't."

Adrian rattles the fence. I can smell him. I've always loved his scent, and this smell of spoiled meat and shit makes my stomach twist. His teeth are still white, which means he hasn't found anything to eat. That was his worst nightmare.

I let the spike fall into Nelly's hand. John catches my waist when I stumble backward and turn away. I won't look again, because I was wrong. I can imagine terrible things—awful, scary things—but nothing could be worse than the reality of Adrian at the fence. Ana's eyes are as soft as Penny's when she passes to help Nelly. I close my eyes to wait for the crunch, and when it comes I can't hold back the helpless sound that escapes.

John murmurs something I don't hear. I push out of his arms. I'm no longer in a holding pattern; the flight has landed. It doesn't seem real, but it is. This is real. It's real.

Peter grips my elbow when I trip to a stop and heave until what little is in my stomach comes up. He gathers my hair and holds it at the nape of my neck. "It's all right," he says. "It's all right."

I don't see how it will ever be all right.

CHAPTER 24

Adrian and Marcus have been brought to the orchard, while the other bodies have gone down to the field where we stack or bury them. They've set him under a tree, but I don't go until they've laid a sheet over top and moved away. I hate how scared I am, how disgusted I am by the body of the person I love so much.

The apple trees are in bloom and petals drift through the air to land on his makeshift shroud. The trees on this side of the orchard are gnarled and old, straight out of a fairy tale, and the air sweet and clean, until I get close. I force myself to breathe through my mouth when I kneel beside him.

"You shouldn't have done it," I say, and realize how furious I am when I hear my clipped tone. I don't want to be angry with him; I want to say goodbye.

I've put on my gloves, and I move the sheet enough to find his hand. His fingernails are crescents of dirt, and the skin is puckered and pale. He's less decomposed than if he had died in an ordinary way three days ago, but the fact that I can't touch him—won't touch him—without gloves makes me angrier. I'd already touched him for the last time; I just didn't know I had.

My stomach threatens to send up its contents again. I try to think of something good, but all I see is his face grinding against the fence. I can't see his smile or his dimple or the warmth in his eyes. I have to see him. I ease the sheet back, chest tight, to find they've closed his eyes. He looks enough like Adrian that I can breathe. The snarl is gone, replaced by a soft jaw, like when he's asleep.

"Okay," I whisper. "Okay."

The *scritch-thump* noise of the shovels stops. We have to put him in the ground. I want him in the ground, safe under the soil. After they died, my parents were taken straight to cremation from the morgue. I said goodbye to their ashes, not their bodies. Since then, I've wondered how someone lets go of a loved one's hand that last time. How they finally, irrevocably let go. But now I know—it must be when holding on to the alternative would be even more terrible.

"What am I supposed to do?" I whisper.

The thought leaves me empty, like there's a great, yawning chasm that starts here and ends when I die, too. I want to tell him that I love him until the end of the world and after, but he already knows, and I don't think I can say it aloud.

His jeans are stiff with dried blood and torn where a mouth or hand might have found an artery. I don't want to know for sure, to relive his final moments with any accuracy. His knife still hangs on his belt. It was a gift to him from my dad, who always said a good knife was worth its weight in gold. When I unclasp the knife from its bloody sheath, a silvery glint beneath catches my eye; the band of my engagement ring has worked itself halfway out of his pocket.

I reach for the ring but then stop myself. I don't want it. His knife still has purpose; it has happy memories. The ring was a promise—one he can't keep now. But I can make him one. I push it down until I'm sure it's secure. It's the same pocket he carried it around in, waiting for the perfect moment. The Underwear Moment. I wouldn't think it possible, but a smile pushes through my tears.

"Hold onto this for me?" The words are barely audible, but I know he can hear. "No changing your mind, though. You can give it back the next time I see you."

I squeeze his hand twice, and then I let go.

CHAPTER 25

The restaurant is full of people speaking in murmurs and wiping away tears, while I sit with dry eyes. I didn't think I would ever stop crying, but while I watched them fill the hole under the apple trees so I would know for sure he was under the earth, the tears dissipated like they were buried along with Adrian. I want them back, though, as awful as they were. Right now I'd like to feel something besides this emptiness that's so dark I can't imagine being able to produce a tear. I can't bear to sit here, I can't bear to get up, I can't bear to think of what the next minute or hour or month will be like.

Ben walks over with Mikayla, who hands me a steaming mug of tea. It's a heavily rationed item, and I know she's trying to do something to make me feel better.

"Thank you," I say.

"If there's anything I can do for you, you'll let me know?" Ben asks for the third time. He looks desperate for an answer. And he's probably worried; he might have been Adrian's partner, but Adrian's the one who kept all this running.

I force myself to sip the sweet, milky tea. "This is good. Thank you."

Mikayla leads him away. She leans into him when he wraps his arm around her waist. Watching them is like being stabbed in the lungs. I need be alone, but I have nowhere to go. I can't go to our room. I'll set up a tent, at least for tonight. I won't sleep, anyway.

Peter sits next to me with Bits in his arms, her face buried in his neck. I rest my hand on her hair and say, "It's all right."

Peter covers my hand with his, and I realize it's what he said to me. Adrian said it, too. Maybe we humans tell each other it will be all right—even when we know it probably won't be, even when we don't believe it ourselves—otherwise we'd never be able to go on.

Bits leaves Peter's arms for mine, and my shirt grows moist from her tears. I rock her and scan the long table. Penny fingers her handkerchief and huddles next to James. Nelly sits on my other side, head in hands, while Ana clenches and unclenches her fist and stares into space. John lays a heavy hand on my shoulder before settling back into his chair. Adrian would have hated this. I hate this. I can't stand another minute.

"Bits, sit with Peter, okay?"

I scoot her back onto his lap and pry myself out of my seat. Caleb sits at the end of the table, staring down into a mug of coffee. Coffee for him, tea for me. Lucky us. Toby moves so I can sit, and I take Caleb's hand in mine. His eyes are rimmed in pink and his lips are puffy.

"I'm so sorry," I say. "He was so funny. You know, he picked on you because he loved you so much. He reminded me of my brother. He could beat the crap out of me, even though I was older."

After my parents died, I'd always appreciated when someone showed me they'd left a mark on someone besides me. Caleb laughs and wipes his nose on his sleeve. He wraps his arms around my neck just like Bits does.

"Adrian loved you so much," he whispers in my ear. "Everyone wanted what you guys..."

It's too much, and I try to stop the strangled sob that escapes. People turn and then look away when they see it's me. I don't want to be this person again—the one everyone looks at apologetically, the one everyone tiptoes around.

The entire room watches me kiss Bits's hair before I leave the restaurant. Her eyes are so blue against the bloodshot whites, but the spark that dances in them is missing. It will most likely return, although it seems to grow a tiny bit dimmer every time she loses one more goddamned thing to this world. How many more before it's extinguished entirely? All that's left is to keep that light shining, to keep her safe, no matter what. It's all I have, until I meet up with that ring again.

***

It's a six person tent, not that I'm planning on a party, but it's nice to have space. Nelly found me setting it up by the greenhouse at the back of the farm and helped me without a word. He brought me bedding, a chair, my bag of toiletries and a lantern. I watch his profile from the chair while he unrolls the sleeping bag and lays a pillow at the head. Adrian was his friend, and he had to kill him. My gut clenches again, but there's nothing to come up.

"Nel—" I say. "Thank you—for...at the fence. I thought I could..."

The hard line of his mouth turns down like he's trying not to cry. "I didn't. Ana..."

If anyone could do it, it's Ana, and not because she's heartless. I remember the sympathy in her eyes as she walked to the fence, the way she was struggling to hold herself together in the restaurant, and know it wasn't easy for her to do, even if she'll pretend it was.

CHAPTER 26

I've spent a week staring up at the blue ceiling of this tent. My friends take turns bringing me food I can't eat and sitting with me in the evenings until I kick them out. John hovered for days in a silent vigil, until I begged Maureen to make him leave. She lost her husband on the way to the farm last year, and I knew she'd understand my need to be alone. She held me tightly, wordlessly, and then led him away.

Bits and Sparky stayed over one night. We played Uno, but Bits got tired of reminding me it was my turn and asked me to lie with her. I held her until she fell asleep and wished there was someone to do the same for me. Barnaby hasn't left my side. He follows me everywhere I go and stretches out alongside me, and although comforting, it doesn't help me sleep.

It's still chilly, especially at night, but if I want to get warm I work in the greenhouse. It's quiet, and when people see me they find another destination. I don't mind; they may not know what to say, but neither do I. Asking how I am is a sure way to make me cry, and I hate to cry in front of people. I'll have to go to my room soon, though. I can't live like a hermit on the back of the farm forever.

The tent ceiling has turned a light blue, which means it's morning, so I leave to use the bathroom and brush my teeth, Barnaby at my heels. I'm surprised to find an eight-man tent behind the outfitter tents, not forty feet away. Dan sits out front and smiles as I walk past.

"Hey," he says. I raise a hand. If I'd known he was out here I would've cried quieter last night. "I hope you don't mind. I pitched as far away as I could. I like having my own space once it's warm enough."

He did this last summer and fall, too. We called his tent The Love Den, just to bother him. I shake my head that I don't mind and continue walking.

"We're heading to Whitefield today, to help out," he calls after me. "Bringing those chickens and some other stuff. You want to come?"

I look back. He's treating me almost like nothing happened, except for the gentle tone of his voice. No one else would ask me to go, except maybe Ana. No one would think I was up for it. But when I imagine getting out of here—away from the farmhouse and the orchard and the concerned expressions—I want nothing more. I've never felt trapped here, but now the circular fence I once loved feels like one of the circles of Hell.

"When are you leaving?"

"Couple hours. We're staying the night."

"Okay," I say. "I'll be ready."

***

The stairs seem insurmountable, and when I'm at the top I stare at my door for a good three minutes before I work up the nerve to push it open. I move to his pillow and press my face into it, even though I know I'm torturing myself. I lie on our bed and stare at the painting I made for Adrian so long ago, of the spot where we first kissed. He'd hung it up even after I'd told him I didn't love him anymore. I would give anything to take that back, to have those years when I could have been with him.

I try to take comfort in his smell, but all it does is make me livid: at myself for being so stupid and at the Lexers for taking away everything we love. It's probably only a matter of time before they take Bits, too. I dry my face and move to the dresser, where I shove clothes in my backpack and grab my knife and cleaver. Adrian's phone is on his desk, fully charged. I zip it into a side pocket and nestle the charger in with my clothes. I shower and twist my wet hair into buns.

I stand at the bedroom door before I head back downstairs. It's like a place from another life—a life where I truly believed Adrian and I would never be separated again. We were meant to be, and deep down I thought that made us exempt from losing each other. I knew we would get our happily ever after, as long as we were vigilant. Why I thought I deserved anything better than the people who've been ripped apart and turned into monsters is anybody's guess. I was a fucking idiot to think I was entitled to a guarantee. There's only one guarantee left in this world—zombies never die, never stop and are never satiated.

CHAPTER 27

"Of course Bits can stay with me," Penny says, "but are you sure you should go?"

"I have to get out of here." I dig my nails into my palms; if I cry, she'll try to Mother Hen me into staying.

Penny bites her lip and studies my face. "Okay, if you're sure."

I hug Bits goodbye. She sits with Sparky curled in her arms on the little couch in the cabin and lifts a finger to her lips. "Careful not to wake her. She's really tired. I think she's sad."

I didn't think it was possible for my heart to crack the tiniest bit more. I don't know how to comfort Bits. I can't even comfort myself. She gets upset when I cry, and I can't stop crying for any decent length of time, so I've been staying away. "Okay, I won't. I love you so much."

"I love you, too," she whispers.

I motion Penny outside. "I was thinking that you and James might want to switch rooms with me."

"No!" Penny raises a hand to her throat. "That's your room. We don't want—"

"I could live here with Ana and Peter. Bits wouldn't have to go back and forth. She could stay with you when we're on guard or patrol. A baby would be so much easier in a house with running water. You already have to pee six thousand times a day and would have a toilet right there." I try to sound like giving up my room is the best idea I've ever had.

"No, really, I don't want you to—"

"I can't stay there," I say with a shrug. "So either you switch, or I'll stay in my tent."

"I don't think you're thinking this through. You don't want to make a big decision right now, you know?"

"I'm going to be on guard and patrol all summer. I'm signing up for nights, since—" I almost say *since I can't sleep*, "no one wants them. Say yes."

"I'll talk to James. I think you need to take more time, you're moving too fast."

I sling my backpack over my shoulder and shrug again. Penny still feels safe here. She has a boyfriend she loves and a baby on the way. She teaches school. She doesn't have to kill Lexers day after fucking day so we can live. That's my job, although I never wanted it. I wanted to be the person dreaming of babies while wrapped in someone's arms, too. I swallow down my resentment, but I can't look at her.

"I have to go," I manage to say before the first tear slips out.

"Cass..." Penny trails off before she begins. Even she doesn't know what to say to me, which is exactly why I want to leave.

I turn and walk to where the trucks wait. Ana ties down chicken crates in the bed of the pickup. She didn't bat an eye when I told her I was coming, just nodded like it was expected. "Ready?"

"Ready," I say.

CHAPTER 28

The roar of the truck's engine lulled me into the longest sleep I've had in days, and I drag myself back into consciousness at Whitefield's gate. Nelly pretends to wipe off my drool when I lift my head from his shoulder. He's trying hard to be normal because he knows I want it that way, even if I can't quite get there myself. I tousle his hair and follow the others onto the tarmac.

Kyle greets us outside of the main hangar. "Glad you all made it. Zeke's scouting out North Conway, so I'm helping set this all up." He looks at me and shifts his bulk from one foot to the other. "Cassie, I didn't know you were—I'm sorry about Adrian."

"Thanks," I say.

Kyle nods and studies the mountains. He's angry; I can see it in his brow and the pucker of his lips. I rage at the injustice of it all, too, but it's like screaming at the clouds for sending down rain. Lexers are just another force of nature. We stand in an awkward silence. My life has become one huge awkward silence.

"So, should we get the chickens in the new coop?" Peter asks.

"Right," Kyle says.

I walk to where Nelly, Dan and Liz unload the extra electrical equipment Henry has asked for. Nelly glances up hopefully every time someone passes.

"Nels, we have this," I say. "Go."

"Well, I'll help with the chickens and then—"

He lifts another box and sets it on the ground. I move between him and the truck and cross my arms. "Go find Adam. We have this."

He looks away, and I realize that he doesn't want to seem too eager. I'd do the same for him, but it makes me feel even worse. "Go," I say again. "I'm not letting you near this truck."

He gives me half a smirk. "Stop bossing me around."

"Never gonna happen."

It's not our usual banter, but it'll do for now. He yanks me into his arms and rests his head on mine. "Love you, darlin'."

"You, too. Now get out of here."

He squeezes me and walks off in search of Adam.

***

It turns out that Whitefield isn't the escape I'd hoped for; it took the whole day to run through the apologies. Henry and Hank were the one bright spot. I brought Hank a letter from Bits, who's decided they should become Safe Zone pen pals. When Hank saw her drawing on the bottom, he insisted he wanted to live at Kingdom Come. It wasn't quite a tantrum, but it's apparent who inherited Dottie's quiet determination. Henry promised they'd move as soon as he'd trained someone to take over.

Darkness has fallen by the time we sit in the living area of the family barrack. Kyle strokes Nicole's tiny pigtails while he runs down the inventory of what we brought today. Whitefield has supplies for now, but a patrol will be necessary soon. Nicole's eyes flutter and her lips move on her thumb while she sleeps. She was glued to her dad's side all day, and I happen to know she kicked her thumb-sucking habit a few months ago. Even the littlest ones, who've been kept from the worst of it, know enough to be scared. Kyle's all she has; she did have a mother, and Kyle a wife, but when they returned home from preschool to head to the base, she'd been on the lawn eating their dog.

After we've made plans to patrol, we spread out our sleeping bags on command's carpeted floor. The green pin remains stuck in Idaho. I'm almost glad it's still there because I can't imagine having to tell Adrian's mom that we've lost him forever.

I slip out once my roommates' breathing becomes regular, nod at the people who man the radio and walk into the night. The dim lights guide me to the spot where Adrian proposed. Sometimes I wonder if I should have kept the ring, but I don't want it without him. The star ring on my right hand means more to me than that little diamond because I like to think it led me back to him.

The roar of Zeke's motorcycle draws near. He parks it by his dental office, which means he'll pass where I stand. I'm blinded by his headlight before the engine sputters off. His boots thud as he nears, and then I'm in his solid arms.

"I thought that was you, sugar. Jesus, I'm so sorry. So sorry. How's my girl?"

I cry softly at first, and then I'm sobbing and my nose is running and I gasp for air. Zeke holds me until it's become hitching breaths and looks down at me with such concern that I want to reassure him that I'm okay.

I attempt a smile. "That was more than you bargained for, I'll bet."

His laugh bounces off the buildings. "Girl, my mama would've loved you. C'mon, let's go shoot the shit in my office."

Zeke's office is built into the last remaining storehouse. He's scavenged enough dental equipment to make it a full service establishment. It even smells like the dentist's office. I recline in the exam chair while he putters around.

"Have you been flossing, sugar?" he asks. I love when he calls me sugar, especially since it comes out like *sugah*.

"Zeke, you are first and foremost a dentist. Yes, I've been flossing. And, before you ask, I still make Bits floss, too."

"You're one of my only flossers. I couldn't stand it if you stopped."

He asks me every time I see him. When he found out that I'm slightly neurotic about tooth care, he was over the moon.

"So, why would your mom have liked me?"

He sits in his rolling chair and puts his feet on his desk. I close my eyes to listen. "She admired spunk. She could find something to laugh about, no matter what, even after Daddy died. She was such a smart-ass. I remember, one time, I must've been nine..."

I'm listening, but his voice gets fainter and fainter, until it fades away entirely.

I wake up under a blanket in the chair. It looks like early morning, judging by the gray light that shines through the window and onto where Zeke's head rests on his desk. The chair squeaks when I swing my legs over the side.

He leans back with a groan. "Glad you got some sleep."

"Sorry, I didn't mean to fall asleep in the middle of your story. I haven't slept much."

"I've put many a woman to sleep with my long-winded stories. I'm used to it."

"That's not possible," I say. "Not someone as rugged and interesting as you." The way Zeke and I tease each other comes so naturally that I feel close to normal, until I remember it's the start of another day. I sink to the edge of the chair.

"How 'bout some breakfast?" Zeke asks, and pretends he doesn't notice. "But first, we brush our teeth."

CHAPTER 29

Penny finally agreed to switch rooms after I'd spent another week in the tent. I kept the painting, his phone and his knife. Some of his things went back to general supplies, and Penny helped me store the rest in the attic. I sat on the bed and watched her do most of the work while I cried. We had it down to a science—I held her hair back while she puked, and she handed me handkerchiefs when the old one was too sodden to do any good.

But I haven't cried for two days straight. It'd been almost three weeks of tears, and I was tired of it. I'm sure everyone else was, too. There have been no more pods, only small groups of Lexers that hit the fence several times a day. I do guard almost every night, and I'm no longer afraid to walk the fence line alone. The Lexers don't scare me, and when I stab one in the eye the satisfaction is immense. Every ounce of hate drives my spike into a brain—but at least instead of wallowing in my misery, I'm putting it to good use.

When not on guard, I stare at the pages of books without reading, I talk to Bits without listening and I lie awake at night, staring. It's only in the morning, when I hear people starting their day, that I'm able to sleep for a few hours. It's noisier on this end of the farm, in amongst the cabins and large tents, but I like our little cabin. The bedroom I share with Bits is big enough for a single bed, a cot and a dresser. The walls are wood, with a window and a row of hooks where we hang our coats when we're not too lazy. Adrian's painting, Bits's drawings and her paper flowers on the windowsill make it cozy and warm instead of spare.

I've just drifted off after guard when Bits hops into bed with me. "Cassie! Are you asleep?"

I crack open an eye. She's so close her freckles are blurry. "Yes. I am asleep."

She giggles. "Will you do art class today? Please? We're so bored. Penny's all like—" I laugh when she makes a face and clutches her stomach, "and we need to finish our portraits."

I feel guilty for putting it off and think of Frida Kahlo's portrait with Diego Rivera on her forehead. Mine would have Adrian, larger than life. "Yeah. I'll be there in a while."

She gets dressed and skips into the main room. Peter, who's also a flosser, makes sure she brushes her teeth before they leave for breakfast. Once they're gone, it's too quiet to sleep. I stare at the wall and try not to think about how I now sleep in a twin bed. Instead, I think about patrol in two days. I used to fear it, but now I crave the escape. Sometimes, when I walk the fence at night, I imagine leaving. I would disappear through a gate for an indeterminate length of time and return as a normal person. But I'd probably return as a zombie.

***

I made it through art class and sit at dinner, picking at my spaghetti. People glance at The Girl Whose Fiancé Has Died, but my eyes are dry.

"We're going to Montpelier?" I ask Dan, who's taken to sitting at our table.

He sucks up a strand of spaghetti. "Yup. Toby mapped it out."

"Who's going?"

"You, me, Caleb, Toby, Ana and Peter."

"I can't wait," Ana says.

"Me, neither," I say.

Peter breathes through his nose and sets down his fork. Penny stiffens but doesn't have enough energy to scold us. She goes back to her ginger lemonade. I make a mental note to find more of both ingredients.

"Shawn's checked the vehicles?" John asks. Dan answers in the affirmative, and John levels his gaze at me. I swear he can hear what I'm thinking when he looks at me that way. "Just be careful."

I nod solemnly, although I've come to the conclusion that being careful is overrated. Adrian was careful, so was I. Bad shit happens anyway. Being careful might extend the amount of time until it finally gets you, but it's going to get you no matter what.

"Then we're going to Whitefield next week, right?" Nelly asks.

"Yeah," I say. "We'll bring them what we've found."

That will be another three days out of here. We need to head to the Quebec Safe Zone at some point, too. And then Whitefield will need more supplies.

"Anything you want, Bits?" Peter asks.

"No, thanks," Bits answers, and concentrates on twirling her fork in her spaghetti. She doesn't want us to go. I know she's afraid, but she doesn't appreciate that this is what keeps her safe. Just imagine how afraid she'd be without a fence and friends and plenty of food to eat.

CHAPTER 30

The ride to Montpelier is over an hour, but we take a longer route in order to avoid Morristown. Most of the gas and food were cleaned out of there late last fall, but there were a good number of Lexers due to the treatment area the government set up. Thankfully, Vermont wasn't very populated, except for the city of Burlington and its surrounding areas. We don't know how many Lexers are in Burlington or what the roads are like; no one ventured that far last summer. Gas is running low, however, and without Will's patrols to supply us through the summer, we might find out about Burlington soon. We have enough diesel to have begun work on the trench that's being dug around the farm, but probably not enough for the whole job.

We usually take two vehicles on patrol. It gives us more room for supplies, and a spare vehicle if one breaks down. I try not to rewrite history, but I can't help but think that if we'd all come back from Whitefield together Adrian would be sitting next to me now.

Peter and Ana sit in the front of the pickup while we follow Dan and the others. Peter refused to let Ana drive, much to my relief and her chagrin. It's warm for mid-May, and the sweet spring air flows in the open windows. The grass is green, and the overgrown fields are a tangle of brown stalks that were bent double under the snow's weight. I wonder how long it will take before it's reclaimed by forest. A hundred or more years ago, much of Vermont was cleared for farmland, and the woods are still crisscrossed with rock walls the farmers built around what were once open fields. One day it will be rock walls, houses and cars in the middle of forest.

We roll through Albany at a snail's pace while I write down the addresses of houses with large propane tanks for future use. A few raggedy Lexers hit the two-lane road after we pass, but they give up once we're a good distance away. A Lexer completely covered in black moss crawls along the shoulder before falling in a heap and going motionless.

"Ew." Ana screws up her face. "Did you see that one?"

It was gross, but it also looked like it was dying. It gives me hope that something besides us is after them; we only have to hold out long enough for it to happen. It's something to look forward to, but a world without Lexers will still be a world without Adrian.

***

The Walmart is outside of Montpelier, in an enclosed strip mall with a brick façade. Ana points at the Bath and Body Works sign with a squeal that makes Peter jam his foot on the brake.

"Christ, could you not scream like that?" Peter asks, but his voice is light.

"There's a Claire's, too! Earrings!" Ana yells. "J.C.Penney!"

"You wouldn't have been caught dead in J.C. Penney a year ago," I tease.

She does a ridiculous dance in the passenger seat. "Beggars can't be choosers. Woo! I'm getting me some spangled jeans! Did you ever think you'd hear me say that?"

Dan backs up the van and leans out. "Everything okay?" I can't stop laughing, and Dan grins at Ana's antics.

"She's a little excited at the thought of lotion and sparkly things," I say.

"We are only going to Walmart," Peter says. "You can get earrings and cheap denim there, if you must."

"But, Da-ad," I whine, "can't you just drop us off and come back in an hour?"

Everyone laughs, including Peter, but he shakes his head and says, "I repeat, we are only going to Walmart."

I don't care what we do. It feels so good to be out here, to have laughed, that I'll go anywhere they want. The parking lot has only a few cars, which might mean the mall is close to empty. We park the trucks outside the entrance and scan the parking lot, while Toby and Dan peer through the glass.

"Okay," Toby says. "These doors go into the mall corridor, and then it's another fifteen feet to Walmart's doors. We're gonna need one person in the lot and one in the hall."

That leaves four inside the store. We really should have more people, but we didn't know this would be an issue.

"I'll stay in the hall," I say. "Just get some ginger and lemonade for Penny. And cat food and flea stuff, if you can." Peter and Ana nod; they like the idea of a flea-ridden Sparky crawling around the cabin about as much as I do.

"I'll stay outside," Dan says, and hands a piece of paper to Toby. "Here's the list. Pharmacy and food are most important. Although it doesn't look like one of the stores with a lot of food."

Toby peruses the list and cackles. "Ah, I see why the pharmacy is first."

Ana giggles when she reads it over his shoulder. *Condoms*, she mouths at me. I roll my eyes, I figured as much.

"It's not *my* list, you moron," Dan says, but it's a cheerful insult. "It's everyone's. And by pharmacy, I meant actual medicine."

"Sure you did," Caleb says, and hops away when Dan's boot connects with his butt.

"Maybe we could look around for zombies?" Peter asks. "This is a great time, but I'd like to finish here and get back."

Ana steps on Peter's boot. "You're such a killjoy."

"Let's check out the hall," Dan says.

Walmart is at the end of the long corridor, and we can see halfway to the other end before our view is obstructed by indoor trees that have died from lack of water. Bags, boxes, clothes and shoes lay in heaps on the floor, along with bodies that were either killed or froze to death. Some of the stores' gates are up, but there's no way of seeing who or what's inside unless we check it out. The fact that it smells more musty and damp than anything else is a good sign—there can't be too many zombies close by or it would stink a lot worse. Maybe living people won this battle and then cleared out to find warmth for the winter.

Toby tears the list and hands half to Ana. Peter and Caleb fit radio earpieces in their ears, while Dan wears the third. "Fifteen minutes," Dan says.

The Walmart is pitch black inside, and I'm happy to be staying out here where light floods through the glass. Peter flicks on his headlamp and walks ten feet into the store, machete drawn. "Clear so far."

We speak in low voices because we'd like to get out before we're noticed by anything. Normally, we'd stand outside and make noise in order to draw any Lexers into the open, but the corridor has changed the plan. The four grab shopping carts and rumble into the darkness. I lean against the windows at the end of the corridor to watch the hall while Dan stands in the outer doorway and examines the lot.

After a few minutes he says, "You know, those aren't for me."

"Okay." I glance at the back of his head and then resume my watch down the hall with a grin. "How's Meghan? Oh, right, it's been over three weeks. How's the next girl?"

"I'm taking a breather."

"But The Love Den looks like it's open for business."

"You and Nel. You guys don't quit."

"You're an easy mark," I say. "We can't help it."

He chuckles and turns to me, eyes squinted in the sunlight. "You seem different today."

"I'm having fun. It's nice to be out here."

This isn't what one would consider nice, but he nods. He raises his hand to his forehead to block the sun and watches the trees at the edge of the lot rustle in the breeze.

"Yeah," he says. "I love the farm, but someti—"

He puts a finger to his earpiece, and what sounds like an avalanche of metal carries out of the store's entrance. I take my cleaver from where it leans on the wall and look to Dan, who shakes his head. A whoop echoes from within.

"They're fine," he says. "Fucking Caleb. I think he's going a little crazy."

Caleb is on guard with me a lot. I like when he's there because we don't ask each other questions. We sit, making the occasional comment and walking the line. We have friendly arguments over who gets to finish off the Lexers. He hates them as much as I do.

The crash has brought something out of the Payless Shoes not far down. It was once a man, dressed in khakis and a t-shirt. He's followed by a woman in a loose coat and two kids who look to be ten and eight years old. A zombie nuclear family. The only thing worse than regular zombies are zombie kids: you want to help them, even though they'd eat you just as soon as the adults would.

"Four coming this way," I say.

Dan shuts the outer door and draws his machete out of its sheath. "Ready?"

"Yup."

The adrenaline, the sense of purpose, fills me. We step through the debris. I don't want to kill the little girl if I don't have to—her long, brown hair reminds me of Bits. But I will, because every Lexer gone is one less to worry about. The man's swollen tongue protrudes from his lips. This family is gray and cracked, lacking the pliability of new Lexers, but their speed increases as they close in. Maybe they were the ones who'd cleared the mall, but it still didn't keep them safe.

The kids hiss. The woman groans and raises a hand that's more like a talon. Dan hits the man's throat with a wet-sounding swish, and I spike the boy in the eye and withdraw in time to get Mom, who lands on her back beside him. Dan squares his broad shoulders as the girl approaches. He takes in her dress and one sparkly shoe and then swings his machete hard enough to obliterate her face. After she hits the floor, he closes his eyes briefly.

"I know," I say. We don't say anything more, and in the silence I hear a small gulping noise. "Do you hear that?"

The hall is empty. Dan cocks his head and follows the sound to its source: Mom. He moves the flap of her coat aside to reveal a baby carrier. Its face is hidden, but tiny, sore-covered gray legs and arms wave through the holes. I've never seen a Lexer younger than five years old; I hoped I never would. Its hands make little fists. The mewling hisses ramp up. That could be Penny on the floor, a hole where her left eye once was. It could be her baby, whom she'll be wearing in a carrier like this sometime this winter.

"Should we...?" Dan asks in a quiet voice.

It's not going to grow up and eat people, but we can't let it stay this way. It deserves to be put out of its misery. My mouth thickens with saliva. He did the little girl. It's my turn. "I'll do it."

"You sure?"

I nod and stand over Mom. The baby has a bald spot on the back of its tiny head. It grinds against its mother's chest as though looking to nurse. It takes two false starts before I bring the spike down. I close my eyes at impact and shudder when the skull gives way with a pop instead of a crunch.

I stride toward the Walmart entrance without a word. Dan follows and takes his post outside. I just killed a baby. I know it wasn't a baby anymore, but that doesn't make me feel much better. We wait in silence until headlamps light the registers just inside the doors. Peter and Ana's carts are filled to the brim.

"We got everything," Ana says. "Well, except earrings, because it turns out Walmart earrings are hideous. Really, really hideous. There's so much stuff in there. I wonder why—" She breaks off and follows my line of vision to the bodies. "Oh, were they the only ones?"

"Yeah." I don't mention the baby. I don't want everyone going over there to see. They won't be able to resist; I know because I wouldn't, and it's just too horrible.

Toby and Caleb appear, heads down and shoulders hunched, pushing carts laden with bags of flour, sugar and other dry goods.

"We're going back in," Caleb says. He drums on his shopping cart handle and clicks his tongue to the beat. "There's just too much good shit in there."

"Cabe," Dan says quietly, "if you pull another stunt like whatever that was in there, you're never going on patrol again."

Caleb's mouth opens. Dan holds his gaze with icy blue eyes. "Sorry," Caleb says. "I just—there was a Lexer, and I wanted to see what'd happen if I crushed it. Why so serious, man? You laugh at them."

Dan takes a step toward Caleb, who backs up a few paces. "Yeah, I do. But I don't make unnecessary noise to pull them out on my friends. And I try not to torture them. They were people, Caleb. They were *babies*. So grow the fuck up."

Caleb nods, lips white. He's half right—we do make fun of them and try to find humor in what isn't at all funny. But you never, ever do something to endanger your patrol. Peter gives me a questioning look. Dan is almost never pissed, and even a stunt like Caleb's would be mostly laughed off since we came to no harm.

"I'll go back in with Caleb and Toby," Ana says in an attempt to make peace. Ana may endanger herself but never anyone else. I'd trust her with my life. I do trust her with my life, regularly. "Why don't you three load?"

They head into the store. I tell Peter about the baby and the little girl who looked like Bits while we stack the food in the van.

"I knew something was wrong," Peter says with a grimace. He throws a bag of cat food into the pickup. "I don't want to see. And don't let Ana, or she'll never want kids. It'd be the perfect ammunition for her argument."

He says the last part with a wink. Dan and I smile at his levity, which is what we needed. I hold up boxes of birth control in every type and size before I add them to a bin. "Looks like you're out of luck for now, but at least you'll be getting lucky."

"That's if Dan doesn't use it all."

Dan throws up his hands in surrender and joins in our laughter. It's the second time I've really laughed today, and I haven't cried once.

CHAPTER 31

Patrol tired me out, but it didn't put me to sleep. I leave Sparky sleeping on Bits's hair and head for the main gate. Nelly's on tonight, and he looks up from his game of cards with Mike's son, Rohan, and Sue. Sue's in her late forties, with long, frizzy hair that's always covered with a baseball cap. She doesn't do patrol due to a bad knee, but she grew up hunting and has no problem taking out Lexers near the fence.

"Want me to deal you in?" Nelly asks.

"What are you playing?"

"Poker. Texas Hold 'Em."

"Sure." I drag a chair to the table. "But I don't remember how to play very well."

"I'll learn ya," Nelly says. "This was huge at the frat house."

Rohan pushes his dark, shoulder-length hair behind his ears. "You were in a frat?" He's more of a Dungeons and Dragons-type guy, and he eyes Nelly with suspicion.

Nelly laughs. "Yeah, but don't worry, Cass here wouldn't have been friends with me if I'd been a real frat guy."

I make a face. "No way."

"Let's walk the fence before the next hand," Sue says. "I'll go east. Rohan, you go west."

After they've left, Nelly says, "So, darlin', how was your day?"

"It was good. I had fun."

He looks up from his card shuffling. "*Good? Fun?* Those are two words I wouldn't use to describe patrol. Tell me more."

"I like being out there. You don't think about anything else."

He gets it, but that doesn't mean he approves, if the look on his face is any indication. "What's going on with you? You went from crying all the time—which was normal, mind you—to almost acting like nothing's happened."

"I'm not acting like nothing's happened! What do you want me to do? Sit around crying forever? There's stuff that needs to be done so we all don't die, Nelly!"

He puts his hand over where mine grips the arm of the chair. "All right, now, darlin'. I didn't mean that the way it sounded. I don't want you to cry forever, obviously. I just want to make sure you're not pretending you're okay."

"Of course I'm not okay," I say in a barely controlled voice and blink to hold back the tears. "But I feel most okay when I leave the farm."

"You should feel most *unsafe* when you leave the farm," Nelly says with a dramatic sigh. "But who am I to argue? Just your dearest and most intelligent friend in the world."

He's made a joke to stave off my tears, and I love him for it. "No, that's Penny."

"Dearest and handsomest?"

"You used to be, but now that I'm friends with Peter he might have that slot." I clasp my hands under my chin and flutter my eyelashes. "Those cheekbones and straight nose? The dark, soulful eyes? I'm thinking no. Not that you're not ruggedly handsome, of course."

Nelly holds his wounded heart.

"Dearest and funniest," I say. "And that's the best slot of all. Don't ever leave me."

He chews on the inside of his cheek and looks away.

"What?" I ask. "What's wrong?"

"I was thinking that when we go to Whitefield this week...I might stay there for a while."

I drop my gaze to the table. If Adrian were here I would've sent Nelly off happily, even though I'd miss him. Now it feels like everyone's happiness is growing but mine.

"Y'all will be coming every other week for a while," Nelly continues quickly. "So it's not like we wouldn't see each other. I'll come here, I promise. And we can talk on the radio—"

"Nels, you know I hate the phone." I cross my arms and pretend to pout. I can tell he's been agonizing over this decision and wish he hadn't been afraid to tell me. "The radio's even worse! I'll visit you, but only if you promise to take me out partying."

"You're asking *me* that? Like the first thing I do isn't going to be checking out the nightlife?" His eyes grow serious. "Thanks, darlin'."

"Why are you thanking me? I want you to be happy, too. But there's one thing you need to do for me before you leave me here all lonely, eighty miles away."

"Anything. Name it."

"Tell me what base you and Adam—"

He slams his forehead to the table. "I knew it! God, I hate you."

CHAPTER 32

❝Big Bend and Gila both fell off the map," Zeke says. He points at the new green pushpins stuck in Whitefield's map in Command. "We haven't heard anything from them in two weeks."

Big Bend and Gila are Safe Zones, in Texas and New Mexico, respectively. And they're both in the middle of nowhere. Even if a pod hit Big Bend, the Gila Safe Zone is so remote it seems unlikely they'd be overcome. When I was twelve, my parents took me and Eric on a cross-country trip, and I still remember the winding roads and steep drop-offs of the Gila National Forest.

"How many days apart?" John asks. "Could we be talking about a large pod?"

"The thought's crossed my mind," Zeke says. "Big Bend was supposed to check in a few days after Gila. We've tried to raise them on the radio every day, but so far, nothing."

Zeke is officially Whitefield's new boss. You can see it in the bags under his eyes and the way he's not as apt to joke as he was a month ago. He twists his beard into a point and tugs. "We've been in touch with the Grand Canyon Zone, and Monte Vista, in Colorado. They haven't seen a thing, besides the usual."

John's bushy eyebrows practically touch when he inspects the map. "Dwayne can only go about six hundred miles in the plane before he has to turn back. Not enough to see anything. And it'd be a waste of fuel. Speaking of which, how's the supply?"

Dwayne's the only pilot left, besides the one at Moose River— the others were in the 157th.

"Low," Zeke says with a sigh. "Will had plans to get more, but the plans were in his head. I don't know where he was going to get it. We've bled all the closest airports dry, and we can't head to Portsmouth without the 157th."

"Well, there's nothing we can do about it," John says, "except check in with Colorado and Arizona more often."

"I've got even more respect for Will now," Kyle says. "The planting's bad enough, forget the other shit. I don't know how he did it."

I slide a sheaf of papers across the table. Kyle looks them over and the lines on his forehead smooth out. "It's Whitefield," he says, and hands them to Zeke. "All the crops mapped out. You do this, Cassie?"

"Adri—" I clear my throat. I haven't said his name out loud. "No."

Kyle nods quickly. "Thanks."

It's time to start the gardens, now that it's the first of June. We brought a truckload of plant starts and extra food with us today, but it's still going to be a tighter spring than we'd anticipated.

"One last thing," John says. "We need a meet-up point, in case we ever have to bug out of the Northeast. Will and I discussed heading north across Canada, to the Yukon or Alaska. There's the Whitehorse, Talkeetna or Homer Safe Zones. No sense going where it's warmer, or where it's flat."

I shiver doubly at the thought. Not only is Vermont cold enough for me, but it would also mean we'd lost the farm. I'm comforted by the fact that Kingdom Come will continue to keep people safe, like Adrian wanted. And I like that he's near, even if I haven't gone back to the orchard.

"Alaska can take us in?" Zeke asks.

"They say the more the merrier. Good group of folks, it seems. Not a lot of Lexers to speak of so far this spring. They think the bitter cold might've killed even more of them than it did here. They still have to deal with stragglers from Fairbanks and Anchorage, but they don't think many will make it over the mountains from the south."

"Not like us," Peter says.

We've had a daily average of thirty Lexers at the fence. Not enough to worry about, but enough to keep us on our toes. Enough that I have an excuse to stay at the fence and blow off things like art class and breakfast shift, where Mikayla's sympathetic glances make me want to throw a pot at her.

"Then what would we do?" Ana leans back, boots on the table, and purses her lips. "It'd be boring."

"Boring is good," Peter says. "Boring is what we want."

Ana throws a wink my way. She keeps me busy with weapons practice and guard. She's tireless and brusque, two qualities that used to drive me crazy, but I now find them appealing. She doesn't coddle me, and she doesn't judge. I pretend I don't see Peter's frown when I fail to hide my smile.

***

Nelly and Adam have set up house in one of the barrack rooms. I gave Nelly a framed photograph that I found in Adrian's things. Adrian, Nelly and I are sitting on a boulder, arms around each other, sweaty from a hike. None of us looks particularly well-groomed, but our smiles are so genuine that it's always been one of my favorites. I took a picture of it with the phone so I'd have it, too.

Nelly holds out his arms. "How is it possible that I'm going to miss someone I hate so much?"

"I hate you, too," I say into his shoulder. "A lot."

Nelly's always taken care of me, even if it's by bossing me around and making fun of me until I'm on the straight and narrow. I know he's here, but it almost feels like he's gone forever. I give him one last squeeze and turn to Adam. "Take care of him. He gets too full of himself and needs someone to cut him down to size."

"Believe me," Adam says with a grin, "I know."

I don't trust myself to speak again, so I wave and walk to our trucks. Henry and Hank are coming to Kingdom Come and have thrown their few possessions in the back. Hank practically shoves his father into the truck in his excitement, and I don't feel as alone as I did a moment ago.

I pull the sleeve of Zeke's black t-shirt. "Get some rest, Zekey."

"Lord knows I'm trying. You too, sugar," he says. "We could go on vacation with the luggage under our eyes."

"Zeke! Are you implying that I look like shit?"

"Never, my dear. I'd elect you Miss Safe Zone if I could."

I can't stand to see him so serious, so I'm pleased to get one of his big laughs when I throw a pretend baton in the air. I blow him a kiss and jump in next to Hank.

CHAPTER 33

I flip over the dark earth with my trowel, lower a tomato plant into the hole and pat the dirt back around it. Bits works next to me, just like last summer. And, also like last summer, we're both barefoot. I soak in the warmth of the sun now that the early morning clouds have burned off.

"So maybe they have special powers," Hank says to Bits, paying no attention to where his trowel ineffectively jabs at the soil. "Like the girl can shoot bolts of lightning out of her hands."

"No," Bits says. "They're like us, but better. Maybe she's a ninja, like Ana."

I laugh. Bits and Hank have become fast friends, as though they'd been looking for each other all their lives. They're collaborating on a comic book about two kids who single-handedly save the world from zombies. I thought it might frighten Bits more, but imagining herself as a zombie killer seems to have had the opposite effect.

"How about they live forever, like zombies, only they're still alive?" Hank takes off his glasses and rubs them with his shirt. "Maybe they took the antidote. Or the reverse virus or something?"

Bits gives him a hug, leaving him flustered. He may have grown up a lot, but he's still the socially awkward boy I love. "Yes!" she yells. "That's totally what they should be! And maybe the first scene is where they find the vials in a secret research lab."

Hank drops his trowel altogether and says, "Yeah!"

It's hard not to think of Adrian as we follow his directions on where to plant. I love growing things, but he loved it so much more. I swipe at the one tear I can't contain and dig a hole for the next plant. By plant number three the lump in my throat is gone.

"How's it going?" We look up to see Dan standing over us. "Bits, I think you forgot your shoes."

"We don't wear shoes when it's hot," Bits replies, and points to my feet. "Our feet need to run free."

"Those are some dirty, free feet."

"Hey, don't knock it 'til you've tried it," I say. "We may be filthy, but we can wiggle our toes whenever we want. Unlike you, all trapped inside your boots."

"Well, now I have to try it." Dan bends down to strip off his heavy black boots and socks, and then moves his toes in the dirt. "You're right."

"See?" Bits says.

She swipes at him with her black toes. Dan catches her foot and tickles until she's lying in the dirt gasping for breath. I can't help but laugh at the belly laugh that erupts when she's tickled, but I shake my head at Dan. "Feet are easy to clean. Dirt in the hair—not so much."

"Do it again!" Bits says. "Please, Dan!"

He kneels to brush off her hair and points his thumb my way. "I would, but I don't want to get in any more trouble than I'm already in."

I smile and move to the next row. Bits and Hank run their latest comic storyline by Dan, who shows so much interest that they end up in a circle discussing the finer points of Lexer slaughter. It looks like I'm the only one in our assigned rows who's going to do any work today. I don't mind, but I've already decided not to come back tomorrow. This lends itself to too much thought.

Dan's feet appear in my row. "Want help?"

"Sure." I show him what to do, and we finish the last row in record time, starting on opposite ends and meeting in the middle. We strip off our gloves and sit on the dirt.

"Thanks," I say.

He waves at the green that surrounds us. "Well, I should probably help to plant since I'm planning to eat. I like it."

"And the tomato plants smell so good. Rub a leaf and smell your hand. I wish I could bottle that smell and wear it."

"They do smell good." Dan leans forward. "And you *are* wearing some. Or some dirt, at least."

He rubs his finger across my cheekbone. It's more a friendly gesture than anything else, but I want to be touched so badly that I can't breathe. I want to lean into his hand and close my eyes. I want him to be Adrian.

I bolt to my feet, cheek tingling and stomach queasy. "Yeah, I guess I really need a shower. Thanks for helping."

Dan looks a bit startled by my abrupt departure, but he shrugs. "Sure thing."

I grab my boots at the end of the row but don't head for the showers. The wrinkled petals of the apple trees are soft under my feet as I walk to Adrian's grave. Someone's put wildflowers on the rock that marks his mound of dirt. I should have been doing that, I guess. I slump against his tree and let two weeks' worth of tears go.

CHAPTER 34

I'm driving because I want to live to see another day, sort of. Ana sits in the passenger seat of the VW bus and rests her boots on the dash. "I wish we could play some music."

"Why don't you see what's on the radio?" I ask.

"Ha ha. You know what I mean."

I keep my eyes on the dirt road that takes us up the mountain to the lookout. "No music. We can't hear anything with music."

"I know. Fine. Did you see how my tomato plants are the biggest?" She hasn't shut up about her plants since we got them in the ground a week ago.

"Yes, Ana. For the thousandth time, your plants are the biggest. Maybe you'll win a blue ribbon at the state fair this year."

"Look who's Miss Cranky today. Geez."

I glance at her. She's raised her hands stick 'em up-style. "Sorry," I say.

"No, it's fine. I like my women feisty."

My laugh is drowned out by the song she starts to sing. This is not a good thing, and not because of zombies. Ana is tone-deaf, unlike Penny, who sings like an angel.

"Stop!" I yell. "You're killing me."

She raises her volume. It's a Top 40 song that almost makes the apocalypse welcome, since I thought I'd never have to hear it again. I whack her on the head, and the last howled note hangs in the air as I pull into the driveway and park at the abandoned house. We wait in silence, but nothing appears.

I follow Ana up the steep trail. It's five hundred feet to the top of the mountain, and though I might be in good shape, keeping up with her makes me winded. The trail opens to a clearing dotted with stumps, which has been enlarged with chainsaws and axes to afford a view of much of the south of the farm.

Ana hands me binoculars and raises hers to her eyes. "Penny's on me about you."

"What?" I ask, and turn to where she continues scanning the terrain.

"She thinks you're all messed up and doesn't like for you to be doing guard so much."

"Messed up?"

"Yeah, she said something about the stages of grief—that you're not doing them right. I don't know." She shrugs. "You know I never listen to my sister. She said I needed to stop encouraging you."

I'm speechless and can't see a thing through the binoculars with the way my hands tremble. I would kill Penny if she were in front of me right now. She's got indoor plumbing, a baby and James. She has no idea what this is like.

I scan the quarry. The man who owned it had high hopes when he started mining, according to Adrian, but it never produced large amounts of granite, and eventually he gave up. The road that separates the three lakes is wide enough for one vehicle, although I think it must have been wider in the past. The fences have long been torn down by people seeking respite from a hot summer's day. Lexers bob in the water. I can't tell if they're finally dead, since none of them are doing the backstroke. I see a Lexer moving across a field, and another standing by a farmhouse, but there's nothing else interesting. I hold my binoculars by the strap and stare at a tree stump.

"All clear," Ana says. She drops her glasses and notices my slumped shoulders. "Hey, don't worry about Penny. You know she wants everything to make sense. She probably read a book about it. I say that if you want to be out here, you should be out here."

I start down the path, wondering if everyone thinks that I'm doing this wrong. I know Bits does. She wants to be held all night. She wants the Cassie who was fun. I can only keep it up for so long before I need to escape. I thought I was doing okay, better than when my parents died, at least. I start the bus and drive down the hill at a snail's pace because I don't want to go back to the farm. I can't shake the feeling that I'm failing everybody.

"Lexers at eleven o'clock," Ana says at the bottom of the hill.

There are five of them heading up the road. They'll probably be at the farm by this afternoon or evening. They'll scare Bits. We'll kill them and then have to drag their bodies far away to lessen the stench. We could nip the whole thing in the bud right now.

I hit the brakes and my chest flutters in anticipation. "Want to take them?"

Ana drops her feet to the floor with a laugh. "Really?"

I lift my cleaver and swing open my door. Ana races around the side of the bus and calls, "Hey guys, where you goin'?"

They turn. I think they were four men and a woman; it's hard to tell sometimes, especially when they're almost skeletons like a couple of these. I steady my cleaver. I have two guns and Adrian's knife as well, so I'm not worried. One heads for me, thinking he's going to get dinner, but he's dead wrong. I take three big strides and the flat blade hits his neck with a crunch. His moans are cut off with his head. Some of them are easier to kill than they were last year, as if their muscles and bones have weakened from cold or time. I turn to the one who's just laid a hand on my shoulder and shove him back. I saw him coming and knew I had time. I banish the thought that I might not have cared that much and push the spike into the soft spot under his chin. Ana's finished two, and the last one stands in the center of the road, blinded by the moss that's grown over her eyes.

"You want it?" she asks.

She grunts and makes a beeline for Ana, but I call, "Yeah, sure, I'll take it. Over here, lady!" It turns for me, arms outstretched movie mummy-style, and walks eye-first into my spike.

"Nice," Ana says. She wipes her cleaver in the greenery and then stares at me. "What was that about?"

I clean my glove with an antibacterial wipe we keep on hand for this purpose and throw my cleaver on the tarp in the back of the bus. "Like you said, I want to be out here. You want to look for some more?"

Ana hangs her arm out the window like we're two girls on a road trip. "You know I do."

The next group is a bit past the turn to Kingdom Come's first gate, heading up the north road toward the noise of the machinery outside the gates. Ben has us getting in a few more acres of crops because of the food shortage, and they're digging the trench that will surround all of Kingdom Come. They'll have to stop work to take care of the Lexers. We might as well do it for them.

"Think we can take eleven?" I ask, but I've already put the bus in park.

"We can from the roof."

We sit on the roof and call to them. They continue staggering up the road. I sit cross-legged near the edge and whistle, to no avail.

"Maybe they want you to sing for them," I say to Ana.

She belts out another horrible song, made even worse by her snorts of laughter as they close in. The van rocks when they hit, but we're safe up here. A woman flattens herself against the bus and growls, her gaping lips a mass of cracks and her tongue black. My spike hits her uvula with a satisfying crunch.

Ana's brought two machetes from the weapons in the bus. I puncture one head, then another. It's almost too easy. We enjoy the lack of guttural moans and listen to the warm breeze rustle the leaves and the steady drone of the tractor. The fury that follows me all day, every day, has abated for now. It lies on the ground with the bodies, but I know it'll follow me home.

"Ana," I say. "Thank you for taking care of—I couldn't."

She wraps her arms around her knees and catches her lip in her teeth. "I didn't want you to. I thought it would make things worse. Look at Caleb."

I watch the Lexers on the ground and say what I've been thinking. "I should have done it. You would've, if it'd been you."

"I don't know," Ana says. She scoots closer so that her knees touch my shoulder. "I've thought about it, and I don't think I would. You'd do it for me."

I think about having to kill Peter or another one of my friends. It's almost as bad as Adrian, but I'd do it so she wouldn't have to. "I would."

"I know. And promise you'll kill me if I don't have time to do it myself. Don't let Peter. You do it—you'll get me in one shot."

"Yeah, right," I say. "Like that'd ever happen."

This is the kind of thing Ana jokes about, but the humorless look on her face tells me she's not this time. "Promise me."

"Fine. I Promise."

She nods and stretches out. I do the same, and we lie in silence until the radio in the van crackles. I slide down and peel off a glove.

It's Mike, at the first gate. "Ana, Cassie, check in."

"We're on our way, Mike. All clear."

"Okay."

We pull through the gate Shelby's opened a few minutes later. Mike finishes scribbling in his ever-present notebook—he was a writer in his past life—leans in the bus and pulls his head back out in disgust. "You ran into Lexers? I can smell it out here."

I'm not good at lying, but Ana jumps in. "A couple on the road to the lookout."

"Really? There are never any up there."

Ana shrugs. "Well, they were making their way up, and we didn't want to be caught out."

"Good thinking."

We wash our weapons and clothes before lunch. I feel good, like I've taken control of the situation. I ignore the guilty voice that reminds me I've broken the promise I made to Adrian. But I promised that I'd never do anything that would keep me from him, and he's not here.

CHAPTER 35

I'm woken by the sound of clanging metal and Barnaby's incessant barks. I went to bed at seven in the morning, and it's only a couple of hours later. I pull the blanket over my head, but when my half-asleep brain realizes that noise is hands on the fence—a lot of hands, from the sound of it—I jump into my boots, grab my cleaver and slip on my gloves.

I run toward the shouting that's been added to the noise. Half of the farm stands watching the east fence. Caleb pushes through them, spike in hand, and I follow. The front of the crowd parts to reveal well over a hundred Lexers at the fence. The chain-link sags under the press of bodies. I don't know how many it would take to push it down, but it looks like if they sustained this in a single spot for long enough, they might be able to do it.

One detaches from the pack and laces his fingers through the fence a bit farther down. He rattles the metal and releases a high-pitched scream that makes my skin crawl. I've never heard anything like it before. There's an answering scream from behind me. I spot Bits in a tight knot with the other kids, hands fisted and face chalk-white. Her eyes are so wild that it scares me more than the Lexers at the fence. The Lexer's mouth opens again, and I end his next scream with the spike of my cleaver.

I hurry to where Bits has buried her face in Hank's armpit. "It's okay," he says. "Cassie got him."

Hank winces when her nails dig into his side, followed by another ear-splitting scream. I wrestle her away and sink to the ground. I fold myself over her head in my lap, but she won't stop screaming and thrashing, no matter how many times I call her name. I'm still wearing the pair of Adrian's boxers that I sleep in, and she sinks her teeth into my thigh hard enough to break the skin. She takes off for the cabins when I yelp and let go.

Peter comes to a halt at my side and does a double take. "She *bit* you?"

"I'm fine. Just see if she's okay." Now that the Bits show is over, the other kids stare at the fence with pale faces. I rise to my feet and turn to where Penny stands. "Why are they out here?"

Penny appears overwhelmed by the kids and the scene in front of us, but I don't care. It's time she joined me in the real world. "Th—They ran out when they heard the noise," she stammers. "I couldn't get them back in."

"That's your one fu—freaking job!"

Penny pushes up her glasses and blinks. I don't think I've ever yelled at her, and even now she flashes me a placating smile. "Cass—"

I ignore her and return to the fence. It's sagging more than it was when I arrived. A fencepost shifts, and the chain-link bulges in a few feet. There are yells from the crowd behind us, which doesn't help at all. Someone needs to get the spectators out of here if they're not going to lend a hand. I stab an eye socket and then a forehead. Out of the corner of my eye, I see Ashley brandishing a spike and shoving it through the fence.

Ana runs her spike across the links and hollers, seeking to get the crush of bodies to spread out. I move down to where she is and bang on the fence. A dozen detach from their friends and move to us. Liz and Dan do the same on the other end. Once they separate, it's easy for all of us to finish them off, and we survey the bodies while we catch our breath. The fence is covered in gore, and the stench is terrible. It's going to take all afternoon to move the stacks of Lexers that lie outside.

"That sucked," Liz says, and rubs her lower back. She glances at the onlookers, who murmur amongst themselves.

"Are you okay?" Caleb asks her.

"I'm fine, but the old back isn't what it used to be."

"Let me help," he says, and winds his arm around her waist.

"Cabe, I can walk." Liz tries to shake him off, but he guides her anyway, pointing out rocks in her path. I can hear her mutters from thirty feet away.

Ashley drops her spike in a bucket and walks to where we stand. Her eyes are huge and she offers us a tremulous smile. "I tried to help," she says, and then she starts to cry.

I put an arm around her. "You did great, Ash. It's hard, though, isn't it? Especially the first few times."

Ashley pulls back and raises a hand to wipe her eyes. Before she can get it there, I grab her hand in mine and hold it up. She looks at the splattered blood and her breath hitches.

"Wash up first and don't touch anything," I say. I haven't heard of anyone getting the virus through blood splatters, but that's probably because they're a zombie now.

She nods and leaves for the shower room that's built onto the laundry. Ana watches her go. "She was good. I wish they would let her do guard."

"Looks like you need a bandage," Dan says, pointing at the blood that runs down my leg into the top of my boot.

"Yeah, well, I didn't think I'd get bitten on *this* side of the gate. I'll help with cleanup, but I want to check on Bits first." I'm still in shock that Bits bit me. It's so unlike her, and I can't help but feel upset that she bit me of all people.

"We got it," Ana says. "We have enough people without you and Peter."

It's a lot of bodies. We need people to load and move them, plus guards to make a perimeter around the ones doing the work. There are some, like Sue, who can't do patrol for other reasons but willingly help with disposal when needed.

"Thanks," I say, and turn to leave.

Dan follows me. "Hold up. I'll walk with you. The other trailer's down there with the truck."

Meghan rushes out of the crowd and rests a hand on Dan's bicep. She's cute, with a sloped nose, dimples and two short, brown pigtails. "Dan! Are you okay?"

"Yeah, sure, Meghan. Just gotta clean up now."

She blinks slowly, wide-eyed. It would be annoying if it was fake, but Meghan's sweet, if a little too adorable and helpless. She could do patrol; she's in her early twenties and all her parts are in working order, but the one time she tried to stab a Lexer, she missed. Through the fence.

"That was so scary, but I knew if anyone could do it, you could. Cass, you were so brave, too!"

Killing Lexers through a fence isn't brave, but I thank her because she's sincere. Sincerity or no, I can't stop myself from clutching Dan's arm after we're out of view. "Danny, you were soooo brave! You're my hero!"

"Don't. Please."

"But, why?" I ask in a perky voice. "I knew you'd save me!"

He pushes me playfully. I've decided to forget the moment in the vegetable garden when I got weird. Maybe he didn't realize; it's not like he knew what I was thinking.

"I think Meghan might be visiting The Love Den tonight," I say.

"No way," he replies. "I told you, I'm taking a breather."

"Mm-hmm." He elbows me in the side. We've arrived at my cabin, but I hesitate before going inside. "You sure you don't need help?"

"Nah, we're good. Just take care of Bits."

"Okay." I stumble up the cabin's steps on the bootlace I didn't take the time to double knot.

"How was your trip?" Dan asks.

"Yeah, like I've never heard that one before," I say.

He laughs as I head inside. Bits is asleep in my bed, curled in Peter's arms, with Sparky in hers. He stares at the wall with a wrinkled brow, but it smoothes out when I enter.

"How is she?" I ask.

"She's okay, but she feels terrible about biting you." I raise the hem of my boxers to show him the bite, now rimmed with the beginnings of a bruise. "Yowch. As well she should. Did you see Doc?"

"I'm sure it's fine." I sit and yank on my boot without success. "C'mon, you old boot. Work with me here."

"Why do you think inanimate objects can hear you?" Peter asks.

It pops off, and I turn with a grin. "They can, see? Sometimes you just have to ask nicely."

I push Bits's cot against the bed so I can lie down and caress her cheek. She exhales with a flutter of eyelashes. Barnaby has followed me, and he hits the floor with a thump and a long sigh.

"Could there be another creature in here?" I ask.

"You might be able to fit a cow in that corner."

I smile, but another look at Bits and it slips away. "She was doing so well. I thought doing the comic with Hank was helping."

His eyes are cautious when he whispers, "She misses Adrian, too. She loved him."

"I know."

I close my eyes. I'm so tired; what I wouldn't give to sleep it all away like Bits can. Peter runs a finger over my eyebrows the way he does when Bits has a nightmare. I can see why she likes it; it sucks all the restless thoughts out. I couldn't stay awake if I tried, so I let myself go.

***

I open my eyes to find Bits staring at me from Peter's arms. He breathes heavily and doesn't wake when I take his hand from where it rests on my neck.

"Hi," I say. "How are you feeling?"

Her lower lip trembles. "I'm sorry I bit you."

"It's okay," I say. "Well, actually, it's not okay, but maybe try not to bite me again?"

She sniffs and whips her head back and forth.

"I thought you were a zombie fighter," I say. "Did you forget and think you were a zombie, so you bit me?"

"No," she says with a giggle.

I reach to touch her but pull my hand back. "Wait, are you going to bite me again?"

"Cassie, I'm not gonna bite you!"

"I know this is all so scary." I take her hand in mine, and she nestles our clasped hands under her chin. "What can we do to make it better?"

"I don't like it when you leave. I want you to stay at the farm all the time."

I want to tell her I will because I want to make her happy, but I can't do it. I guess I could, if I didn't want to remain sane. "I know, honey. But that's what keeps us all safe and fed. How about if I'm here when you go to sleep, at least when I'm not on patrol?"

It may not be good enough, but she nods. When she's not biting people, she's a sweet, accommodating little person.

Peter's eyes open. "Good morning, baby girl."

Bits murmurs hello and buries her face in the pillow; she hates to disappoint Peter. He doesn't pass judgment, which forces you to evaluate yourself. It can be really annoying. I try not to think about how let down he'd be if he knew what Ana and I do when we're outside the gate. I've broken my promise to keep her reined in. It may not have been a real promise, but I still feel guilty.

"You know," I say to him, "I think it was that nickname you gave her—Bits. Because Bits bit me."

"So it's my fault that *Bits* bit you?" Peter winks at me over her head and tightens his arms around her middle. "Hey Bits, you're not going to bite me, are you?"

Bits makes an exasperated noise and lifts her head. "No, Peter!"

"Well, I'm going to tickle you, Freckles."

She's in hysterics before he's touched her. I think of the Peter of a year ago compared to this one, who looks at Bits with such tenderness even while he tortures her. He's become one of the kindest people I've ever known. I know it was always in there, but I don't know that he would have become the person he is now if it weren't for all of this. And it strikes me that he's quite possibly the only good thing to come out of the end of the world.

CHAPTER 36

I find John sitting at the desk in the radio room, where he does a morning shift. His hands are laced behind his head, and he stares at the map on the wall above our radio. It has pushpins just like Whitefield's, and the south is turning green, slowly but surely.

"What'd Zeke have to say?" I ask.

"They can't get Grand Canyon on the radio," he says. "I wish we knew what was going on."

"Will Monte Vista go check it out for us?"

His jaw bulges, and he bumps a fist on the desk. "Nope. They're too scared. Part of me doesn't blame them, but it's foolhardy to stick their heads in the sand. You'd think they'd want to know if something's coming."

"You'd think." I would want to know. "How's Nelly?"

"He's fine. He told Zeke to say hi. Zeke says they really needed the help. Everyone loves Nel, as you know."

No one more than me. I can't wait to see him tomorrow, when we go to Whitefield. I've taken to bothering Peter and Dan now that I don't have Nelly, but it's just not the same.

"Well, no matter what, we've got to finish that trench," John continues. "We're putting up extra posts, but we need this whole place surrounded as soon as we can." He leans forward. "How are you, hon? I feel like I only ever see you at dinner."

That's probably because I avoid people, between guard at night and trips to the lookout. "I'm okay."

What I should say is that it's been six weeks, and I still feel like I'm sucker-punched in the gut multiple times a day. That Ana and I have taken to secretly hunting down parties of Lexers and the fact that I like it so much scares me. That I have to restrain myself from screaming at Bits when she clings to me during the night and wakes the moment I move. I don't—but I'm sure she can feel my frustration, no matter how hard I try to hide it. I can't breathe around all these people who want things from me. There's no oxygen, not even in my own bed.

"It takes time, but it'll get better," he says. "When Caroline passed, dying didn't seem like such a bad idea. I didn't see the sense in sticking around when she was gone."

I stare at the radio. I don't want to die; I'm just not all that invested in living. It's a fine distinction, but at least it's there.

"I found strength in God," John says. He raises a hand. "Now, I know we have differing religious views."

Seeing as how he's Christian and I'm agnostic, it's a big difference. He smiles and continues. "But God didn't do all the work. I had to find the strength from within. You can lie down on the road in front of a pod of Lexers, but if you don't help yourself by getting up and getting out of there, they're going to eat you, no matter how loud you pray. You have that strength, hon."

He clears his throat and tugs on the collar of his shirt with a thick finger. "I also thought I'd never love anyone again, but I was wrong. And the only reason I'm telling you this is because I want you to know that life does go on, even if it doesn't seem like it right now."

Maureen. I let out a whoop and plant a big kiss on his cheek.

"That's enough," he says, but his eyes aren't stern. "Do you hear what I'm saying?"

"Yeah, I do." I'm not lying in the road—more like standing in the road, cleaver at the ready. It's the only kind of strength I can manage right now. I change the subject. "So, what can we do about Arizona?"

"Not a darn thing, unless Colorado decides to man up."

Oliver, a guy in his forties with thinning hair, comes in to relieve John. "Anything interesting happen?"

John gets him up to speed, and I take his arm as we leave the building. "Thanks, John."

"It'll be all right, hon. Just hang in there."

John may have found love again, but I'll never love someone like I did Adrian. I don't see how it's possible. I don't want it, anyway; I have enough people left to lose.

***

I stiffen when Penny sits beside me at dinner. We've barely spoken in weeks. We're not in a fight, but I can hardly look at her, knowing what she thinks of me.

"I'm feeling so much better," she says, and takes a bite of salad. The greens are growing like crazy in the spring weather, and even the people who used to turn their noses up at salad have been eating it like chocolate.

"That's really great," I say, and lapse back into silence.

"Are you okay?"

"I'm fine. Just thinking about going to Whitefield tomorrow. Have to get ready. Oh, and Bits has had a lot of trouble sleeping since the fence thing, so you have to stay with her until she falls asleep. It can take a while."

I honestly didn't mean it as a dig, but she flinches. "Listen, I'm sorry that Bits saw the Lexers at the fence. I should have kept them inside, it just happened so fast..."

"I know. It's fine. I'm just doing everything in my power to keep her from seeing it again."

Penny tugs on the end of her ponytail. She's about to say something I don't want to hear, so I push back my chair. "I'm going to go pack."

"Okay."

We've been best friends since we were ten, and I know when her feelings are hurt. Well, so are mine. "See you later."

I walk out of the restaurant feeling justified in my anger, but it doesn't make me happy or less lonely. I may have lost Adrian, but I feel like I'm losing everyone else, too.

CHAPTER 37

I leap out of the truck into Nelly's arms. "I'm stealing your boyfriend," I say to Adam.

"He's all yours," Adam says. "Just give him back when you're done, in approximately the same condition. Except for his hair. Whatever you can do to fix that would be great."

I put my forehead against Nelly's and whisper loud enough for Adam to hear, "I love him. He's just perfect."

"Nel says I'm a lot like you," Adam says.

"Number one being that he's a slob," Nelly says. "I thought I got away from it, and here I am again."

Nelly lowers me to the ground with a long-suffering sigh, but his eyes are crinkly, and when he looks at Adam they soften even more. I feel the tiniest bit envious, but mainly, I'm happy for them. Nelly catches me smiling at the way he watches Adam and shoves me. I shove him back.

"Well, I left the kids working silently," Adam says, "and I have a feeling they are no longer silent, so I'm going to head back. I'll leave you two to your third-grade antics, although maybe I need to stay here and supervise."

I shove Nelly again. He grabs me in a headlock and asks, "What do you mean?"

Nelly releases me after Adam's strolled away, shaking his head at our mature behavior. "So, I hear we really are going out partying," I say.

We're heading to North Conway tomorrow. Whitefield's greens are growing, too, but they could use more staples. And they need practice; it's the first patrol for everyone but Nelly, Kyle and Zeke. Ana thinks she's going to the outlet mall to get clothes, but she's living in a dream world.

"Yeah," Nelly says. "I'd rather not, though." He waits for me to agree, and when I don't, he makes a sound deep in his throat. "You want to go, don't you? Penny thinks—"

"Don't tell me. C'mon, we brought beer."

He drops the subject and rubs his paws together. Whitefield's alcoholic beverages were burned along with the food.

"Maybe we'll get some more tomorrow," I say.

"Now you're speaking my language."

***

"I know I asked yesterday," John says. His eyes land on each of the Whitefield patrol volunteers. "But I want to make sure that if you don't think you're up for it, you stay here. It's a crapshoot—we could run into nothing or find ourselves up the creek without a paddle, and we need to be sure we'll have each others' backs."

Christine pulls her hair into a ponytail and murmurs assent. She was in the Air Force years ago, which is where she met Brett. I watch her holster her gun with a trembling hand, but of course she's nervous—she should be.

Besides Zeke and Nelly, there are five men, Christine and Margaret. Margaret is in her forties and holds a gun in her ropy arms like she was born with it there. The guys I don't know well except for Kyle and Tony, a former dockworker with dark hair and deep-set eyes.

Jamie's dark, curly hair is in a bun atop her head and her green eyes sparkle. "So, who's going where?"

"The Hannaford supermarket is near Shaw's, and they're both near Walmart," Zeke says. He looks at the crudely drawn squares on the map. "So, half of us to Shaw's and half to Hannaford's. Last we knew, the Hannaford still had baking supplies and stuff in the back, and the Shaw's was in decent shape."

John points a finger. "Cassie, Peter, Ana, Christine, Margaret, Kyle and Tony will come to Hannaford's with me in the bus. The rest are with Zeke in the van."

We pile into the small school bus and pull out of Whitefield. Christine listlessly watches the state forest go past from our bench seat.

"You okay?" I ask.

The sunlight emphasizes every sleepless night and crying jag she's had in the past weeks. I probably look the same, although out here I don't feel like I do.

"I'm fine," she says, but her eyes are flat. "Did you know it's been over a year since I left the gates? I had to get out of there."

"Maybe if you like this it could be one of your jobs. Maybe it'll help."

I nod encouragingly and Christine returns her gaze out the window. "I had friends like you in Iraq, Cassie. People who could find the positive in everything. I tried, but I had the worst nightmares. Brett made them so much better, but now..."

If she thinks I'm Little Miss Sunshine, then she must be bad. I touch her gloved hand and lie through my teeth. "It'll get better. It has to get better, you know?"

I try unsuccessfully to think of something else to say that isn't a cliché. Her lips move while she fingers the gold cross around her neck. It's not the praying—if I were a praying kind of gal I'm sure I'd be at it all the time—but something tells me she's not up to this.

The forest gives way to residences and then the town of North Conway. Rows of wooden houses-turned-tourist shops have shuttered or shattered windows.

Ana calls out the store names as we go past. "Leather—Dansko, Ugg—tell me that's not necessary! We need boots, don't we? Toys. Oh, my niece needs toys!"

John gives a firm shake of his head at every outburst, until Ana's arms are crossed and she mutters every store's wares to herself. I know she's saving her nuclear argument for the outlets, but there's no way it's going to happen with John in charge. Peter watches from his seat behind her, mouth half lifted and hands behind his head. She's amusing when you're not the one being bombarded with whatever scheme she's cooked up.

I can't blame her, though. There's so much stuff here for the taking—useful stuff and stuff that would be nice to have, like overpriced handmade-by-an-artisan-out-of-sustainable-wood baby toys and boots that aren't just functional. I remind myself that there are only three things worth dying for: other people, food and water.

There are a few Lexers roaming around, but the 157th killed a lot of them off this winter. So many charred bodies are piled in the center of the village green that the air still smells vaguely burnt and fatty when we pass. Cars are parked haphazardly along the two lane road, many pushed out of the way to create the center lane along which we follow Zeke's van. The houses and businesses become more dispersed until we finally enter Consumer Heaven. The hotels that boasted park-like grounds are overgrown with weeds and decorated with broken windows. Maybe people tried to take refuge in the rooms, or maybe they were escaping.

When we near the turn for the outlet village, Ana's shoulders tense and her mouth opens. John keeps his eyes trained on the road and says, "No."

Ana turns with a grin when Peter and I snicker. "You win some, you lose some, right?" She rests her chin on the back of her seat, brushes Peter's hair behind his ear and whispers, "Be careful, okay?"

"*You* be careful," Peter says.

He cups her face in his hands and leans in for a kiss. I feel the ghost of Adrian's hands on my cheeks. The wave of longing is so intense that I dig my nails into my palms to distract myself. The gloves make it more ineffective than usual, so I pinch my thigh until it hurts. Adrian's everywhere on the farm, but he rarely follows me past the gates, which is how I like it.

"Here we are," John says, and turns onto a side road.

"We should hit EMS and L.L. Bean sometime." Kyle points out the two stores that sit behind a Starbucks on the main road. "And I wouldn't mind a coffee."

"I'd kill for a latte," I say. "There's even a drive-thru, so we wouldn't have to worry about being eaten alive." Everyone but Christine laughs.

"I'll take a cappuccino," Tony says with an Italian accent. "And a cannoli. My mother made the best cannoli."

He kisses his fingers and raises them to the sky. Last year he'd had a round belly to match his round face, but the work and lack of extra food has left him only with the spiky, dark hair and cherubic cheeks that make him look younger than his forty-some years.

"We could make cannoli," Peter offers. "We already make ricotta cheese. The rest is easy."

"You could? I'm gonna hold you to that," Tony says. "You Italian, Pete?"

Peter grins. "No, just your run-of-the-mill whiteboy."

Tony slaps the seat in front of him, his cheeks puffed out with laughter. The bus slows to a stop next to the van, and Zeke points to the Hannaford on our right. It's at the closest end of the shopping center, which is good in terms of a quick getaway. I can just make out the village-type buildings of the outlets through the trees to our left, but Ana doesn't glance that way now that she has a new mission.

Zeke rolls down the road. He radios that the rear is quiet and continues on to Shaw's. Splitting up isn't always smart, but since we have two patrols' worth of people, we should be okay. The parking lot holds cars and two kinds of bodies—ones that were stripped of their meat and the ones who ate them and then froze to death.

Whitefield killed off the Lexers in the store, and they were waiting for the roads to clear to pick up what they didn't bring back on snowmobiles, but they hadn't gotten around to it before they were attacked. The plywood they'd nailed over the shattered doorway has either been pried off or fallen, so there's no telling what's in there now.

"Let's get them up here first, then we'll worry about opening the back," John says. We push the wood out of the way, and John shows Christine, Tony and Margaret how we make noise at the front of a store. "It's better to call the Lexers to you and finish them off."

After a few minutes of quiet calling, footsteps sound from inside the store and ten Lexers appear from out of the gloom.

"This is easy," John says. "Back into the lot, and get them as they feed out."

All three hold a spike or blade of some kind, as well as wear a gun. Margaret's spike hits a Lexer through the missing lens of his glasses. She takes a couple more and lets Tony do the next few. Christine watches with a pale face.

"Do you want to try?" I ask. She shakes her head like she's in a dream.

"Perfect," John says, once they're all down. "You never want to be surprised. Take them one at a time, if you can."

Peter and Ana keep watch while we go shopping. The sky has been growing darker by the minute and now it starts to drizzle, although it was a beautiful day when we set out. This might be good for hiding our scent, but rain doesn't help when you need to hear what's going on around you.

The inside of the store has no skylights, and everything not in the direct beam of a light takes on a menacing shape. Overturned carts and exploded bags and boxes of food litter the linoleum. We skirt around bodies to the carts. Our feet crunch over the debris when we head to the center aisles that hold dry goods. We ignore the unprocessed, perishable foods of the outer aisles. Now that they've had plenty of time to perish, there's a faint, not-fully-composted odor mixed with the scent of the Lexers that have spent the winter in here.

John takes Margaret to the back while we hit the baking aisle. Kyle loads his cart with bags of sugar that have turned to bricks from moisture. The flashlight that rests in the seat of his cart illuminates Tony a few feet away, taking what's left of the flour. I point to the remaining oil and cans of shortening, and Christine places them in her cart after inspecting each label.

"Anything's fine," I say, and place four bottles in my cart, then four more. "Just load it up. Pretend you're on Supermarket Sweep."

Her headlamp blinds me when she looks up from her can of Crisco. I can't see her face, but the light moves up and down, so I guess she's nodding.

"Okay. Good job," I say, like she's a toddler.

John and Margaret walk down our aisle. "There are some pallets in the back," he says. "Let's get the loading doors open for some light and have Peter and Ana pull around. The canned food aisle is almost empty, save for a few cans."

When people came looking for food, before the store was overrun, I would imagine they took the things that didn't require cooking: the cereals and canned foods, chips and crackers.

I lean in to John. "Christine isn't doing too well. How about I take her back with me to open the doors?"

Once he has radio confirmation that the rear lot is still clear, he points the way. I lead Christine through the butcher department and into the storeroom. All the meat has rotted, frozen, thawed and rotted again. The smell of old decay is thick, almost as bad as Lexers, and flies are everywhere. Christine gags, and I hear her vomit hit the floor with a *splat*. I've smelled worse, though, and I pat her back and move her to where pallets of dry goods sit.

"I'll get the doors," I say. "You just keep watch."

"It's so empty," she says in a small voice. "Everything's gone."

Peter and Ana help raise the loading bay door and waste no time hauling the boxes of pasta and rice mix through the bus's rear exit. The daylight is bright enough to make out Christine's dazed expression. I don't know what she expected to find, but this isn't it, obviously.

"I have to get outside," she says breathlessly. "I'm going to throw up."

I nod and stack boxes by the door. Normally, I'd help her, but there's no time out here for babysitting. The first carts arrive, and they wheel them to the exit and leave for fresh ones to fill. I open a smaller door and roll the carts down a ramp. Christine has climbed onto the concrete loading pad of the adjacent store. She seems safe enough, and she's dry under the overhang.

"What's with Christine?" Ana asks me.

"I don't know." But I do know, a little. She was looking for something to fill her time and her thoughts, but this seems to have made it worse. Large, cold drops of rain spatter on the ground. I wipe my arm across my face and hand boxes to Peter in the bus. The space where they've removed the back seats is loaded top to bottom; this must be a couple of weeks of food for Whitefield.

John leans out of the doorway. "We have the last of the food here. Just going to check on batteries and such. Don't want to press our luck."

We're emptying the final cart when a yelp echoes through the rain. Christine stands on the loading pad and watches five Lexers move toward her from a door I don't remember being open. All she has to do is drop off the platform to the ground, but she doesn't move.

"Christine!" I call. "Jump!"

"Chris!" Tony yells.

We run. We have a hundred feet to close, and the Lexers have ten. They may move slow, but not that slow, especially when they have prey in sight. Christine looks at her feet.

"Jump!" I scream.

She closes her eyes as a tall, thin Lexer sinks his teeth into her neck. Her face turns to the sky, mouth open in a silent scream. A fleshy woman takes the other side, and then Christine's on the ground. With five of us here, the Lexers are dead before they know what's hit them. Christine lies in a pool of blood and chunks of flesh, mouth in an O. I'm used to the smell of death, but this smell is fresh—fresh blood, ripped intestines. I manage to keep down my food, but Tony isn't so lucky.

She's dead, but not for long, since her head is intact. We've had varying reports of how long it takes someone to turn. Some people have seen it happen in minutes, while others say it took hours or days. It seems to depend on where you're bitten and whether or not you're dead or have to first die of the virus. I've never seen it happen, and I watch, stomach churning, for movement. It takes only half a minute, but it happens slowly, like she's waking. Her lips move, and then her eyes blink open. The blue has gone gray. Ana's cleaver hits just as mine does.

"Shit," Tony says, and wipes his mouth on his sleeve. "Holy Mary, mother of God."

Kyle looks to me. "The fuck happened? Why couldn't she run?"

"She could," I say, and turn away. "She just didn't want to."

CHAPTER 38

The mood in the main hangar is anything but celebratory, even though the trip was a success in terms of food. Once word got out, Whitefield was eerily quiet. Most people retired to their rooms early, and we've spent much of the night gloomily sipping at the beer Zeke's patrol crammed into the van's trailer.

Zeke stares into space while he works on what must be his sixth beer. "Danielle said Christine gave her a bunch of her things yesterday. She never thought that it might mean...I never should've let her come."

"Zeke, she would have found another way," I say. "She could've slipped out the gates, used a gun. I think she chose this way because she didn't have to make a decision."

"Suicide by zombie," Tony says. His bloodshot eyes roam around the group. "Like suicide by cop."

"She said she had nightmares and couldn't sleep without Brett," I say.

Nelly glances at me with a frown, and I peel the label off my bottle and squish it into a ball. I shouldn't have said anything. I can't stop replaying the way Christine's eyes closed, the way she let go. That I understand the feeling, at least partly, makes me uneasy, like it might be contagious.

Zeke's eyes are at half mast; maybe that was beer number ten. John lifts him by the armpit. "C'mon buddy, let's get you to bed."

Zeke kneads his eyes with a hand and allows John to lead him out of the hangar, followed by Tony and the rest. I'm drunk and in no mood to play fifth wheel to Peter, Ana, Nelly and Adam. "I'm going to bed," I say.

I unroll my sleeping bag and mat on the floor of Command. Now that they've repaired the damage, there are enough beds that I could sleep in the barracks, but I like the noise of the people on night duty.

Nelly enters the dim room and lowers himself next to me. "Are you okay?"

"I'm peachy," I say. "How 'bout you?"

He runs a hand through his hair and sighs. "I'm worried about you, Half-pint. You're always out on patrol and guard. You don't sleep. You gave Penny your room."

"I gave her my room because I didn't want it, not because I'm going to feed myself to zombies. And, no, I don't sleep a lot, so I do guard at night."

I keep my voice calm and measured. It's dim in here, so he may not pick up on how I skip over the truth in a few places.

"Relax. I'm not going to lecture you. Just promise me you don't have some sort of gory goodbye planned."

My laugh is short. "No gory goodbyes, promise. Only killing Lexers."

"Good," he says, and nudges my side. "Scooch over."

He lies under the sleeping bag and puts an arm beneath my head. I wish I could make Nelly sleep with me every night. My eyelids are lowering from the mixture of his warmth and the beer.

"This is just like old times," Nelly says after a few minutes. "Except we're not zipped in like sardines."

"You like being sardines with me," I rouse myself enough to say. "Admit it."

"Fine. And I'd be very sad if my favorite sardine got eaten. Promise you'll be careful?"

I nestle into him and murmur, "Don't worry, I won't get eaten. Ana and I have killed tons of them, and we're always careful."

He asks something, but I'm too exhausted to answer.

***

I come to with Nelly's arm still under my head and poke him in the side.

"What the hell?" he groans, eyes closed. "Why are you poking me?"

"I'm waking you up. Adam's going to think you cheated on him."

"He told me to stay with you so you'd get some sleep."

"Well, thanks. Although it makes me feel like I've become a freak."

He opens his eyes. "Darlin', you were always a freak."

"I don't miss you at all," I say, and poke his side, hard this time. He yells and grabs my hand in his fist.

"Likewise. Now let's go get some breakfast before you leave. I can tell you what else is wrong with you while we eat."

"Great. But I might need to stay through lunch if we're going to do all that."

CHAPTER 39

There have been no repeats of a group as large as the one that scared Bits, but smaller groups numbering at least twenty come to the fence each day, and they make her just as upset. There's no way to keep it from her. If she doesn't hear the commotion, then the kids are talking about it the next day. The only recourse is to kill any Lexers before they get here. Ana and I try, but there are just too damn many of them.

It takes me an hour to get her to sleep and then another hour to put her back to sleep when she inevitably wakes again. Peter usually takes over when I'm on guard, but for the past week she won't settle for anyone else. I've had to leave the fence almost every night, and I've learned it's possible to love someone more than life itself and want to strangle them at the same time.

She lies in my bed, sweaty and tangled in the sheet. I've barely made it to the door when she calls, "Cassie! Where are you?"

I close my eyes. I could have sworn she was back asleep. "Bits, I have to go back to the fence."

"I want you to stay with me," she whines. "Don't leave me alone. Why can't you stay? You're so mean."

I sit on the edge of the bed and put my hand on her shoulder. "Bits, I'm not trying to be mean. I just—"

She responds with a wail; she won't reason at all these days, like a two year-old. I leave her wailing and knock on the wood frame of Peter and Ana's curtained doorway. "Peter?"

The wailing becomes a screech. Peter stumbles out, and we sigh at each other the way my parents used to when Eric and I were being pains in the ass. It makes me feel better that even Peter's a tiny bit frustrated.

"Go," he says. "I got her."

He moves into my room, and the wailing lessens at the sound of his quiet voice. She wants me there all night long. I tried it a couple of times, but there are only so many hours you can stare into the dark before you begin to lose your mind. By the middle of the night I was seething in frustration and angry that I never get a single moment to myself. Every morning I tell myself that the next night I'll be patient and understanding, and every night I lose my patience in record time. I hate myself for it.

I make my escape before I'm roped back in, although guilt for saddling Peter with the job colors my relief. Dan, Liz and Caleb sit at the table at the first gate, wearing t-shirts and shorts. The nights in July are warmer than January, but it's still sweatshirt weather, if you ask me.

"Did you get her back to sleep?" Dan asks.

"Yes, then no, and now Peter's trying."

"I had nightmares all the time when I was a kid," Liz says. "I could hardly sleep by myself. I was afraid of everything."

"Really?" I ask. Liz isn't afraid of anything. I can barely imagine her as a kid. Maybe there's hope for Bits; right now I'm afraid she'll never make it.

"Yeah. I still have nightmares sometimes, but I think that's just how I work things out, you know? I'm not so scared when I'm awake, but I must be inside, so it comes out at night. Cheaper than a shrink, anyway."

She dips her head at having expressed so much emotion. Caleb licks his lips and tentatively places a hand on her knee. "You know, you can wake me if you ever need company in the middle of the night."

Caleb likes Liz. He *like* likes her. I turn to Dan in amazement, and he runs a hand over his scruff. We watch as Caleb's hand massages her knee.

"Cabe, what the hell are you doing?" Liz asks.

"I was just saying—"

Liz stands. "Time to walk the fence. I'll go west." She puts on her gloves and grabs a spike and flashlight before beating a hasty retreat.

Caleb looks at me and Dan, who sit with our mouths agape. The almost invisible blond lashes that frame his eyes make him look like a baby. "What? I like Liz."

"Cabe," Dan says. "You're more than ten years younger than her."

"So?"

Dan looks at me for help, but I shrug, so he says, "Well, I guess, nothing. As long as she likes you."

"Do you think she does?" Caleb asks, like a hopeful puppy.

"Oh, I couldn't say, Cabe," Dan says. He works hard not to laugh. "You'll just have to ask her yourself."

"I will. When I get back from the fence."

He leaps up and marches down the fence line. I lay my head on the table and bite the sleeve of my sweatshirt so I don't make too much noise. When I come up for air, Dan is wiping his eyes and shaking his head.

"I am so glad I was here for that," I say, between gasps. "God, this world makes for strange bedfellows, doesn't it?"

"It does," Dan agrees. "Although maybe it happened this way so that the people who belonged together would find each other."

"Then Adrian would be here." He goes silent. I realize I just said Adrian's name aloud for the first time in two months. "Sorry. Let's talk about something else."

"It's okay to talk about it."

"I don't want to. But thanks," I say. A breeze has risen, and I pull my hands into my sleeves.

"So, I'm thinking your middle name's not Cold," Dan says. I look at him blankly. "You said that once, that your middle name was Cold."

I laugh. "No, it's Mae. It was my grandma's name, on my mom's side. She died when my mom was little."

"Cassandra Mae."

"Yep." I put on an Appalachian accent. "Cassie Mae, nice to meetcha. My mom was from West Virginny."

"A pretty name for a pretty girl."

I let my head fall to the side and groan. "Please tell me you don't use that line often. It's terrible."

"It's worked once or twice," he says with a laugh. "I would never try it on you, though."

"Oh yeah? So, what would work on me?"

I hear the flirty tone in my voice. I'm flirting with Dan. I almost feel guilty, but it's not like it means anything. It's nice to feel normal sometimes.

"I'm still trying to figure that out."

He tilts his head and assesses me. The way he stares makes me warm and prickly, even with the breeze. This was a bad idea. I've flirted with Dan before, but that was when Adrian was here. When it *couldn't* mean anything. My chest tightens, and I busy myself with my water bottle while the silence drags out. The awkward moment passes when Liz appears out of the shadows and takes a seat at the table, once she's made sure Caleb's still absent.

"So, Caleb likes you," I say. "And he's going to ask if you like him, so you'd better have your answer prepared."

"What's wrong with him?" Liz asks. She steeples her fingers and looks at us in desperation. I've never seen her flustered.

"Nothing's wrong with him," Dan says. "You know, you are a catch."

Liz snorts.

"What?" he asks. "Not everyone goes for the typical girly type. And he'd do whatever you asked. You could boss him around all you wanted, he's practically begging for it."

I crack up when Dan swipes a cougar claw through the air. Liz hides her face and moans.

"All the picking on you suddenly makes sense, you know?" I say. "There's an age difference, but—"

"I'm thirty-one and he's nineteen!"

"Twenty! I'm twenty now!" Caleb's voice rings out. He comes out of the woods looking embarrassed but hell-bent on convincing her.

"Caleb," Liz says, and looks at him steadily, "we are not talking about this right now."

Caleb nods obediently. Dan was right; she could have her own manservant if she wanted.

I change the subject. "So, who's going to Quebec next week?"

All three say they're going. We're bringing them seeds, since their tomatoes were hit with early blight this year, plus some electrical stuff James has promised them. In return, they're giving us some of what they say is a large supply of maple syrup. Then we're traveling down to Waterbury and Stowe for electrical supplies and whatever food we can find. The crops are doing well, but farming holds no guarantees, and we're not taking any chances on starving this winter.

CHAPTER 40

Ana and I are in the weapons room of the barn looking for something interesting with which to kill zombies on our way to the lookout. Blades of all sizes and types hang on the walls above bins of spiky implements. The guns are mounted on a wooden frame that Dan built, and the ammo takes up two shelving units. It looks like a lot of ammo, but it's all we have. Maybe one day we'll be able to travel down to John's old house and collect some of the ammo we left behind, if no one's gotten to it yet.

Ana pulls a medieval axe-looking thing out of a bin. "How about this?"

"That looks like it weighs a ton. Who uses that, anyway? Conan the Barbarian? How about that sword?"

I point to a slim, razor-sharp sword. Ana pulls it from the sheath and slices the air, then grins and sets it by the door. I spot something on a corner shelf that looks like the love child of a pistol and crossbow. It has a slim, rectangular metal box that rises up from where you would normally string the bolt.

"Have you seen this before?" I ask.

"Nope." She picks one up and makes laser gun noises. I stick my head into the radio room and ask John where they came from.

"Oh, we got those from Whitefield," he says. "Will had the guys modify a pistol grip crossbow. This box is like a magazine. Holds ten bolts. I've been meaning to have you try them out. Why don't you girls bring them with you? If you do any target practice, try to get the bolts back. There's extra, but I don't know when we'll get more."

He shows us how to cock the lever in the back to string the next bolt. The bolts are shorter than the average arrow, maybe six inches long, and have wicked-looking steel tips.

"Cool," Ana says.

John goes back to the radio. We make our way to the vehicles and find Peter leaning against the ambulance, arms crossed.

"Hey," Ana says. "What are you doing here?"

"Jamie and Liz already left for the lookout."

"Why?" Ana asks with a frown. "It's our time."

He stares her down. I get the feeling we're in trouble—it's the same look he gave Bits when she used the f-word one day. "Because I asked them to."

"And why did you do that?" Ana asks slowly.

"Because you're doing stupid shit when you go out there, aren't you? Nelly told me you're killing Lexers, when all you're supposed to do is check for pods and come back."

Ana looks at me, eyes wide. I have a vague recollection of mentioning that to Nelly after too many beers. I make an *I'm sorry* face and step backward a few paces.

"Jesus, Ana," Peter says. "What the hell is wrong with you?"

She sets her weapons down and stands with her feet apart, ready for battle. "What's wrong with me is I want to keep everyone safe. You're not my fucking father, Peter! You don't get to tell me what to do."

I'm very close to escaping through the back door of the restaurant when Peter turns to me. "What about you, Cassandra? You, at least, used to have more sense than this."

Well, he's definitely not my father, or my boyfriend, and I glare back. "Ana's right. You've seen Bits. How much more do you think she can handle?"

He looks away first. "You're right, Ana, I can't tell you what to do. But I can tell you that I love you and want you safe. Both of you. For whatever that's worth."

He pushes off the ambulance and walks past her without looking back. I expect to see her eyes fill, but when she turns to me she's livid. "I can't believe him!"

I know Peter's right, but it doesn't make me want to go back to sitting behind the fence. It's us or the Lexers, and I want us to win. I want Bits to win. Maybe she can grow up in a world where she won't have to be afraid, if we work hard enough.

Liz's voice squawks out of the radio on Ana's belt. "There's a pod, around two hundred of them, nearing the quarry. We'll be at the gate in three minutes."

Ana's eyes flick toward the ambulance. I know what she's thinking—she wants to give her quarry idea a try. The combination of not wanting Bits to see the pod, wanting to get beyond the gate and wanting to give Peter and Penny something to really be pissed about makes me acquiesce. I hold up a finger. "Okay. But if it doesn't work, we turn around right away."

Ana hugs me and grabs the keys. When we get down to the gate, she leans out the window and says, "Going to make sure Liz and Jamie get back okay."

Toby slides open the gate at the same moment as Liz and Jamie arrive. Ana flies past with a wave, and I watch Toby shrug before closing the gate again.

There aren't many roads out of Kingdom Come. There's Trunk Road, which runs east-west, with the turnoff that dead-ends at the farm. Another, smaller dirt road—the one on which we killed the Lexers from the VW's roof—heads north from Trunk Road after the turnoff. Trunk Road continues east until it meets up with a paved road that runs north-south. But we're going west, toward route 100 and the roads for the lookout and quarry.

Ana bangs on the steering wheel. "This is gonna be awesome!"

I've broken out in a cold sweat and can barely swallow, but it doesn't deter me. I kind of like the feeling. This is what Ana lives for, and the smile she flashes is slightly crazed, with eyes to match. I feel a moment's hesitation; I did make a semi-promise to Peter. "Ana, we need to be careful. Peter would be—I know how he'd feel, okay?"

She turns onto the quarry road with a shrug. "Promise. But, you know, I'm not going to live forever, so I might as well take out as many as I can."

"That wasn't very convincing. And no one's going to live forever, Ana."

"Well, some of us don't even get to live to be old, you know." She cups her mouth with her hand and glances at me. "Shit. I'm sorry."

I ignore her *faux pas* and say, "Don't start all that going out in a blaze of glory crap. It doesn't matter how you die, you're still dead." It's not totally true—how you die is important—but you are still dead.

She bounces in her seat. The quarry is on our right, and a large group of Lexers walk in the fields to our left, heading straight for the farm. I imagine them at the fence, the nightmares they'll cause, and push any second thoughts out of my mind. We're here to kill these fuckers, and that's what we're going to do.

"Okay, here goes," she says, finger poised at the siren control. "Wait, *now* can we play music?"

The radio has a CD player and a few CDs, but they're country-western. "I'm not dying to—" I look at one of the CDs, "Shania Twain. Sorry. I could do Patsy Cline or Johnny Cash, but not Shania."

Ana laughs like a madwoman. The Lexers have noticed us, but they've got a field to walk across. Ana hits the lights and sirens and blasts the air conditioner. We're going to use as much gas as humanly possible in the next ten minutes, I guess. But I angle the vents and drink in the deliciously cool air.

"How did I ever not love air conditioning?" I yell over the siren.

"You didn't wear leather in the summer!"

She throws her head back and screams in delight. Her excitement at the prospect of death may be foolish, but she's the only one who understands the drive I feel to rid the world of all of this. I don't want to hide away. I'm not afraid of dying, not anymore. She turns toward the quarry and waits for the Lexers to join us. When they hit the back of the ambulance, she rumbles to the road that intersects the lakes.

I study the rock road. The edges have crumbled away, but it looks more than wide enough. I give Ana the go-ahead, and she makes a left onto the road. The mob shuffles after us. I look down and decide not to do it again. It's a vertical drop into deep, cold water. Most of the floaters look dead, or bloated so badly they can't move, but aside from the useless remnants of a rope ladder, I don't see any way to climb out without mountaineering equipment.

The ambulance kicks up dust and gravel for twenty feet, and then Ana slams on the brakes. The Lexers won't fit on the road all at once, but they don't know that, and the ones in back push forward. I feel a wave of satisfaction at every plop, every splash of the Lexers into the water. They're killing themselves, and it's such a beautiful sight that it makes me want to do this all day, every day, until the quarry is full.

"This was a great idea!" I yell.

Ana's eyes gleam. "I told you!"

She waits until they meet up with the ambulance. Twenty splashes, thirty splashes. We inch forward until we hit where the road splits in two to form a V.

"Left or right?" Ana asks. "Lady's choice."

"Right."

More plummet into the water at the sharp turn, and the seventy-five that are left follow us back onto shore. Ana circles onto the other road and taps her fingers impatiently on the steering wheel. "They're so freaking slow."

Ana brakes and backs up with a swerve when they finally reach us. It serves the purpose of knocking ten more into the water, but it also gives me a heart attack.

"Ana! What the fuck?"

"Just wanted to see if it would work," she yells.

Ana speeds up and turns left again. More fall in as they round the bend. Forty left. She presses her lips together in concentration and reverses up the first road. A Lexer presses his face to my window. The others pound on the metal.

"Ana, go straight!"

Ana cackles and continues backward. She's left the real world for Crazytown. I was afraid this might happen. I can't hear over the siren, but I feel a jolt as the ambulance shifts and the rear driver's side drops. Ana jams the accelerator. We jump an inch and slide back.

"Shit! It's crumbling!" Ana says.

The Lexers are closing in, and if the other rear tire goes off the road when they reach us, we're going for a swim. I don't panic, though I probably should. I flash back to the helpless feeling of the ditch, of watching Adrian die for me, but I don't feel helpless now. Maybe this is why I'm still alive, to kill as many of these things as possible. There has to be a reason why I've been left here without him.

"Put it in low gear," I say in a calm voice. "Go slow, or we'll end up in the water on the other side."

"What the fuck is low gear?" Ana screams.

She didn't have a license before Bornavirus. I reach over and slam the gearshift into low. I hope the ambulance is front-wheel drive, and that Ana will go easy on the gas pedal for once.

"If we start to slide, jump out and fight," I say, hand poised over the door release.

The first of the pack hits. Ana presses the accelerator. We scream at a momentary backward slide, but the tires bite rock and we level out. Ana moves slowly through the Lexers. They slap at the metal in frustration and follow us to solid ground away from the water. I turn off the siren, and then the only sounds are their groans and our rapid breathing. I grab the crossbow, lower my window and line up a head in the sight. The bolt punches through its nasal cavity. I cock it and send out another. The crossbow has a bit of a kick but no worse than a rifle.

"This thing is great," I say to Ana from where I kneel in the foot well. "You should try yours."

She climbs onto my seat and levels it out the window. She gets off three shots, taking down three Lexers, and says, "I'm in love."

We run through the remaining bolts until there are less than ten. There's no need to keep quiet at this point, so we pull out our pistols. A woman with a missing nose hits the door with a snarl. Ana pushes her backward before firing.

They're close enough that head shots are simple. And it's good target practice, something we don't get often. When they all lay on the grass, we exit into the heat of the day. Ana leans on the ambulance and surveys the scene with satisfaction. Her hair is wet, and her face shimmers with sweat, but she looks as happy as I feel. We just killed two hundred Lexers, and near-death experience or not, I'm pretty proud. But it was the first and last time; the road that crumbled is now barely wide enough for one car.

"Well," I say, "you almost killed us."

"Cassie! I did not—" She turns to see me grinning. "Shut up! It worked, like I said it would."

"It did, but it won't again. Look at the road."

"We could fit," she argues.

I shield my eyes from the sun and stare her down. "No. Now it'd just be stupid, not that it wasn't before. And, since you're going to be grounded forever, it doesn't matter anyway."

Ana's eyes are so wide I can see the white all around. "Peter's going to flip, isn't he?"

"Oh, yeah," I say. "That's one way of describing it."

CHAPTER 41

"You two are crazy," Rohan says as he passes by our dinner table. "Nice work."

I keep a straight face because we're sitting with a slew of pissed-off people. Peter is pissed beyond belief, Penny is super pissed, James is whatever Penny tells him to be, Maureen is concerned and John is perturbed. It's been a fun dinner thus far. Ana eats her chicken pot pie in silence, glancing at other tables with a quick grin that makes Peter's jaw grind. Dan and the others haven't dared to sit with us tonight, and Bits is having a sleepover with Jasmine.

I can't take it anymore. "Okay, we know you're mad. But it worked, and we're fine. No one else is angry."

"It was two hundred," Ana adds. "That many might be able to knock the fence down. The south trench isn't done."

Penny flashes me and Ana the dirtiest look I've ever seen and rises. "C'mon, James."

She stalks out and James follows, but not before turning back eagerly. "You'll tell me all the details tomorrow, right? I wish I could've seen it." He gives a thumbs up at our nods and races out.

"You could have died," John says, his face severe, "and for what? We could have outlined a way to do something like this, with more safeties in place. We have enough fuel to start the south side. You guys'll get more while you're in Quebec, and we'll be good to go."

"You're right, John," I say, and push my food around my plate. He's managed to make me repentant without yelling. "I'm sorry."

I'm not that sorry, though, because Bits never would have gone on her sleepover had the Lexers reached the fence. She'd be sitting here right now, face pinched and pale. And later she would have been up screaming.

"We love you girls, that's all," Maureen says gently. "We don't want to lose you."

I look away. My bags are packed for a guilt trip, but I don't hop on the train. No matter how much they love me, I still end up in bed alone. But I guess I can't expect them to understand. We've all lost people, I know, but no one but Caleb and I has lost anyone from our new life. I kick back my chair and bring my plate to the empty seat at Liz and Dan's table.

"Girl, you in trouble," Liz sings.

"Tell me about it," I say.

I glance back. Everyone at the table watches me with disappointment, except for Ana, who looks jealous. I stick my tongue out at her. She pretends to scratch her chin with her middle finger, and my new table breaks into laughter.

"It *was* dangerous," Dan says. I turn to him and sigh. He lifts his hands. "Just saying. It was also awesome, but no one at this table wants you to fall into the quarry, either."

"That was a huge pod," I argue, "and if they came to the fence it'd be a mess to clean up. And I know the fence is strong, but just a single Lexer—look at Whitefield."

"I would've come if you hadn't blown past us," Liz says. She takes a bite of dinner. Caleb watches the fork move to her mouth and head to her plate again. He averts his gaze when she stops, fork halfway to her mouth, and catches him in the act.

"I'm thirsty," she says. Caleb takes her cup and heads to the back without a word. Liz sighs. "No matter how many times I tell him no, he won't stop."

"Well, at least you're putting him to work," Shawn says. He strokes his new goatee and adds, "You know none of us would care, right? If you guys hooked up?"

Jamie nods, her eyes bright. "I think it'd be cool. Who else are you going to date? Dan?"

"Hey!" Dan says. Jamie blows him a kiss.

Liz closes her eyes and shudders. "Absolutely not, you guys. He's like my little brother."

CHAPTER 42

I've finally dragged myself to art class. I keep promising Bits I'll do it, and then I sleep through. She finally stopped asking, which makes me feel even worse. It's not like there's much to do; all the kids are working on comics and graphic novels now.

"I'll try to get some comics when I'm on patrol in a few days," I tell the kids, and ignore Penny's glare.

"And some paper," Hank reminds me from where he and Bits sit.

"You got it."

Hank thanks me, but Bits acts like I'm invisible. Her relief that the Lexers didn't make it to the fence has translated into several nights of unbroken sleep, but that doesn't mean she was pleased with me once she heard. I thought she would be, since there was nothing to fear. Everything feels wrong between us, and I know I'm to blame. I've changed, not her. But what's better—a sad, crying mother figure, or one who at least does her best to protect you? It appears they both suck.

After class, I walk through the vegetable garden and come upon Ana hiding under the tomato plants. She has bags under her eyes, probably due to the heated conversations I hear from the other bedroom every night.

"Fancy meeting you here," I say.

"Help me up." I pull her to her feet. If Ana's not bouncing around, she's definitely miserable. "I was talking to the plants, but I think they're mad at me, too."

"For the love of all that's holy, just apologize and get it over with. I'm sure that's all he wants."

She throws her arms in the air and looks like she might cry. "No, he wants a promise that I won't do anything stupid or dangerous. How can I promise that?"

"I promised Adrian, and he promised me. It's not crazy to ask, Banana. You do some stupid shit. Put yourself in Peter's shoes. How would you like it if he did the things you've done?"

"I wouldn't," she admits, and her eyes glitter. "But I'm so much better at everything than him."

I put my arm around her shoulder with a laugh. "One of the things Peter loves about you, besides your modesty, of course, is the way you're fearless. You're not afraid of anything—zombies, tomato plants, or even to love with your whole heart. When you do something, you do it all the way, and that's rare. But you have to temper it a little because honestly, if I were Peter, I'd have killed you by now."

She exhales. "Okay, I know. Now what should I do about Penny? She's so angry."

"Beats me," I say. "But when you figure it out, let me know."

***

My backpack is ready, my hair is in buns and I've ventured to Penny's room to say goodbye to Bits. It looks different, but I'm still slapped in the face by Adrian's scent when I walk through the door. I pick up Sparky and bury myself in her neck until I'm composed.

"Hey, Bits, I'm getting ready to go. Can I have a kiss?" She lies in her bed by the window and stares at the ceiling. I sit at the edge of the bed and tuck her hair behind her ear. "Please?"

Her lips thin. "I don't want you to go."

"I know, but I have to."

"Why? Why do you have to?"

"We've talked about this, sweetie. We need food and gas. We need to protect ourselves."

"You're always leaving," she says. "You don't want to be with me."

It's not that I don't want to be with her; it's that I don't want to be here. I love her as much as I ever did, but I don't know how to be the way I used to be with her. Sometimes it feels like too big of an effort, too much of a responsibility.

"I love you so much, Bits. It's just been hard these last months. It's not—"

She narrows her eyes. "You ignore me all the time! You're so selfish. I hate you!"

I try to stop myself, but between hearing the words I know I deserve and sitting in this room that reminds me of everything I've lost, I lose the battle with my temper.

"How do you think you get clothes and shoes? How do you think you get things like candy? The cookies you like to eat are made with sugar, Bits! They don't just fall out of the sky, you know." My voice is rising. I've never spoken to Bits like this. I should stop, I want to stop, but I don't. "Why can't you let me go without making it a huge deal? Do you want me to let zombies come to the fence? Would you like that?"

Her eyes grow round, and she faces the wall with shaking shoulders. I want to kick myself for ruining the only positive thing I've done in the past months by scaring her.

"Bits, I'm sorry. I'm sorry I said that, okay?" I try to kiss her, but her arms fly up and hit me in the nose. The van's horn beeps twice.

"Bits, I have to go. Can I please have a hug?"

"No." Her voice is muffled. "I hate you."

"Okay. I know you're angry, and I'm sorry. But I love you." I kiss the top of her head, and she scrubs at the spot with a hand.

"Bye," I whisper.

Penny stands in the hall, arms crossed and face hard. I brush past her and clatter down the stairs to the porch. The screen door slams open behind me.

Penny follows me onto the grass and stops with her hands on her hips. "Cassie!"

"I can't talk," I say.

"Why? Because you have to go fight zombies?"

Her voice is sarcastic, and she waves her hands in the air like *big fucking whoop*. I want to punch her, but I fold my arms instead. "Actually, yeah, Penny. That's exactly why."

"That's bullshit. You barely speak to me even when you're here. And now you're yelling at Bits?"

"I need to leave. Bits won't let me go without screaming. What do you want me to do?"

Penny moves closer. "Oh, I don't know. Maybe stay? She needs you, and you escape every moment you can like she has the fucking plague."

The comment hurts, probably because it's true, and I think of something to shoot back that saves me from answering. "The world has the plague, in case you didn't notice. I'm doing my best to keep us all from getting it."

"Oh, right." Penny rolls her eyes. "Saving the world. Is a box of crackers worth making that little girl inside miserable? She doesn't want candy, she wants you."

"I'm keeping her a lot less miserable than she'd be otherwise. Bits has lots of people to help take care of her. Why is it all on me?"

I feel horrible after the words leave my mouth. I know I'm failing Bits in every other way. Keeping her safe is the one thing I don't fail at.

"Because you're closest thing she has to a mother," Penny says. Her cheeks are pink, and she speaks low, but it has the same effect as a scream. "Do you know that sometimes she calls you her mom to the other kids? You don't get to be her mother only when you feel like it. You spend all your time racing off to kill Lexers, and I know you don't care if you come back. You have a death wish."

I shrug, even though every word she's saying is true. The knowledge that Bits calls me her mom is a knife to the heart. I want so badly to go back in, but I'm too stubborn to do it. "I prefer to think of it as courting death."

"Oh, that's real funny. Who are you—Ana? I expect this shit from my sister. I know one day she won't come back, everyone does. But what am I supposed to tell Bits when *you* don't? 'She loved you, but not enough to stick around?' What's wrong with you?"

"What's wrong with *me*?" I ask. "You're the one who disapproves of everything I do. I can see it every time you look at me. I'm sorry that you think I'm fucking things up, but we're not all as lucky as you, you know!"

She steps forward with a small laugh. "Lucky? Really?"

I guess we're getting into this now, and I'm more than ready. "Yeah, lucky. You have James, you have a baby, you teach at a pioneer school like you're Laura fucking Ingalls. You don't have to get your hands dirty. You don't have to worry about anything."

"Right." She drags out the word.

"Yeah. Right. You're as close as you can get to a completely normal life. You don't know what it's like—you have everything. You know what I have? I have nothing." I hold back the tears. I am not going to cry. I'm not going to let her know she's getting to me.

"You're right," Penny says. "I don't know what it's like. But you don't have nothing. How do you think that makes the rest of us feel when you say that? I'm not saying you have to be happy, but you need to at least *try* to stay alive."

Penny's eyes redden, and she swipes at the tears that plop onto her cheeks. "You think I don't know this baby's a crying, screaming zombie magnet? I'm scared, Cass. I need my best friend back."

I want to be back, but I can't find my way. I've been envious of Penny's contentment and angry at her disapproval. But Penny has always been good at hiding her fear, and maybe the reason for her disapproval is that I'm one of the things she's afraid to lose. The thoughts flit through my mind, mixed up and unclear. Someone calls my name, and I'm thankful for the distraction.

"Are we done?" I ask. It comes out more harshly than I'd intended.

Penny sighs and turns away. "Sure, Cass, we're done."

I risk a glance at the house after I'm in the van, thinking maybe I'll wave or try to smile, but Penny's already back inside.

CHAPTER 43

The ride to Quebec is almost three hours, what with having to clear out the customs booths that were jam-packed with cars and temporary fences. Thankfully, they weren't jam-packed with Lexers, although we had to take care of a few. The authorities tried to cordon off Canada, but obviously that didn't work out. The farther away we travel from Kingdom Come, the worse I feel. I know I don't have nothing—I have Bits. Right now I may not be fully invested in living, but if Bits were gone I don't think I could muster the energy to keep fighting. There would be nothing left to fight for.

I sit in the back of the van, book unopened on my lap. Dan drives, while Peter, Toby and Ana scan the countryside. Shawn, Jamie, Liz and Caleb are in the pickup, pulling the trailer. The trailer holds our fuel drums, and we're hoping to fill the rest of the empty space with food in Stowe and Waterbury tomorrow. Empty farmhouses and overgrown fields flash by, broken by the occasional copse of trees. It's not as mountainous here compared to Kingdom Come, although the ground moves up and down in gentle waves that look like someone took a fuzzy green blanket and carelessly threw it over the dirt.

"Earth to Cassandra," Peter says.

I look up. "What? Sorry."

He joins me in the back. "I saw you and Penny talking. You both looked upset."

I look around the van, but the others are busy pointing out a group of Lexers caught in a barbed wire fence. "She was just telling me what an awful mother I am."

Peter looks like he's about to argue, but I nod and lean my head on the seat back. "No, she's right. I've been a shitty mother. The worst part is that I told myself I was doing some great thing for Bits by protecting her and was annoyed that she wasn't thankful. But I was being selfish."

"You're not selfish. You're always doing things for other people."

"No, that was Adrian."

"And why do you think he loved you? You're just like him."

I don't feel like him. Adrian was what I aspired to, but I'm too flawed, too prone to fucking things up. And then he went and did the most unselfish act a person can do for another. He did it for me, and I don't deserve it.

"You always offer to take a shift when someone doesn't want it—even the laundry," Peter says. "On poop day. You make a huge deal out of everyone's birthdays. You want everyone to be happy and go out of your way to make people laugh, especially when they're sad."

I shrug. "Who doesn't do all those things?"

"Lots of people, that's who."

"You do."

"Well, that's because I'm a pretty amazing guy."

I roll my head his way to find him grinning at me. "Well, be that as it may, I've still been a shitty mother."

"Cut yourself some slack, as John would say. It's been a rough few months. You've done your best."

"No, I haven't." I watch trees flash by. "It should've been me, in the woods. At the fence. People needed him more than they need me."

"What?"

"I've ruined everything that was good. Adrian wouldn't have done that."

"Adrian kept you alive because he didn't want to be without you," Peter says in a forceful voice that makes me turn to him. He almost looks angry. "You haven't ruined everything. You just forgot to keep on living. That was all he wanted—for you to keep living. Believe me, I know."

I picture Peter standing on the dumpsters as we drove away that day in Bennington. He'd looked happy, he *had* been happy.

"It feels wrong," I whisper. "Like a betrayal."

He puts his arm around my shoulder. "I know that, too. But it's not. Do you believe that?"

I nod, although I don't yet. Not fully, anyway. "I yelled at Bits before we left. I scared her. She was worried, and instead of trying to make her feel better, I made it worse. She hates me, and I don't blame her."

"No, she doesn't," he says, and squeezes my hand. "She loves you. And she needs you, but you've been...missing."

It hurts to hear him say it, but it's the truth. I'm getting a lot of truth today. "Well, I'm not anymore. When we get back, the first thing I'm going to do is apologize to her."

I want to turn around. I want to fix this. I'm not sure how to do it, but I'm starting right now. I rest my head on Peter's shoulder and watch a Lexer meander in a field. I still hate them, though. That's never going to change.

"Anyone know French?" Toby asks. "How are we going to know what they're saying?"

"Toby, you're an idiot," Dan says. "They talk to us by radio. How do you think that happens?"

"Oh, right."

"I think we should have turned a minute ago," Ana says, and studies the map in her lap.

Dan slows, and the truck pulls alongside. Shawn leans out the window. "What's up?"

"I think we were supposed to turn back there," Ana says. "Can you turn with the trailer?"

"I can do anything," Shawn says. "Haven't you figured that out by now?"

Jamie rolls her eyes from the passenger seat. "Are we lost?"

"I don't think so," Ana says. "But all the French names are throwing me off."

"Google it!" Caleb yells from the back of the pickup.

"That joke never gets old, Cabe," Liz says.

The next road is paved, and we follow it alongside a lake surrounded by a fence made of rope, barbed wire and wood until we reach the turnoff. A short dark-haired man in his sixties stands behind the chain-link.

"Kingdom Come?" he asks in Quebecois-accented English.

Dan nods, and the man smiles, his broad-featured face breaking into a network of lines. "Hello! I'm Gabriel. I'll take you to the main house."

He nods to an older man in a driver's cap, who unlocks the chain that secures the fence and swings it back. Gabriel straddles a bike and motions us to follow him down the dirt road. It's heavily wooded, except for a large house in a clearing every four hundred feet or so. They're beautiful houses; most are two-story, with back porches on which to sit and enjoy the lakefront view. The lake is still, reflecting the blue sky and puffy clouds of the sweltering day.

We gape at the mown grass around the houses. We have weeds or mud. The only thing that gives away our new reality are the vegetable gardens, the outhouses set back from the lake and the stovepipes that have been fitted onto roofs. In front of one house, a few kids kick a ball while a woman watches from a chaise lounge with a yawn.

We pass four houses before Gabriel stops and gestures at a stone house in a clearing the size of a small park. More than a dozen people sit at picnic tables on the grass to the left, and to the right is a vegetable garden that has gone haywire, in a good way. We pull to a stop in the circular driveway and step into the fresh-smelling air. I love Kingdom Come, but it doesn't always smell clean like this— farm animals and giant compost piles really stink.

The people at the tables rise and follow us through the French doors of the stone house. The first floor is a wide expanse filled with tables and chairs, a central fireplace, mullioned windows and a gleaming wood floor. A tall, thin woman Gabriel's age comes out of a door to our left and wipes her hands on a towel. Her gray hair is in a severe bun, emphasizing sharp cheekbones and a face that's lined but still beautiful.

"Hello! We are so happy you came. My name is Clara."

"My wife," Gabriel says, obviously proud of that fact.

We make the introductions, and she says all of our names as if committing them to memory. And she must because seconds later she's assigning us seats at one of the long tables. "Now we'll get lunch, and we can talk."

The people who've followed us sit at nearby tables and wait as food is brought out on plates, like a restaurant. A plate of something that looks like French fries with white globs on it is set in front of me by a smiling teenager. Whatever it is, it smells delicious.

"What is this?" Shawn murmurs next to me. "Did a bird poop on—" Jamie's elbow hits his ribs.

Clara sits at the head of the table. Thankfully, she didn't hear, or she's tactful enough not to let on. "This is poutine. A famous dish here in Quebec. French fries with gravy and cheese curds. We thought the last of the potatoes should be made into something special. You're our first visitors."

I think I may have entered another dimension. Not only did I just get served like I'm in a restaurant, but I just got served French fries with cheese and gravy. It makes me miss Penny: in high school we spent many a sunrise in diner booths eating fries with cheese and gravy, giggling about what had happened earlier in the night.

"Please, eat," Gabriel says, and lifts a loaded fork to his mouth.

The fries and gravy and cheese curds are salty and rich. Peter needs to make these for everyone back home. These people know how to live.

"Where do you keep your animals?" I ask. I know they have them, since they have cheese, but this place is so clean I could almost believe they conjured it out of thin air.

"There are nine houses here," Gabriel answers. "The largest two were made into barns. They're farthest from the entrance, on the east side of the lake."

"This is delicious," Jamie says with a pointed look at Shawn, who nods emphatically. "Thank you. Do you always eat like this? Like, with waitresses?"

All the Quebecois laugh, including the ones at the other tables. "Oh no," Clara says. "This is for your benefit only. Usually we're lined up at the back of the room, fighting for our food. We cook here in the summer, but in the winter most houses cook their own food since they're heating them, too."

That's more like it. I was beginning to think that they were too perfect.

"There are ninety-eight people in total," Gabriel says, "spread throughout the other houses. You're welcome to stay anywhere you choose tonight. There are no extra beds, but plenty of room to make beds on the floor."

That many people spread among seven homes must be crowded, even if they are big. But at least they're houses and not outfitter tents, like us, although Dan's drawn up plans for larger cabins on which work has begun.

"We brought tents," Dan says. "We don't want to put anyone out."

"Nonsense," Clara says. "Although I do enjoy sleeping outside in this weather. It's much cooler."

The day is hot and humid, so hot that even with every window open my shirt is glued to my back. Whoever spent the morning frying potatoes deserves a medal. I look out at the lake and almost salivate at the thought of dunking myself in the cool water.

Peter follows my line of vision and asks, "Is the whole lake fenced off?"

A guy in his twenties, with auburn hair and freckles, answers. "Yeah. We used rope and barbed wire, mostly. We didn't want the lake contaminated. We fenced off about four miles." His voice is unaccented, and his about is more like aboot.

"So we can go swimming?" Ana asks, and throws her head back in ecstasy when he nods. "That's it, I'm moving here."

"We have bathing suits you can borrow," Clara says with a laugh. "Why don't we show you around, and then you can swim?"

CHAPTER 44

We hit the familiar smell as we near the two log homes built on a rise that leads down to the lake. The walkout basements have been partitioned into stalls for cows and goats, with several holes cut into the ceiling to act as haylofts. We follow Gabriel to the main floor of one of the houses, where hay and bags of feed are stored on the once-beautiful wood floors that now boast rough-sawn holes.

"This house cost almost a million dollars. The owners would cry if they knew." He leans forward. "But we were happy when they didn't arrive. Such a terrible family. Horrible children."

He says something in French that includes a word that sounds like *tabarnack*. Clara gives him a reproving look, although she turns away as though to collect herself.

"Did you pass the farms right before the lake?" Gabriel continues. "That's where we plant our crops. It's dangerous to harvest, but there's nowhere in here to do so."

"Ours are outside the fence too," Peter says. "I wish we had a lake. We use spring water, although it's gravity-fed."

Clara nods. "Gabriel and I moved here after he retired. The stone house is ours. When this began we thought about leaving for a government zone, but the lake is what decided us to stay. And the children. Our two sons came here with their families."

He nods up at her, since she's a few inches taller than him. They seem to like each other, the way my parents liked each other. The way Adrian and I liked each other.

"Come," Clara says. "Enough business. Let's swim."

***

The lake is cool and deep. I swim to the floating raft and lie on the warm wooden planks, where I can allow myself fifteen minutes of sunbathing before I die of sun poisoning. I close my eyes and listen to the others splashing and laughing at the shore. They're so loud that I don't hear someone arrive until drops of cold water snap me out of my stupor. I open my eyes to find Dan shaking off like a dog.

He sits down. "This is nice, huh?"

"This is amazing." I prop myself up on my elbows. "I'm thinking we really should move here. Swim in the summer, ice skate in the winter. Or we could organize vacations; this could be the Quebec Safe Zone Resort and Spa."

"People could pay in food. They'd never have to grow anything. Just concentrate on full-body massages."

I laugh and roll onto my stomach. "A massage would be awesome."

"Just say the word."

He crinkles his eyes at me. I roll mine back and watch two of the Quebecois girls make their way to the raft. I know why they're here—they've been eyeing Dan all afternoon.

"Your fan club," I say.

He makes a noise of dismissal, but Alice and Sofia climb up the ladder and deposit themselves on either side of him. They're both in their early twenties, with dark blond hair that matches their tans. Dan greets them in a business-like fashion, but it doesn't put them off. He's fresh meat, and he's fresh meat with tanned muscles and a killer smile.

"Dan, we were wondering if you'd stay at our house tonight," Sofia says, and licks her full lips. She has an accent, but I could swear it wasn't this heavy and sultry an hour ago. "It's the next one down." She points to a house with a back wall made entirely of glass. "Everyone there is young. We'll have fun."

Alice, an English-speaking Quebecker, nods and angles her chest at him. "We made liquor from maple syrup, and it's so good. Like mead. We can hang out."

"Um, maybe," Dan says. He looks to me for confirmation, or possibly help, since he looks uncomfortable. "Cass, don't we have to be up really early?"

I sit up and dangle my legs in the water. "Oh, yeah. Crack of dawn. But if you got started now, you'd have plenty of time." The girls look at me in delight. Dan stares me down. I've made him suffer enough, so I put on an apologetic face. "Oh, but there's that thing you have to do with the van."

Dan sighs. "Right, the van. I probably won't have time."

Alice and Sofia make disappointed sounds, but I can tell they aren't going to let him off that easy. I slip into the water and hang on the edge of the raft. "I'm going back."

"Stay," Dan says. "It's nice out here."

"I really can't. I'm roasting. See you back on land."

I grin at his look that says I'm a traitor and push off into the water.

CHAPTER 45

D inner was salad and pasta. For all its civilized ways, Quebec is good at patrolling, and they've made their way to both the outskirts of Montreal and Quebec City this summer. They figure they have enough food for the winter, even if they lose part of their crops. It can be unsettling when you think of how close to the edge we live—we've become subsistence farmers and hunter-gatherers.

They can always drink maple syrup. They've given us gallons of it and have plenty more. Alice gave us her mead recipe after she finally came to terms with Dan's refusal to party at their house. Toby agreed, though, and was happily dragged off a couple of hours ago. The rest went with him. The sun is going down, and the hot day is quickly becoming a cool, humid night. I sit by the lake and warm my feet in the last patch of sunlight before I head in to where we've spread our sleeping bags on the dining room floor. I take a picture of the lake to show Bits. Maybe next year I can bring her here to swim, if she's talking to me.

"You're like a lizard," Dan's voice comes from behind me.

I glance over my shoulder and point a finger at him. "Now, *that's* a line. See? I knew you could do better than 'a pretty name for a pretty girl.' It's not very flattering, but it gets points for originality."

Dan laughs. "I meant you soak up the sun like a lizard."

"I thought maybe you were encouraging the use of more moisturizer."

He sinks into the chair next to me. "Nah, you're perfect."

"You really get a kick out of bothering me, don't you?"

"I'm complimenting, not bothering. You just don't take me seriously."

"Very true," I say.

He opens his mouth but then closes it and watches the puffy salmon and pink clouds. Happy voices from the party house carry to where we sit.

"Listen to what you're missing," I say.

"Thanks for saving me. I thought you were throwing me to the wolves for a minute."

"They're hardly wolves. Although I hear Sofia is pretty good with a rifle, so you might not want to tangle with her. You'd never have to see them again. And yet here you are, sitting by the lake like an old man who's forgotten how to have fun."

"You're fun," Dan says.

"Yeah, I'm a barrel of laughs. Maybe I should go drink so I can fall asleep." I remind myself that no one needs to hear me bitch. That will be step one of the new Cassie—a moratorium on self-pity. "Sorry. Insomnia."

"Yeah, I know, dingbat. I'm on nights with you all the time."

"My dad used to call me dingbat," I say with a laugh.

"Mine, too." He reaches into his coat and pulls out his silver flask. "Here, drink some of this. It'll help you sleep."

"Aha, the flask! I've been wondering, why do you carry that around with you? You never drink from it."

"Just in case," he says and looks away, tight-lipped.

It ups the mystery. Now I'm dying to know. "In case of what?"

"In case I'm totally fucked and have to finish myself off. I figure it'll be a little easier if I down this first." He sighs, and I can see the uneasiness beneath the happy-go-lucky facade.

I shake my head slowly. "That is the most depressing thing I've ever heard. I think you may be worse than me. You know what you are? You're the St. Bernard of Death."

His laugh is so loud that the birds pecking on the shore rise into the air with a mad flapping of wings. "What the hell is the St. Bernard of Death?"

"You know the myth that St. Bernards carried a cask of brandy to help stranded travelers in the snow?" He nods but continues looking at me like I'm nuts. "Well, I've been thinking that you're like a St. Bernard with that flask, but now I know it's to be used for death, not rescue."

I lean over and pat his head like a dog. When his laughter subsides, he says, "What goes on in that head of yours?"

"You don't want to know. It's a strange place."

He hands me his flask. The alcohol burns like crazy going down. I wipe my mouth and hand it back. "That's horrible. What is it?"

"It's strong. That's what's most important."

"Well, for death, maybe. But not for enjoyment."

Dan stands. "Be right back." He disappears into the darkness of the trees and returns five minutes later with a wine bottle. "Here, try this. Maple mead."

It's delicious, with a nice alcohol bite to cut the sweetness. I chug some before I hand it back. "Yum, thanks. How'd you get it and escape so quickly?"

"I said I'd be back in ten minutes."

"You didn't! Now they'll be waiting for you all night."

"They're drunk. In ten minutes they'll have forgotten I was ever there."

I grin and slap at a mosquito, then another. They won't leave me alone. I don't want to go inside because it's nice sitting out here with Dan, but I'll regret it in an hour when I'm covered with welts.

"I set up my tent," Dan says. "We could hang out there to get away from the bugs."

"Why aren't you sleeping in the house?" I ask to avoid answering. I feel a little weird about going to his tent even though his suggestion didn't seem like a come-on.

"I like my privacy, always have."

"Me, too. There's not much of it these days." I try to stealthily slap my arm and scratch a new bite that's formed on my ankle.

"You're getting eaten alive," Dan says. "Let's go to my tent. It's cooler than in the house. You can sleep with me, if you want." I look up from my ankle, eyebrows raised. "I meant in your own sleeping bag."

I laugh. "I thought you were inviting me to The Love Den."

"I would, but I get the feeling you'd say no."

"Right you are." The thought of kissing Dan rises in my mind. There's a split second where my body tingles at the idea of someone's touch, but I quash it before it can gain traction. It's just the idea of not being alone tonight that's attractive. "Okay, sure. I'll go get my sleeping bag."

I grab my stuff while Dan visits the kitchen. The others aren't back from the party yet, so I don't have to explain. I'd never hear the end of it, completely innocent or not. He's set up his tent by the picnic tables, and I follow him in once he's turned on the lantern. A sleeping bag covers the floor and his backpack sits beside it, book peeking out of the top. I sit on my sleeping bag and watch as he pours the mead into two cups from the kitchen.

"For the lady," he says, and hands me one.

"Thanks."

He unlaces his boots and sets them by the door, then pulls a self-inflating pillow out of his pack and puts it behind me on my sleeping bag. He digs around in his pack again and comes out with his toothbrush and toothpaste.

"All the comforts of home," I say. I pour more mead for myself and drink it down. It doesn't take much; I'm already feeling buzzed. I lie back and close my eyes.

"You can go to sleep," Dan says. "I don't mind. I'm going to read. You don't have to be alone."

It's exactly what I need—to feel like someone's watching over me—and I'm surprised that Dan understands. I never know what he's thinking. He always keeps it light, which is why I've spent so much time with him lately.

The pages of his book rustle, and I open my eyes to find him reading *A Walk in the Woods*. It's not the same copy I took with me when we left Brooklyn a year ago, the one that burned along with my parents' cabin, but Adrian's copy is in the farm's library. I try not to think about that part and say, "I love that book. Do you like it?"

"You recommended another one of his books, remember? I really like it. I'll read out loud if you want."

I don't even consider brushing my teeth. If I fall asleep now, I might get eight hours. I listen while Dan reads about Bill Bryson's adventures on the Appalachian Trail and laugh when his voice cracks at the funny parts. Adrian and I wanted to hike the Appalachian Trail. It was one of those things we'd planned to do before we had kids. Just us, and two thousand miles of bears and blisters and wilderness.

A rock forms in my throat. I'm so tired of missing him, of feeling lonely. I concentrate on the words until I can breathe again and open my eyes. Dan looks up from the book.

"That life is over," I say. "Hiking a trail for fun. Eating at restaurants. Not having to be afraid of anything except a black bear."

"It has to end sometime," Dan says, and lays the book down. "They can't live forever."

"But maybe not before we all die. One by one."

I want Dan to convince me he's right, but he only shrugs. "If it's your time, then it's your time."

Well, that definitely wasn't helpful. I shake my head and say, "I don't want to die. I want to see Bits grow up. I want to kiss Penny's baby."

I want both of those things a lot. A light warmth blossoms in my chest. It almost feels like happiness.

"I want things," Dan says. "But there's no guarantee. I try to remind myself of that, so I'm not disappointed."

"Hence, the flask," I say, and sit up. He gives me a small smile. "So, what do you want?"

I hold out my cup, and he fills it silently. At first I don't think he's going to answer, but then he raises his eyes to mine and his Adam's apple bobs. "Right now I want to kiss you."

The heat that floods my stomach has nothing to do with the mead. I want him to kiss me. I don't want him to. I freeze, cup in the air, until he makes the decision and leans forward. He tastes like maple and smells of lake and leather. I consider pretending he's Adrian, but I think about Adrian enough. I want to feel something real.

Dan pulls back and his eyes flicker between mine uncertainly. "Are y—"

I cut him off with another kiss. I don't want to talk. I don't want anything gentle. I don't want the spell broken because I know I'll leave, and I don't want to leave. I pull off his shirt and move my teeth to the smattering of freckles on his shoulder. When I look again, I'm glad to see the softness in his eyes is gone.

He unhooks my bra one-handed faster than I could. Dan's unhooked a lot of bras in his life, I'll bet. I run my tongue along his bottom lip, still sweet from the mead, and trail my hand down his chest to the button of his jeans. He pants into my mouth and sweeps me onto the floor.

The weight of his body is good. It anchors me, keeps me from feeling the way I have—like one of those helium balloons on a strand of curling ribbon I'd get as a kid. It always seemed that they slipped away so easily. I'd watch them after they escaped, becoming a smaller and smaller dot against the blue of the sky, until they were too tiny to see. I've been afraid that's where I was headed, up to where no one could see me or reach me. But right now the ribbon is tied around Dan's wrist. I'm tethered to the earth.

And then there's nothing but the two of us. There's not even room for Adrian. There's only this tent and Dan and the slippery nylon of the sleeping bag under me, all glowing in the golden light of the lantern.

CHAPTER 46

Dan is asleep, arm draped over my chest, but I still struggle for air after I've laid it back by his side. I wish I could take last night back, but all I can do is leave and pretend it didn't happen. Pretend I'm not the kind of person who sleeps with someone mere months after her fiancé has died. I pull on my clothes and slip out of the tent. The sun is rising and mist swirls along the lake's shore. I walk to a tree and lean my forehead against the bark. Once my breathing steadies, my stomach revolts. It could be the mead, I guess, but I know it's not.

I walk toward the stone house, hoping to pretend I spent the night there and am already up for the day, and almost turn in mid-stride at the sight of someone on the deck. I brave a look and sag with relief to find it's Peter. He's at the table, bent over a backpacking stove. I walk up the steps and plop into the chair next to his.

"Hey," he says.

I duck my head. Peter doesn't say anything more, only places his steaming mug of coffee in front of me. I don't like coffee, but I need to wash the taste of last night out of my mouth. I take a sip to find it's a latte, loaded with sugar.

I lift my head in awe. "Don't even tell me this place has a Starbucks."

The last latte I had was the day before we left the city, over a year ago. He pulls out a tiny stovetop espresso maker from near his feet.

"I wanted to try it out and knew you'd want one," he says, and raises a finger to his lips. "But it's a secret. If everyone knew they'd be ordering drinks like I was a barista."

"They totally would." I laugh and take another sip. "This is so good. Thank you, Petey. I've been dying for a double-tall, caramel macchiato, ex—"

"Extra hot, extra caramel," Peter finishes.

"How do you remember that?" I ask. "I guess you bought me enough of them, huh?"

He used to bring me one whenever he came to my house, or have one waiting at his place. They were too rich for my blood to buy every day.

"Thanks for all those, by the way," I say. "I know you were incredibly wealthy and all, but it was still nice of you."

I hold the cup out, but he nudges it back. "It's yours. Maybe one day I'll surprise you with some caramel sauce."

I toast him with my cup. If anyone in the apocalypse could make caramel sauce, it'd be Peter. "Oh man, if you do that, I'll love you forever."

"So, Dan?" Peter asks, and puts on more espresso.

"So, I'm a horrible person." The latte sloshes in my stomach. "What was I thinking? Adrian..."

Peter looks up. "Adrian would want you to be happy."

I watch the flame hiss under the coffee pot. He's probably right; if Adrian's watching me, he knows how much I miss him. How much I wanted to join him. He would only smile and wipe my tears away. Maybe that's the worst part: that someone like that is gone.

"I just needed—I don't know—someone? Something?" I wrap my arms around my knees and watch the ripples on the lake where the fish have come up for their bug breakfast buffet. "It's nice to have someone who really loves you, inside and out, you know? Who appreciates the weird things you do, even if they're slightly crazy-making."

"I know all about the crazy-making," Peter says.

I laugh at his long-suffering expression. "Yes, yes you do. More than most. I mean little stuff. Like how Adrian would throw or drop the last bite of food onto his plate, as if it were a grenade about to go off. Most people save the best bite for last, but he'd eat until the last bite and then—BOOM!—done. It killed me every time because who does that?"

"So that's why you always ate his last bite," Peter says. "I wondered."

"You thought I was pilfering his food, didn't you? What do you people think of me?" I shake my head at his laugh and continue. "And about four times a year, he'd fold all my socks and underwear and arrange them in my drawer in these orderly rows. He'd show it to me like it was this amazing feat and then get all irritated when I wasn't impressed. But I thought it was sweet how excited he got over that dumb drawer, even though I knew it was going to lead to a lecture on the importance of organization.

"And it used to drive him crazy how I'd get out of his car. He said I used my foot to push the door open. I'd try not to, but I'd forget and there'd be a footprint on the door. He was always like, 'My car's already a piece of shit, you don't have to kick it.' "

"I know all about that, too," Peter says. "You have no idea how many times I wiped your shoeprint off my door."

I cover my mouth when a huge laugh escapes. "Really? Except your car wasn't a piece of shit."

"It was a beautiful piece of German engineering."

"I'll get you another. I can afford it now. I'll trade you for caramel sauce."

Peter watches me, waiting for more. Now that I've opened the floodgates, I can't stop talking.

"And I miss the silly things. We had an ongoing game where we'd sing an awful song, just to make the other person get it stuck in their head. And we'd act super annoyingly in love, even when we were alone, just to amuse ourselves. It all comes up and smacks me in the back of the head when I least expect it. There are all the big parts of missing someone, but there are a million little parts."

"I know," Peter says, and I know he does. He's spent his whole life missing people. "It's okay to want that again. It doesn't take away from what you had with Adrian."

"It won't happen again."

"What won't happen again? What you had, or last night?"

"Both."

"Does Dan know that?" Peter asks.

I laugh despite myself. "Do you think I really need to tell *Dan* it was a one night stand? Dan *is* a one night stand."

"I think he likes you."

"Dan likes everyone. Name one girl Dan doesn't at least partially like."

"You don't know how easy you are to love," Peter says with a shake of his head.

"Oh, please. What does that even mean?"

"There're no games, no craziness. You're just you. You're easy to be around."

Nelly once said everyone's entitled to one crackup in their lifetime. I'd already used mine, and here I've gone and had another. The first was three years. At least this time I've whittled it down to around three months. A personal best.

"I'd say I've been pretty crazy and difficult to be around."

"Why must you argue when someone says something nice about you? It's really annoying." I hide my smile because that's another thing that drove Adrian crazy, and Peter's eyebrows are up at his hairline. "It means that you make it easy to love you. Speaking as someone who was once in love with you, I can attest to that fact."

"No, you were not."

"Yeah, I was." He looks at me intently and then places a cup under the espresso spout. "And you thought I was oblivious."

I shift in my chair. Maybe he once loved me, but that was a different Peter. For a moment, I wonder what would've happened if he'd been this Peter when we met, if there'd been no Adrian, and I can't say for certain that I wouldn't have loved him back. But that was a long time ago. I love Peter with all my heart, but it's the way I love Nelly.

He snorts at what I can only imagine is my deer-caught-in-the-headlights expression. "Don't worry, I'm not anymore."

"You totally freaked me out."

"Sorry. More than sleeping with Dan?"

"No. That's in the number one freak-out spot." I sigh. "Thanks for the pep talk, Petey. But as much as I'd love to discuss the wonder that is me, I need to go brush my teeth and get my life together."

"In that order?" he asks.

"Of course."

Ana strolls onto the porch and perches on the edge of the table. She yawns and looks at me with interest. "Good morning, Cass. So, how was Dan? I hear he's really good in bed."

I kick her from my chair, but she's undeterred. "Please don't talk about it. I'm an awful person."

Peter puts a tiny pot of milk on the stove and waits for it to heat. "No, you're not. Time is different now. We don't know how much we have. We never did, but we could pretend. Now we know, and we don't have the luxury of mourning the way we used to."

"Yeah," Ana says. "I'd want Peter to hook up with someone. I wouldn't even make him wait two months."

"So, how long do I have to wait?" Peter asks.

"You do whatever you want, baby," she says with a grin. "But I'm waiting a month, tops."

"You could find out about Dan for yourself," Peter says. "No more wondering."

Ana licks her lips. "Good point. So, maybe a week." I love to see them tease, but it also makes my heart hurt. Another thing to miss.

"You have nothing to feel guilty about," Ana says.

I try to believe her. We enjoy our lattes as the sun rises, and by the time the mist has burned off I'm feeling better than I did.

CHAPTER 47

W e're eating eggs when Dan finally appears. I make a split second of eye contact and give him a quick smile. I'm not good at this kind of stuff; I'm already sweaty and my eggs are stuck in the back of my throat.

"Good morning," he says to the table and pulls out a chair. "How was the party?"

Shawn groans and rests his head in his giant hands. "I probably could've done without the last nine drinks."

"You're such a lightweight," says a bright-eyed Jamie, despite the fact that she's a third of his size and, from what I hear, drank just as much. She turns to Dan. "So what'd you do? I can't believe you didn't come."

"I read a little and went to sleep," Dan says, and takes a bite of eggs.

"Dan? Is that you?" Jamie teases. "How old are you again—sixty? I thought you were thirty-three."

Dan chews his eggs and doesn't take the bait. No one asks why I didn't go, at least. I guess I've been so antisocial that it's not suspicious.

By the time Shawn's fixed a problem with the trailer hitch and we've said goodbye to Quebec, it's late morning. We pull out, girls in the van, guys in the truck. It was Ana's idea, and I know she suggested it to spare me an awkward drive.

We find a truck full of what's probably a year's worth of sugar at the Ben and Jerry's factory in Waterbury, after killing the few Lexers in the parking lot. We take as many sacks as we can fit, but we'll have to make another trip to get it all. It's late afternoon by the time we've stocked up on gas and made our way into Stowe.

The quaint stores look the same as they ever did—except for the broken glass, garbage and human remains that litter the streets. The weather has worn the bodies down to bone covered with scraps of fabric. Liz tries to weave around the bodies, but the crunching is unavoidable.

"Stop for a sec?" Ana asks. Her sights are locked on a yellow clapboard store, and she opens the van's door. "We're going shopping."

Ana saunters back to the truck and points at the signs, one of which says *Boutique*. But she's purposely picked a boutique-slash-gourmet foods store, so there's a reason to go inside besides clothes. A Lexer rounds the corner and heads for the voices that argue behind us. Jamie beats me to the sidewalk, slices her machete into its head and uses what looks to be an abandoned jacket to wipe her blade. The street is quiet after that. The good thing about pods is that it seems you're less likely to run into smaller groups. The bad thing about pods is everything else.

"We're going," I hear Ana say. "Send Caleb and Toby down while we're in there." She strides to the boutique's door and stops with a hand on the knob. "C'mon!"

The brass bell dings when we enter. It's completely untouched. The walls are lined with handmade soaps, gourmet goodies and Vermont souvenirs. Jamie slides behind the long counter on the back wall. The wooden shelves behind her are loaded with jars of jam and chutney. Some have burst from the cold, but many are intact. In front of her are large glass jars of candy.

"Help you ladies with something?" she asks.

It all looks so delicious that I don't know where to begin. The gummy worms are rock hard, but they taste perfect. Jamie unwraps a tube of Smarties and lets the entire row of round candies fall into her mouth. I follow her lead and then cram a Mary Jane in after them.

"This is awesome," Jamie says. "We need to take all of it."

My teeth are glued together with peanutty goodness, so I nod. The kids are going to scream with pleasure when they see this haul. Zeke will kill us, or at least bore us to death with lectures on tooth decay, but I don't care. The joy on Bits's face will be worth it.

"You have to see this!" Ana calls from an opening off to the side.

I tear myself away from the candy and step into a room full of clothes. The walls are lined with gauzy shirts and skirts, and the racks hold spring dresses.

Ana closes her eyes while she glides her hand along the fabrics. She'd just started her career as a fashion buyer before the world ended. Saying she likes clothes is a bit of an understatement.

"Look at this one!" she says.

The dress is light orange with gold embroidery on the skirt. She pulls a black and white-striped dress off the rack and holds it under my chin. It looks like it's from another world—a world where you don't have to wear elbow-length leather gloves and boots. A world where you can skip down the street on a beautiful summer's day and never once have to glance behind you.

"This would look great on you," Ana says.

It could be from the 60's, with off the shoulder sleeves that form a deep V-neck and a gathered skirt. Ana slings dresses over her arm. When the clothes are higher than her head, she leaves for the van. Jamie and I bag up the soaps and what's left of the food, followed by every last scrap of candy, while Ana makes a return trip to the children's section.

The front door is open, and we listen to the guys argue with Ana about the necessity of the clothes. I'm inclined to agree with them, but I don't know why they bother—she's going to get her way. Sure enough, when Jamie and I step outside, the clothes are in the van and Ana wears a triumphant smile. We lug our bags across the lot.

Shawn opens the van's door with a resigned sigh. "More clothes?"

"No," Jamie says. "Food, soap and candy. There are more bags inside."

The word *candy* elicits a response not unlike when a Lexer spots a human. Dan, Peter and Shawn dig through the bags. We're not much better than the kids. Dan bites off the end of a candy stick and winks at me. The heat of the sun is nothing compared to the flames in my cheeks, and I escape to get the rest of the bags while I try not to think about last night. Whenever I do, I'm filled with a mixture of guilt and desire to do it again. The guilt is winning, but it's a close race.

Toby and Caleb pull alongside the van. Toby leans out the window. "We found a fully-loaded RV. All gassed up, keys in the ignition, generator, hot water—all still working. We should camp tonight and hit the other stores in the morning."

It's an hour's drive to the solar power company that, as of last summer, had plenty of equipment we need. The sun's still up, but it's early evening. Traveling at night with a heavy trailer and no idea of what's ahead of us is a lot less appealing than hot showers and beds.

CHAPTER 48

We park the RV in an open field surrounded by barbed wire. I emerge from the shower to find Ana sitting on the bed, holding my clothes hostage. The orange dress she wears makes her skin glow and catches the gold highlights in her hair and eyes.

She wiggles the black and white dress in the air. "We're playing dress up."

"No way," I say. Not only am I not in the mood, but I feel too exposed out here in something so flimsy. "I'm supposed to be able to kill things in that?"

"We're in an RV, nothing's going to happen! You can change quick. Please?" She pouts, but that doesn't work on me. She tugs on my towel and attempts to look sad. "Pretty please? Jamie has one on already."

It is a pretty dress. And if I don't wear it, I'll spend the rest of my life hearing about The Time You Didn't Wear That Dress. She squeals when I take it and order her out. When I enter the living area, I get friendly whistles and catcalls that make me want to retreat to the bedroom. Jamie's hair is down and her dress is green to match her eyes. Ana knows what she's doing when it comes to personal shopping.

"You look purty," I say to her. We don't often get glimpses of what people might have been like before we all wore boots and holsters.

"Thanks. So do you. Although I'm not sure why I let Ana talk me into this."

Liz wears her own clothes, of course, and she says, "Suckers."

Dan's eyes skate up and down in such a way that I touch the bodice to be sure I haven't forgotten to put it on. "Nice dress."

"Thanks." I try to sound casual and curse the cheek capillaries that always give me away.

I help Peter with dinner so I have something to do besides blush, and then take my turn at watch on the RV's roof. I sit in my dress, rifle across my knees, and wait for Liz to join me.

Footsteps sound up the ladder rungs, but Dan appears. "I switched with Liz, hope you don't mind."

I shake my head. I'm going to have to talk to him at some point. I may be twenty-nine, but in these situations I have the awkward tendencies of a teen.

He sits facing me, but off to the side, so he can watch in the opposite direction. "That dress looks even better with a holster."

"Yeah, accessories make the outfit."

The light moment ends. I've run out of things to say. Crickets— real crickets—chirp in the silence.

"So, I feel like things are weird," Dan finally says. "I don't want them to be weird."

"Me neither. Can we just forget about last night?"

He watches me, face lit orange by the setting sun. "If that's what you want."

"It is." Dan looks away with a curt nod, so I try to explain. "It's too soon. I'm not good at this, anyway."

"At what?"

"At being with someone without it meaning something. And that's impossible now. Not that I was thinking this was a whole *thing* or anything. It's just... I think I should steer clear of...anything. And I should probably stop talking since the more I say, the crazier I sound."

Dan gives me a half smile when I make the universal finger-by-the-ear crazy signal.

"I meant that I know this isn't a big deal for you," I continue anyway. He lowers his eyebrows. "You, um, date people a lot. So, it's on to the next girl for you."

"Right. Okay."

I wait for more, but he watches the field silently. I smooth my skirt and replay what I've said until I want to dig a hole under the RV and get in it. This watch shift is going to last forever.

"It's beautiful up here," Dan says suddenly. "I never thought I'd live in the country."

I jump on the conversation. "I love it here. I always thought I would live in the country one day, but I had a bit of a different scenario in mind."

"I'll bet. I thought I'd live and die in Boston. I still can't believe I didn't die there."

"When did you leave?"

The setting sun has left a purple sky and shadows that shade his expression while he speaks. "I was watching the news, same as everyone. It wasn't until I finally spoke to my brother, Mike, that I knew how bad things were. He was stuck in his basement in Chicago. He got through on some sort of radio linkup—he said they'd been blocking internet and phones for days. He told me how bad things were, how they were zombies. I laughed when he first said it, but Mike wasn't much of a jokester. I was at the shop and couldn't get in touch with anyone, so I decided to walk to my girlfriend Diana's work."

He talks in the past tense about his family. Not everyone does that. I don't want to, but in my heart I know Eric's dead, and it just slips out.

"The streets were full of looters. I avoided anyone who looked infected. When I watched a group of them attack some poor kid, I realized Mike was right. An army truck went past, and the soldiers opened fire. They didn't stop—just blew the shit out of those Lexers and kept going. I was about ten feet away when they got up again. They just got up, like nothing had happened. I've never been so scared in my life.

"I ran to the hospital. I couldn't get anywhere near the door, so I went around to the ambulance entrance, but it was blocked. They came at me, so I jumped in an ambulance and took off. The only reason I got out was because I had the sirens going and they let me past. I tried to find my parents and sisters, but I didn't. I didn't even get close. And Diana...she was trapped in the hospital. If she was alive."

I think of Maria; the people in the hospitals were at ground zero.

"I wasn't the greatest boyfriend, but I tried to save her when it counted. I thought about her first. She never would've believed it, but it's true." He says the last part in a way that makes me think he hopes she can hear him.

"We all have things we could have said or done," I say, "but we have to forgive ourselves and believe that they forgive us, too."

I did apologize to Adrian and make things right; that's something to be grateful for. I can imagine how I'd feel had I never gotten the chance, and I want to pat Dan's knee, but I don't.

"Live like you'll die tomorrow," Dan says. "That's what they say, right? But I didn't until it was too late."

"None of us did," I say. "And it's hard, even now. We're human. We get bogged down in all the little things. Maybe it's impossible to do all the time, you know?"

He nods and everything about him slumps. And then I do rest my hand on his knee. I promise myself I'll do my best to remember this moment, to never forget that I could lose Bits at any second of any day. We watch the moon rise in silence.

The RV door opens, and Jamie and Shawn climb to the roof.

"Your relief crew is here," Jamie says. "You're missing the party—again."

"Let's go party," Dan says, and pulls me up. He climbs down the ladder and waits for me.

"Don't look up my skirt," I say.

His teeth flash in the moonlight. "Been there, done that."

It may not be that funny, but relief at his joke makes me wheeze with laughter. I knock him with my shoulder when I reach the bottom. "Thanks, Danny."

"Anytime, Cass."

CHAPTER 49

The RV's beige and gold interior is littered with empty candy wrappers and gourmet soda bottles. Drinking last night, with guards and a fence, was one thing. Tonight it's sugar only. Ana sits at the dinette wearing a green visor that says *Barb*. This rig had to have contained someone's grandparents, if the visors and sprays of fake flowers are any indication.

"Cass!" she yells, waving an unlit cigar. "Come play poker."

"I don't have to strip or anything, do I?"

"Nope," Peter says from under his visor that says *Bill* in puffy paint. "We're playing for watch tonight, these year-old Twinkies and the big bedroom."

I'm on the late watch shift, so I've got nothing to lose, and the Twinkies will be edible in another ten years. "Deal me in. I could use some hydrogenated vegetable shortening and/or beef fat." I look to where Dan leans against the kitchen counter. "You in?"

"You had me at beef fat," he says.

A couple of hours later the yawns have taken over. Liz has my watch shift, and Caleb lost on purpose so he'd be with her. I've got a full night of sleep and a package of Twinkies, thanks to Nelly's lessons. I'm so flush with winning that only when it's time for bed do I realize I'm going to sit up all night anyway. Peter and Ana head to the bedroom they've won, while Jamie and Shawn turn the couch into a bed. I sit in the driver's seat and watch the dark field.

"Can I talk to you for a second?" Dan asks.

I follow him outside. He stands in the light that shines through the window and rubs the back of his neck, looking so serious that I cross my arms to hide my shaky hands.

"I was thinking about what we talked about," he says. "About things we wished we'd said."

He fiddles with the walkie talkie he holds, and I notice his hands aren't steady either. "So, here goes—I don't want to move on to the next girl. I know what you said, and I understand completely. I'm just putting it out there so that you know, so I don't regret it."

I look down at my feet to hide my unease. I'd thought this was done, and now he's thrown the door back open. "Oh, okay," I whisper.

The light in the RV switches off. I can no longer see his face, and I'm very glad he can't see mine.

"Okay," he says. "Goodnight, then." He turns and walks toward his tent.

"Goodnight," I call softly.

***

I sit in the passenger's seat with my feet on the dash until I hear nothing but the small movements of Liz and Caleb on the roof and the others' gentle breathing. Dan's tent glows with lantern light. It reminds me of last night. Of Dan's mouth on my throat, his weight, of the way I fell asleep and slept until dawn, something I haven't done in months. The idea of tossing and turning in the dining table-turned-bed makes me feel worse than the idea of joining him again.

I don't so much make a decision as I follow my body where it wants to go. The tall grass is cool on my bare feet, and I clutch the Twinkies like a security blanket. He's set up his tent far away, and I wonder if it's because he'd hoped I'd be with him. I freeze when I reach his door, one foot pointed toward the tent and the other at the RV. Divided down the middle.

I don't know how to begin this. You can't knock on a tent. Maybe I should whisper, but that would mean admitting I want to be here. I spin around—a dining table bed is where I should be. There's a rustle and the sound of a zipper, followed by the soft light of the lantern. Dan smiles; not his confident smile, but a pleased one. "Hey."

"Hi," I say. He waits for more, but that's all I've got. I hold out the Twinkies, which are slightly squashed from my grip.

"You're dropping off Twinkies?" I shake my head. I really should've rehearsed this better. He looks at me a few seconds more. "Do you want to come in?"

"Okay."

He moves back to give me room. I kneel inside, taking my time to zip the door, and turn to face him. I think even my cheeks are trembling. I want him to touch me so badly that I can't think about anything else, and it's such a relief to not think.

"You still have your dress on," he says.

I smooth down the skirt and move forward to rest a hand on his chest. It rises and falls quickly, keeping pace with his heartbeat. Barb's berry-scented body wash rises off him in waves.

He runs his hand to my shoulder and laces his fingers in my loose hair. I exhale in frustration when he hesitates before our lips meet. "So, what does this mean?"

I don't have an answer; I think I can do this, after all. "Does it have to mean something?"

"No," he says. "I guess not."

Our kiss is gentler than last night. His breath is warm on my neck when he leans over to unzip my dress. I let it fall to the ground, and we pick up where we left off the night before.

***

The light tells me it's just dawn when I wake abruptly to the sound of a hand rasping along the nylon of the tent. No one on patrol would come this close without announcing themselves, even as a joke. Not unless they wanted to get shot. My hand reaches for my cleaver and holster down by my side, where they should be, but comes up empty. I came out here with Twinkies, like an idiot.

Dan's body stiffens beside me. The sleeping bag slips down his chest when he raises himself to a seated position. I reach for my dress, slide it over my head and zip up the back as far as I can. I'm so exposed. My hair is loose. I have no armor, no weapons, nothing at all.

Something brushes against the tent. Slow footsteps drag through the grass. One of them groans. It's answered by more noises and a wet, slopping sound. Dan reaches for the radio and connects the earpiece, then shakes his head—the batteries must be dead. I'm sure they've been trying to call us on the radio. They would have seen the Lexers coming, but didn't want to shout. There's always the chance they'll keep walking, as long as we don't attract them with movement.

Dan slides into his jeans and boots, shoves his arms through a flannel shirt and dons his leather gloves. He picks up his leather jacket and holds it behind me. I thread my arms through the sleeves.

If he gets bitten through the fabric of his shirt, he's dead. It's his coat—he shouldn't be punished because I'm an idiot. I start to shrug it off, but he pulls the lapels tight with a shake of his head. It's bulky and may be hard to move in, but I'll take it over bare skin. I squeeze his hand in thanks. He hands me one of his pistols, points a finger toward the window and mimes unzipping it. I watch as he painstakingly pulls the zipper to reveal a triangle of tent screen.

Ana stares through the window glass of the van. They're waiting. They won't start the engines until they have to. They won't leave until they know we're dead or we're with them. We've gone over it before, but we haven't ever had to put it into action.

Dozens of Lexers trample the grass between us and the vehicles. The ground behind us crunches with the footsteps of more. They haven't caught our scent or movement or whatever it is they do. Their shadows on the tent's nylon are made huge by the sun, like we're trapped in the middle of a dozen zombie giants. A body bumps on the tent and almost takes the side of it down. My hand flies to my mouth. Dan grips my forearm.

Peter's in the pickup, eyes trained on the tent. I freeze when a bloated leg passes the window and then wave a hand. I'm unsure if he can see me, but he nods and moves the radio to his mouth. A moment later, the van's engine roars to life. The window lowers and Jamie leans out the passenger's side.

"Hey, shitheads!" she calls to the Lexers. The horn beeps twice. "Come on! Come over here! Cassie, Dan, meet with the RV once they're out of the way."

If they drove this way, the Lexers would converge on them, on us. Now that they know we're awake, they'll lead them away. We'll be safe. The Lexers trudge after them. There are hundreds. I hold my breath at the passage of bodies. One hits the nylon with a swishing noise and an interested grunt. The stumbling legs of a dozen more turn our way. One of the rain fly's elastic cords is pulled out of the ground with a *twang*. More stop, attracted by the sound, even over the calling and honking.

I mime unzipping the tent door and running. Dan nods quickly. We're dead if the tent goes down with us in it. We're probably already dead. Dan's eyes are fierce when he takes my face in his hands and shakes his head. I breathe deep. I'll get home to Bits; there's no other option.

I raise the door's zipper tooth by tooth until it's wide enough to fit through. We leave everything but our weapons and crouch at the door. Lexer hands run down the nylon. The rain fly slithers to the ground, leaving the screen roof of the tent exposed. Decomposed faces appear, and a Lexer with a terrible perm and missing nose makes a hissing screech, just like the one at the fence. We scramble through the door just as she attempts to dive through the screen and the tent collapses.

The honking continues, but the Lexers who'd taken the bait have found something more interesting. They move toward us, but so do the vehicles, now that the initial plan has changed. They're coming for us, but we're going to have to stay alive until they get here, and with the number of Lexers that surround us, that's impossible. We have to move. Our friends will have to follow. We zigzag through the rotten bodies, first running left, then right. There's no time to aim and fire, to stop and slice, just the endless dodging of hands and arms and bodies.

The RV door flies open and Toby hangs out as it moves toward us, firing at the ones he can hit without hitting us. The other vehicles follow suit. It sounds like a war zone, and a flock of birds spirals up into the early morning sky. I jerk back and almost hit the ground when a hand tangles in my hair from behind. The Lexer pins me against his chest, and I sink down, away from the rotted mouth that's close enough to see his fillings. I scream with the effort of pushing him away and jam my pistol just below his ear. A clump of my hair goes with him when he drops.

The sweet smell of the field has been replaced with decay that I can taste with each gasping breath. Dan spins in a circle, machete hitting open mouths and withdrawing with a metallic *ching*. The RV is twenty feet away, pushing Lexers out of its path on its way to us.

I take Dan's free hand in mine. His grip is tight enough to hurt, but I couldn't bear it if he let go. I run barefoot to where Toby screams, urging us on. Dan follows me in, and Toby slams the door just as a Lexer hits.

"They're in! Go!" he yells at Shawn.

I land on the floor next to the easy chairs. Dan pants, face flushed, elbows on the kitchen counter. We bump and thump over grass until we hit the paved road and roll smoothly.

"Holy shit!" Shawn yells from the driver's seat. "We thought you guys were dead. We really did. Holy shit."

Toby falls into the chair. I take his trembling hand in mine. "Thanks, Toby."

He gives a shake of his head and opens his mouth but can't get out a word. The sweat pours down his temples like he just ran through a pack of Lexers himself. A week ago I might have thought that was fun, in a twisted way. Now all I can think of are the people I would've left behind. And the way I left things with Penny, she would have thought that I wanted to die. Bits would've believed I didn't care.

I release Toby's hand, pry myself up and lather my hands at the sink. Dan removes his blood-splattered shirt and takes the soap I offer when I'm done. Dan's leather jacket sticks to my bare skin, and when I pull it off something heavy hits my side. I remove his silver flask and wiggle it in the air. "You want?"

He turns it over in his hands in contemplation until his entire face is alight. "Not this time."

I laugh; it's the laugh of having cheated death, of being alive. I touch the spot on the back of my head, and my fingertips come away wet with blood. Dan spins me around for a look. "That one tore out a chunk. It's small, but I bet it hurts like hell."

It's starting to, but it's no match for the relief I feel. "It's fine, nothing a ponytail won't cover."

He pulls me close by the nape of my neck. "I prefer the buns."

They've stopped the vehicles. The others spill into the RV, but Dan doesn't glance at them. I think he's going to kiss me, right here, in front of everyone. A dalliance in a tent and off the farm is one thing, but we're not a couple, and I'm not going to be the new girl visiting The Love Den. I feign ignorance and turn away.

Ana flings herself into my arms. "I thought that one had you, I really did. Maybe you should cut your hair."

She flips her hair with a grin. I smack her lightly and point at my wrinkled dress. "Don't ever ask me to play dress-up again, Banana. I swear I'll kill you."

Ana laughs uproariously. Peter squeezes me tight and whispers, "I would have told Penny you were sorry, but I'm so glad I don't have to."

The thought makes my knees weak and the room blurry. "Me, too."

CHAPTER 50

W̶e come back with solar panels and enough sugar, in real and candy form, to kill us all. We bring the RV—I think that John and Maureen might want to shack up together and, with the addition of a wood stove, it'll be the perfect place. I find Dan waiting when I step out of the RV. Somewhere between the field and the solar store he'd switched vehicles. I've made it a point not to ignore him, to treat him the way I always do, but today he's the one who's aloof.

"Can we talk for a minute?" he asks.

Bits stands with Penny in the gravel lot behind the restaurant. I want to run to her, but I follow him around the back of the RV. He traces the seam of the window frame with a finger. "Just so you know, I won't say anything about...us. Neither will anyone else. In case you were worried."

"Thanks," I say evenly, not wanting to sound too relieved.

"If you want to hang out, you know where to find me," he says, and studies the trees. "I'd like to."

"Hang out?"

Finally, he looks at me, and his mischievous expression returns. "Yeah, you know, play Parcheesi or something."

"Ah, Parcheesi." I shake my head slowly. "I don't think it's a good idea."

"Maybe not. No big deal."

He leans against the RV, hands in pockets, and shrugs. I'm not being entirely truthful—I do think it's a bad idea, but that doesn't mean I don't want to.

"I should go see Bits," I say. "But thanks, Danny. You saved my life today, when that one had my hair."

"You got him yourself."

"Yeah, but you kept the others away. You gave me your jacket. So, thanks."

"You would've been okay," he insists. "I shouldn't have set up the tent so far away. I almost killed us both."

"Would you just say, 'You're welcome?' " I hold out my arms for a hug.

"You're welcome," he murmurs into my neck.

His lips brush just behind my ear. I stay a moment longer than necessary before I break away and round the corner of the rig, my neck still tingling. Peter kneels in front of Bits, listening to the latest Sparky news. I kneel beside him and reach for her. She stares at me accusingly, the tip of her nose raw. She might have cried for the past three days, all because of me.

My heart drops and my arms fall when she doesn't move into them. "I'm sorry, Bits. I'm sorry I scared you and said mean things. I'm sorry I haven't been around. I've been really sad, and I know that's not a good excuse. I don't have an excuse, I just hope you can forgive me."

Bits's chin trembles. I lift my arms again, and she hugs me tight enough to cause lasting nerve damage, but I'll gladly take it over any damage I might have caused her had I not come back. I've let this little girl flounder for the past months, thinking she had the farm to make her feel safe. But Bits is smart—she knows that a school protected by the sheriff, a log cabin surrounded by barbed wire and a farm bordered by fences only afford her so much safety. Her safety lies with me, with Peter and the others. With feeling loved as well as protected. I'm so glad I figured that out—or had it screamed at me by my best friend—before it was too late.

I glance at where Penny stands with James. "How're you feeling, Pen?"

"It moved," she says, and rubs where her stomach has become more pronounced. Maybe it happened in the past few days or maybe I hadn't noticed, or hadn't wanted to because I was so jealous.

"The baby? Really?"

"No one else can feel it yet, though."

"I sat there for forever," Bits says. She pulls out of our hug and purses her lips. "It was so annoying. Every time I took my hand off, she'd move, and then I'd put it back on and she would stop."

"It's probably too early, anyway," I say with a laugh. "I'm sure you'll feel her soon."

There's really somebody moving around in there; a little person, like Bits. I should've known that Penny would be terrified. "I'm sorry, Pen."

"I'm sorry, too," she says.

"You have nothing to be sorry for. You were right."

"But I'm sorry for the other stuff. I had no right to tell you what to do."

"You had to take over Nelly's job, since he isn't here." I stand and speak my next line into her belly. "We got you some really cute clothes, so you'd better be a girl."

"This poor kid. He's going to have a complex," Penny says.

We both have tears in our eyes, and we sink into each other and laugh the way we always do when we cry at the same time. I rock her side to side while making *whooshing* noises. "Whoa baby, hang on! Think she's dizzy?"

Penny giggles and pushes me off. "No, you maniac, but I am. Let's go eat."

We walk to the restaurant, Penny on my arm and Bits's hand in mine. I know the pain of losing someone never completely abates, but that warmth—the happiness at having these people to live for—is also here to stay.

CHAPTER 51

John stands beside the wide trench that now surrounds the farm and rubs his beard. "I didn't think it would ever be finished."

It runs like a dark brown scar across the grass and borders the woods on the east and west sides of the fence. They've included a ladder every so often, in case someone not dead falls in. It's ugly, but it's beautiful to us because it should catch a pod. And the large pods are growing. The other Safe Zones are reporting that no groups fewer than thirty have been spotted in recent weeks.

"We can go even wider," John says. "But that means more fuel. That excavator burns through fuel like you wouldn't believe, when it's not breaking down. Thank God Shawn can repair it."

The racket it made called plenty of Lexers up for a trial run of the trench. And between Lexers, breakdowns, removing the extra dirt, shoring up the trench walls to avoid collapse, tree roots and boulders, what should've taken a week or two turned into over two months.

"We need more diesel to have on hand. I hate to send you out again." He looks tired and the wrinkles under his eyes are more pronounced. Like Zeke, he's taken up leadership and it's wearing on him.

I put my hand on his arm. "Are you feeling okay?"

"Nothing a little rest won't fix," he says. "I was worried when you were out there, didn't get much sleep."

"I've been back for three days, you goose. You should go to your new rig and relax." I wrap my arm around his side. "You'll need it, if you're sending us out again."

"I hate to do it."

"It has to be done. I'm not looking forward to it, either."

It's true; I don't want to go. I'd like to see Nelly, but that's it. No more zombie hunting for me. I'll let the trench capture them and kill them in safety.

***

I haven't done guard in the past few nights because I thought that maybe I'd finally sleep. But as it turns out, optimism is purely a daytime outlook. Bits is sound asleep for the fourth night in a row with Sparky nestled on her chest, rising with each gentle breath.

I read the same line of my book over and over and finally toss it to the side. Ana, Liz and Jeff are on guard at the main gate tonight, and maybe one of them would appreciate sleep. I use my windup flashlight to find my clothes and leave a note for Peter, who's here if Bits needs something.

I walk along the graveled paths, past the other cabins and laundry. The grass is still green, mainly because of the rule of You Must Not Walk on the Grass. Otherwise, this place would be a dust bowl. I round the restaurant, shuttered tight until my morning breakfast shift, and see Dan walking toward me.

I'd thought I'd timed it well; he was off guard an hour ago, but he must have stuck around to chat. He still sits with us at dinner, and we joke the same as we used to. But I get all flustered when he looks at me across the table like he'd rather have me for dinner.

"Hey," he says, and stops a few feet away.

The solar powered lights throw off enough light to see facial expressions, but only if you're standing on top of one. His voice sounds happy to see me, although his body language yells uncomfortable.

"Hi," I say. We stand for another minute in silence. "So, you just got off guard?"

"Yeah," he says. "You on?"

"No, I was just...bored."

"Stupefyingly bored?" He moves closer, and now I can see the smile on his face before his eyebrows lower. "Couldn't sleep?"

I flap my hands dismissively. "No. I mean, yeah. It's much better, though. Just not right now. It's fine."

"You can sleep in my tent," he says. "Just sleep."

"Okay." It comes out before I think about it. Even Dan looks surprised. "If nothing—"

He holds two fingers in the air. "Promise."

I walk beside him while he tells me about the Lexers who fell into the trench this evening. You can hear them; a series of thumps every night. It's made watching the fences boring, but as Peter says, boring's good. We thread through the pants, shirts and towels on the clotheslines behind the laundry.

Dan's hand touches my waist to guide me past a flapping sheet, and my pounding heart overrides the ache in my chest. Loneliness is stronger at night, in the same way that things are scarier. Maybe I can have it mean nothing for a little while longer, so I don't have to sleep alone. I was lying when I said I wanted nothing to happen. I hope he was, too.

***

I creep out of the tent for my shift, leaving Dan asleep on his mattress. It doesn't escape me that I'm the girl leaving the Love Den, but at least I know the score. I have three weeks, and by then I'll be ready to sleep alone.

In the restaurant, Mikayla stands at the stove. "I missed you! I was so happy to see you were on this morning."

"I missed it," I say, and stow my gear by the door.

"You look good." Mikayla tilts her head. "No, really. You weren't looking so—"

"Yes, I looked like shit," I say with a laugh. "Why does everyone feel the need to mention that to me?"

"Cass! You know that's not what I meant. You look different, happy."

"I got a good night's sleep."

And I barely got through the tent door before Dan kissed me and his hands were everywhere, the liar. I start on breakfast. I think I might even do art class afterward.

CHAPTER 52

"Colorado," John says, after he sits at the dinner table. He looks like shit—maybe I should share that with him, it seems to be the thing to do. He picks up a forkful of corn salad. "Colorado's gone. Off the air. So is Arkansas."

"Big Bend, then Gila, Utah, Colorado, then Arkansas..." James says, and sets down his fork. I can practically see the gears in his head spinning as he continues. "They're moving northeast. It's probably the mountains. But they might swing due north now that the land's opened up. And, shit, they'll be here before the winter if they keep coming this way."

"Who's moving northeast?" Maureen asks. "Lexers?"

James nods. "We're losing Safe Zones in geographical order. Like a pod or pods are moving north and east. The Rockies might have forced them east. I think Lexers will choose the path of least resistance, if they're not after something. But there are mountains to the east after Arkansas, and north through the Dakotas is flat. Let's hope they head north."

James carries around an amazing amount of information, like the computers he loved so dearly. And he's a walking, talking map, apparently.

"Hmm, let's say—fifteen hundred," he says to himself. He shakes his head. "No."

"Share with the class," Penny says.

He uses his long fingers to tuck back his hair. "Sorry. Assuming that it's a pod and if—and it's a big *if*, because they can walk faster—they walk at one mile per hour, twenty-four hours a day, for fifteen hundred miles, straight here—"

"Two months," Penny says. "They'll be here in two months."

I don't question the math; these two are math whizzes. The cold starts in my chest and runs to my fingers and feet.

"We've got the trench," Ana says. She looks around the table. "Right?"

"We do," John says. "But it might not be enough, depending on the number."

I look out the picture window at the leafy green mountains. They seem so sturdy. "Maybe it'll take longer, even if they do come this way. They'll have to get over the mountains. If we have an early freeze it will slow them down, maybe, at least at night."

"If they are coming, when would they be within six hundred miles?" John asks.

James thinks. "Forty-five days, give or take."

That's early September. All we need is for them to move a little slower, if indeed they exist, and not hit us until November or December.

"There's no Safe Zone after Arkansas," Dan says. "Not until Pennsylvania and New York."

There are other pockets of people, we know because we've heard of them, but they don't have radios. Dan gulps from his glass of milk; I thought only nine year-old boys drink milk with dinner. I've been at his tent every night for the past weeks. I go after Bits is asleep and leave before dawn so I'm there when she wakes. I swear I won't go back, but when the farm is quiet, I leave my bed for his. We didn't sign up for night duty this week, without even discussing it. Dan catches me staring and lowers his cup to the table, eyes locked on mine. I busy myself with my napkin.

"So we won't know anything concrete until they're close enough for Dwayne to do a flyover," John says. "We've got enough fuel for two runs. Maybe one in early September and another in mid-to-late September. I'll have to talk to him about it."

"Why wouldn't they have sent out a distress call?" James asks. "It doesn't make any sense. I mean, Colorado knew we wanted to know what was going on."

"People do strange things when they're scared," John says. He puts his hand over where Maureen's rests on the table. "Or there could be bad weather. They could have had tornadoes, electrical trouble, who knows? Let's not jump the gun."

We pick at the rest of dinner in silence. The tables around us are full of talk and laughter, but they won't be once people know. Bits giggles at Hank and Henry's table. I wave and force myself to make a silly face. She's so perceptive, and if she knew she might not sleep at all.

CHAPTER 53

I help clean up dinner and get the kitchen ready for breakfast in the morning. I wasn't on kitchen duty, but there's a bonfire in back of the barns tonight and people wanted to get a jump on the festivities.

"Go ahead," I tell Shelby, "I'll close up."

"Are you coming?" she asks.

"I don't think so, but thanks."

"Okay, well, if you change your mind. I think Dan's coming."

I freeze. "What?"

"I thought you and Dan..." She shrugs. "You know. I'm on the west fence a lot."

"Oh," I say. "Right. Well, we hang out sometimes."

"Cool. Maybe I'll see you later."

She takes her blond hair out of its ponytail and leaves with a wave. I watch her go with a sinking heart and lower my forehead to the countertop.

"What's so awful?" Dan's voice floats out of the dining area, and I scream in surprise. He leans against the doorframe with an eyebrow up. "Wow, you're easily startled."

"Why the hell are you lurking around in the dining room?"

"I wasn't lurking, I was waiting to walk you home." He moves closer and pins me against the counter. "My home."

I push him off and cover my face. If Shelby knows, then who else knows? I've become the girl I make fun of. If Nelly finds out, he'll never stop torturing me. Everyone must think I'm so cold-hearted that I jumped right into Dan's bed. Or tent, as it were. I press my lips together to stop their trembling.

"Hey. Oh no, don't cry." Dan puts out a hand. "Why are you crying?"

I can't tell him. He pulls me to his chest and smoothes my hair. I breathe deep, wanting to be comforted, but his scent is all wrong.

"Come," he says.

I follow when he pulls my hand. I shouldn't go, but I want to. Things are easy with Dan. In his tent we laugh and talk about nothing of great importance. I feel safe and desired. It's only when I'm out of the microcosm of his tent that I regret going. He leads me through the flap, and I perch on the edge of his mattress. I'm already loosening up at the thought of what comes next—the mindless feel of our bodies connecting, a few entertaining words and then blissful sleep.

He removes the knife on his belt and kneels in front of me. "Do you want to talk?" I bite my lip and shake my head, then lean forward to kiss him, but he pulls back. "Are you sure?"

"I don't want to talk," I say. "Do you?"

I grab a fistful of his shirt and pull him closer, giving him no time to respond to my question. His mouth is hesitant at first. I don't ask why because I don't want to know, and after a minute he doesn't seem to care.

***

I pull the sleeping bag up to my chin and turn on my side to face Dan. "So, how are the cabins coming?"

Dan's drawn up the plans and is in charge of building the long cabins that will replace the outfitter tents. The tents kept people warm during last winter, for what we hoped would be the only winter. But now that we know we have years to go, the tenants need a modicum of privacy.

Dan's head is propped on his hand, and his other traces circles on my stomach. "They're fine. I wish I could say I was excited, but it's basically framing things out and telling people where to put nails. Nothing like what I used to do."

"So, what'd you used to do?" I ask. There's so much I don't know about him. "How did you become a carpenter in the first place?"

"My dad. I used to help him in his shop. He'd get these wood deliveries where they'd dump a whole bunch of wood out front. I'd help him stack the pieces by type and size. They were rough and dull, but he'd run his hands along them like they were already beautiful things. Like he could see what they were before he even started. And one day I realized I could see it, too."

I know what he means. Sometimes a blank canvas looks like that; I just have to fill in the spaces with what I can already see. "So what kind of things did you make?"

"We made furniture, boxes, bowls, whatever we saw in the wood. We sold at a lot of galleries. My favorite things were these carved boxes I made. We were more woodworkers than carpenters, but we filled in the quieter periods with general carpentry. My dad could do anything."

His voice is soft and eyes faraway. I run my fingers along his tightened jaw. He kisses my fingers and holds them there. It feels more intimate than what we've just done and a nervous clatter starts up in my stomach.

"I'd love to see one of those little boxes—I love boxes," I say, in order to cut through what's quickly becoming a moment I can't handle. "My mom used to build stuff, more utilitarian things like shelves and bookcases, but they were always pretty. The one time I tried to build a table, it looked like a baby deer. She laughed her ass off."

Dan snorts. "How can a table look like a deer?"

"You know, all spindly legs and wobbly? Like Bambi."

"You see things differently, you know. I guess that's why you were a painter—are a painter."

"I was a painter. Then, after my parents died, I stopped. I started again last summer."

"So what'd you paint?"

"Whatever struck me. It could be a landscape, or the kids I worked with in Brooklyn, or something beautiful, or something so ugly that I wanted to show its beauty. And the kids and I did murals in the neighborhood."

"Maybe you should do a mural here. In the restaurant or something."

"I was thinking that. I have it all planned out—unicorns and a rainbow, with mountains in the background." His smile becomes forced, and I shake with laughter. "I'm kidding! I like unicorns as much as the next girl, but really?"

"I thought you were serious, Dingbat," he says, and gives an exaggerated wipe of his forehead.

"Well, you would've figured it out when I got to the part about the robot battle in the background, right?"

"I'd like to think so, but you are kind of strange." He laughs when I push his chest. "So, were you good?"

"Some stuff I was really proud of, but some stuff I hated. I guess other people thought so."

"So they wanted your paintings?"

"Yeah."

Dan runs his fingers up my side. "Maybe you'll paint me something one day. That corner of the tent is kind of bare."

"Maybe you'll make me a box to put my treasures in. We can trade."

I'm already thinking of what I could paint for him. Not what I want to paint, which is the ambulance on a dark night, siren lights illuminating the cables of a bridge. Bold strokes, blurry and murky and bright at the same time. I think I could convey the fear, the rush, the terror he must have felt as he sped out of Boston and left everyone behind. I won't paint him that, but maybe I'll paint it for myself one day. Future generations—if there are future generations—will want to know what happened. They'll want to see, just like we want to see what came before us.

"It's a deal," he says. "So, tell me something else I don't know about you."

"You know everything, I'm sure." I remember Shelby's comment. "Everyone here knows everything."

I roll onto my back and look at the mesh of the tent's roof. Dan turns off the lantern and moves next to me. "I took off the rain fly so we could see the stars. The Perseid meteor shower starts every year in mid-July. It hasn't peaked yet, but if you watch long enough you'll see them."

I stare at the sky until a tiny trail of white zings through the stars, followed by another.

"Make a wish," he says, but I don't answer. His hand finds mine and squeezes. "What's the matter?"

"Nothing." I wanted this to be uncomplicated and secret, but it's not. Nothing here ever is. I haven't even told Penny. She and I may have cleared the air, but I'm still nervous about her reaction.

The mattress bounces when he faces me, but I continue to watch the sky. Two more meteors shoot past. "What about us?" he asks. "What we're doing."

"We're hanging out. Right?"

"Well, how do you feel about it?"

I tear my eyes away from the stars. I can only see his silhouette. "I don't know. I guess...I have fun with you?"

I wait for him to press me further, praying fervently that he won't. He switches the lantern on and shrugs. "I'm having fun, too. You're okay with that?"

"That's all I want," I say. "Really."

I don't know what Dan is like with any of the other girls he's been with. I certainly can't ask, but I assume he must be as nice to them as he is to me. Otherwise they'd hate him, and none of them do. I don't want there to be any confusion, though. He leans forward and kisses me slowly. My body responds, although my heart is silent.

CHAPTER 54

The fifty Lexers that fell in the trench last night have to be finished off, which is like shooting fish in a barrel. I stand ten feet from the edge. I'm not taking any chances—all I'd need to do is trip and then I'd be dinner. The trench is five feet deep; deep enough that they can't escape, but not deep enough to keep their hands and heads below ground level. To get close enough with something short is to get within arm's reach, which is why I have my trusty crossbow.

A long spike would do, but even though my arms are strong, driving things through bone isn't easy. And when it gets stuck, it can take tremendous effort to get it out again. This is easier, and we can retrieve the bolts when we're done. I'd go as far as to say it's fun, if you don't think about it too much. It's become an impromptu target practice out here today. I pull back the cocking string, unclick the safety and line up the sight on the eye socket of one with long auburn hair. I'd bet her eyes were green once, but now they're a yellow-gray rimmed with black-edged eyelids. Her arms are stretched out, filthy fingers making troughs in the dirt beside the trench. The bolt twangs and hits her square in the eye.

"Nice," Ana says.

"Thanks," I say. I hand the crossbow to Peter. "Take a shot. They're great. We used them at the quar—Day Which Shall Not Be Named."

Peter laughs and smacks Ana on the backside. She punches him in the arm. "It's okay to talk about it. She's not doing it again. Are you?"

"I promised," Ana says. "Except in certain emergency situations. On an as-needed basis."

"Which must first pass my approval," Peter says. Ana sucks her teeth and glares. "I'm kidding."

"Would you shoot the damn crossbow already?" a familiar voice says.

I spin around. Nelly stands behind us, arms crossed and mouth curved. I scream in joy and run to him. "What are you doing here?"

For once, Nelly doesn't act blasé. He lifts me in the air and spins me around. "I missed you, Half-pint."

My scream has caused our trench zombies to lose their minds. It's impossible to hear over the din. Ana and Peter unload their crossbows into the Lexers and hug Nelly when they're done, but they don't seem surprised. We walk back to the side gate and lock it behind us. The newly formed Body Removal duty will clear the bodies and clean the bolts. I'm not looking forward to my next shift on that crew.

"Why didn't anyone tell me you were coming?" I ask.

"I wanted to surprise you," Nelly says. "We need fuel at Whitefield, and when we heard y'all were going on a run we thought we'd join. We brought the tank truck to load up and fill your tanks before going out again."

I hop up and down in excitement. Peter and Ana look as happy as I do. We're all back together again, which is the way it should be.

"You'll stay at our cabin, right?" I ask. "We can squish in my bed. Or Bits can sleep with me, or Ana and Peter."

"I thought I'd have your bed all to myself, since I hear you're sleeping elsewhere these days," Nelly says with a smirk. "And here I thought you were immune to his charms."

I cover my face with my hands. I know he's so been looking forward to this conversation. He probably spent the past hour working on his opening line. "Please," I beg. "Please don't torture me. I can't take it."

"I can't pass up this opportunity, Cass," he says sadly. "I wish I cou—"

"I saved your life! You owe me. This is all I want in return."

He turns his face to the clouds and shakes his head slowly. "No. I'd rather die than not be able to bother you about this."

"I can't believe you!"

He wraps his arm around my shoulders and drags me toward the cabin. "Now, come and tell me all about it. I suppose I know what base you've gotten to—" I kick him, hard, and he laughs, "but I'm gonna need more than that."

I look to Peter and Ana for help. Ana looks at her watch and says, "I'm late for the garden." She flashes Nelly a grin tinged with evil. "Every detail. Later. She doesn't talk to anyone."

Peter edges away, but I grab his arm. "You have nothing to do. I know you don't. You aren't leaving me alone with him."

Peter stops struggling. "Okay, but I reserve the right to cover my ears."

"You won't have to," I say, and stick my tongue out at Nelly.

***

Nelly's been grilling me, in between my annoying him about Adam, but all I'll say is that I sleep in Dan's tent. Nelly sits beside me on the loveseat, my feet in his lap, and curls his lip.

"That's it?" he asks. "That's all you're giving me?"

"It's nothing, I swear. We're just hanging out. It's been a few weeks, so it'll end soon. It's almost over. Of course, I was hoping that would happen before the rest of the world knew."

"So you don't *like* like him? To use your first-grade terminology."

I shake my head. "He asked me how I felt about us, and I said we were friends and I was cool with it. The end."

Peter's been leaning back in a table chair, head against the wall. But now the chair legs hit the floor, and he and Nelly exchange a glance. "Darlin'," Nelly says. "*Dan* asked *you* how you felt about things?"

I roll my eyes, but I remember the way Dan seemed different last night and take a sip of water to moisten my mouth. "Stop. You're making it out to be a bigger deal than it was."

Nelly looks unconvinced. I turn to Peter. "Did you put this in his head? Dan likes everyone. You both know that."

"I didn't say a word," Peter replies. "Not a syllable."

"You need to—" Nelly begins. He drops the subject and holds out his arms when Bits runs through the door with Penny. "There's my most favorite kid in the world."

"Nelly!" Bits throws herself on the couch and kisses him all over.

"Did you know that none of the kids at Whitefield are as smart as you?" Nelly asks. He puts a hand up to his mouth and whispers, "They're all pretty dumb, actually."

"They are not!" Bits giggles. "Want to see my comic book so far? I'm a zombie hunter. Come!"

She drags him to our room. Penny gives him a big kiss and parks herself next to me with her hands on her belly.

"So, when were you going to tell me?" she asks. I throw my head back and sigh. "I'll forgive you this once. But don't ever think you can not tell me something like this again."

"This is ridiculous. I'll just sleep in Peter and Ana's bed. You'll rub my eyebrows until I'm asleep, right?" Peter chuckles. "You think I'm kidding."

"Are you mad?" I ask Penny. I have my best friend back, and I don't want to lose her again.

"For what?"

"For not telling you about Dan. For anything. I don't know, pick something."

"No, I'm not mad. And don't break it off unless you want to." She sticks a finger in my face. "But, either way, you have to tell me."

"I will." I lean on her shoulder and rub her bump. "How's little Cass doing?"

She lets out a snort. "*Cass?*"

"It was worth a shot."

"If it's a girl, we were thinking of naming her Maria."

"I think that's perfect. Your mom would love that."

Penny sniffs. "I know."

CHAPTER 55

"I missed you last night," Dan says. The words are serious, but the creases by his mouth aren't. He tosses his backpack into a pickup.

"Nelly's here," I say.

The creases disappear. "Right. Got it."

"That's not what I meant. He's staying with me, and I want to spend time with him."

I don't owe him an explanation, but I don't want to hurt his feelings. "He knows about—" I wave my hand between us. "It's not that."

I shiver when Dan runs his fingers up my bare arm and says, "I missed your cold feet."

"Well, maybe they'll be back on you soon."

"Can't wait, Dingbat." The day grows ten degrees warmer when he lifts his hand to my cheek and stares at me without blinking.

"Is that my new nickname or something?" I ask.

"Yep. It fits you, in the best possible way."

"I'm not sure if that's a compliment or not, but okay."

"It is. At least the way I mean it."

I walk past the small tanker truck. It holds about a thousand gallons and if we get that, we'll be set. Nelly stands beside our pickup and shakes his head. "That doesn't look like it's over."

"Stuff it," I say.

***

We make quite a caravan on the way to the outskirts of Burlington. We have the small tank truck, the trailer with fuel drums, and another two pickups with in-bed tanks that hold a hundred gallons of fuel each. We don't know what to expect. Burlington had a population of 40,000, plus college students, at the time of infection. Even with the winter, that's a lot of zombies.

I've come to regret my decision to ride in one of the pickups with Nelly, who's been hounding me ever since he put the truck in drive, much to Ana and Peter's amusement. John drives the tanker with Zeke. Dan, Caleb and Toby are in the trailer truck, and Kyle, Tony and Margaret follow in the last pickup.

"I saw you!" Nelly bangs a hand on the steering wheel for emphasis. "He was not looking at you like he was 'having fun.' And you weren't much better."

Heat rises in my cheeks. "What do you want from me?"

"Admit you like him."

I look out the window at the two-lane road. "I don't like him that way. I really don't."

It's not entirely true. I do like Dan—he makes me laugh, he's smart and a nice guy—and that's as far as it goes or will go during this little escapade. I don't plan on falling in love with him. With anyone. Dan said he felt the same, but if Nelly and Peter are right I'll have to end it. I hope they're wrong because I don't want it to end just yet. I don't want it to intensify, either. I'm happy with the status quo.

"Well, what was that look on your face? You should have seen her, y'all. She was all—" He turns and makes his eyes big and melty. Ana giggles. "So what was that?"

If I could throw Nelly out the door without killing him, I would. "It's...He's..."

Ana screams. "I knew it! He *is* good in bed!"

It may be true, but that's not what I was going to say. I don't even know what I was going to say, but it definitely wasn't that, especially with Nelly and Peter in the truck. She wiggles one of my buns and jumps back before my seat belt stops me from smacking her. I always wear my seatbelt. It's not like they can rush me to the nearest hospital if we crash.

Nelly sobs with laughter. Peter covers his ears jokingly. Maybe I should throw *myself* out the door.

"So how does he compare to Peter?" Ana asks. "It's the only way I'll ever know."

"Ana!" Peter and I scream at the same time.

I'm roasting in embarrassment, and out of the corner of my eye I see Peter drop his head in his hands. She and Nelly high five, which causes Nelly to swerve to the shoulder before he straightens the truck out. This is why seatbelts are important, especially when your friends are jerks.

"Everyone okay back there?" Zeke asks over the radio.

"Yeah," Nelly gasps. "We're better than okay." He can barely get the words out. "We're having the most enlightening conversation. Did you know that—"

I rip the radio from his hand and press the button. "We're fine. Nelly's being a dumbass."

"Well, just be careful," Zeke replies.

I set the radio on the seat between us and turn to the back. Ana's teeth are dazzling against her tanned face, and she wipes tears from her eyes. Peter looks like he'd rather be anywhere else in the world. I'd like to be there with him.

"This conversation is over," I say. "Forever."

Nelly and Ana go silent, apart from the occasional chuckle. I never think about sleeping with Peter, and I'm sure he does the same. I don't want our friendship to be strained, and I want to kill Ana for being so oblivious. Nelly puts a hand on my leg and frowns when I move away.

The two-lane road widens and becomes a small town. Besides the few abandoned cars, including one flipped on its roof, it looks relatively untouched. A farm equipment store is across the road from the service station, and a church sits another hundred yards down the road, door hanging on its hinges. The steps of the few small houses are choked with weeds.

The trucks ahead slow to a stop and Nelly pulls onto the shoulder. John steps on the running board and leans his arms on Nelly's window. "We'll check here first," he says. "Maybe we won't have to go much closer to Burlington."

We walk to the pumps. It's a fairly large station for such a small town. Zeke wrestles with the lock on the ground tanks. There are so many of us to watch that I head inside the small convenience store to see what's left. There's not much, although I find something I think Dan would appreciate. I stuff it into my coat pocket and pull bags from behind the counter. I'm in the process of taking all the toiletries when I hear Peter clear his throat.

"Sorry about Ana," he says with a quick glance at me. His hair has gotten longer, and he pushes back the shock that's fallen over one eye.

"You're not your girlfriend's keeper," I say. "You'd have to be a lion tamer for that."

His lips twitch at the crack of my imaginary whip. And like that, we're okay again. He looks at what I'm putting in the bag, which at the moment is a box of condoms.

"Can we not discuss what you're holding?" he jokes, and I thump him with my hip. "I'm glad you're happy. Or happier."

"I am happier, and I feel like shit about it." I look out the store's window to where they feed a tube into the hole in the ground. "I still can't believe he's gone. Sometimes when I wake up I think everything's fine. Then I remember and I have to go through it all again. It doesn't happen when I'm with Dan."

Peter takes the bag from my hands, sets it on the floor and pulls me to him. My cheek presses into the zipper of his jacket. I breathe in his scent and then I do remember him, us. But it's not a big deal; it's like another life, a movie I once watched.

"That's why I don't end it," I say.

"You don't have to. You deserve to be happy."

I nod and pick up the bag. He takes an empty bag and fills it with the remaining bottles of mouthwash and boxes of Motrin. "But I'll rub your eyebrows, if you need me to."

I laugh. "Thanks, Petey. I know you majored in business, but you're turning out to be an excellent therapist. When's our next session?"

"Let me check my sched—"

Ana knocks on the window to let us know they're done. We bag the rest and meet them outside.

CHAPTER 56

There wasn't much in the tanks, and John thought the fuel might have gone off, based on its color and smell. We head to Winooski, where the road widens into four lanes. At first it's more of a highway, with glimpses of houses through the trees, before it opens up on the usual stores: Pizza Hut, Dunkin' Donuts, and then an assortment of large old houses and office parks. A group stands under the awning of one office building on what looks to be a zombie smoking break.

We see one here and there down the road, but not enough to scare us off. We can take care of a few, even a dozen or twenty, but after that it isn't worth the risk. We drive under an overpass and come upon two gas stations, side by side. John and Kyle pull their trucks into the first, and we pull to the underground tanks of the other station. Caleb and I stand in the back of the pickups to watch for signs of movement, but the kiosk in the center blocks my view.

"I'm going out to the road," I say. "I can't see a thing."

Ana follows me, leaving Toby and Caleb to watch the back. I'm encased in leather and sweating like crazy. I take a swig from my water bottle and shield my eyes with my hand; even with sunglasses the glare is intense.

Ana swivels her head and takes in the wide road. "This doesn't look too bad."

"Mm-hmm," I say.

"I'm sorry." She removes her sunglasses and squints at me. "I thought it was funny, but you didn't."

"It's fine," I say, and resume scanning the road.

"Don't be mad at me, Cass. Please?"

"Why? Since when do you care if anyone's mad at you?"

"I care if *you* are. You may be Penny's best friend, but you're mine, too. Please?"

She's made an art of begging to get her way, but I hear an authentic tone of misery in her voice. I let her stew a minute longer and turn to her. "I'm not mad anymore. It's just that I love you and Peter, and I don't want things to be weird."

She shrugs. "Well, it's not weird for me."

"That's because you're not human. It's usually not weird for me, and I want it to stay that way. But you bringing it up like that *was* weird, okay?" Ana looks properly scolded, so I wrap an arm around her. "You know you're one of my best friends. It'd be a shame if I had to kill you."

Ana kisses my cheek before we break apart to watch in opposite directions. There's not much to do. The road has only the occasional abandoned car and the adjoining streets are residential and empty. The roar of the tanker's pump and the portable pump we use to fill the tanks drown out any noise, so we have to rely on sight alone. The only other movement is Kyle, who stands out front of the Mobil. He lifts his chin and makes his way over to us.

"How's it going?" he asks. "The ground tanks are about full over there. John says the color looks good. It'll take ten minutes to fill the truck."

"Same over here," I say. "It'll be nice if we can go home after this."

Kyle nods and stands at attention, rifle against his shoulder. He wears dark sunglasses and his usual serious expression. One day I'm going to make him laugh his ass off, if it's the last thing I do. I look to where Peter, Dan and Nelly hold the hoses into the rectangular tanks in the pickup's bed. The drums are done, and the tanks won't take much longer. Caleb and Toby stand like tightrope walkers on the guardrail that separates the station from the vine-covered trees behind. Caleb points two fingers to his nose and does an arabesque.

I nudge Ana with my elbow. "Look at those idiots."

Kyle snorts and Ana laughs, but if Dan or Peter catches them they're never going on patrol again. Caleb hasn't been all there since Marcus died. I may not be the poster girl for sanity, but I've regained my sense of self-preservation, whereas Caleb hasn't.

"You guys okay here?" I ask. "I'm going to tell them to knock it off."

Toby wraps an arm around a spindly tree. At first it looks as though he's lost his balance in whatever game they were playing, but then I see the hands tangled in his dreadlocks, and he goes down with an open-mouthed scream I can't hear. Shadowy figures appear in the spaces between the trees. Caleb tries to leap, but his ankle is pulled out from under him. He slams face-first into the guardrail before being dragged back into the foliage.

Ana and I take off at a run. Our shouts are drowned out by the pump's motor. Finally, Nelly looks up when we're twenty feet away and follows our fingers to where Toby and Caleb were a moment ago. They're gone now, and in their place are a dozen Lexers. They spill over the guardrail one by one, first falling on the ground, and then slowly staggering to their feet.

Ana and I fire at their heads when they hit the asphalt. There are more than I thought. Too many. Another dozen trip over the guardrail at once, and then eight are on their feet, with more behind them.

The pickup slams to a halt beside us, and Peter leans across the seat to pop the passenger door. Ana and I cram ourselves into the front and watch the Lexers follow. A couple have faces smeared with the bright red of Toby and Caleb's blood.

"Where's John?" Ana yells.

"They're okay," Peter says.

He pulls out of the lot and stops in front of the Mobil, with Nelly and Dan behind in the other pickup. I breathe a sigh of relief when I see John and the rest moving toward us in the trucks. We roll down the road for a quarter of a mile and stop side by side with the tanker.

Zeke says, "What happened? Is everyone okay?"

Peter looks to us. There hasn't been time to explain, but he knows not everyone is okay.

I pop open the door and stand on the running board. "Caleb and Toby—" I choke on their names. "They weren't looking. They got pulled into the trees."

Zeke hangs his head, and I see the disbelief on the others' faces. John leans into my line of vision. "Could they be—"

I shake my head. There's no way they're alive. Stupid, stupid Caleb. He was only twenty, and Toby wasn't much older. If they were okay I'd smack them first and then hug them. I look down the road. The pod has hit the pavement and they're coming our way.

"There's nothing we can do," Zeke says. "Let's go."

The words may sound cold, but his face is haggard and his shoulders slump as he says them. And that's what we do: We leave people behind.

CHAPTER 57

There's nothing to bury, and neither of them had family left, so their belongings have gone to their closest friends or back into the general supplies. Dinner was a subdued affair, and we sit in shock at the tables after most people have left.

Liz's face is streaked with tears. She wipes at her face and inspects the wetness on her hand as though it's a foreign substance. "He was so annoying. Like a pesky, incestuous little brother." She sob-laughs. "I loved that kid."

I give her a hug. Her tough, sinewy body yields, and she holds me tight. We're having a bonfire in their honor tonight: our post-apocalyptic version of a wake. Caleb never got his birthday party, and Toby was always trying to arrange a bonfire and score alcohol to make it livelier. He rarely got the alcohol, but tonight we're going to drink it for him.

I help bring bottles of wine to the spot behind the first barn, up near the orchard. It's far enough away from the sleeping quarters that it won't wake the kids. We have all kinds of wine here; Jeff appropriates any uneaten or un-canned fruit for wine-making.

He takes a bottle out of the crate I set down and holds it up to the sunset. It matches the gold color of the sky. "Watermelon wine. It's just ready now, after a year. It's a tough one to make, but if it's done right, it's delicious. I make it sweet. Man, Toby wanted some in the worst way." He sets the bottle down and sighs. "I'd let him drink it all if he were here."

Meghan and some of the other girls drop their crates before they sit on a blanket. Usually they're big gigglers, but not tonight. Even the older folks are here, and some kids. I wave Bits over and find a spot on an old sheet with Henry and Hank.

Hank's eyes are gigantic. "Cassie, is it true that they just grabbed them? Right off a fence?"

Bits watches me closely. Henry shushes Hank, but there's no taking the question back.

"Yes," I say. "But they weren't being safe. They weren't paying attention. They were supposed to be watching their own backs, and ours, and they forgot how serious a job that was."

Hank shakes his head at Bits, who looks upset but not frightened. I take her hand in mine, and she looks around furtively; she doesn't want to be seen holding my hand. Henry gives me a join-the-club look, and I laugh. It's a good thing: I was afraid I was going to have to snuggle her to sleep when she was twenty.

"Bits and I would never do that," Hank says. "We have each others' backs. Right?"

"Even if you were trapped, with no hope of escape," Bits says, "I'd come for you." She squints into the distance, her smooth, freckled face screwed up in determination. Hank nods in satisfaction.

"I'm glad to hear that," Henry says. "Now I won't worry."

He coughs into his hand. The image of these two small-for-their-age kids saving the world is both incredibly sweet and hilarious.

"How are the new digs?" I ask Henry.

Two of the long cabins have been completed. Families get first dibs, and Hank and Henry moved into the second cabin a week ago.

"Great," Henry says. "And seeing as how I'm one of the electricians, I'm working out a way to get us some power for the winter. Those skylights are nice, but it's still gonna be dark."

"How about you hook up my cabin after that?" I ask with a wink.

He leans back and watches a young guy named Troy light the wood in the pit. "James and I already have the plans drawn up."

"I knew you were a keeper," I say. "One of the best things I ever did was to meet you, Henry." I'm joking, but that doesn't make it less true.

"We wouldn't have survived, Hank and I, without that gun you gave us at the campground."

This is America, land of the armed, and I'm sure they would have found something. But if his belief gives me electricity sooner rather than later, I won't argue.

"I wish Dot were here," he says. Bits and Hank are busy discussing something school-related, so they don't hear. The lines around his mouth turn down, and he shrugs in apology.

"I understand. It's a beautiful night." Even though we're gathered to mourn, it's also a celebration that we're alive. And we want the people we love at a celebration.

"I'm all he has left," Henry says quietly. "What if something happens to me?"

"You know I'd take care of Hank," I say. "I'd do anything to keep him safe. I promise you that."

Henry watches me, his brown eyes solemn. "You would, wouldn't you?"

"You would too, for Bits."

Henry puffs up his cheeks and releases a breath. "Yeah. I would."

"So we have a deal," I say, and hold out a hand.

He takes it in his. "Deal."

I take a sip of watermelon wine. Jeff wasn't kidding about the sugar. The sun has dipped behind the trees, and the woods beyond the fence and trench are already dark, but rays of sun still angle over the barn and orchard.

"I'll be back in a minute," I say.

I walk to the edge of the orchard, out of sight of the fire, and stand at Adrian's grave. At least he has a grave. Dot doesn't, neither do Caleb and Toby. I feel bad that I don't visit more often, but I can't find him here. I don't know where else to talk to him, though. Talking to the phone seems weird, although I feel him more when I hold it in my hands.

"I'm sorry," I whisper.

The apology slips out. I'm not sure what I mean at first, until I understand it's for trying to be happy without him. It's what I would want, if our roles were reversed, but I can't shake the feeling that it somehow belittles what we had. I should be tearing my clothes, throwing myself on his funeral pyre, but instead I keep on going. Because that's what we do.

CHAPTER 58

The bonfire is at full-tilt. There's no way all this noise isn't drawing Lexers, but no one seems to care. I know I don't. My face is flushed with wine, and when Nelly tries to talk to me on the blanket, I point a finger at him.

"I'm still mad at you," I say. I sound sloppy drunk.

Nelly doesn't look much better than I sound; even his hair looks drunk. He kneels and puts a heavy hand on my knee. "C'mon. You know I love you, Half-pint."

"Promise you'll stop bothering me about this, then."

"Not fair! You bother me all the time."

I press my forehead against his. "That's different. You don't feel like a bad person. You can tease me about something else."

We're so close that in the firelight he has four eyes, and all of them blink slowly. His forehead rubs mine when he shakes his head. "You are not a bad pershon. Did I just say *pershon?*"

I crack up. He pulls me down so we're lying on our backs. "Per-sssson," he says. "You know what I mean. You're not a bad one."

Penny sits next to us and hands me a canteen of water. "Drink, both of you. Do you know how annoying it is to be missing the first full-on drinking party in a year?"

I put my hand on her stomach. "You're creating a person, Pentastic. You're beautiful and brimming with life. It's a miracle!" I enunciate each word clearly, but it still comes out sounding like a drunken sorority girl.

"You should be high on life!" Nelly yells. "All we have is this here delicious wine." He attempts a sip, but since he's lying down, half of it runs to his neck.

"And you have no idea how annoying drunk people are when you're not drunk," Penny mutters. "Promise me a party after I pop this kid out."

"Absolutely," I say. "Abso-fruitly!"

"I'm going to bed," Penny says, looking somewhat mollified. "Want me to take Bits? Or are you so drunk that you've lost her?" The corner of her mouth rises.

"Hey! What are you trying to say? She went with Henry and Hank. They stopped to get her cot so she could sleep over. I know where my kid is!"

"It's ten p.m. Do you know where your children are?" Nelly says, like the gloomy voice in the old PSA. Penny sighs when we roll around in drunken laughter.

She bids us goodnight, and we lie on the blanket and talk until Nelly begins to yawn. "Today sucked," he says. "God, it sucked."

"That's why we're drunk."

"Uh-huh. And that's why I'm going to bed. Tomorrow's another day."

"What? Don't leave me."

Nelly sits up. His smile isn't his usual smirk. "Don't worry, there's someone waiting in the wings. He has been all night. Good night, darlin'."

He kisses my forehead and slowly rises to his feet. I'm about to follow when Dan appears next to me. I take the full cup out of his hand and swig.

"Haven't you had enough?" he asks.

"Nope," I say. "I'm just getting started. The fun has just begun." Except it comes out as *hash jusht begun.*

He nods, straight-faced, and I push him. "You're right. Okay, I'm done. Do you want your prize?"

"What prize?"

"I got you a prize today. Don't get too excited, though. It's not that great." He stares at me without blinking. "What? Is that weird?"

"No, it's not weird. It's nice."

His whole face shines. It makes me wonder if I should have said anything, and I try to play it down. "Well, like I said, don't get too excited. It's in my cabin. Walk me to get it?"

Dan pulls me to standing. I walk beside him, chattering about everything and nothing, partly because he's so quiet, and partly because it keeps my mind off of Caleb and Toby. I run to the cabin to grab my leather jacket and meet him at his tent. The tent floor trips me on my way in, and I giggle when I sprawl on the ground.

"You are very drunk," Dan says.

"I am very drunk. Are you?"

He looks down at his feet. "Sober as a judge. I didn't feel like drinking."

"I didn't feel like sobering," I say, which gets a small laugh. "I don't want to think. It's a night off from thinking. Hey, it's a slogan— Drinking: a night off from thinking!"

"I like you this way. Maybe I should get you drunk more often."

I hold out my hands for him to pull me up, but instead he hooks his arms under my knees and shoulders and hoists me onto his mattress. I scramble to a sitting position and pull his prize out of my coat. "Ta-da!"

He holds the Red Sox baseball cap in his hands and turns it over carefully, like it's made of china. "Thank you, Cass," he says softly.

He looks so pleased, and while I want him to be pleased, I don't want him to think of it as anything more than a friendly present. "It's just a hat. I know how much you miss the Red Sox, and when I saw it in the store today I thought of you."

"Thanks for thinking of me."

"Sure." I drop on my back. There was a lot of wine consumed tonight, and I'm starting to pay for it. The room has begun a slow rotation that is kicking into high gear. I turn on my side and close my eyes to stop the spinning, but it throws it even more off-kilter. "Not feeling very good. Have to sleep."

"Okay," Dan says, and strokes my hair. It slows the spinning and gives me something to concentrate on.

"Don't stop," I say. "It makes the world straight."

"I won't. You're a funny one, Dingbat."

And then I remember nothing, until Dan climbs under the blankets and pulls me to his chest. I only wake for a second, but it's long enough to hear him murmur, "Love you."

Now I'm the one who's sober as a judge. I don't love him back. I won't ever love him back. I stare into the dark until his breathing is deep, and then I gather everything, including my spare toothbrush and jeans that live in the corner of his tent, and return to my cabin.

CHAPTER 59

"I wish you didn't have to go," I say to Nelly.

He brushes his hair back and glances to where Zeke waits in the tanker truck. "I was thinking that I could convince Adam to move here."

I grab his hand and jump up and down. "What? Really?"

He forces me to a stop. "Calm down, you. That doesn't mean Adam will say yes. Even Zeke was talking about combining Safe Zones this morning at breakfast. Which reminds me—why were you curled up on the loveseat when I left?"

"You were hogging my bed." It's not the answer he was looking for, and he waits expectantly. "It's over. Not a big deal, okay?"

"Something happened."

"You have to go," I say, and give him a friendly push. "Go get your stuff and move back. We'll talk more then."

He steps backward reluctantly. "It won't be right away. Before winter, though. Are you all right?"

"Of course," I lie. "I hate you, a lot."

"I hate you more."

With a light heart, I watch the trucks rumble down the driveway. Nelly's coming back.

***

I've switched with Liz for guard tonight. It's been difficult to avoid Dan all day, but I've managed it by working in the garden picking tomatoes and eating dinner in the cabin. I'm on the east fence with George, an older guy with thinning hair and a beer gut that must be caused by something other than beer these days.

"I went to the zoo the other day," George says. "There was only one dog in it. It was a shitzu."

I laugh even though it's ridiculous. He's been telling me terrible jokes for the past thirty minutes.

"I have one. It's my favorite," I say. "Knock, knock."

"Who's there?"

"Interrupting cow."

"Interrupting co—"

"Moo!" I whisper-yell.

George chuckles. I lean back in my chair and drum my fingers on the armrest. Guard is boring, but I don't feel like testing out my new sleeping arrangements.

Dan appears in the lamplight. "Hey."

I mumble a greeting and look away with my chest thumping. He and George talk for a few minutes before Dan looks at me. "Can I talk to you?"

"Well, I'm on guard. I can't leave."

"Oh, go ahead," George says. "I can hold down the fort. That trench has almost made guard a waste of time, not that I'm complaining. I'll think up some new jokes while you're gone."

"Thanks," I say, although I want to bonk him on the head with my spike.

"We'll be in the school if you need us," Dan says.

I follow him to the little building. He lights a lamp and turns to me. "What's up?"

"What's up?" I repeat. "You're the one who wanted to talk."

I fix my gaze on the projects hung on the wall of the reading area. The self-portraits came out great. Bits has drawn herself dressed like Ana, but with a tiara and fairy wings.

"You left last night," he says.

"I always leave."

"But you don't take your toothbrush and avoid me all day."

"Well, it has been three weeks," I say lightly, although this moment is anything but funny.

He looks dumbfounded before he realizes what I mean, and then his shoulders harden. "I didn't ask you to leave. In fact, I don't want you to leave. So, what's going on?"

"I just think it would be better if we didn't see each other anymore," I say. "I need some time."

I finger papers on Penny's desk. Dan moves closer and touches my arm. "Maybe I can help. I don't want to not see each other. Talk to me."

I'm going to have to tell him. I take a breath and say, "I heard what you said. Last night, when you got in bed."

He stares down at his boots before he looks me square in the eye. "It's true."

"You can't. It's only been a few weeks."

"I've known you since last summer."

"That's not what this...thing is about," I say.

"So what's it about? You using me as a sleeping pill? Thanks for that."

His tone is sarcastic, and his mouth settles into a hard line. I thought what we were doing was pretty clear. He's changed the rules on me, and now he wants me to feel guilty about it. I don't need one more thing in my life to feel guilty about.

My laugh is unkind. "Using *you*? This is what you do. What am I—girl number four, six, eight?"

His face is red, but he takes a deep breath and says, "It doesn't matter. You're the girl I want."

"I told you I couldn't do this. That I wasn't ready. You said we were just having fun."

"I lied." His glassy eyes meet mine for a long moment before he breaks contact. "I lied because I thought you might have feelings for me, but you won't even try."

"I won't *try*? I shouldn't have to *try*, Dan. Feelings are either there or they aren't."

"You won't let yourself have feelings. The minute we get close, you back off. I can see it happen."

He's trying to argue me into this, and it's not going to work. I don't know why he won't let me off the hook. Of course I back away from feelings; the person I thought I'd spend my life with has been dead for a few months, and all of that died with him. I'm angry at Dan for putting me in this position, but I can't help feeling sorry that his pained expression is because of me.

"I like you, and I don't want to hurt you, but I don't feel that way. It's not you. I won't ever feel that way about anyone. That's why we shouldn't do this anymore."

"All right. Fine." He gives a humorless laugh and spins to the door. I breathe a sigh of relief that we're done, but then he turns. "Are you sure?"

This is torture. He's torturing us both. "Yes," I whisper.

He slams the door behind him. I'm only telling the truth. He made me tell the truth. And although I know I did the right thing, I wonder how satisfying it'll be to sleep with a ghost for the rest of my life.

CHAPTER 60

I don't have to avoid Dan because he has that covered. His name has been erased from the schedule and put on shifts where I won't be. It hurts my feelings, which is ridiculous, since I don't want to be on the same shifts either. But knowing that he's purposely steering clear of me makes me feel worse. He eats dinner later and at a different table. I didn't realize how used to him I was, how much he was a part of my day, until now.

I haven't done much guard the past week, anyway. Caleb and Toby's deaths have made us more careful, more afraid. We haven't done any patrols except a local trip to salvage some lumber and blueberries from one of the abandoned farms. We have plenty of fuel, and the garden must be tamed, so I've spent most shifts canning the produce we don't eat.

My fingers are stained purple from the blueberry jam I've been making the past two days. We've set up two cookstoves in the gravel lot, and I stand at one stirring the blueberry pulp. It's hot labor, but nothing compared to what it would be in the kitchen.

"We ran out of pectin," I explain to Meghan. "Which means you have to cook the fruit longer so it will set up in the jars. We could add apples, if we wanted. They have a lot of natural pectin."

Meghan bobs her head and lifts her spoon to check the thickness of the fruit. "I don't think it's done yet."

"A few more minutes, it looks like."

She sneaks a glance at me. "Can I ask you something?"

I nod, but I don't like the look on her face. It's the look of someone who's going to ask you something personal.

"Are you and Dan still seeing each other?" she asks.

"Nope," I say, and bang my spoon on the pot's edge.

"I was just wondering. You know how we saw each other for a while?" She giggles. I hope she gets to the point soon. If she doesn't, she might end up wearing a pot of blueberry puree. "Well, I thought maybe we would again, but I didn't want to get in the middle of anything."

"Go for it," I say brightly.

I've been able to sleep in the past week, but it's not as nice as having someone next to me. And maybe not just someone—it's nice to sleep next to Dan. I miss him, but I wasn't lying when I said I wasn't in love with him. That kind of love isn't something I can do right now. I shouldn't have jumped into anything in the first place.

"I think it's ready," Meghan says when the jam is thick on the spoon. I show her how to ladle it into the jars and place them in the canner.

"Now, we wait," I say. "Then we take them out and—voila—jam."

Ana walks up wearing a floppy garden hat and a dress. If it weren't for the dirt up her arms, she could be going to a tea party. Normally, I would make fun of her outfit, but her face is tight. "Another Safe Zone's gone. John just heard."

"Which one?" I ask.

"Iowa."

I picture a map of the Unites States. "That's north. Maybe they're heading north, like James said."

"Yeah, but this one broadcasted. They said something about a giant pod before they lost communication."

"They didn't say how big?"

"No," Ana says. "Whoever was on at Whitefield says they might have said 'thousand' or 'thousands,' but it wasn't clear."

My mouth drops. A thousand. Maybe even thousands—plural. The trench would never catch them all. The fence would collapse for sure. I'm cold suddenly, even with the heat of the cookstove and midsummer sun.

"What does that mean?" Meghan asks. She wraps her fingers around Ana's wrist. "Are we safe?"

Ana pats Meghan's hand. "We're never safe, Meghan. Never."

***

James has tried to calculate where the pod might be, based on how long it took them to get to Iowa. "Maybe halfway here, if some came this way. I wouldn't send Dwayne out yet, not with his range of six hundred miles. Maybe next week."

John and Ben nod. It's after the dinner hour, and all the adults who were interested stayed to talk. Enough people were interested that it's standing room only.

Mikayla sits next to Ben, hands in her lap. I don't know that I've ever seen her so still. "But that doesn't mean they are coming here, right?"

James shakes his head. "We don't know anything other than the fact that Iowa's gone and they said a lot of Lexers were there. That's it."

People murmur. Josephine tightens her hand on her throat. I look to where Dan stands, Meghan beside him. He glances at me and then away in time to miss the smile I offer.

"There's nothing we can do but wait," John says. "And have our plan in place. You've all got a bug out bag in your assigned vehicle. If you don't, see me after the meeting. The plan is to head north through Canada, to Alaska or Whitehorse. Everyone knows that, right? In case we get separated."

John's voice is steady, and the murmurs lessen. I'm not the only one he makes feel safe. After a few more questions, to which there are no good answers, everyone heads to bed. We walk into the night. Not knowing what lies in the darkness behind the fence is bad enough, but tonight's discussion has made the night seem darker and more foreboding than usual. James guides Penny by the small of her back. She pulls away and glares at him.

"I know how to walk," she snaps. James lifts his hands in apology. "I'm sorry. Guys, I'm scared. What if they come? I can't run. I'm as big as a freakin' house, and I'm not getting any smaller."

"You won't have to run," Ana says, and puts her arm around her sister's shoulder. "We'll get you out of here. *I'll* get you out of here. You and my niece. James, you're on your own."

James laughs. "That's good enough for me."

"My God, what has the world come to?" Penny asks. "My bratty little sister has to protect me from zombies." She ignores Ana's yell of protest and pulls me to her other side.

"The fact that Ana protects anyone from anything other than bad fashion is mind-blowing," I say.

We cackle when Ana screeches. We've teased her like this since she was little. I tug on her hair, and she joins in our laughter. I may no longer have a brother, but I'm so lucky to have my sisters.

CHAPTER 61

I leave breakfast early to attend to the fall vegetable starts that will go in the ground soon. For the first time in my life, I wish it were December with a huge ice storm on the way. The farm has always had something of a nervous undercurrent running through it, which makes sense when you consider our circumstances, but now there's no *under* about it. You can feel it, like the low hum of electricity through wire. You can see it in the nervous way people watch the south fence.

I duck my head when I pass Dan's tent, but someone chooses that moment to exit the door. I will myself to be invisible and look straight ahead.

"Good morning, Cassie!" Meghan calls. She waves and heads for the other end of the farm.

I wave and speed to the greenhouse, where I busy myself watering the plants. It didn't take them long. I know I can't expect Dan to agree to an arrangement that doesn't work for him, but I'm resentful that Meghan gets the uncomplicated relationship I wanted.

Dan clomps into the greenhouse wearing unlaced boots. His hair is messy, like he spent the morning in bed. Which he did, of course. "That wasn't what it looked like," he says.

I set down the watering can. "It didn't look like anything except Meghan leaving your tent in the morning. You don't owe me an explanation."

He leans on my potting bench with an earnest expression. "She stopped by to say hi, even though she knew I was on guard last night. She woke me up."

"Don't you love when people do that?" I ask, to keep the conversation going. I don't want to go back to not speaking to each other. "They say, 'Are you awake? No? Well, I just want to tell you one little thing, then you can go back to sleep.'"

Dan laughs and sticks his finger into a pot of soil. "And Meghan can talk."

"She's very chipper."

"She's extremely chipper." Dan looks at me sideways. "I'm all for being a morning person, but she takes it to another level."

"Yeah." I chew on my lip, not sure if this conversation means we're friends again.

"I'm sorry," Dan says quickly.

"You don't have to apologize."

"Yeah, I do. You told me what you wanted. You never promised me anything. It wasn't fair of me to get angry. It's just that you put me in the friend zone, and I didn't like it."

"The friend zone?"

"As opposed to the boyfriend zone."

"Right," I say. "I like having you in my friend zone, you know."

"I like being there."

"So stay and help me?"

He takes the watering can and looks to me for instructions. Things still feel strained, and I don't want them to be.

"Can you sing?" I ask, because there's no better way to break the ice than a sing-along, except maybe a dance party. But Dan might not be up for a dance party first thing in the morning.

"What? Um, I'm okay, I guess. Why?"

"Because we sing to the plants here. What song do you want to sing?"

He laughs, but when he sees I'm dead serious, he thinks and says, "You like Radiohead, right?"

"Is it possible to only *like* Radiohead? Name a song."

" 'No Surprises,' " Dan says.

"That's the perfect song for our lives."

Dan knocks on his forehead. "It's been in my head for a year."

"Not only is it perfect, but it's one I have." I reach in my pocket and pull out Adrian's phone.

"I'm actually going to get to hear it?"

I scroll through and press play. The lullaby-like beginning of the song starts. Dan closes his eyes. "Shit," he says.

We go through all of *OK Computer*, *The Bends* and *Amnesiac*. The plants have long been watered, and we sit against the bench, phone balanced on my knee, when the battery finally dies.

"These were some of the best hours of my life," Dan says. "This, right here. Thanks."

It was up there, in terms of finding something beautiful, something you'd never thought you'd have again. A few hours where the old world was so close you could almost believe it still existed.

"Thank *you*. It's better to listen with someone who loves it as much as I do."

"I could go all day," he says wistfully.

"Well, we're not done. We still have more albums and the B sides. I can charge it now so we can listen later."

"Yeah?"

"If you want." I stare out the glass and feel stupid for being presumptuous. We might be friends, but that doesn't mean he wants to hang out with me; there are other girls he could play Parcheesi with.

"I want," he says.

His answer makes me happier than I'd anticipated. I push his leg with mine. "See? The friend zone isn't all bad."

Dan pushes me back. "Dingbat."

***

It's dark when I announce myself at Dan's tent. He looks up from where he sits on the bed, a board game covered with colorful squares and circles in front of him.

"Parcheesi," he says with an impish grin. "For real. I found it in the game stuff."

I laugh. "Do you even know how to play?"

"Nope. But we're gonna learn."

I plug the phone into the tiny speakers I found in Adrian's things and set it on the bed. "Sounds good. But I suck at every board game but Scrabble. I lose Monopoly one hundred percent of the time. Seriously, I never, ever win."

"You let people live rent-free, don't you?" Dan asks.

"I feel bad when they don't have enough money. How'd you know?"

"I knew it the moment I saw you, when you all pulled up in the VW last year. You had your hair in buns and that green shirt with the gloves pulled up—"

"I don't even remember what I was wearing. How do you remember that?"

Dan looks at me like I should already know the answer. "Because every guy my age has a thing for Princess Leia. So, anyway, I thought, 'That girl right there is a terrible capitalist.' "

"That's the first thing you thought?"

"That's what I always think of the first time I see a pretty girl—economic systems."

"And you say I'm weird." He laughs when I toss a piece of the game at him. "Okay, deal me in or whatever one does in this game."

A while later we're tied 2-2, and I can't stop yawning. Dan packs Parcheesi in its box and sets it on the floor. "The meteor showers are over, but you can still see a lot this time of year."

"I know. I've been watching."

"You have? Do you want to watch now? You can sleep here if you want—friend zone only, I promise. I'd like it..."

He trails off and picks at a thread on his jeans while I ruminate on his invitation. I should probably go home. We made up hours ago and already I'm having a sleepover. But I want to watch the stars and fall asleep under his blankets. I just don't want to give him the wrong idea.

"Forget it," he says, at the same time as I say, "Okay."

"But," I continue, "since it's a friend zone sleepover, does that mean we do facials and paint each other's nails?"

"I had two bossy older sisters. I've done it all. I can give a pedicure like nobody's business."

"I'm filing that away for future reference. Bits is asleep, but I'll just sneak in and grab my stuff."

When I get back from washing up and changing into pajamas, he's already in bed with the lantern off. I get under the covers. "Do I still get to put my feet on you?"

"Nope. That's a boyfriend zone perk."

I shake my head and smile up at the stars, but he moves his leg so I can tuck my feet under anyway.

"Maybe you'll watch the Leonid meteor shower with me," Dan says.

"When's that?"

"Mid-November. Sometimes, when the moon is bright, you have to wait for it to set before you can see them. My dad used to wake us before dawn. We'd bundle up and drink hot chocolate while we watched."

November's months away. Maybe he's asking if I'll still be here. I jiggle my toes under his thigh. "That sounds fun. Bits would love that. If there's hot chocolate involved, she's there."

"It's a date." There's a drawn-out pause, and then he says, "Sort of."

He quizzes me on the constellations until we're too tired to keep our eyes open. I turn on my side and drift off, feet pressed against his leg. I may be using Dan as a heater, but I'm not using him for anything else—I want to be here.

CHAPTER 62

The next morning, we wake to loud voices and footsteps. Outside, we follow the people walking hurriedly toward the orchard. I hear the Lexers before I see them—a cacophony of hissing and grunts, followed by thuds. There must be a hundred already in the trench, with another couple hundred bringing up the rear. They stagger forward and fall in, then rise and wander the hole, looking for a way out.

Thank God for the trench. If three hundred Lexers focused all their energy on one section of the fence, we might not have time to kill them before it caved. The trench may be a savior, but killing all these Lexers is going to suck. I mentally cross off all the things I've planned for my free afternoon.

"Wow," Bits says. She sidles up and takes my hand in hers. "That's a lot of Lexers!"

"Bits, go back to school!" I say. "Why are you here?"

"I had to go to the bathroom. I wanted to see what was going on."

"Okay, you saw. Now, c'mon, let's go back."

She plants her feet apart and stares, but she looks more intrigued than terrified. "Wait a second. I'm getting some good ideas for the comic."

"Bits, as much as I love for art to imitate life, you shouldn't be here."

Dan picks up Bits and swings her around. "You need to be in school, kiddo."

Her peals of laughter cause the Lexers in the trench to move to our side and howl. They may be stuck in a hole thirty feet from the fence line, but Bits's cheeks lose some of their color. I'm glad—a little frightened is good. Toby and Caleb weren't frightened enough, and look what happened.

"Okay," Bits says, "but I want Dan to walk me."

She bats her big blue eyes at him, and he gives her his full-wattage grin. I swear she swoons. I don't care, as long as it gets her away from the fence. We drop her at school, and Dan walks me to my cabin.

"I had fun last night," I say. "Thanks."

"So did I. I'm glad you stayed."

"Me, too. I'll see you in the trenches. Literally."

Dan groans but walks away laughing.

***

There are a couple of bright spots to spending your afternoon killing three hundred Lexers. The first is that it makes three hundred fewer Lexers in the world. The second is that we've seen the black moss on almost all of them. Most have a small patch or two, but some are half-covered, and a very few drag themselves along the ground like snails, leaving a trail of slimy flesh juice. The last take almost no killing; they separate from the bone like pulled pork.

A few people use arrows, but no one here is particularly skilled in archery, and most of the arrows glance off skulls and onto the ground. The crossbow bolts we have are shorter, which makes them difficult to remove from a brain cavity for cleaning. Ana and I sit close enough to the edge to pierce them in the eye with one of the longer spikes. By number twenty it's become routine. By number forty my arm is numb and my mouth tastes rotten from the stench. Finally, they all lay motionless in the trench, and we sit against the fence and guzzle water.

"What are we going to do with all these bodies?" I ask John.

"We'll cart them down to the field, same as always," John says. "We might need a new one soon, the way things are going."

We can't let them stay here. Not only do they take up too much room, but they also stink to high heaven. And that's not going to get better before it gets much, much worse. I pull my gloves back on. The trench doesn't span the whole farm; areas like the driveway before the first gate and a few other places were left as solid ground to drive machinery through. It's in one of these spots that we lower a metal ramp for John to back the first trailer down.

Even with using every truck, it's almost dark by the time we've removed the bodies and tossed them into the field that's become our graveyard. My muscles ache from swinging dead weight around. I rest my head on the pickup's seat and close my eyes.

"I'm guessing you're not in the mood for Parcheesi," Dan says, after we've driven through the gate for the final time.

"Shower. Sleep. I need to make sure Bits is okay. I want to stay with her tonight."

"Yeah, of course," he says, but I can tell he's disappointed.

Dan's heading to his empty tent after this long and discouraging day, while I'll be in a cabin filled with warmth and company. He has friends, but not ones like I do—people I knew before all of this, whose companionship I'd choose even if the world hadn't ended. I've been holding him at arm's length. If we're going to be friends, I'm going to have to let him in.

"Why don't you come to the cabin for a little while? Hang out with Bits while I shower. I told Ana and Peter I'd grab food from the kitchen. Mikayla saved dinner for us."

He pulls the truck into its spot. Someone else is going to clean it out; we've done enough for one day. "I'll clean up and be there in ten."

By the time I've showered and brought back pasta and bread, Dan and Bits are deep in conversation at the table. Sparky sits in his lap and pushes against his hand while he rubs the magic spot behind her ears. Ana and Peter shoot me amused glances from the loveseat.

"Cassie," Bits says with a frown, "Dan told me you don't like him."

I set down the bowls and bread basket. "What? I like Dan."

"No, *like* like. I asked him who he likes, and he said you. And that you don't like him back, but it's okay because you're friends."

My own words are coming back to haunt me. Next she'll be asking me about bases. Dan stands to help me dish out the food.

"Hey, she asked," he says. "I wasn't going to lie." I could be irritated he's telling Bits this stuff, but Dan makes it hard to be angry with him.

"Well, now that you've answered one question, get ready for the third degree," I say. "You deserve it."

"Bring it on."

Ana takes a bite of her pasta salad and says, "There's ham in here. Who are we eating?"

"Gus," I answer.

She puts down her bowl with a grimace. "I liked Gus. He was cute."

"Ana won't have anything to do with the butchering," Peter explains to Dan. "She cries whenever they kill one of the animals."

"I do not cry!"

"No, she just leaks water from her eyes," I say. "She spends butchering day on the other side of the farm with her fingers in her ears."

"Who knew the Queen of Death had a soft spot?" Dan says. Ana smiles and rips into a piece of bread.

Bits shoves a bite in her mouth and grins. "Mm, Gus!"

"Bits, on the other hand, has absolutely no problem with it," Peter says.

I take a bite; Gus really is tasty. Dan leans back with his bowl in his hand, completely at ease. He drops a piece of ham for Barnaby, who gobbles it up, and then feeds Sparky one.

"So, do you like dogs or cats better?" Bits asks Dan.

"Both. I like cats because they're easy, but they have personality. I like dogs because they're goofy and loyal."

"Barn's really goofy," Bits says, and rubs Barn's back with her foot. "But we love him anyway. What's your favorite color?"

"Green."

"What's the worst thing that ever happened to you? Besides zombies."

Dan looks at me. "You weren't kidding. Um, when my aunt died."

"Best thing?"

"When I was seven and my brother broke my collarbone while we were wrestling."

"What?" Bits asks, mouth open. "How could that be the best thing?"

"I was in Little League, which meant I had games and practice on the weekends. I liked playing, but my brother got to stay home and watch cartoons."

"Why didn't he have to play?" Bits asks.

"Because Mike was older. He'd already played for a few years. Anyway, on the same weekend as what was going to be the biggest Little League game of the year, my dad got invited to Fenway Park before it opened. That's the Red Sox stadium."

"I know," Bits says. "My dad loved the Red Sox."

"I knew I liked you," Dan says, and Bits grins. "Well, I got to go instead of Mike because he'd broken my collarbone and I didn't have the game. It was first thing in the morning. I got to stand on the field. It was the most beautiful thing I'd ever seen in my life. I got to touch the Green Monster."

Bits and Peter nod like they have any idea what he's talking about. It sounds vaguely indecent to me. I ask, "What the heck is the Green Monster and why did you want to touch it?"

"The scoreboard," Dan says. "It's a huge wooden board, painted green. It's still changed by hand. It's amazing. It was one of the best days of my life."

I shake my head. "The scoreboard has a name? Who gives a scoreboard a name? I'll never understand sports."

"How many years of watching the Super Bowl did it take for you to realize they didn't always start in the middle?" Peter asks. He was never much of a sports watcher, but he laughed at me the whole night when I finally figured that out.

"Twenty-eight," I say proudly. "And that's because I see the Super Bowl as a food and drink event with annoying noise playing in the background."

"That doesn't surprise me," Dan says, and eyes my second helping of pasta. Like he should talk: he's on bowl three. "So that's why it was the best thing. I also got to choose which cartoons we watched that whole spring. All I had to do was pretend to be upset about missing baseball."

Bits leans across the table with shifty eyes. "That was kind of sneaky."

"I know," Dan says with conspiratorial wink.

Bits sighs, probably because she would give anything for some Saturday morning cartoons, of anyone's choosing. So would I. We eat by the light of the lantern while Bits interrogates him more. He asks her a million questions, and only after she's run through every one of her likes and dislikes does he stand.

"I should go," he says. "It's been a long day."

Bits hangs around Dan's neck until Peter tickles her off. I follow Dan into the night and stand on the bottom step. "You have a not-so-secret admirer."

"She reminds me of you, you know," Dan says. "Down to the freckles."

"I wish I still had face freckles. They're pretty much gone, except for the gazillion on the rest of me."

"You're perfect."

My stomach churns at the affection in his voice. I'm so far from perfect it's not funny. "Please don't say stuff like that. It's not true, first of all, and it makes me feel weird."

"Isn't that what you once said? That the other person should be perfect for you?" I focus my gaze on the neighboring cabin, and he turns my chin back his way. "Sorry. I won't say it again. Okay?"

"Okay."

The smile that's probably won more women than I can count spreads across his face. "But I'm gonna wear you down one of these days."

I turn to the door to hide my own smile. "Goodnight, Danny."

"Goodnight, Dingbat."

His footsteps crunch toward his tent. I wouldn't mind being worn down by Dan and almost dared him to try. I don't think it's possible, but he'd be my first choice.

CHAPTER 63

The sound of the air horn makes me jump, even though I knew it was coming. I leave my crate of zucchini in the garden and walk toward the school. There's another burst, and then another. Three bursts means move straight to your assigned bug out vehicle. Do not pass go, do not collect two hundred dollars.

The kids pour out of the school with Penny herding behind. She has a list in her hand and reminds everyone where they're to go. They chatter, but when I raise my eyebrows they quiet down. I take Bits's hand and head for the VW bus. Peter, Ana, Penny, James and Maureen join us. We only need John and we're all accounted for. It's a lot of people to cram in the bus, but we refuse to separate; too much can go wrong out there. Shawn souped up the VW's engine this winter, and it zooms up and down hills like a dream. Or at least better than it did.

I wave at where Hank and Henry stand near the large school bus. The bus holds half the farm and enough diesel to get them far into Canada is strapped to the roof in metal cans. Josephine stands beside Henry with her hand clamped on Jasmine's shoulder. Jasmine winces and pats her mother's hip, but, if anything, it makes Josephine more anxious.

Dan leans against the ambulance with Mike, Rohan and three others. All of the vehicles have been stocked with a week's worth of supplies and sharp weapons. Some have guns, but most of us wear ours, now that it's summer. Our packs are small; otherwise, we'd have no room for passengers.

The last stragglers meet up with their vehicles. John checks his watch and calls out, "Ten minutes, not bad. But three bursts is serious. You might not have ten minutes in a real emergency. Remember, I'll always announce a drill beforehand. If you hear those three bursts, and there's been no announcement, it's not a drill."

Heads move up and down. The sun filters through the trees that border the lot, and birds call to each other. It's so peaceful, unlike what it would be if this was for real.

"Okay," John says. "Good job, everyone."

People walk away from their assigned vehicle, the somber mood replaced by laughter. Barnaby and Gwen, another dog, sit on the gravel, tongues lolling. There's no way Barnaby can fit in the VW with us, so he's been assigned to the small school bus. I'm glad—I want Barn to make it, but I'd prefer he shed and slobber somewhere else.

"What about Sparky?" Bits asks. "I have to get her."

"No, Bits," Peter says. "You come straight here. If it's two bursts, you still come straight here and one of us will find her."

Her eyes fill immediately. "But we can't leave her here! She'll die!"

"Bits, this is very important," I say, and take her shoulders. "I'll get Sparky, okay? You get to the VW. That's your only job, understand?"

"Promise you'll save her?"

I can't promise that, but I don't mind lying this once if it'll get her here. "Promise. Now back to school, Bitsy."

I shrug at my vehicle partners after she's left. "You know there's a good chance she'll go after Sparky anyway, right?"

Peter watches her skip up the steps of the school cabin. "She doesn't want anyone to die, including that cat. I'll get Bits. You get Sparky, but only if you can."

"And I'll drive," Ana says. She takes in everyone's horrified expressions and sighs. "Kidding. Relax, people."

***

There haven't been any more giant pods like the last, but dozens of Lexers fall in the trench every day. We've taken to leaving them until there are enough to warrant a trip down the road.

"Let's take them to the new field," John says, while we load the trailers with the latest bodies. "The holes are dug. We'll use it until they're full and then find another one."

The field to which we move the corpses is devoid of grass and dotted with deep holes. We used to burn the bodies when a hole was full, but it takes a lot of fuel to get a hot enough fire going. Otherwise we end up with barbecued Lexer and no space to burn the next group. Now, with so many Lexers, it doesn't make sense. We just make sure they're far enough away not to contaminate anything useful.

We drag and toss them into the deep holes. I can usually distract myself from what I'm touching, but I gag when the meat of a particularly mossy one's arm slips off the bone and remains in my grip.

"That's disgusting," Jamie says from the corpse next to mine.

I gingerly grab the wrist bones and pull. The woman slides to the ground, and her shirt falls open. The moss has eaten a gaping hole in her belly that's filled with writhing maggot-type bugs. I gag again, but it's good news, no matter how disgusting. I've never seen a single insect on a Lexer.

"Look," I say. "Something's living in her."

By the looks on everyone's faces you'd think we were staring at a newborn baby or something miraculous. But it is miraculous, if you think about it—it could mean the birth of a world without zombies.

CHAPTER 64

Nelly sent a message yesterday saying he needed to talk during John's radio shift. I stand next to John and pick up the handset at the sound of his voice. "Hey, Nels."

"How goes it, Half-pint?"

"It goes good. How about you?"

"I have some news." He pauses for a full minute. I'm about to shriek at him to tell me already, when his voice comes again. "So, do you want to hear it?"

"Nelly, stop messing with me!" I yell into the radio. John chuckles at my look of exasperation.

"We're moving back in October."

I jump up and down with a squeal. Nelly can't hear me, but John sticks a finger in his ear like I broke his eardrum.

"Adam found someone to take over the school," Nelly says. "You guys are going to need a teacher anyway, with Penny having the baby."

"Oh, that's cool." I say in a bored voice and wink at John.

The radio is silent. I can almost see Nelly's expression of bewilderment. "You're fucking with me, aren't you?"

I press the button. "Yes."

"And on our precious radio time, too."

"You started it."

He laughs. "So, less than two months."

"Two months," I repeat. "I can't freaking wait!"

"That's better. I almost changed my mind for a minute."

"Don't you dare. I'll come get you myself if you try."

"Don't worry, we're coming," he says. "Come hell or high water. I have to go, they need the radio. I just wanted to let you know. Hate you."

"Hate you back," I say. "Bye."

I hang up the handset and turn to John. "Well, that's good news," he says.

"It's the best news."

I leave to tell Penny, who was looking for an excuse to let the kids do whatever they wanted for the rest of the afternoon. We decided to run school all summer to keep the kids away from the fences, but it's more like summer camp.

"I was worried about the kids. I mean, I knew between everyone here they wouldn't end up dumb, but still," she says with a grin. "What if she's colicky or something? I couldn't teach with her screaming all day."

We all refer to the baby as a girl. They haven't even picked out a boy's name.

"If she's colicky you'll hand her off to me. That's the nice thing about commune living—there are plenty of arms."

"Maureen's practically salivating at the thought," Penny says. "Her daughter had just had her first grandchild last spring. She'd only seen her once."

"You'll be lucky if you get to hold her an hour out of every day."

"You can have nights."

"Thanks a lot." I pat her belly. I'm allowed to pat at will, unlike the rest of the farm who have to ask first. "She can stay with me anytime because she's going to be a perfect angel. Right, Maria?"

"That's the first time anyone's called her Maria out loud." Penny looks down, but not before I see her lips tremble, and I touch her arm in apology. "It's okay. I just wish my mom were here. I'm scared, especially for when this kid wants to come out. I don't even want to think about that part. You know she's going to have to come out, right?"

I wince and then laugh at the terror on her face. "I know. But I'll be with you the whole time."

"Promise?"

Now that's one I intend to keep. "Promise."

CHAPTER 65

The morning of my thirtieth birthday is hot even before the sun's up. I lie in bed and stare at the ceiling. I've been dreading this day. A twin bed, alone, is definitely not where I saw things going, but the ache in my chest is no longer suffocating. It's more of a gentle ache most days, something I never thought I'd get to, especially not in so short a time. I guess Peter was right when he said we move on more quickly than we used to, and I've made a decision to embrace thirty instead of feeling guilty. Birthdays used to come whether you wanted them or not. These days you have to work for them, and I'm going to enjoy the fruits of my labor—Adrian's labor.

I head to breakfast, where I make pancakes and receive birthday greetings. The first few are hard, but it gets easier. By the end of breakfast shift I'm more than ready for my fourth decade.

Dan enters the restaurant, paper bag in hand, while I'm finishing the cleaning. "Happy birthday, Dingbat. How's it going so far?"

"Thanks. It's good. And when I'm done here, I get to do nothing for the rest of the day."

"Lucky. I'm on my way to guard, but I wanted to give you something."

He hands me the paper sack. I want to tell him that he shouldn't have, but he's practically glowing with excitement. I pull out a wooden box, no more than four inches long. The dark wood has been so finely sanded and shellacked that it gleams like polished stone in the window light. A border of itty bitty stars runs around the lid, and in the center is a constellation I recognize.

"Cassiopeia," I whisper. I'm in awe of how beautiful the craftsmanship is, and I run my finger along the perfect shapes of the stars that must have taken Dan hours and hours to carve.

"This is gorgeous," I say. "I love it. Thank you so much."

Dan's been rocking from foot to foot while I admired the box, and now he asks, "You really like it?"

"Are you kidding me?" I yell. "It's beautiful! No wonder you're bored building cabins."

His nervous smile becomes a real one. "Open it."

I laugh at the tiny unicorn figurine inside. It's two inches long at most, but it's been given the same attention to detail as the rest of the box. The bottom of the box is a carving of two mountains with a rainbow running between their peaks. He's captured the corniness of my pretend mural, but even so, it's lovely.

"Thank you." I wrap my arms around his waist. "It's my new most favorite thing in the world."

"So you like it?"

"If you ask me that again, I'll punch you. I really, truly, absolutely, swear-on-anything love it. You're so talented, you know."

I go to kiss him on his cheek, but he turns his head and presses his lips on mine. I leave them there for an extra second, if I don't exactly kiss him back. He grins when I push him away.

"Dan," I say. It's the half-hearted scolding I'd give to a little kid.

"Sorry," he says, but we both know he's not. "I have to go. I'll see you tonight?"

"Are you going to behave yourself, or will I have to kick you out of my birthday party?"

"I'll be on my best behavior."

He swaggers out the door. I don't trust him as far as I can throw him, and if the glimmer of excitement swirling in my abdomen is any sign, I kind of don't mind.

***

Everyone's in high spirits. I'm the only August birthday, and it's been too long since a party was thrown that wasn't a wake. The kids are watching their movie in the radio room, and we're in the restaurant eating and drinking. I pull out the phone to snap a few shots and end up at the picture I took of Adrian by the woodpile. He looks so peaceful, the way he almost always did, and I swallow down the lump in my throat. Most of the time it might be a dull ache, but right now it's more of a wallop.

I close the photo. Adrian's gone, and I'll mourn him forever, but I won't tonight. He left me here to live, and he was probably pretty pissed that I hadn't been doing the greatest job of it. I imagine there were a lot of his trademark sighs in the afterlife. The thought makes me laugh. I pick up my beer and wander the room until I find a seat next to Peter.

He rubs my back. "How's the birthday girl?"

"She's great," I answer. "She really is."

I clink his beer with mine and take a picture of him and Ana. Jamie and Shawn are playing quarters, and I catch her in a triumphant yell when she wins a round. I try to get everyone in at least one shot. Dan moves my way, but stops when I hold up a palm to take one of him.

"Happy birthday again," he says.

"Thanks again. Guess what I have in my pocket?"

I pull out the unicorn and pass it around so everyone can admire Dan's handiwork. They exclaim over the tiny details until Dan begins to fidget, so I put it away.

"Is that a unicorn in your pocket or are you happy to see me?" Dan asks.

"I don't even know what to say to that, so I'm going to pretend it didn't happen." He guffaws and pulls up a chair. "Bits wants one. Actually, Bits wants a whole unicorn family. So be prepared for that. She said you have plenty of time to make them before her birthday in November."

"I think I can handle that."

Dan rests his hand on my knee. I glance down and then up at him in a pointed way. Dan pointedly ignores me back while he talks to John. I shrug and join in the conversation. We don't talk about zombies or trenches or anything important. Funny stories, like how I spilled an entire bowl of pancake batter this morning, are the kinds of things we discuss on birthday nights.

We end the festivities when the kids come back from their movie. Bits sashays beside me and gives me a rundown of the entire plot, which, more often than not, takes longer than the length of the movie.

"I really loved my cake, Bitsy," I say, during one of her few breaths. "Thank you again."

"Dan said it should have stars because you love stars. Like your ring and the constellations."

Dan walks on Bits's other side, and I smile at him. "He's right. And you did a beautiful job."

"Cassie's teaching me the constellations," Bits tells everyone. "I knew the one on her box was Cassiopeia when I saw it."

"I'm passing along your knowledge," I say to Dan. "You can quiz her soon. She's excited for the next meteor shower."

Dan tousles Bits's hair. "I know it's late, but if you two lovely ladies want to watch the stars tonight—"

"We do! Right, Cassie?"

"Sure we do."

We sit on a blanket outside Dan's tent. After he's pointed out a few related constellations, he takes Bits's hand and holds her finger to the sky. "Follow your finger while I tell you the story. There's Andromeda, Cassiopeia's daughter. Cassiopeia bragged that Andromeda was more beautiful than the sea nymphs. The sea nymphs demanded that Poseidon, the sea god, punish her by sending Cetus, the sea monster, to ravage the shores of Ethiopia. Andromeda's father, Cepheus, asked for mercy for his kingdom. He was told to chain Andromeda to a rock so the sea monster could eat her instead—"

"Did he?" Bits asks incredulously.

Dan nods and moves her finger to another spot. "But Perseus came along and saved her, using the head of Medusa to turn the sea monster into stone. Then they lived happily ever after."

"That Cassiopeia was a real piece of work," I say.

"I can't believe he did it!" Bits says. "My dad never would've done that. And Peter and Cassie wouldn't either."

"You never know," I say, and pull her braid. "That depends on how well you were listening that day."

Bits giggles. We sit out until it's too chilly—even the mid-August nights have the bite of autumn up here—and move into Dan's tent, where Bits snuggles between us and listens to Dan tell the constellations' myths. He's a better storyteller than I am, and she stares through the mesh roof in fascination.

"I love the stars," she says dreamily. "I didn't know they had so many stories. It's like a book up in the sky. Is that why you love them, Cassie? There's always something to read."

"I never thought of that," I say, and marvel at her cleverness. "Maybe that's part of it. I love that there are other worlds out there, maybe other beings. It scares some people, how small we are in comparison to the rest of the universe, but it reminds me that there's always something beautiful out there, something bigger, even if it doesn't seem that way here sometimes. But do you know what I really love?"

"What?"

I press my lips to her temple. "You. More than all the stars in the sky."

"That's a lot of stars," Bits says. "Like infinity. Right, Dan?"

"Well," Dan answers, "as far as I know, they were never sure about whether or not there are an infinite number of stars, but I like to think there are."

I pull Bits closer. "So do I."

"Me, too," Bits says.

"Then it's agreed," Dan says. "After all, who's going to argue?"

CHAPTER 66

Dan, Jamie and I sit around the fire at the main gate. We still walk the fence, but with the trench we never have anything to stab. Until morning, that is. It's somewhere in the fifties, and I have a feeling this signals the end of our unusually warm summer. I hold my mitten-clad hands over the fire. I know I said I wanted winter to come, but that doesn't mean I have to like it. Jamie's hat almost covers her eyes. Dan wears a light jacket and keeps complaining about how hot he is, just to annoy us.

"Hello?" a voice calls from the other side of the gate.

The wind has covered any footsteps we might have heard approaching. We scramble for the platforms and shine our flashlights over the edge. An older man with a trim, graying beard stands on the dirt road. He wears hiking clothes and a massive pack that he carries easily on his compact frame, as though out for a Sunday stroll with nothing more than a fanny pack. He shields his eyes from the light and waves.

"Hi," Dan says. "Are you looking to come in?"

I hold my pistol at the ready. I'm wary of visitors since Whitefield. We haven't had many people come this year, but the few who've made it have all been perfectly nice and uninfected, if a little shell-shocked.

The man strokes his beard. "Yes. I'm not infected, if that's what you're worried about."

"Okay, I'm coming down. I'll have to look you over."

Dan steps off the platform and opens the small door. The man carefully lowers his pack to the ground to protect the bow that's strapped to the side. He takes off his jacket and shirt to show grimy but unbroken skin. He reaches for his belt with a glance at where Jamie and I stand with our guns ready.

"Pardon me, ladies," he says, and drops his pants.

He's healthy, which seemed the case, considering his bright eyes and demeanor. Dan motions for him to dress, and says, "Welcome to Kingdom Come."

The man bypasses Dan's outstretched hand and hugs him with a cry of joy. I holster my pistol and join them on the road.

"I made it!" the man yells. He begins to cry, big, gulping cries that make his shoulders shudder. The tears stream, but he beams at us as he wipes his nose with a handkerchief. I giggle when he hugs me and dances a jig. He smells terrible, but we've all been there at some point in the past year. And besides, nothing smells as bad as a Lexer.

"I'm Cassie," I say, once he's let me go.

"My manners! Where are my manners? Mark Golden, teacher of high school history."

He shakes our hands while Dan and Jamie introduce themselves.

"Nice to meet you, Mark," Dan says. "Have a seat. Or one of us can walk you up now and get you settled in."

Mark's feet dance on the ground even after he drops into a chair. "I'll have a seat. I want to sit and revel in safety with people. How I've missed you, People! I ran into some on the road, but they were heading elsewhere. I always wanted to retire to Vermont. Retirement's come early, but I've done it!"

He punches a fist in the air, and his eyes light up more when Dan pulls out his flask and offers it to him.

"Ah, a libation," Mark says. "How wonderful!"

I sit next to him. "Where are you from?"

"Tennessee. It's been a long trek, my dear."

This guy is a character. I love him already. "We're happy you're here, but why didn't you stop at one of the other Safe Zones?"

He frowns. "Aside from the fact that I love Vermont—as the bumper stickers say—I ran into people from Oklahoma. They said the monsters are moving north, like a tidal wave from the south. Said they'd heard the bridges of the Panama Canal were full, day and night. Traveling north and east made sense."

All the blood rushes to my feet. I make eye contact with Jamie and Dan and see that they look just as stunned. "They're coming up from South America?"

"That's what they said. It must be taken with a grain of salt, though. They were very agitated about everything, always on the verge of a fistfight amongst themselves. This is news to you all. I'm sorry to be the bearer of such bad news. If indeed it's true, I would think the monsters will freeze before they reach us."

"I'm going to wake John," I say. "Mark, will you come with me? I have someone who needs to hear this."

"May I bring the flask?"

Even with the fear tugging on my insides, I manage a laugh. "Of course. We're going to need it."

***

Mark's answered every one of John's questions, but we still have no solid answers. He was told that thousands of Lexers are heading north but can't say whether or not they're heading northeast. From what he's heard, they were toward the west.

"They can't be walking fast," Mark says from one of the easy chairs in the RV. "I walked as briskly as possible. It's true that's not as brisk as it once was, but unlike the monsters, I had to rest, and I still beat them. They'll go...if not forever, then damn close, I'd say."

He gives a dramatic wave of his arm. I can picture him in front of a class, making the Revolutionary War come alive for a bunch of seventeen year-olds.

"We'll be sure to make three runs to the lookout every day," John says. He looked tired when we woke him, but now he looks exhausted. "We can see for miles on a clear day. It should give us time to bug out."

Mark takes another sip from the flask and swallows before saying, "And where will you go if you have to leave?"

"Alaska."

"Well, I've always wanted to visit Alaska," Mark says. He lifts a finger in the air. "That is, if I may come along for the ride?"

John laughs. "How good are you with that bow?"

Mark's teeth are stained with years of teacher's lounge coffee, but his smile is bright. "Oh, I've won my fair share of competitions. I was a bit rusty, but I've gotten a lot of practice recently."

"You'd be welcome to anyway, but we could use a good archery instructor. If you're willing."

"I have a suspicion that the days of American history being fundamental knowledge are behind us. Archery, now, that's another story."

"You must be exhausted, Mark," Maureen says from the other end of the couch. "Why don't you stay here tonight, and I'll sort you out in the morning?"

"That would be wonderful." He turns to where I stand by the door and holds out the flask. "Take this back to your friend. Please give him my thanks."

I say goodnight and leave. On my way to the gate, I take a sniff of the flask, but whatever's in there smells terrible. When I hand it back to Dan he holds it by his ear and swishes the contents.

"He'll be sloshed in ten minutes," he says. "Looks like I'll need to refill."

"You and that flask," Jamie says. "Why do you have it, anyway? It's not like you ever drink it."

"I'm like a St. Bernard," Dan says. "I use it to rescue people like Mark, who were lost in the wilderness."

I laugh when Jamie shakes her head in confusion. It's a much better use than he originally intended.

CHAPTER 67

It's been a week of canning with no end in sight. I find myself half-wishing we'd run out of jars, but the upper level of the barn is still stacked with boxes. Jamie lifts the blanched tomatoes out of the water and takes a knife to the skins.

"Tell me why you like this again?" she asks.

"It's food. I like food. You can starve to death this winter if you'd rather."

"I might, just to get out of this," she says, and holds up her pruned fingers. "Any more news from the Safe Zones?"

"Nope. Everyone else is fine so far."

"When's Dwayne going out?"

"In two days."

It's just September, but Mark's news has unsettled us enough that we need to know if anything's close. Dwayne says he'll run almost half the tank down and turn around, so he'll be able to go anywhere from 450 to 600 miles. We'll do another flight in a few weeks, and that will be the end of our fuel.

"I hate this." Jamie throws a tomato skin into the compost bucket. "Not canning—well, I hate that, too—but waiting for something that we don't even know is coming. Everyone's so stressed. I tried to talk Doc into giving everyone antidepressants."

I laugh at her wicked expression. Jamie works with Doc when he needs help. She isn't trained as a nurse, but she's close to one now.

"I just wish the kids didn't know about it," I say. "But at least Bits is doing okay."

"That's great. Doc says Chris is having nightmares, even."

"Did you and Shawn ever want kids?" I ask. Jamie seems like she'd make a great mother, and they both love the kids, but neither of them has ever said a word about it, although they're in their mid-thirties.

"I'm not having kids until every single one of these motherfuckers is wiped off the Earth." Her knife slips through tomato and slices her finger. I hand her a towel and she smiles, although it's more like a baring of teeth. "Sorry, can you tell I feel strongly about this?"

Her reaction wasn't strong, it was feral, and what I can tell is that she doesn't want me to ask anything more. "I don't blame you. I feel the same way. I've just got to keep Bits safe until it happens."

"I'm here to help," Jamie says. "No matter what."

I put an arm around her shoulders and feel her tension start to subside. "Thanks, lady. But don't go thinking that cut's gonna get you out of canning."

"Fucker!" she says.

***

The day is bright and sunny, but the weather six hundred miles southwest is a mystery. Dwayne and Jeff stand by the plane. Dwayne's found a couple of small airports they might be able to land in and refuel on the way, which would mean he could go farther. They're unknown quantities, but he has one of the pumps we use for fuel on board, just in case.

"We'll be back before sundown, most likely," Dwayne says. "You'll hear from us when we're close. But if we're not back, assume we stopped for fuel."

"I'll be at the radio," John says. "Just come on back if you hit any bad weather. Don't chance it."

Dwayne nods. Peter and I watch the field for Lexers while the two climb into the plane. We head back behind the fence and watch them roll down the runway and into the air. When they've disappeared from sight, John turns to us. "Maybe they'll find out something."

"Maybe," Peter says, still watching the sky with a frown.

"We'll go out again in a few weeks. If they aren't close by then, they probably won't make it by winter."

I link my arms through theirs as we walk to breakfast. "There's nothing we can do about it, right? So let's go eat pancakes."

"Someone took her happy pills this morning," Peter says.

"Someone took his morose pills this morning," I say. "What's wrong with being happy to be alive?"

"Absolutely nothing. Being alive suits you."

"But I'd be an awesome zombie, right?" The words come out of my mouth without forethought, and Peter glances at me quickly. I would feel bad, but Adrian would only laugh if he heard. I chomp my teeth. "I'd eat you all up!"

Peter smirks. "Well, you're certainly pale enough."

I trip him with a carefully timed foot. "Whoops! Careful there."

He trips me back, which isn't difficult to do. I don't have any happy pills, but maybe Jamie has slipped something into the water because I haven't been able to shake this feeling of contentment. Not that I want to. Now that Bits has been in Dan's tent, she asks to sleep there every night. We slept there once, and true to his word, Dan painted our toenails, but only after he made us scrub our feet. I've made it a point to stop by Adrian's grave. I still miss him more than I've ever missed anyone in my life, but my pedicured feet are planted on terra firma.

CHAPTER 68

"Wake up, Sleeping Beauty," Dan says, and tickles my side. "It's almost ten."

There was no plane last night. Dan and I stayed up late in the radio room with John, but as of three in the morning there was still no word. I came back to Dan's tent to sleep for two hours until breakfast shift.

Dan sits on the side of the bed, dressed and wide awake. Rain patters on the tent roof, now covered with the rain fly to keep out the cold night air. The light that filters through the fabric is dim from the overcast day.

"Ten?" I ask. "Shit. I had to do breakfast."

I start to rise, but he tucks the covers back around me. "I did it for you."

"Really? Thank you. You didn't have to do that. Is everyone still alive?"

"Mikayla told me I was beating the bread dough to death, instead of kneading, but other than that, no one died." He holds up a mug and my toothbrush, complete with a dollop of toothpaste. "And I stole you tea, but I thought you might want to brush first."

"I'm going to throw caution to the wind," I say, and take the mug. "Thanks. That was really nice of you."

He spreads his arms. "I'm a nice guy."

"I know that." I touch the hand that rests on the sleeping bag. "Believe me."

"But I'm still in the friend zone."

"The other zone is closed for business. You *were* in the Friends with Benefits Zone." I wave a finger side to side. "But did that work for you? Nooo. So, tough."

"I should've kept my mouth shut," Dan says, and pretends to punch himself. "That's okay, I'll wait."

"Well, you're first on line for the grand opening."

Those creases appear alongside his mouth; I've never said anything like that before. I look down and wish *I'd* kept my mouth shut. I shouldn't make any promises, even vague ones.

Dan coughs. "Dwayne still isn't back. Pennsylvania said they had a storm yesterday afternoon. I guess it's the one we're getting now."

"Did he radio them on his way?"

"Yeah, when he passed by yesterday morning. Said all was well."

"Shit."

"Yeah."

I get out of bed and pick up my jeans. "I have to get ready for art, but I'll see you at dinner. We're on guard tonight?" Dan nods absently, and I tilt his chin up in question.

"It just gets to me sometimes, you know?" he says.

"Yeah, I know," I say.

There's nothing more to say, and I don't stop myself from planting a kiss on the top of his head before I leave.

***

Rainy days are usually fun days. We still have meals to make, fences to guard and clothes to wash, but the outdoor canning can wait until tomorrow. And although I spent a cozy afternoon in the school with the woodstove burning and the kids doing art or playing quietly, every boom of thunder and bolt of lightning made me jump. I imagined Dwayne and Jeff up there, with no experienced air traffic controller to talk them down and no weather reports to guide them somewhere safe. Now it's evening, and our dinner table has been quiet until Hank and Bits show off their finished comic.

"They haven't saved the whole world yet," Bits says. "Just the Northeast, for now. Their power is running out, so they have to find more juice."

Hank opens the comic to the last page. Comic Book-Bits stands, dressed in black leather, brown hair streaming behind her, next to Comic Book-Hank, who still has on glasses but has suddenly sprouted muscles. The hills behind them are dotted with bodies. The entire table applauds.

"That was excellent," Henry says.

"Cassie helped us," Bits says.

I shake my head and say, "No, guys, that was all you. It's wonderful."

I was reluctant when they asked me to show them how to make the bodies more realistic. But the kids giggled as we pretended to fall to our deaths and observe how our limbs splayed out. It's not like they don't see dead people every day, but I almost couldn't stand the sight of Bits sprawled on the floor, as though letting her pretend to be dead would be tempting fate. And that fate might be marching our way right now from South America. Ana's stepped up PE, and the kids can run faster than they ever could. They try harder too, as if they know their lives might depend on it. Maybe they do know.

"Didn't Bits do a great job on the artwork?" Hank asks.

"Well, you did the writing," Bits says. She twists a dread on his head that's frizzing out. "I mean, I helped, but you're much better with words than I am."

They grin at each other and start to talk about their next issue in low voices. They've both grown so much in the past year. They're still kids, but sometimes I get a glimpse of what they'll be like ten years from now—maybe as close as brother and sister, or maybe more than that. There are so many possibilities, so many things I want for them. But those things can only happen if we're still alive. If they can run fast enough.

CHAPTER 69

M ark Golden, history teacher, may be sixty-five, but he has more energy than I do after seven lattes. He stands by the east fence and rocks on the balls of his feet while showing us how to take apart and reassemble a recurve bow. "I'll demonstrate later how to string without a stringer, but let's get our feet wet. Who wants to be first?"

He looks around the group of us who do patrol. Everyone at the farm will learn archery eventually, but we're his first students. In keeping with every annoying teacher I've ever had, Mark notices my attempt to become invisible and points at me. "Cassie, why don't you go first?"

I sigh and take the bow. I hate doing things like this in front of people. It makes me all flustered and hot. Mark has me string the bow with the stringer and then points to the target he's set up. At least it's close. He explains the proper stance, and I do as he says. There's no sight, nothing to help me figure out how to get an arrow anywhere near the target. I want my crossbow.

"Good," Mark says, and lifts my right hand. "Now use the tips of your three middle fingers to draw back the string. Your hand will come to your face, elbow level."

It's harder than I thought, and this isn't even a bow with a high draw weight. Mark tells me to let go and hands me an arrow. I fit it onto the string and follow his directions to draw it.

"Now how do I get it there?" I ask.

"Aha," Mark says. "You're used to guns, as evidenced by the way you're gripping the bow to keep it steady. Loosen your left, my dear. There are a few ways to aim, but I use the instinctive method."

"What's that?" Shawn asks from behind me. "Point the arrow and hope for the best?"

Mark gives him a talking-out-of-turn-in-class look and raises a finger. "If your stance is correct, young man, you'll be able to tell where the arrow will go. Now, Cassie, let it fly."

The arrow misses the target, but hits the hay on which the target rests. Between all the eyes on my back and being first to go, there's no way I'll ever hit it.

"Okay," I say. "Who's next?"

"Keep going," Mark says. "Get the feel of the bow. Tell the arrow where to go. It will do your bidding if you work at it, that I can tell you."

I turn to the others. "Don't watch. Face the other way."

They stare at me before Dan winks and spins. The others follow suit, until it's just Mark and me and the target.

"Again," he says. "Let your middle finger touch the corner of your mouth when you draw back. That will be your anchor point. When it hits your mouth, release the string."

I take another arrow and draw the bow. This time I hit the blue. I loose another arrow, and then another. Three more and I've hit the red. I see what he means: sometimes when I shoot a gun I know when I have it; the bullet does my bidding. The tenth arrow hits the yellow center, and a cheer rises from behind me. I knew they wouldn't stay turned, but I could pretend that they were.

"Wonderful!" Mark says. "You got the feeling, didn't you?"

"Cassie can shoot," Ana says.

"Two very different methods," Mark says, "but the same zone of concentration. Now, who wants to go next?"

I hand off the bow and watch the others take a turn. My fingers itch to try again, although my shoulder tells me it'd like to rest. When archery lessons are over, I ask Mark if I can practice more.

"Yes, my dear," he says. "I didn't want to say anything earlier, but I'm impressed. I know you like that crossbow of yours, but those bolts are short and quite impractical to retrieve out there. I left home with three dozen arrows and arrived here with two dozen left."

"And it's quiet," I say, "without having to get close. Do you think we can practice in the trench tomorrow, if anything's in there? Moving targets are harder."

Mark's weathered face is alight. "We most certainly can. Nothing makes me happier than an eager pupil."

CHAPTER 70

Dwayne and Jeff have been gone for over a week and not a single Safe Zone has heard from them. Everyone hopes that they had engine trouble and landed somewhere safe, and I secretly hope they found a nice, zombie-free tropical island on which to drink Piña Coladas. Sadly, the first is as unlikely as the second.

We've sighted some large groups of Lexers from the lookout, but they number in the hundreds, not thousands. All we've done so far is waste the gas that could be used in the winter. One day we're going to have to wash our clothes without the use of generators, and I've read enough Little House books to know how much that's going to suck.

Dan knocks on the side of the ambulance. "Ready?"

"Yep," I say, and hop in the passenger's seat.

We pull out of Kingdom Come on the morning run to the lookout. It takes less than ten minutes to get to the trail that leads to the top of the mountain. I spot a few Lexers in the woods, tripping their way over downed branches and rocks. Then I spot another ten, fifty feet down the road. They're moving toward Kingdom Come, or at least in a northerly direction.

"Small groups," Dan says. "Good."

He turns up the hill. A squirrel sits on the grass that borders the dirt road, munching on a squirrel snack. At the last moment, it darts in front of the ambulance. There's a tiny thump as we plow it down.

"Crap," Dan says. He slows to a stop and looks in the side view. "I think I squished him. I don't want him to suffer."

I follow him out of the ambulance. The squirrel is indeed squished, with his paws up by his head. Dan lifts it gently by its tail and moves it to the side of the road. A lump rises in my throat at the pathetic sight.

"What's wrong?" Dan asks. I shake my head because only an idiot cries over a squirrel during the zombie apocalypse, and if I speak, I'll cry. "The squirrel?"

"Yes," I say. It comes out as a sob, just like I knew it would. "No. Why the hell did he run out like that? We're the only car for a million fucking miles, and Squirrel Nutkin has to run in front of us?"

I take out a bandana and blow my nose. Dan looks at me like I've gone crazy. "Well, he's a squirrel. He doesn't know about cars."

"Everyone dies. They keep dying, and we can't help it. But Squirrel Nutkin didn't have to die."

Dan gives me an understanding nod, but he still looks baffled.

"I'm tired of it," I say through my tears. "I'm tired of the smell. Of the bodies. He didn't have to run out in the road like that, and he's all cute and furry—"

I stop when Dan moves to the back of the ambulance. He grabs the folding shovel and digs a hole in the dirt by the side of the road. After a few shovelfuls, he lifts the squirrel into the hole and then replaces the dirt.

"Come here," he says.

I take his outstretched hand. He clears his throat and looks down. I start to thank him for burying the squirrel, but he speaks before I say a word.

"I'm sorry," he says to the tiny mound of dirt. "If you'd run out a little sooner, I could've stopped in time."

I wipe my face one last time. It was stupid to lose my shit over a squirrel, of all things. And although what Dan's doing is sweet, it's insane to be standing out here in Lexer country over a squirrel grave. It's also kind of funny. I put my handkerchief to my mouth to stifle the laugh that threatens to burst out. Dan must think I'm crying, though, because he squeezes my hand.

"Oh, Squirrel Nutkin," he says, "we'll never know why you decided to run across the road."

He may not mean to, but he sounds like a Southern preacher, and that does me in. I duck my head as a snort escapes. It's followed by giggles, and then I can't help it, I'm doubled over and struggling for air.

Dan drops my hand and crosses his arms. "Are you laughing at me?"

"I just...you were so serious. And...and...you called him Squirrel...Nutkin." I hold my stomach and collapse into laughter again.

"That's what *you* called him! I didn't make up that name. I was trying to make you feel better."

"I know." I force a giggle back down. It wasn't in the way he intended, but he did make me feel better. "You did, see? Thank you. That was so sweet."

"Yeah, yeah."

"Hey, I'm done now, promise."

He examines my face warily. "That's the last time I invite you to a squirrel funeral."

I don't crack a smile at his joke, and he frowns. "Am I allowed to laugh?" I ask out of the corner of my mouth.

"You are a pain in my ass, Dingbat."

"Well, you are a wonderful person. Thank you."

He scratches the back of his head with a shrug. I can see how pleased he is by my comment, though, and I like it. I think maybe he's worn me down just a little. And maybe he was partly right—I didn't want to let him in. Another person loved is another person to lose, and I'm afraid there's a limit to how many people we can lose before our hearts are destroyed. But maybe if they're overflowing there will always be someone left to help us through.

"We should get up there," Dan says. "What's wrong?"

I've been staring at him, and now I look away. "Nothing at all."

"Okay."

We ride in silence the rest of the way to the trail and hike to the top. There's nothing to see but the occasional Lexer in the distant fields. Only a few trees have begun to change color, but the gold of the rising sun has made them vibrant.

"Isn't it pretty?" I ask.

"Uh-huh," Dan says. He sounds distracted, and I turn to find him watching me with an expression I can't read.

"Did I really make you feel bad?" I ask. "I'm sorry."

"No. You made me feel good."

His hair is gold, his skin is gold—everything about him is lit by the sun. I want to run my thumb along his golden jaw. I want to kiss him. My heart pounds when I imagine leaning forward and taking him by surprise. I'm a second away from doing just that when he speaks.

"Let's go. We wasted enough time with Squirrel Nutkin's service. They'll start to worry."

I tell myself it was just that the moment seemed perfect, but the urge follows me through the trees and into the ambulance. He starts the engine. It's now or never. I don't want to regret not saying something.

"I meant what I said—I think you're a wonderful person." I face him and take a breath. "Thank you for waiting until I was ready."

It's as close as I can get to saying what I want to say. I can't make any promises. I can't promise that I'll love him, especially the way I loved Adrian, or that it will be easy—but I can promise that I want to be here right now. I want to try. I run my gloved palms along my jeans and hope he caught the past tense of my last words.

Dan's no dummy, though. He drops his hand from the gearshift and turns to me. "What?"

"Thanks. For waiting."

He doesn't move when I lean forward; maybe he wants it to be my decision. I close my eyes when my lips touch his, and I know it's the right one. His taste is familiar now. I've missed it. Everywhere else he's ever touched clamors to be included, and I climb onto his lap. His hands run down my back, around my waist and to my neck. He grunts in annoyance when he fails to open my jacket on the second try. It's ridiculous how many layers I wear out here, and there's no way they're coming off easily in the front seat of an ambulance.

"Cassie, Dan, where are you? Check in," the CB squawks.

Dan groans and holds me to him when he leans for the handset. "All clear. We're coming back now."

"Okay, see you in ten."

He hangs it up and leans back, eyes closed and hands tight on my waist. "I have laundry, anyway. And then I'm on the afternoon run."

"And here I have the rest of the day off," I say. "Too bad."

Dan opens his eyes and his lips curve. "I'll see you tonight, though?"

"Yup."

He's going to see a lot more of me tonight. I press my forehead to his before I return to my seat. He backs onto the road and starts for home, hand on my knee. I lace my fingers through his, fluttery with excitement and fear. But it's a good kind of fear, like just before you jump off the high dive into warm blue water.

Once we're through the gates and standing in the lot, Dan asks, "So what are you doing on your day off?"

"This and that," I say. The truth is I'm working on his painting. I found a photograph of Fenway Park in a book and a small board to paint it on. It's almost finished, and I want to give it to him tonight even though it won't be dry.

He brushes my lips with his. "I'll see you at dinner."

"Yes, you will." I watch him walk away. I can't wait.

***

I've dragged the table to the door of the cabin, so the light is decent enough to paint by. Fenway Park is empty, and the early morning light streams onto the grass. You can just see the Green Monster, which is a silly name for a scoreboard, but those sports fanatics are all crazy. It looks timeless, glowing and magical, which is just how a little boy would have seen it all those years ago. I stick my brush into the turpentine for the final time and admire it for a while. A shadow comes up the steps and blocks the light.

"Hey. Oh—" Dan says.

It's too late to cover it, so I smile and say, "For you."

"Really?"

"No, I painted Fenway Park because I love it so. Of course it's for you. Careful, it's wet."

Dan bends over and inspects it for a full minute, until I start to wonder if I'm wrong, if it's horrible. His eyes are moist when he finally looks up.

"It's—" he begins. He screws his mouth to the side and looks away with a shake of his head. It must be the kind of day where squirrels and paintings can bring you to tears.

He cries like a guy—a few tears, a couple of sobs and hands that clutch me as though he's sinking. Then he's done, although he doesn't move out of my arms.

"You know," I say with a rub of his back, "you made me tell you a hundred times how great that box was. And here I spend every spare second on this and you don't even thank me?"

His shoulders jump when he laughs in my ear. "Thanks."

"You're welcome. Now, why were you sneaking up on me?"

"I thought you might want to come on the midday run to the lookout."

"Why on Earth would I want to do that?"

"Oh, I don't know. The company?" He nudges me back against the wall and kisses me softly. "Thank you. I love it."

"I'm glad. And I'd love to come with you. Let me get my gear and Princess Leia myself."

"Nice. You don't happen to have a gold bikini laying around, do you?"

I laugh because it's a *Star Wars* reference I actually get and duck out from under his arms to get ready.

Twenty minutes later, Dan pulls into the driveway of the abandoned house. He glances at the clock and then at me. "We're early."

This time neither of us waits for the other. In the silence I hear the breeze and the clicking of the engine cooling and something else I've never heard out here before: A low hum. A distant crowd.

Dan stops inches from my lips, his face slack. My desire is replaced by a steady beating of dread. We jump out of the ambulance to the trail, and then we run.

CHAPTER 71

My parents once took me and Eric to a march on Washington. Even having grown up in New York City, I had never seen that many people at once. We walked, en masse, through the streets to the National Mall. A hundred thousand people moving in unison, all bent on a common destination.

What we see when we reach the peak resembles the news footage we watched later that night. A mass of people, moving slowly. Voices that merged into a low hum. But these are no longer people, and the hum is the drone of thousands of moans. There must be tens of thousands of Lexers. West of the quarry is packed to the woods behind the fields, and more spill out of the trees as the front line moves forward. I can't even see the weeds that cover the fields. The east has a pod or two, but there's a dark mass a mile or so back. We don't need binoculars to know we're fucked.

"Holy shit," Dan murmurs.

We slip and stumble back down the trail. Dan starts the engine and calls into the radio until Oliver answers.

"We have thousands of Lexers coming our way. Thousands, Oliver. We need to evacuate. Now." He hands me the radio and backs onto the road.

"Are you sure?" Oliver asks.

"Yes," I say, "Oliver, tell John three blasts. Three blasts. Call Whitefield and the others."

Dan takes the corner to the main road so fast I'm thrown against the door. But he wasn't just turning, he was swerving to avoid a group of Lexers in the road. He tears east, toward the farm, and I look in the side view mirror. The road is clear, but the Lexers to the west had already reached the southern woods and could be only minutes away. They'll block the road, and if we're caught in it we might not escape.

"Shit!" I thumb the radio. "Oliver!"

"John's going for the air horn now," he answers.

"They can't head west. We have to head east. Tell them to go east!"

"Okay." I hear a blast over the line. "I'm going now. Out."

"Oliver!" I scream. I wanted to make sure he called Whitefield, but he's gone.

Dust trails behind us when Dan screeches to a halt at the first gate then races up to the farm. I jump out in the lot and run to the VW. Penny, James, Ana and Maureen wait outside, bodies tense. The first few vehicles pull down the driveway, and the school bus lets out a burst of air and follows. I breathe a sigh of relief as it disappears; most of the farm is safe.

"Where's Bits?" I ask.

"We're waiting for her and Peter," Ana says. "We're picking up John at the front gate."

Peter rounds the corner of the restaurant and moves to the van. "Okay, we're clear. Everyone's out."

"Where's Bits?" I ask.

Panic rises when he looks behind me into the VW and his chin drops. "She was here! I put her in the van and told her not to move."

He looks again, like he might have missed her the first time, and turns to me with giant, dark eyes.

"Sparky," I say.

"I'll look here," he says.

I run for the cabin, but Sparky is curled up on Bits's cot, completely unperturbed. I throw her in her box, grab my extra bag and run outside. I hear the others calling, and I do the same.

"Bits!" I scream. "I have Sparky! Bits!"

There's nothing but the noisy silence of the rustling leaves and grass. If we hadn't seen what was coming our way, we would have been lulled into thinking it was a beautiful fall day. I hold Sparky's carrier to my chest and sprint for the van.

Ana stops in front of me, panting. "Bits is in the big bus. Mike saw Josephine take her and Jasmine. He thought she was supposed to be there."

It doesn't make any sense. Josephine knew we had the job of checking the farm; we were to be the last ones out. It doesn't matter why, though—all that matters is that Bits is by my side. Dan paces outside the ambulance with Mike and Rohan, the only other people left. There are supposed to be others in the ambulance, but maybe they were too scared to wait until Dan and I got back.

Peter pulls out of the lot and speeds to John at the gate. I throw open the door. "Bits is on the bus. We have to catch up."

John ducks in. Peter turns west at the main road, and my body ices over. "East. We have to go east," I say.

"West," John corrects.

"We told Oliver to tell you east! They're going to reach the road in the west!" My voice is a screech. We could turn east and radio the others, but there's one person I'll never leave behind, and she's on that bus.

"He didn't tell us," John says. He speaks into the radio. "Everyone, turn around. We're going east. I repeat, turn east. Lexers will block the west road."

Something unintelligible crackles out of the radio in response. The small school bus and a pickup speed toward us over the rise a half mile down. We meet them halfway, and Shawn stops the pickup alongside while the small school bus speeds east. I keep my eyes on the road, willing the big yellow bus to crest the hill, but it doesn't.

Shawn rolls down the window, face drained of color. "Everyone ahead is surrounded. They swarmed onto the road right before you called. The big bus went into a tree. I think the radiator's busted. There's no way to reach them without going into it."

The last words are barely out of his mouth before Peter slams on the gas pedal. Once over the rise, we see the school bus sitting angled off the side of the road, engine smoking and motor revving. It's surrounded by Lexers thirty feet deep in the rear and as far south into the forest as I can see. A couple of vehicles ahead of the bus are drowning in a sea of Lexers. A van's back doors are open; whoever was in there must have tried to run. Screams echo out of the bus's open windows, and I might be imagining it, but I'm almost certain I hear Bits among them. I clamp my hand over my mouth to stop the answering scream that rises in my chest.

I sink my fingers into Peter's shoulder. I don't have to tell him I won't leave without Bits: he would never consider it either. He leans out the window. "You have room in the truck? We'll meet you in Quebec."

"There's room in the bed," Shawn says.

Mike and Rohan leave the ambulance and crouch on the cargo in the pickup. Mark Golden steps out of the backseat and motions for Penny to get in the cab, but she shakes her head. "No, I'm not leaving."

James opens the VW's door, the planes of his normally placid face sharp. "Yeah, you are."

"Get in the truck," Ana says to her sister. "Now."

"Go with Penny," John says to Maureen. "We'll meet you there. James, you're with them."

James starts to argue, but John cuts him off. "Go."

The look on John's face silences the both of them. James helps Penny and Maureen into the truck and jumps in the bed.

"You want me and Jamie?" Shawn asks. "Someone else can drive."

John shakes his head and waves them on. Penny presses her face against the window and looks at me and Ana helplessly, and then she's gone. We turn to where the bus rocks from the hundreds of hands. Shrieks filter through the air. Peter rolls forward until he's as close as he dares, about half a block's distance away. So far, with all the noise coming from the bus, we hold no interest for the Lexers.

The ambulance pulls up alongside. Dan runs to John's window. "What's the plan?"

"You don't have to—" I begin.

Dan's jaw is set. "I'm staying."

I'm so grateful that I don't argue, even though Bits is Peter's and my responsibility, and I know it's probably a lost cause. I don't care—some things are worth dying for. Adrian thought I was. And while I might not agree, I understand the feeling.

"We'll make as many trips as we can," John says, "then go back to the farm for the other trucks."

A few Lexers draw near the VW. One makes a beeline for Dan, who drops him with a machete to the jaw. The noises intensify to screams of terror and muffled gunshots. The bus's front door hangs to the side, and the Lexers crawl up each other. They're inside. I thought we had at least a few minutes. And that they couldn't get past the doors and up the stairs—up to Bits. Black spots threaten to take over my vision, and I grab the seat to stay upright.

I've always known that watching Bits die would be unbearable, but I'd hoped that I'd be there, able to give her comfort, if I couldn't save her. And I can't even do that; she's going to die alone. I can only sit here and watch, and this choking helplessness is worse than anything I've ever encountered.

The rear hatch on the bus's roof swings up. Hank's head pokes out, and he pulls himself onto the roof. He turns quickly and lies on his stomach, arms dangling back into the hole. I don't dare breathe as Bits's brown hair emerges.

"Please," I whisper. My feet press to the floor as if I can give her a boost. "Please."

Hank drags her alongside him, and then turns back to the hatch. Henry gets his torso through and braces his hands on the roof. He sinks a few inches and struggles to straighten his arms. Bits and Hank grasp his jacket, bent backward with the effort of pulling against whatever's down there. Henry's mouth opens and he shakes his head. Bits releases her grip, but Hank holds on a moment longer before he lets his father drop, and then he flops to his belly and hangs into the hatch. I don't want him to see, and I exhale when Bits pulls him to his feet. She knows what it does to you.

Ana's fingers tighten around my arm. "We'll get her."

Ana is more like Bits's favorite aunt than a mother, but she adores Bits as much as we do. She won't leave until every hope of saving Bits is gone. And this is our one chance, slim though it may be. We have to get them out before the road to the east is blocked, too.

Dan leans out of the ambulance window. "Get on the roof. I'll drive you in. John, stay here in case we need you."

Ana, Peter and I scramble up the hood and lie on the roof. We hold tight while Dan drives into the mob, nudging Lexers aside. They move at first, but then they go wild. The ambulance is buffeted as we inch forward. Dan angles to pull alongside the bus. Bits and Hank look so small on the roof, arms dangling by their sides.

"Stay there!" I yell. "We're coming!"

But I don't know how we're going to get there, not with the seven solid feet of Lexers wedged between our vehicles. Bits nods, mouth open in an O. She looks as though she might faint.

"Closer!" Ana screams.

Dan backs up again. Peter lies on the roof of the cab and flings Lexers out of our path. He picks them up by their hair or tattered clothes and tosses them to the side until Dan's managed to close the gap to three feet. The driver's side window shatters, and Dan fires at the ones wedged between the two vehicles. Ana and I stab at their heads until they're upright and motionless, forming a barrier to keep the others away.

I look up at the roof. Hank's glasses reflect the trees and sky, but I can see the desperation in Bits's eyes. "Cassie!" she screams. "Peter!"

Hank takes Bits's hand in his and moves to the edge of the roof. "Not together!" Peter yells. "I'll bring you over."

It takes him one stride to get across, where he catches Bits by the waist. She wraps her legs around him and shuts her eyes while he leaps back. And then she's in my arms. I thought it impossible, but she's in my arms. Peter and Hank land on the van with two thumps. Dan backs up slowly and then turns for the east. He gets another few feet, bumping over bodies on the ground. The front of the ambulance rises and doesn't come back down. The tires squeal, but we don't move.

Ana peers over the side and curses. I move Bits off my lap and crawl to the edge. The front of the chassis is caught on a hump of bodies, tires spinning two inches above the road.

"We're stuck!" Ana yells over the roof's edge.

A moment later, Dan climbs out of the window and onto the roof. The number of Lexers we'll have to fight our way through is many more than that day in the woods, or the one in the field. There are so few openings in the first ten feet that we'll have to push our way through.

"I'll carry Bits," Peter yells over the din.

I don't want to let her go, but I could never carry her weight and run the way he could. Peter lifts Bits to his hip and covers her with the flap of his jacket. He grips his machete in his other hand and meets my eyes with a nod. If there's anyone I trust with Bits, it's Peter; he'll die before he fails.

Hank has a thick jacket, but nothing to protect his ink-stained hands. I strip off my gloves and point to the VW. "Put these on. We're going to run to John as fast as we can. Can you do that?"

Hank's eyes are white all around, and his head shakes in what might be a nod or what might be fear. I take him by the shoulders. "Don't let go. Unless I go down. Then you run. Don't stop for anything."

Hank slips into the leather. I take Adrian's knife off my belt and put it in his hand. "Use this if you have to," I order, and this time his nod is firm, just like his dad's.

Ana holds her cleaver in one hand and a small machete from the VW in the other. "I'm with Peter. Dan, you're with Cass."

Dan puts a hand on my arm. His eyes are fierce, just like that morning in Stowe. They say there's no alternative, we will get out of this. Ana raises the hood of the sweatshirt underneath her coat. She flashes Peter a smile I've seen before—the one that means she'll do anything, no matter how risky.

"Careful," I call to her.

"Stay close," Peter orders Ana. "Don't do anything—"

"Promise." She pulls her hood's drawstring tight. Ana and Peter slip down the hood and into the fray. She slices with her blades, shoving and kicking the mass of bodies. Peter shoulders his way through the crowd, knife out, stopping to use it on one who spins Ana to the side.

Dan and I hit the dirt. I have to drag Hank at first, but within steps he's matching my pace. Hands rip at my coat as I move through the space Dan leaves behind him, careful to keep Hank just ahead of me. I stab at a head that's too close. Dan fires at one who dives at his side and hangs there, arms around his waist.

We've almost caught up to Peter and Ana when a surge from behind knocks me and Hank to our knees. His hand slips from mine. I make myself as small as possible while they trip over me and land on the road. I struggle out from under the weight of bodies and shake off the one who's latched on to the arm of my jacket with its teeth. The surge has pushed this patch of Lexers to the ground, but I can't find Hank among them.

"Hank!" I scream.

Dan shoves a Lexer aside and pulls Hank to his feet. A hand grabs my thigh and another grips my ankle. I kick them off with a grunt and run across the Lexers attempting to rise to their feet, smashing spines with my boots. There's no time to ask if Hank's bitten. And anyway, I wouldn't leave him if he was. There are now two people I'll never leave behind—Henry would've made it out of the bus had he not kept his word to protect Bits, and I'll be damned if I renege on my part of the bargain. I grab Hank's hand and spin straight into a skeletal face. The skin is dry and sunken, its teeth immense. They snap, half an inch from my nose, before it crumples to the ground.

Dan stands behind it, and he throws three more to the ground. "Go!" he yells.

The Lexers aren't as thick here, but that's changing quickly. We have less than ten feet before we're out. Another few feet and my cleaver is batted out of my hand by a Lexer who lunges to lock Hank in an embrace. I press my palm to its forehead a second before his mouth connects with Hank's face, but I can't push it off. I jam two fingers into its eye socket. It's cold and wet and viscous, and at another time would be too disgusting to contemplate, but I don't care. They're not going to get Hank. They're not going to win, even if I have to punch my bare hand into the brain of every single one of them. I dig my thumb through the rotten cheek for leverage and ram my fingers in until it drops to the dirt.

Dan grunts behind me; he's kept the others away to give me time. A high-pitched curse comes from Ana, ahead to my left, and she spins to slam her cleaver into the one who's grabbed her hood, but she misses. She fumbles with her coat zipper and kicks another away. We make it past as she slips out of her sweatshirt and jacket.

Hank and I break through the crowd and run the final feet to where John has pulled the VW. John slides the door open, pistol in hand, and throws Hank inside. He reaches for me, but I shake my head and turn. I think I see Dan heading in Ana's direction, which is where I'm going now that Hank is safe. "Ana's back there!"

"You stay," John yells and hits the dirt. "Get inside!"

I slam the door and watch John's red jacket disappear into the crowd. I don't see Dan or Ana or Peter. I can hear gunshots, although I can't pinpoint their location. I need to find Peter and Bits.

I crouch in front of Hank. We're both panting, and I know my eyes must be as huge as his. "Are you okay? Did any bite you?" His lips move in a silent No, and I nod in relief. I look out every window again. Trees and Lexers are all I can see.

"Stay here, okay?" I grip his knee when his lower lip trembles. "I'm only going on the roof. I won't leave you."

Hank nods slowly and raises his knife at the lone Lexer who shows interest in the VW before continuing on to the school bus. Somehow Hank's managed to hold on to both his glasses and the knife.

Peter calls my name when I step out the door. He's coming out of the empty woods from the east, Bits still around his waist. How he managed to get so far away is a mystery, but my legs almost buckle before I scramble for the steering wheel and reverse the hundred feet. Peter shoves Bits into the VW. She's disheveled and terrified, but the sight of her is so very beautiful.

"I got pushed into the woods," Peter yells. "Where are they? Where's John?"

"He went for Ana," I say. "She was okay when I last saw."

I climb to the roof and catch a flash of red. John is in the midst of them, fighting his way back alone. He hacks with his knife, but the crowd has become a solid mass.

"John's coming!" I scream to Peter. "Move us closer!"

But before Peter reaches the door, hands wrap around John's face, and he's pulled to the ground. A muffled gunshot echoes under the bodies that have followed him down. I wait, and when he doesn't rise, hear myself shriek with the breath I've been holding. I'm not sure what I've said, but Peter drops his hand from the door handle and stares at me in shock.

"Ana?" he yells.

I shake my head numbly and search the crowd for Ana and Dan. There's a chance they're still okay. Not like John. Peter puts a boot in the window frame and hops to the roof. Something fast pushes through the back of the mob, and Dan runs up the hood of the ambulance to the roof. His jacket is unzipped, and the bottom of his gray shirt is a dark stain. I tell myself he can't have been bitten, but the way he stands with his head lowered and chest heaving tells me otherwise. He raises his eyes to mine.

"No," I say, and then say it again, although I know it's true. He's alone up there, just like he'd feared. I ache to do something, anything, to make this easier for him. I wish he'd come this way; he shouldn't have to do this alone. He shouldn't have to do it at all.

It only takes a few seconds for the thoughts to flit through my mind, a few seconds in which Dan nods and his mouth moves in words I can't discern. He points a finger my way before raising it to the sky. I don't know exactly what he means, but I nod anyway. Those are our stars up there.

"Ana!" Peter's voice is so frantic that I tear my eyes away from Dan.

He jumps off the roof and races toward the Lexers who've spotted us and are coming our way. I slide down after him and fire at one who breaks from the pack, then another. Peter doesn't seem to notice until one gets close and he flings it out of the way.

I scream his name, but he doesn't answer. We've got two minutes before we're swallowed by the crowd. We have Bits and

Hank, and we have to get out of here. If Ana were okay she'd be here by now, I know she would.

And then I spot her, moving more swiftly than the other figures, but nowhere near as fast as she was. Her neck is shredded and shirt soaked with blood. She makes it to the forefront of the crowd, unsteady on her booted feet, and Peter stumbles back like he's been shoved.

She's fifteen feet away. The lips that were so expressive—pursed or grinning or saying something completely inappropriate—hang slack. I remember the promise I made on a sunny day, the one I never thought I'd have to keep. My hands shake when I aim my pistol between her dull eyes. I know I have her, though. Head shots might be hard, but I'm good at them. And while she's close enough that I barely have to try, it's the hardest shot I've ever taken. She hits the ground, and my shaking becomes a full-body shudder. If there were time to run to her, I would, but the rest of the pack is twenty feet away. I shout to knock Peter out of his stupor and drag him by his coat. I can't do this alone. He walks the first few paces backward, in a trance, and then runs for the driver's side.

Peter reverses in a wide arc and pulls east. I scramble to the rear window and look to the ambulance. Dan sits on the roof, watching us go; his flask flashes silver in his hand as he raises it to his mouth. I fall to the side when Peter swerves around a few Lexers who have reached the eastern road. By the time I'm up, we're over the rise and Dan is out of sight.

CHAPTER 72

My hands are filthy. They're black and brown and rust colored. The brain of the Lexer I killed coats my fingers with slime. I stumble to the sink and lather the soap until my hands are raw. I try not to think about the virus seeping into the cut on my finger. It's five days old and scabbed up, so I should be safe. I hope.

I try not to think of Ana and John and Dan and Henry, all those people in the bus, whether Whitefield got the call. How to tell Penny that I killed her sister. What to say to Peter, who stares at the road with a look of utter desolation on his face. What to say to Hank. You'd think I would know.

We've hit the empty road that will take us north. I dry my hands and turn to where the kids sit on the bench seat. Bits is okay, stunned but not in shock. Hank mashes his lips together and raises his bloodshot eyes to mine. He slides into my lap when I kneel before him and buries his face in my chest. His sobs are so forceful they must hurt, but this isn't something you hold in; it'll eat you alive if you do.

"I know, honey," I say. "I know."

I know and Bits knows and Peter knows. Everyone knows what it's like to be an orphan now. Hank's new to the club. I rock him while tremors pass through his body and whisper that he'll be all right. We'll be all right. It might not be true—it likely isn't—but it's what he needs to hear.

My voice cracks and the tears I've tried to restrain break free. I want to be here for Hank, to be strong, but I've just lost a father for the second time. I've lost my beautiful and fearsome sister. I don't know what Dan would've been to me, now I never will, but he was a friend and perhaps a future. The day that felt like a new beginning has ended before it ever really began. I hold Hank as tight as he holds me and murmur promises I'm not sure I can keep.

Peter slows when we're fifteen miles out. He doesn't say a word after he pulls to a stop, just moves between the seats to Bits. His pain is so raw that I have to force myself not to look away. I take his slack hand in mine, and he lowers himself to the VW's floor, mouth buried in Bits's hair, and leans against me.

The Lexers are coming north, but we have time. Not much, but some—if every mile equals an hour of zombie walking. We sit in the silence of the dead world and take a few precious moments that might be better used running. But in order to run fast you have to want to live, and we need this moment in order to go on, I know we do.

CHAPTER 73

Now that we're a few miles from Quebec, we could raise them on the radio. They'll ask who's with us, though, and I don't know what to say. Peter doesn't suggest it either, just grips the wheel and stares straight ahead. I sit silent in the back, kids in my arms, and wonder how I'll find my voice to tell Penny. A man I recognize from our trip this summer runs the gate open. Peter crawls along the main road, partly to avoid boxes, bags and discarded belongings, but also, I suspect, because he doesn't want to reach Penny any faster than I do.

He pulls into the lot, next to the pickup Shawn was driving. The small school bus has also made it. Penny rises from a picnic table at the sight of our vehicle. I take a breath and step through the door. I hear the kids' shoes hit the gravel and Peter's footsteps, but I don't break eye contact with Penny. Her face crumples when she moves her gaze to the empty road behind us, and she sinks to the bench with an open mouth. James stands with his hand on her shoulder as I walk across the impossibly mown grass and kneel in front of her.

"No." She shivers and folds her arms. "No."

"We couldn't help her," I whisper desperately. "We couldn't."

She inhales sharply, her face wild. "Did she turn? Is she..."

I shake my head so hard that a bun tumbles down my shoulder. "No. I—" I try, but I can't say it. "I promise."

Penny's eyes widen, and she takes my hands in hers without asking more. I'll tell her if she wants to know, but I don't ever want to talk about putting a bullet dead center in her sister's head. She sobs quietly, and I know Penny well enough to know that she wants me here but doesn't want platitudes. I watch the reflection of the clouds move across the lake. The chairs Dan and I sat in on that first night are still by the shore. I wonder if he's done it already—how long he waited, if whatever was in that flask made it any easier—and the burn in my throat is worse than when I drank that awful liquor.

"John?" James asks, although he already knows the answer. His face is drawn and eyes wet, but he's not surprised that we all didn't make it back. He's probably surprised any of us did.

"Dan. Henry. Everyone on the bus. We think everyone in front of the bus."

Bits sits at the table, hair a knotted mess, and watches Hank trace a gouge on the tabletop with his finger. Peter stands alongside us, his gaze on his feet.

"I'm sorry," he says in a whisper. "I shouldn't have let her—"

Penny jumps to put her arms around his neck. "You couldn't have stopped her if you'd tried. I knew it would happen one day. I did."

Penny may not be a fighter, but she's one of the strongest people I know. Instead of falling apart, she'll try to keep us all together. James wraps his arms around Penny's waist, and she leans into him with her eyes closed.

"We have to leave soon," he says, like he's reluctant to bring it up. But no one looks at him askance; we know we have little time to mourn. "We're just waiting on Whitefield."

Maureen comes out of the stone house and picks her way across the grass. Her cheeks hang alongside her mouth. She holds us each in turn, like my mother would have, and I sink into her embrace.

"I'm sorry," I whisper.

Maureen sniffs and hugs me tight, then pulls Hank into her lap. She removes his glasses and wipes his eyes gently. She doesn't cry, and I rub away my tears. I'm not going to cry anymore. Crying won't get us fuel or food or drive us the thousands of miles to Alaska. I'm going to concentrate on what comes next, on keeping those who are left safe. I'll cry when we're behind fences again.

"Is Whitefield coming?" I ask.

"Gabriel said Whitefield called here when they couldn't get us," James says. "Said the pod had reached them and they were leaving."

Pod isn't the right word. It's more like those armies of ants you see on nature shows, the ones that march forward unrelentingly, eating everything in their path. Or the swarms of locusts that used to plague pioneers. Whitefield might be caught in that swarm. I'm not sure I could stand to lose Nelly today, too.

"Quebec's not going to Alaska," Maureen says. "They're heading up to northern Canada somewhere."

"There's no Safe Zone," James adds. "They don't know what's up there. Some of the others from Kingdom Come want to go with them."

"What?" I ask. "Why?"

James shrugs. "It's closer. I don't know."

Gabriel comes down the porch steps with a large box. Clara follows behind with winter parkas. I meet up with them at their van.

"Cassie," Clara says. "I'm so happy you're here and all is well. Your friends were very worried."

I nod. They don't need to hear what's happened. "You're not going to Alaska?"

Gabriel stashes the box and says, "It's too far. We're taking the James Bay Road to Radisson. There may be survivors there, and there's the hydroelectric dam."

James has followed me over, and now he shakes his head. "But it's flat. I think mountains would be better."

"There's only one road between here and there. And many lakes," Gabriel says. He looks to Clara, who nods. "We think the water will protect us. We can get there on the fuel we have, rather than finding ourselves out of fuel halfway to Alaska."

"The western mountains are a better bet," James says, and looks to me. "There's a reason John and Will chose it, right? We'll have the Cascades, the Rockies and the Alaska Range in our path. Alaska's had a quarter of the Lexers we've had."

My heart stops at the mention of John. I'm not sure we can make it to Alaska without him, but if it's where he thought best, then he must have been right.

Gabriel sighs. "Yes, as you say, it is probably better. But this is our decision."

Clara smiles apologetically and turns back toward the house.

"We leave in ten minutes," Gabriel says. "You're welcome to stay here as long as you like, of course. You'll tell Whitefield they're welcome to join us?"

James and I walk back to the table, and Gabriel resumes his packing. Two men pull down the rear door of a box truck loaded with food.

"They don't have enough food for the winter," James says. "I think we should stick to the plan. We know where we're headed is safe. They *think* it's safe up there. By the time they find out it's not, it'll be too late to turn around. I want those mountains around me."

I want them, too. All the pictures I've seen of Alaska, where the smallest mountains are the height of the tallest here, flash through my mind. Alaska has food and warmth; they told us to come.

James explains the situation to the others, and Bits pulls Peter's hand. "I want to go to Alaska."

"That's where we're going, baby girl," Peter says, and absently runs a hand down her hair.

The other survivors from Kingdom Come walk toward the small school bus. Jamie and Shawn come our way, followed by Barnaby. I kneel to throw my arms around him; I never thought I'd be so happy to see this dumb dog. He spins in a circle and his tail hits me in the eye hard enough to make it water.

Shawn's normally jovial expression has been replaced by sloping eyes and a downturned mouth. Jamie checks over Bits and Hank. Doc is gone, too; he was on the big bus with Chris. Liz, Mikayla and Ben were in the first vehicles, but I don't remember which. Maybe a truck got through to the west, and they're heading for Alaska right now. It's a slim hope, but it's a possibility.

"Almost everyone's going north," Shawn says. "Mike and Rohan are coming with us. And Mark. That's it."

Mark sets his pack on the ground. "If it's all right with you. I've secured the bows in the pickup, just in case."

"Of course," James says.

Ashley walks up and throws her pack on the picnic table. "I'm coming to Alaska."

"Where's Nancy?" Penny asks.

"We got separated," Ashley says. She swallows and blinks. "She was on the big bus. I want to come with you." Her hair is in a bun and she wears a knife on her hip like she's one of us. She juts out her trembling chin in a tough girl act.

"Of course you'll come with us, Ash," I say.

Ashley sighs with relief, all her bravado spent, and glances at the little yellow bus. "Meghan and the others say I should go with them, but I don't want to."

We look to where over a dozen of the others stand. Meghan and her closest friends are huddled together, wide-eyed and unarmed. I can't believe none of them is wearing a gun or knife. Maybe it's good they're going their own way. We have enough to worry about. I feel mean as I think it, but I can only protect so many people, and those people need to be able to help themselves if they're over the age of eighteen.

We jump when Peter curses and strides across the grass, pushing through the remainder of Kingdom Come to where Oliver cowers in the back. He doesn't say a word, only takes Oliver's shirt in his left hand and draws back his right. I arrive just as his fist smashes into Oliver's face. The crowd murmurs in surprise, but, honestly, I can't believe that somebody else didn't beat Peter to it.

I pick Oliver's bent glasses up off the dirt. Oliver shrinks, but Peter doesn't let go. I've seen Peter angry, but I've never seen this blank, murderous rage. There's another meaty thud, and blood rushes over Oliver's eye before dripping off his chin. I consider stepping in, but I want Peter to get a few more in—one each for Ana, John, Dan and Henry.

Oliver gasps, his mouth open in a rictus of fear. He fixes his good eye on Peter's fist. "I'm sorry!"

Peter's fist stops before it connects. He drops Oliver to the ground and bends over him. "Do you know how many people you killed today?" he asks in a scarily quiet voice. "Do you? I hope you have plans to go with Quebec. I guarantee you won't make it to Alaska."

Oliver hugs his knees and blinks up at Peter. I hold out his glasses, and it takes him three tries to get them on with the way his hands quiver. The crowd has reassembled around us. Penny, who usually abhors this kind of violence, wears a satisfied expression, but Meghan and her friends look at Peter in shock. Well, fuck them. Fuck everyone who was so scared to leave the farm, the ones who are going with Quebec. They're going to find out what it's like out here, and God help them if a fistfight is enough to cause such alarm.

"I forgot!" Oliver says with a whimper. The tears mix with blood to form a watery soup. "I—I was scared. I f-forgot. It was all so fast!"

Peter's fist retightens, but then he takes in the pathetic mess that lies sobbing on the ground and splays his fingers with visible effort. I take his arm and walk him to the lake. If he punches Oliver again, he'll regret it. I rinse the blood off his knuckles with a plastic bucket and dry it on my shirt, then seat him in one of the chairs by the water.

"Stay here until they leave," I say.

Peter nods and watches the lake with a tight jaw. I sit next to him until I hear the engines fade into the distance. We've lost so many today that it almost feels the same as when the world ended a year ago. But we hadn't let that destroy us—we'd built a new world, and now that's ended, too.

CHAPTER 74

Quebec took all the food, but they didn't take the time to completely pick over the gardens. While we give Whitefield a few hours to arrive, I pick green tomatoes and snap hidden cucumbers off their vines. It may take the Lexers days to get up here, but we need more than days to cross the thousands of miles to Alaska. Our travels will take us across northern Canada, where the terrain might slow the Lexers down and the roads are less likely to be impassable.

Bits and Hank fill containers with anything that looks remotely edible in the garden we've been assigned to plunder. I'm glad we have something to do because the waiting is torture. Peter pulls a carrot out of the ground and tosses it into a bag. The next one's stuck, and he curses and kicks the greens that rise aboveground until there's nothing but a tiny stalk. I bring over my trowel and carefully dig up the carrot. My hands are steady, although my insides are so unsettled I can't imagine a time when I might ever want to eat it.

I look up from where I kneel. "Why don't you go rest? We can get this."

Peter shakes his head and crouches to rip a carrot from the earth. He wipes his face with the back of his hand and furiously tears out another. His fingernails are black, and blood runs down his knuckles where his cuts have opened up.

"You're bleeding," I say. "Why don't we clean you up? You need a band-aid."

"Fucking stop already!" Peter yells. "I don't want a fucking band-aid!"

Bits and Hank look up, mouths open. Hank takes Bits by the hand and leads her to another row. I'm not surprised by his outburst, though. Of course he's angry.

"Then you don't have to have a band-aid." I hand him the trowel. "Use this."

He stabs the trowel into the soil. I know about the anger that boils beneath the surface. The blame. The rage at the unfairness of it all. Sometimes it rises up and chokes you. Other times, you put it to good use. Right now, I'm doing neither of the two. The anger is in there, along with grief and despair, but I've buried it all with my resolve to think only of the practicalities of survival. Peter's seething with it, though. It's choking him. He's not an angry person. He spent much of his life sad, not angry. The only person he's ever hated with any intensity is himself.

"I'm sorry," I say. "I didn't know you were so vehemently opposed to band-aids, or I never would've offered you one."

The trowel pierces the ground and stays there. I raise my eyes from my carrot to find him staring at me. My semi-joke to defuse his anger was a gamble, and I'm relieved when his shoulders soften and jaw unclenches.

"Sorry," he says. "I just...I should've gone and—"

I look into his red-rimmed eyes. "No. It's not your fault. Don't do that to yourself. We got Bits. Ana wanted to save her as much as we did."

He lowers his head and yanks me forward by my shoulder. I hold him as he cries, his breaths coming in hot bursts on my neck. I know what it's like to need someone to cling to. I should've asked my friends for comfort after Adrian died.

I hear a rustle and spot Bits peeking at us from behind a bean bush.

"It's okay, Bits," I say, and hold out my hand. She steps softly on the earth but halts when Peter raises his head.

"Come here, baby girl," he says. "Sorry I scared you."

She balls up in his lap and he rests his chin on her head. The blood is still running, but it's slowed to an ooze. I take out my handkerchief and press it to his knuckles.

"I think I might need a band-aid," Peter says. He doesn't exactly smile, but some life has returned to his eyes.

CHAPTER 75

The VW and pickup are stuffed to the gills, and those of us who are left cluster beside them. We're giving Whitefield one more hour to arrive, and then we'll leave a note with their two options of destinations. It's late afternoon, but we won't stop for night. The plan is to drive straight through, taking turns behind the wheel as long as it's safe to do so. In a perfect world, it would take four straight days of driving at highway speeds. But this world is highly imperfect.

"We need zombie Doppler," Mike jokes. He cringes and his eyes dart around our group. "Sorry."

"It's okay, Mike," Penny says with a weak smile. "Ana would be the first one to laugh."

Mike puts an arm around Rohan and sucks in his cheeks.

"My dad said we had to joke after my mom and sister died," Hank says from where he sits on the edge of the VW's cabin. "He made me tell him every joke I knew. I didn't want to, but he made me. We laughed so hard we had to stop in case we attracted zombies." He kicks the dirt with a sneakered foot.

"So it worked?" I rest my arm around his shoulders. He leans into me with a nod. "Well, then—Knock Knock."

He throws his head back with a groan. "This isn't the interrupting cow one, is it?"

I push his foot with mine and pretend to be disappointed. "Am I that predictable?"

"You only know one joke, Cassie," Bits says.

"Well, we'll have plenty of time on the road for Hank to teach me more."

Everyone wears a smile now. They range from Rohan's fully-toothed grin to a tiny crease at the corner of Peter's lips. Maureen winks at me. She knows I know they've all heard my one joke a thousand times.

A tiny meow comes from the VW's interior. I scramble behind me for the box I stowed in the back and forgot, but Bits beats me to it with a cry of pure joy. She holds Sparky under her chin and looks at me with glowing eyes. "You really did get her! I didn't think you would. It was three bursts."

I nod noncommittally. I wouldn't have done it had Bits been at the VW, not with what was coming. I can't take any credit for Sparky's survival.

Peter scratches a finger under Sparky's chin. "Of course she did. We couldn't leave Sparkle behind." His raised eyebrows order me to agree. "Right?"

"Absolutely," I lie.

"Anyone hungry?" Maureen asks. "I was planning to pack up—"

The rumble of a motorcycle drowns out her next words. Zeke pulls into the lot and stops, followed by a camper and a truck. There's no way all of Whitefield is in those two vehicles, and my only prayer is *Nelly*.

Zeke takes off his helmet and hollers, "Y'all are a sight for sore eyes, let me tell you."

He steps over his bike and moves to Penny and Peter. I hear him say Ana's name and then turn to Maureen. Jamie and Shawn must have given them the news at the gate. Tony and Margaret leave the pickup, followed by Kyle, who swings Nicole to the ground. The camper door opens and a woman named Marissa emerges with her two children, along with five more adults I don't know well. I take a steadying breath that escapes in a rush when Adam steps out, followed by a flash of blond hair and familiar broad shoulders. I'm through the assembled people before Nelly's shoes hit the dirt. He picks me up in a bone-crushing embrace and sets me back down.

"Jamie told us. I don't...." Nelly runs a hand through his hair. "Are you..."

"We're okay." My lips tremble, and I take a deep breath. "Better, now that you're here. They're okay, for now."

"I didn't think we were going to make it." I start to ask why, but he squeezes my hand. "I'll tell you later. I need to—" He points his chin in the direction of the others. I watch him walk away, and I turn to Adam.

"Hey, you," I say. "Come here."

"Hey, yourself." Adam steps into my hug. "Nel was so worried."

"What happened? Where's everyone else?"

"We don't know." His voice cracks. Unlike Nelly, Adam wears his heart on his sleeve. "We had almost no warning. The fence went down before everyone could get to their spots. We got split up. No one answered the radio. We called the whole way here."

I look around our group of twenty-odd people. It's such a sorry number. It makes me despondent, until I see Nelly raise Bits in the air and draw a smile out of Hank. It may be a sorry number, I tell myself, but maybe quality, not quantity, is just as important.

CHAPTER 76

The sun is rising over the flat expanse of Who Knows Where, Canada. I've spent the night alternately staring at the road while driving or staring at where Penny and the kids sleep on the pullout bed. The outskirts of Montreal were nerve-wracking, but the last couple of hundred miles have been fairly easy since it was barely populated before. James spent the night driving or poring over our maps. He finally passed out with his face mashed against the sink.

We've managed to eke out some gas from cars. We'll need a lot more of it to get to Alaska, though, even with the tank in the truck bed. Tony and Margaret began fumbling with rubber hoses in the dark, until we showed them John's end-of-the-world siphoning method—a screwdriver into the gas tank with a container underneath. He would've been proud.

I rest my feet on the dashboard and watch the pickup and RV ahead. Besides Nelly and Adam, only Tony, Margaret, Zeke, Kyle and Nicole came west from the Whitefield group. It almost killed Zeke to leave his motorcycle in Quebec. He was afraid its roar would attract Lexers from miles away. I know it's only a bike, but I understood. Another thing left behind.

Peter's at the wheel. He glances behind us to make sure everyone's asleep and then speaks. "I shouldn't have done that to Oliver. I told him he was a murderer. I could see how sorry he was."

His face is tight. I knew he'd feel guilty and don't want him to, so I swing a fist in the air. "If you didn't punch him, I would've."

"I might have sent him to die up there."

"He was going north with the others, anyway," I say. "Maybe we should have gone, too."

"To nothing? Not enough food, no fences? Lexers coming straight for us?"

"What if we can't find more gas? Or the roads are blocked? Or—"

"Or we run into a pod," Peter says. "Or crazy people. Or there's a tornado. Or a flash flood. Or the bus breaks down. There—now we've named everything that could happen."

"Nope," I say, and caress the VW's dash, "Miss Vera won't break down. Will you, Miss Vera? You know how much I love you, don't you?"

"Miss Vera? You named the bus Miss Vera?"

"Vera the VW. Miss Vera Winifred Bus, get it?"

"You are a very weird person," Peter says. But he laughs his first laugh since yesterday, which is what I was going for. "We know where we're going and that they'll take us in."

"We know where we're going, but we might not get there."

The orange of the sun makes even this lonely stretch of highway look like something special, so I reach into my jacket and pull out the phone. I take a picture of the road stretched out before us and then snap a picture of Peter's hands glowing orange on the wheel, the knuckles on his right slightly swollen and scabbed.

"What are you doing?" he asks.

"A pictorial essay of our trip. That way they'll know our story when they find the bodies." I lean over and take a picture of myself with Peter.

Peter shifts the gears with more force than necessary. "Cassandra, stop being so pessimistic."

If the past day has shown us anything, it's that the worst is always a possibility. A probability, actually. I don't want to be pessimistic, but you won't get hurt as badly if you expect and prepare for the worst. That's what I'm hoping, anyway.

"I think the word you want is *realistic*," I say.

Peter sighs. I know I'm being argumentative, but if we're going to get to Alaska we need to be practical. We don't have room for fairy tales and blind faith. I can't believe this will end well, not when all the signs point to the truth that it won't.

The truck's blinker flashes and we slow to the side of the road. Nelly stretches his arms above his head before strolling to our window. Barnaby follows, but not before eating something disgusting off the road and then coughing it back up.

"Pit stop?" Nelly asks.

"I have those terrible coffee packets," I say. "Want me to make some?"

"Oh, God, yes."

The others wake at the sound of Nelly's voice. Sparky roams around the bus with plaintive meows. "Sparky needs to pee," Bits calls. "And maybe poop."

"How are we going to do that?" Peter asks me. There are no fences here, and we can't waste time searching for a scared cat if she runs off.

I sigh. "We've got to deal with a half-grown cat and the world's dumbest dog, and you're telling me to be optimistic?"

"Pete, don't bother," Nelly says with a chuckle. "She's too stubborn."

I make a face at him and tell Bits to find the twine in my bag. Bits hands it to me and asks, "Are we making a leash?"

"No way. Have you ever tried to walk a cat? If I can give you one solid piece of advice in your life, it's this: Never tie something around a cat's neck and try to take it for a walk. I speak from experience."

I kiss her cheek when she giggles. Sparky attacks the string as I try to fasten it around her, but in the end I fashion a rudimentary harness. "I'm sure she still won't like it, but at least she won't strangle herself."

"I love you," Bits says, and throws her arms around me. It's so unexpected and genuine that my eyes fill. I'll get her to Alaska, to safety, if it's the very last thing I ever do in this miserable world.

"I love you," I say, and try not to choke on the words. "More than all the stars in the sky."

Bits takes Sparky from my lap and smiles at Peter. "That's infinity, you know."

She and Hank set the cat down in the grass and stand guard. Sparky makes a run for it, only to be yanked back by the harness. I can't help but laugh; I knew it would happen.

"I like that," Peter says. "More than all the stars in the sky."

"Me, too."

I think it's time to retire *Until the end of the world and after.* The world has been over for a while, and we live in the after. It's become completely attainable.

Peter gazes out the windshield at the orange-streaked sky. "Are they really infinite?"

I picture Dan on the ambulance roof. Maybe he was telling me to keep watching, or that he'd be up there, or maybe even that he loved me. I wish I knew because they were his last words, and somebody should have heard them. I ignore the rock in my stomach and say, "No one knows for sure, but we've decided they are."

Peter nods and continues his watch of the clouds. I imagine he's thinking about Ana, and I touch his shoulder before I leave to set up the stove.

"Coffee?" I ask Penny.

Penny looks longingly at the coffee packets. She slept last night but doesn't look as if she has. "I'm not supp—"

"I'll take that as a yes."

Penny offers to finish the coffee in her enthusiasm for a cup. I brush my teeth, visit the Ladies' Bush, and then stretch out in the grass. Everything aches. I'm exhausted and weighted down. I look around at the faces we have with us, but all I see are the ones who aren't here. The holes they've left. The emptiness.

I know we all won't make it to Alaska. Some of us will, maybe, but not all of us. Not by a long shot. There will be more holes, more empty spaces. The thought is so disheartening that I want to stay in this spot and let the grass grow over me. My forced determination evaporates, leaving only the belief that we're going to die, one by one. I wish Ana were here—she'd screech at me to buck up and then make me run a mile, for fun. And John might have been able to get us all to Alaska or at least give me faith that it was possible.

Peter walks over and nudges me with a foot. "Coffee's done. Ready to go?"

He follows my line of vision, and I can tell by the way he slumps that he also sees those empty spaces. But then he straightens his shoulders and extends a hand. I don't know how he manages to conjure up a smile. Years of living with ghosts, perhaps.

"Everything'll be all right," Peter says.

I can see that he believes it, as crazy as that may be. And that he needs me to believe. Maybe it's something you can choose to believe. You make it all right, no matter what gets thrown at you. Maybe happiness is something you can decide on. It has to be better than the alternative. I don't think pessimism suits me. He pulls me to my feet, and I hold tight on our way to the bus.

Bits laughs at something Hank whispers in her ear, maybe one of his jokes. He blinks like an owl, and I feel my fierce protectiveness for Bits expand to include this smart, funny little boy. He may act older than his ten years, but he still needs a mother.

I look down the westward road. It's so barren, so lonely-looking, so filled with the unknown. It looks like it stretches on forever. It certainly feels like it does. I don't see how it can possibly be all right.

But then I see Nelly and Adam share a kiss before they climb into the pickup. I watch Jamie put her arm around Ashley's shoulders and guide her to the camper. Kyle flashes me one of his rare grins when I smile at Nicole, who plays the drums on her father's head from her seat on his shoulders.

There's still so much love in the world. So much to hope for. And so much to lose. But if I concentrate on the former hard enough, I can almost believe it, too. I've had my chance to break down, to fall apart, to be overcome by helplessness and hopelessness. But not anymore—I'm never going to let this world get the best of me again.

"Yeah," I say, and squeeze Peter's hand before I let go. "It'll be all right."

ABOUT THE AUTHOR

Sarah Lyons Fleming is a Laura Ingalls devotee, wannabe prepper and lover of anything pre-apocalyptic, apocalyptic and post-apocalyptic—or anything in between. Add in some romance and humor, and she's in heaven.

Besides an unhealthy obsession with home-canned food and Bug Out Bag equipment, she loves books, making artsy stuff and laughing her arse off. Born and raised in Brooklyn, NY, she now lives in Oregon with her family and, in her opinion, not nearly enough supplies for the zombie apocalypse. But she's working on it.

Visit the author at www.SarahLyonsFleming.com

The *Until the End of the World* series:

Until the End of the World (Book One)
So Long, Lollipops (Peter's Novella)
And After (Book two)
All the Stars in the Sky (Book three—coming winter 2014)

ACKNOWLEDGEMENTS

Thanks to the usual suspects, and some new ones:

My many parents, who read, reread and love my work. For my mom and dad, who read it so many times they must have it memorized. And Mama P, who caught many of those last sneaky typos. I'm so grateful for all of your love and encouragement.

Jamie, whose enthusiasm rivals my own, and who hasn't yet stopped answering the phone when I call for moral support. Seriously, you're the best. And Jamie's friend, Tracy, who also treats my drafts with a ton of excitement. You ladies are my first fangirls!

Rachel Greer, who gave me some great advice to stop smiling all. the. damn. time. She knows what I mean.

Danielle, for reading and proofing. Not only is she excited for the story, but she tells it like it is.

Rachel Aukes, for her helpful comments and for happily (I hope!) answering a few pesky emails.

Linda Tooch, for proofing and giving her honest opinion.

Will Fleming, husband and editor, both jobs at which he excels. Once again, he kept me on the straight and narrow in terms of grammar and clarity. When it comes to writing, he doesn't let me get away with anything. But he lets me get away with plenty in real life, and that's just the way I like it.

59429098R00211

Made in the USA
Lexington, KY
07 January 2017